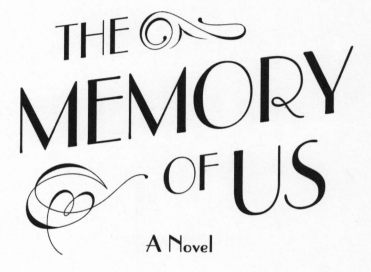

THE MEMORY OF US

A Novel

THE MEMORY OF US

A Novel

CAMILLE DI MAIO

LAKE UNION

PUBLISHING

Published by Lake Union Publishing, Seattle

www.apub.com

Amazon, the Amazon logo, and Lake Union Publishing are trademarks of Amazon.com, Inc., or its affiliates.

ISBN-13: 9781503934757
ISBN-10: 1503934756

Cover design by Danielle Fiorella

Printed in the United States of America

For my husband, Rob. You are my personal romance story. Your encouragement, support, and wild ideas were essential to this book happening.

For my dad, Pete. Without you introducing me to the beautiful music that inspired the story, this book would not exist. Your contributions over breakfasts and coffees were invaluable.

For my mom, Chris. You believed, even when I wrote silly stories as a little girl, that there was something publishable there. Thank you for sharing your love of reading, and for drilling me in vocabulary lessons!

Abertillery, England—1961

The commotion outside startled me, and the pills in my hand spilled out onto the carpet. My palm was stained a sickly ochre from the dye blending with perspiration. How long had I been clutching them? Across the room, the face of the clock was blurred. But it must have been hours.

I ignored the knock at first, determined to swallow the rest of the little capsules, each one bringing me closer to the sleep from which I would never wake. Surely, two decades was enough penance. Maybe tonight I could do it.

But whoever was at my front door was persistent. I left the pills on the floor to be considered later, and fumbled around the top of the chest of drawers until I found my spectacles. My hand brushed against the side of a tarnished silver picture frame, teetering it until it landed faceup. It was the only photograph I possessed. The sepia-toned visage of a young man looked back at me, mouth bent to the side in a whistle, captured unknowingly. The only evidence I would allow of my sin.

My feet found the slippers, laid symmetrically beside my bed, and I picked up the housecoat folded over the chair. With the habit of a distant vanity, I ran my fingers through my hair. But I had long since learned to avoid mirrors, and did not glance at the one that came with the rented rooms.

I flipped the switch and grimaced at the flood of light. The knocking stopped. I slid the chain off its track, and opened the door just enough to peer out at the intruder.

It was one of the Campbell children. There were so many, but this towering boy was one of the older ones. Thomas. Tommy. Timothy. It didn't matter.

"Miss Bailey?"

"What do you want at this hour?"

The moon was high in the sky, and the night had already taken on the stillness that invites ghosts and nightmares.

"It's my mum. She's sick. Bad."

"Is it the baby? It's not her time for another few weeks."

"I guess God thinks differently. It's coming. But something isn't right this time."

"God has nothing to do with it."

He disregarded my blasphemy. Most people did when the demand for my nursing skills in these nothing towns outweighed their desire for pious company.

"I brought the truck."

It was a charitable word for the sad scrap of metal that awaited us. It caved under our collective weight, with his being woefully undernourished and mine making up the difference. I thought for a moment that it would be faster—and less perilous—to walk the four miles to the Campbell farm. But I said nothing. Perhaps it would combust into a fiery pyre, and the pills would be rendered unnecessary.

We drove in silence, save for the sputtering of the engine and the crackle of the poorly paved road beneath the tires. In the illumination of the stars I studied my hands, their spiderweb scars mangling them into something that still appalled me, even after so much time. My nails remained incongruously pretty, although they hadn't seen polish since the war.

The boy spoke only once more, words that were innocent enough. Words that brought me back to the aged photograph lying abandoned at my bedside.

"My brother went to fetch Father Trammel, but he was out of town. He had a houseguest, though. A Father McCarthy. He's coming straight away."

McCarthy. I froze as the words possessed my ears. Of course there were thousands of people with that surname, but I had not encountered one in some time. And there was only one McCarthy who had meant anything. Who had meant everything.

Chapter One

"Good afternoon, Miss Westcott. How nice to see you." The soft garnet cheeks of the secretary matched my own, though hers were painted on with enthusiastic strokes and mine were the consequence of an unintended sprint through the pockmarked streets of Bootle.

"And the same to you, Miss Ellis," I replied. "Are you feeling better? They said that you were out sick last time I came."

"Doing much better, and you're an angel for asking." She glanced at her wristwatch. "You're a bit later than usual, aren't you, my dear?"

"The bus got a flat down on Southport Road, and I came the rest of the way on foot."

"That's quite a hike for a young lady."

"They didn't know when a replacement would arrive, and I wanted to catch Charles before his nap." I had been unsuccessful in avoiding the asphalt cavities filled by a rainstorm the previous day, and the left side of my skirt displayed fan-shaped remains of mud kicked up by a motorcar in a hurry of its own. But, seated behind the opaque glass window that she had opened at the jingle of the front door, she was unable to see below my waist.

Miss Ellis nodded in a robust motion that emanated from her shoulders. "Aye, you've not got long. He ate just a bit ago and should be out on his walk now."

I glanced at my own wristwatch. I couldn't miss the last bus back home. How would I explain what I was doing outside of Liverpool?

Miss Ellis's attention returned to the shiny black typewriter in front of her, and I watched as her fingers danced across the keys. They paused midair, and she looked back up at me. "Did you need anything else, my girl?"

"I just wanted to ask you a favor."

"Anything for you. You know that. Now, what is it?" She patted my hand in her familiar fashion.

"I'm going away at the end of the summer. If I write to Charles, would you read my letters to him?"

Her brow furrowed in confusion, as if I had forgotten that my twin brother was deaf and blind.

"Oh, don't look at me like that, Miss Ellis. I know it sounds absurd. But I want to believe that he'd feel the vibrations of your voice, and it would comfort me to know that he had a bit of companionship in this place."

"Heavens, dear—of course I will. But you don't have to worry about him being lonely. He's made a friend."

"He has? Another resident?"

"No, no, not one of them. It's the gardener. Well, the son of the gardener. Weekend help. He spends a bit of time with your brother when he's here. It's not much, but it's a bright time for the poor boy. I've even seen a smile pass on Charles's face. Twice now!"

I stood up straight, heartened by this revelation. My brother could be difficult at times, and his care was generally relegated to the newest orderly, like an unwanted midnight shift at a factory.

"Yes, it's true," she added. "You'll see soon enough. But, tell me. Why the letters? Where are you going, love?"

The envelope had arrived in the post just two days before, and I had not yet told my parents. Nor had I seen Lucille to break it to her, since she was needed at her father's shop now that school had ended. So this was the first time the news would cross my lips.

"I've been accepted to the Nightingale School at Saint Thomas Hospital in London."

"Oh, if that isn't the best thing I've heard in a long time. You stay right there!" Miss Ellis vaulted from her seat, leaving a concave impression in its tweedy fabric. She swept open the door to the lobby and encircled me in an embrace far warmer than any I expected my news to earn me at home.

Just as I thought I would never again draw breath, I was released. "We will surely miss you around here, you know that, but you will be the best and most lovely nurse in the country, I'm absolutely sure of it. Don't you go forgetting all of your old friends now that you'll be living down in a fancy city."

I took her hand in mine. "Of course I won't. I'll write to you as well."

"Never mind. I will learn all I need to know from the letters to your brother. You need to spend your time studying. So, don't you worry. Just make us proud." She squeezed my arms and then looked down, concern spreading across her face as she saw the grim state of my skirt and shoes.

The telephone rang, sending her back to the room behind the wall. She picked up the receiver, only to cover it and point her head in the direction of the hall.

"Towels," she mouthed, "in the room marked 'Laundry.'" She returned to her call. "Bootle Home, how may I help you?"

It was the same conversation I'd heard nearly every time I visited. Another desperate couple on the other end, willing to cover great distances to come here. Their child was not what they expected, and they were anxious for a place to relieve their burden. To tuck them away on a shelf, rarely visited and often forgotten. Except for the regular invoices that assuaged their consciences, satisfied that the opulence of the institution was a reasonable substitute for the loving care of a family.

At the beginning of the century, the only recourse for such a disappointing birth was the government-run Institution for Idiots and the Feeble Minded. But now, those with burgeoning coffers could select the marble halls and lavender-scented air of the Bootle Home. Leaded-glass windows, the best doctors. Their child surrendered to lonely luxury.

I found the correct room next to the lavatory, and marveled at the ceiling-high piles of perfect white towels on wooden shelves. My hands floated along their soft, rounded edges. Most were larger than I needed, but I found one that was suitable. I was pleased to see a sink located in the corner. I held the towel under the tap, wringing the excess, and dabbed it fruitlessly on my skirt. The mud only darkened, with edges that had now spread into an oval smear.

I sighed and found a bin for soiled towels. I adjusted my clothes so that the stain was only evident from the back and smoothed the new front until I was satisfied that I could do no better.

Miss Ellis was still on the telephone when I returned, taking notes and nodding her head. I passed the magazines laid out in rows on an elaborately carved cabinet. I made a game of noticing something different about it with every visit, and this time I spotted the profile of a cherub on a drawer to the left. Its face was enigmatic, and I was unable to decide if it was a happy angel or an angry one. Mother would love this. The cabinet no doubt had great value, and could stand with the best of them on the pages of a Christie's catalog. Such was Bootle Home.

I reached for a *Vogue*, but it was an issue that I had already seen. So I closed my eyes and sank into the plush cushions of the sofa, my toes just skimming the floor. A clock across the room clanged a throaty sound once to mark the hour. I needed to leave by the time it rang twice in order to make it home before my visit was discovered, and there was still no sign of Charles.

I looked down at my nails and pulled at a snag. They were glossy, polished by Lucille last Sunday with a delicate pink that reminded me of strawberry chiffon. She had a steady hand, and though she chided me for having "twenty thousand colors," my oldest friend smiled as she tapped the brush on the lip of the bottle.

The quarter-hour chime of the clock clanged the progression of time. But just as I was beginning to lose hope, I heard the twittering noises of adolescence beyond the large exterior doors.

They opened to reveal a motley collection of residents, some young, some fully grown, all suspended in an ageless innocence that still found delight in ladybirds and soap bubbles. I watched as they filed in, then I looked for my brother and found him, at last, near the back. He was being supported by a young man, one whom I hadn't seen before. My breath caught uncharacteristically as I studied the stranger. He was tall, with wavy locks and malt-colored eyes. He wore heavy canvas trousers and a rumpled white shirt, a departure from the starchy, crisp uniforms of the orderlies. He held Charles's arm with all of the patience that I could hope for, and with a tenderness more pronounced than I'd seen in anyone else I'd encountered here since beginning my secret visits.

I stood up and took another magazine, peeking out over its pages, and watched as they turned toward the dormitory wing. Everyone passed them by, but the young man took unhurried steps that matched Charles's as he shuffled along.

A file cabinet drawer slammed next to me, and I jumped at the sound.

"Sorry, dear," Miss Ellis said, whirling and opening another.

"Not at all," I said, setting the magazine aside only to realize that its subject was fox hunting. And that I'd been holding it upside down.

"Going shooting anytime soon?" Her eyes grew large, and my smile was unconvincing.

"Who is the man with Charles?" I caught my faint reflection in a nearby window and tucked an errant strand of hair behind my ear.

"Ah, that would be the young McCarthy. The one I was telling you about. A good boy he is, and a handsome one, too. Such a shame, though. He's a—"

But the telephone interrupted us before she could finish.

"Just a second, dear," she said as she bustled to her desk. She caught it on the fifth ring. "Bootle Home. How may I help you?"

Her voice blended into the symphony around me, comprised of the dull whirring of a distant hoover and the clatter of plates being collected in the dining hall. The building was returning to life, awakened by the arrival of the residents from their daily exercises. My attention, however, was acutely focused on the retreating figures of my brother and his companion.

Before my precious minutes could disappear, I started down the hallway and up the stairs after them.

My steps were muffled by the immense Oriental runner, and I arrived at Charles's door unannounced. I expected to find him being prepared for a nap, as the severity of his condition excluded him from many of the activities that the others enjoyed. My monthly visits were intended as a break from what must be a succession of monotonous days. Not to see, not to hear. Not to even think like others. Just following as he was led.

He was not in his bed, however, but next to the window, whose oversized sill was now accented with a row of colorful pots and budding greenery. He was leaning awkwardly on the young man. McCarthy.

He took Charles's hand and touched it to the soil of each pot, one at a time. A smile appeared on the familiar face, one that, until now, had been reserved for my visits. His fingers caressed the softness of the leaves and traced the lines of the stems. He poked them into the soil again and again with the fascination of a child.

I stood transfixed, enchanted by his reaction to such an elementary thing. Then McCarthy pinched one of the leaves and pulled off what looked like a worm. He laid it on Charles's arm, and my brother laughed. My hand flew to my heart in response to this delightful sound, which I had never heard from his lips. The worm crawled from his elbow to his wrist and back, finally stopping. McCarthy returned it to the pot and ushered Charles to his chair. He patted a cushion and placed it behind my brother's back. Then he looked up, suddenly aware of my presence.

He smiled at me, and I was overcome with an unexpected feeling. Like the glow of a fireplace in a chilly space. I tried to convince myself that I was flushed merely by the warmth of the summer day. Certainly not because of those eyes, or the way his hair wasn't committed to a style. I searched the room for anything that could divert my attention, but the unadorned walls were no help at all, leaving me nothing to do but return his glance.

"Good afternoon," I managed. "Thank you. I mean, I couldn't help but see how kind you are with him."

"With Charles? Oh, he and I are buddies. Aren't we, now?" He patted him on his shoulder, and I caught my breath in delight at the gesture.

"I'm Julianne Westcott. Charles is my brother." The words were foreign to my tongue. Lucille was the only friend who knew I had a sibling, a revelation that I had shared through tears after discovering the documents in Mother's dressing room just two years ago.

"I'm Kyle McCarthy. I'm helping my father with the gardens." He reached for my hand.

Hoping he wouldn't notice the quickening of my heartbeat, I took it casually, pulling back as soon as etiquette would allow.

"So you're not an orderly?"

He laughed. "Oh no. Charles and I met a few weeks ago out on the lawn. He was sitting on the ground, running his fingers through the grass. The orderly was trying everything to get him back on his feet, but Charles was obstinate. I came over with a bucket, scooped some of the grass into it, and placed his hand into it. Then I raised the bucket a little bit, and of course he had to rise with it to keep hold of the grass. Bit by bit he rose to his feet, and then we walked that way all the way back to the dormitory."

"You did that for him?"

"Well, it was better than the straitjacket. I think that was going to be their next move. He can be rather stubborn sometimes."

Stubborn. That was what Mother had called me as a child when I refused to stop swinging my legs during tea. And what Father called me when I wouldn't give up during a futile chess match. It saddened me to think that my brother and I could have had so much more in common if we were not separated by geography and the chasm of his inabilities. Real companions, we could have run through the wings of the manor house on Newsham Park, hiding and seeking until Mother or the newest governess instructed us to sit still and behave.

"In fact, it's a little game we play now. Isn't it, Buddy?"

The face of my brother reverted to the same blank expression that it always did, but I had to believe that somehow he was aware of the company of friends.

"Anyway, I brought some pots to his room this week. I thought I'd see if he can tell the difference as they grow." He shrugged. "At the very least, it gives him something to do when he's in here."

"And the worm?"

"It's a caterpillar. I found it last week and added it to our collection. The little dodger tried to crawl out, but now it seems he's settled in just fine."

"Whatever it is, I've never heard Charles laugh before."

"It's fantastic, isn't it?"

I only nodded, pursing my lips before a sob could escape. For there were no words in existence that could do justice to the sound that had taken too many years to reveal. We spoke instead with our eyes, limited by the inadequacy of language. Until Charles moved in his chair and shifted our attention.

"If you'll excuse me," Kyle said then, "I need to get back outside. It was a pleasure to meet you." He pulled a cap from his back pocket and tipped it politely after placing it on his head.

I backed up against a wall so that only the clean side of my skirt was visible. As he passed by me, I detected a pleasant, earthy scent, like grass and soil. When he was gone, I crossed the room to the window and watched until he returned to the gardens, side by side with an older man who looked like an older version of him.

Charles and I settled into our own routine, one that usually coaxed a smile to his face. "I. Love. You." I spoke the words as I squeezed his hands three times in a cadence. He recognized me, if only from the rapport that we had created, and not from the time that we had shared in the womb eighteen years ago. He squeezed mine back in the same manner. I had been told that it was only a reflexive motion, but I chose to believe otherwise.

His almond-shaped eyes and listless features suppressed any resemblance that we might have otherwise had. We did share an identical shade of golden hair, however, and our mutual love of chocolate was evident. I slipped a Cadbury's out of my handbag. Our favorite. Dark chocolate and walnuts.

I was wiping the corners of his mouth when Miss Ellis peeked in.

"Indulging in contraband, I see?"

"Don't tell the doctor."

"You'll have to bribe me." I pulled a second bar from my bag, and she grinned. She broke it in two, giving me the other half, and we tapped them together lightly.

"Cheers, my girl."

"Cheers." I nibbled at it as my eyes turned to the window, which had claimed my attention once again. Miss Ellis saw where they landed.

Kyle was hauling mulch bags over his shoulder effortlessly, even though they must have weighed a great deal.

"It'll do you no good to moon over that one."

I jerked my head around, embarrassed. "I don't know what you're talking about."

"You know exactly what I mean. The McCarthy boy. He's not . . . available."

"Available?"

"Well, let me put it this way. He's on summer break from school in Durham. But not just any school. It's called Ushaw College." She rested her elbow on the bureau and regarded me with a strangely apologetic expression.

"I've never heard of it."

"I wouldn't have expected you to. It's a seminary."

"A seminary? You mean, he's going to be some kind of minister?"

"Not a minister like we know it, you and I. He's a Catholic, Miss Westcott. He's going to be a priest."

The clock downstairs chimed twice, its baritone echo hollering all the way to the second floor, calling me home.

Chapter Two

I stood in front of my mirror and held the two dresses at my shoulders. Flowing white eyelet dress: innocence. Clingy tan ensemble: sophistication. That would be the one. The sleek skirt came just past my knees. I pulled out a green scarf and played with the variations, deciding I'd wear it in a knot under my neck. The green accentuated my eyes, or so I was told. I turned right and left, assessing my reflection. Just right. This was what I would wear to Bootle.

I heard a wolfish whistle behind me and turned toward my door with a start.

"Father!"

He leaned on the door frame, arms crossed. "Well, look at you. I thought you were just going to the talkies with Lucille."

I slipped my foot into a gold-toned low heel and grinned.

"No one calls them talkies anymore. You're funny." I pulled the other shoe out of its box, parting the layers of pastel tissue, and wriggled my foot into it. There was no room to move my toes, but the salesgirl had said that the leather would stretch in time. And, more important, they looked sensational.

"Well, I'll never understand women. I certainly wouldn't want to sit for a couple of hours in a skirt and heels."

"I should hope not! That would be a sight."

We laughed, and his face reddened. He moved over to me and placed his hands on my shoulders. "I'll save you that humiliation."

I pecked him on the cheek and wiped the trace of gloss that was left behind. "I have to go."

He put his hand on my arm. "Hold on there, Princess. I came to tell you that there won't be any movie today."

His jovial tone had turned grave. I froze. Had he discovered my trips to Bootle? I didn't think so, though sometimes I wished that he would. Then I could at last ask the questions that hesitated on my tongue.

"Some IRA hoodlums were arrested outside one of the warehouses last night," he said. "Mavis is overly nervous, as usual, and won't come in to work today. I need your help with the bookkeeping."

They hadn't yet terrorized Liverpool, but the growing rumors indicated that commerce along the coasts was in jeopardy. Father's warehouses and customs clearance office at Albert Dock would certainly be desirable targets. His unflappable demeanor had lately given way to anti-Catholic rants and staunch support of war with Germany.

"I'll come with you," I said through a forced smile. I hid my dejection over this new plan. He never asked me for much, and we did usually enjoy days at the docks together. We would have lunch delivered from a place of my choosing and sit on packing crates in a makeshift picnic.

"Good. Meet me downstairs in ten minutes. Betty is making breakfast, and we can head out after that." As if on cue, I could smell the sausages frying downstairs.

He turned toward my door and then back to me. "There's always tomorrow. I'm sure Lucille will understand."

Of course she would. If that had been the actual plan. But Bootle couldn't wait another day. If I didn't go now, it would be another week. Kyle worked there only on Saturdays, a titbit I'd learned from Miss Ellis after subtle attempts to mine for more information. And having learned this, I was prepared to visit more often than I had in the past.

I was surprised by this preoccupation with the gardener who was so attentive to my brother. Lucille often reproached me for my resigned indifference to that sort of thing. "Dogs will fly and monkeys will talk the day that Julianne Westcott chooses a beau," she'd say. "And elephants will sing," I'd agree.

Her ribbing was lighthearted, but she knew the truth. I existed in the shadow of my mother, a woman enlivened by invitations extended and received, darling of society. Painstakingly preserving her legendary beauty with creams and ointments. Delaying the day when time would steal it away. And when it faded, I was to be her successor among the elite. The hostess. The wife. The replica. No detours on the path she paved.

Now my practiced detachment was failing me, and my mind had become saturated with thoughts of Kyle. His genial eyes, his strength of body and character. The way the corner of his mouth upturned, confident and lively. Even the pale, pinky-sized birthmark that I'd noticed along the side of his neck. I daydreamed in scattered images where his kisses grazed my skin and the clandestine giggles of girls who read petticoat novellas tucked inside schoolbooks suddenly made sense.

But the precaution that Miss Ellis had laid upon me infected the visions. One word: *priest*. I didn't fully understand what that meant, as I didn't know any Catholics. Father wouldn't even do business with them if he could help it. It was my understanding that a priest couldn't get married. They were celibate. Did that mean that they couldn't fall in love?

"Julianne!"

"I'll be right down!" I shook off my broodings and exchanged the dress for a white blouse and navy skirt more appropriate for a day at the docks.

❧

I made it to Bootle the following week, arousing the amused curiosity of Miss Ellis, for whom my feeble protestations of "I just wanted to visit with Charles" were all too transparent. I had never come out there more than once a month. And then there was the dress, the shoes.

"I drove my father's Aston today," I said, leading the conversation before it could go anywhere else. "He's rather progressive about those kinds of things."

"I see that."

"Of course, he thinks I'm on a picnic with friends."

"Undoubtedly."

"Would you care to ride in it later?"

"Miss Westcott, if you think that a ride in your motorcar will—"

"Chocolate, Miss Ellis?"

I pulled one with a caramel in the center from a handbag full of bribery.

"You're a sly one, you are." But she took it anyway. Between mouthfuls, she added, "He's in the kitchen, taking a break."

"Charles?"

"I'm not as blind as your brother, no offense meant towards him, missy. I know it's that McCarthy boy you're here for."

"No . . ."

She looked at me with exaggerated sternness, and I knew the pretense was over.

"Oh, Miss Ellis." I released a resigned sigh.

"And I can't say that I blame you. He's a looker. Dreamy—is that what you girls call it? I just don't want you to get your heart broken."

"I won't, I promise. I just couldn't help myself."

"Sure, now." She leaned in, and I had to move closer to hear her. "I think he has until half past until he goes back out. You'd better get a move on."

"Thank you." I gave a grateful wink to my conspirator.

"One more thing, Miss Westcott." She looked right and left in the empty hallway. I think she was enjoying this more than she would be inclined to admit.

"Yes?"

"I hear he likes cricket."

"Don't all men?"

"And gardening."

"Naturally."

"And Miss Westcott—"

"Hmm?"

She pulled a tattered copy of *The Adventures of Sherlock Holmes* from her desk drawer. "I saw him with a copy of this last week. I brought mine from home. It doesn't hurt to have a prop."

"Miss Ellis, you are positively wicked!"

She sat up straight and raised her voice to a normal tone, feigning offense. "Now, Miss Westcott, I am not wicked. I am a God-fearing woman."

"Well, genius, then."

She beamed. "Yes. I like that. Just call me a genius. And name your firstborn for me."

"I'm afraid your thinking is a bit overambitious. I have to talk to him first. Can you please show me the way to the kitchen?"

She pointed to her left, opposite the hall that led to Charles's room. I had not been over here before, and I opened a few closet doors before I heard the cacophony of pans and dishes and found the right one.

The kitchen was rather ordinary, a different aesthetic from the public rooms. It contained all of the necessary things that I supposed a kitchen should. Two large ovens, double sinks, pots of various sizes. Its checkerboard floor made me wonder where the kings and pawns were hiding. The supper hour was over, and the dishes were being washed by a wrinkly skinned man in preparation for dinner later on. A white-aproned woman lingered over the stove, and I gathered by her generous profile that the food here was good. She barked at the man, who was finishing off the last of the drying.

"Hurry up. I need them potatoes peeled and the apples cored. Cobbler don't just make itself."

"Yes, Mrs. Smythe."

"What are you doing here?"

It was not immediately apparent that the cook was talking to me. My attention had been stolen when I saw Kyle sitting at the far end of a long table, facing the windows with one knee pulled to his chest. He was balanced on the back two legs of his chair and had an open book propped against the table's edge. I tightened my grip on the newly obtained copy of *Sherlock Holmes* and wished that I could absorb its contents through touch.

"I said, 'What are you doing in my kitchen?'"

She was brandishing a wooden spoon, which looked as if it was intended for me. I took one step back, but was paralyzed beyond that.

"I'm—I'm just touring the facilities."

"Well, there isn't nothin' here to see but me and Archie, and you'd best get on your way."

I was surprised that Bootle Home employed such a wretchedly dispositioned person.

"She's with me, Ethel."

The voice came from the table, and I saw that Kyle was now observing us. I felt my cheeks warm and hoped he didn't notice their glow.

"She's here to find out how Charles is coming along with his plants."

"Well, don't you be talking business in my kitchen. That's what the meeting rooms are for."

"You're right. It will be just this one time."

He stood up and pulled out the chair opposite him. "Miss Westcott?"

I walked toward him, stunned into silence, my eyes never leaving Ethel and her culinary arsenal. She turned back to the butcher board counter as I passed, and I quickened my pace at the whack of a knife beheading some unfortunate parsnips.

I jumped when I felt a hand on my arm, but it was only Kyle, leading me to the table with an amused grin. "Don't mind her," he whispered. "She's always like that before dinner. And supper. And breakfast, come to think of it. But she's a pussycat the rest of the time."

"At midnight, perhaps?" I offered.

"Yes. At the stroke of midnight, the spell is broken—"

"And she's a cuddly little kitten—"

"Curled up before the fireplace like a ball of yarn."

"Exactly. Thank you." With that, I forgot all about her and was engulfed in the friendliest eyes I had ever seen.

"Nothing to it. She might have had your head on a platter for dinner, and we can't have that, now, can we?"

"It is rather useful to have a head!"

"A perfectly reasonable expectation." He smiled.

I took my place next to him and remembered the so-called reason for my visit. "So, how *are* Charles's plants coming along?"

"Quite well, actually. Some of them have grown an inch or so since you were here."

"And the caterpillar?"

"It's in its chrysalis stage now."

I tried to recall a long-ago course in science, but came up with nothing.

"The chrysalis stage. That's where it curls up into itself and its skin is hardened into something like a shell," he offered.

"That sounds unpleasant."

"Not at all. Not when you know what's happening underneath."

"Can Charles understand the changes in the plants?" I found myself hoping desperately that he could.

"I wouldn't know. Maybe he does. But he does enjoy having them in his room. Miss Ellis told me that she often walks by and sees him holding them."

"Why, that's wonderful!"

"I agree. It's at least something different for him, isn't it?"

"Yes."

I glanced at the book on the table. I pulled mine out of my bag slightly, making sure that the title was visible. He was not reading detective stories, however, which was just as well, since I wasn't, either. I was two chapters away from finishing *Gone with the Wind*. He closed his book, and I saw, with some trepidation, that it was titled *Advanced Latin II*.

He caught me staring at it. "Not exactly light reading, is it?" he said.

"It's for school. I'm just getting a head start on next term."

"Aren't you the smart one?"

"I had better be. I'm on scholarship, and I don't want to take any chances."

My mind raced back to Miss Ellis's single word, the one that had plagued my thoughts for a fortnight. *Priest.* Could she be mistaken? She must have seen him reading this colossal tome and jumped to conclusions. Surely, lots of people studied Latin besides priests. That had to be it. Just a misunderstanding.

"And I don't want to disappoint my father."

"Your father?"

"Yes. It's all he lives for, to see me become a priest."

My heart sank, though I'd known all along that this was the truth of the matter. "Yes, I'd heard something like that. A—a priest." I could barely say the word, and I felt my face prickle with emotion. *Dogs are flying, Lucille,* I thought. *Monkeys are talking.*

"Yes. Two years down and six to go."

"So many?" I asked. "That's how long it takes to become a doctor."

"Well, I will be one, in a certain way. My father says it's like being a doctor for the soul." He paused, placing his elbows on the table. "What about you?"

Archie dropped a pot at the sink, and the clamor echoed in my ears. But not as shrilly as Ethel's voice: "Archibald Smythe, you had better pick that up and get to the potatoes before I—"

"You'd never believe that they were married, would you?" Kyle had leaned in so close that I could feel his breath in my ear, and I became light-headed.

"I beg your pardon?" I couldn't decide if he was joking. But his face looked sincere enough.

"For better or worse!"

"In dishes and in grease."

"'Til dinner do they part."

"Quite so."

"A fine example of wedded bliss," Kyle said. "Makes the seminary look all the more attractive." He grinned, and I pulled away and looked out the window, afraid of what my expression might reveal. "What about you?" he said. "Are you going to university?"

"Yes. In September. I'm going to London. To study nursing."

"Well, how about that? I'll be tending to people's souls, and you'll be tending to their bodies. Together, we're a full service shop."

Like a fool, I couldn't help but like the way he said *together*. "Yes, I suppose we are." I glanced at my hands, my nails painted a champagne color just for the occasion. "Well, I should go see Charles now. It's been nice talking with you."

"You, too, Miss Westcott."

"You can call me Julianne."

"Julianne."

My name lingered there between us, like a musical note whose exquisite sound lingers at the end of a song.

"Let me walk you to that wing. Somebody's got to protect you from the creature with the wooden spoon."

I did my best impression of a damsel in distress. "I would be ever so grateful, Sir McCarthy. It seems that I am forever in your debt." I touched my fingertips to my heart for effect, but stopped short at batting my lashes.

"That's Kyle to you, m'lady. And I don't think the throne will be knighting Irishmen anytime soon, no matter how long I've lived here."

His laugh put me at ease, and I followed him out the door. I would have followed him to the moon.

As he escorted me down the hall, I thought I saw Miss Ellis wink at me.

Abertillery

I quickly forgot the name spoken naïvely by the Campbell boy. It was of no consequence anyway, for its significance belonged to another woman, another life. We approached the farm, easily recognizable by its drooping fences and yards of clotheslines, sagging in the dead of night from abandoned shirts and blouses, skirts and trousers of various sizes, all colors muted by the well-worn thriftiness of hand-me-downs.

I had been here twice before, and had been duly impressed by the efficiency of the large family, if not by their condition. The wash was done by two of the girls and folded by another, while the smallest played hide-and-seek underneath the freshly laundered piles. Most of the boys worked in the field, although one was handy with tools, and brought in a small income repairing furniture.

But tonight was different. Even in the dark, I could see that the chores lay forgotten, foreboding like a canopy hung over the land.

The boy got out of the truck and was at my side before I knew it. He opened my door and offered me his hand. It was a touching gesture, one that took me by surprise. It had been some time since I was treated like a lady, and I couldn't help but be moved.

"She's this way."

He led me through the front door. I expected to find the downstairs empty, as it was well past anyone's bedtime, but the children were scattered across its corners. Most of the younger ones had fallen asleep. Those who were awake were fidgeting. Only the oldest three were alert, aware of the drama unfolding in the next room.

The tallest girl stood up and held out her hand. I did not recognize her, and I thought that she must have been otherwise occupied when I had called here previously. "Thank you for coming," she said, as if I had popped in for a spot of tea. "I'm Emily. Please let me know how I can help."

"What is her condition?"

"She's bleeding. She always does, but not like this."

"Let me see her."

She tapped lightly on the door of the adjacent room, then pushed it open. The room was lit by a single low lamp at the head of the enormous iron bed in its center. The bed was covered by several quilts that were now tainted with a sea of bright crimson. Mr. Campbell knelt at the side of his wife, one hand holding hers and the other clutching a rosary.

He looked up when I entered and nodded in acknowledgment, but his lips continued to move without sound as he prayed repetitively.

"Mrs. Campbell," I said. Her eyes flickered, and I could see that her usually pale skin was now spectral in its whiteness. I stepped close and stroked her face, which was burning with fever. "Emily," I said without looking away, "get cold towels for her head, and prepare warm ones over the fire for the baby."

The mother let out a weak cry as a contraction waved inside her. Her back arched in pain. I pulled away the blankets and her nightgown to see that the baby had already crowned. It had a full head of hair, matted by blood. Another contraction began. I put one hand on her belly and pressed down, willing the baby to come out quickly.

"Push," I said, although the mother had no energy left. The task was left to me, and I worked my hands with every contraction until the miniature

face revealed itself. My finger swept its mouth, removing the sludge of birth. It let out a hearty howl, and I saw a glimmer of relief on Mrs. Campbell's face.

"Almost there. The head is the hardest part." Not that I needed to tell her that. Three more pushes, and the shoulders slipped out with ease. Well practiced, Emily brought me a pair of shears to cut the cord.

"You have a girl."

Mr. Campbell paused in his prayers and looked up. I expected him to be troubled, both at the condition of his wife and at the thought of another mouth to feed. Instead, he looked at his daughter with a radiance that I couldn't comprehend.

I wrapped the baby in a clean towel. Born several weeks early, she seemed to weigh nothing, but she surprised me with her apparent health. It was my routine to bathe the baby before presenting it to its parents. But the mother clung to minutes that faded with each breath, so I handed her over straightaway.

She pulled down her nightgown to reveal an engorged breast, the blue of the veins especially prominent against her chalky skin. She suckled the baby into a calm stupor. What a sweet scene it could have been in other circumstances.

"Thank you," she mouthed, the strain of the words possessing the rest of her strength.

"I did nothing. I—I can't do anything." I paced the room, searching for something that could spare the family this tragedy. I could feel the foundations of my cultivated indifference begin to betray me.

The oldest boy cracked the door open, and Mrs. Campbell covered herself with a blanket. He put his head in. "The priest is here."

The husband left the room to greet him, leaving the door ajar.

"Mr. Campbell?"

I picked up a towel, freshly heated.

"I'm Father McCarthy."

Chapter Three

My hopes for an opportunity to talk with Kyle again were not realized. Miss Ellis told me that his father's health was declining, so he did the work of two men rather than see the old man dismissed. I watched him from Charles's window as he manicured the rosebushes, then cut the lawn in diagonal lines that revealed the dark and light shades of the grass in crisp, alternating bands.

Miss Ellis slipped in and proudly disclosed the further results of her voluntary reconnaissance as we watched him wipe the sweat from his brow with his shirtsleeve and return to work.

"He lives in Liverpool, dear. In fact, he works there during the week."

"Doing what?"

"Same thing. His father has jobs there most days, and only comes out here on the weekends."

"I've never seen him in town."

"Well, it's not likely that you would, is it? Being that he's doing double duty right now. He probably hasn't seen the inside of a pub or a cinema in weeks."

My heart raced at the thought that he was nearer to me every day than I had known. "Anything else?"

"Only that he came from Ireland with his father when he was just two years old. If he has a mother, I don't know anything about it."

She left when her break was over.

That was to be my last time in Bootle for a while. The increased IRA activity on the coasts required more attention from Father, and in turn, he expected more of my help at the warehouse. It was no secret that he wanted me to follow him into business, overseeing the shipping empire that had elevated our family for three generations. It didn't seem to matter that I was a girl. He grudgingly acknowledged my intention to become a nurse, hoping, perhaps, that enough exposure would acclimate me to the idea of working alongside him. "It's all yours, Julianne," he'd say, "since I have no son to leave it to." I loved my father, but it pained me to hear him deny the existence of Charles so effortlessly.

Mother made demands upon my time as well. The annual Ladies' Society festival was close at hand. She was chairing it this year and had tasked me with management of the booths. So far I had deftly avoided any outings with the "nice young men" with whom she was more than willing to arrange social engagements. Her ambition was for me to be the wife of a prominent businessman or politician, replicating her own position in the coterie of the upper class.

I doubted very much that she wanted me to follow her into the private despair that kept her closeted in her rooms with scotch when evenings turned into midnights. But as with the existence of a brother, I wasn't supposed to know about that. I thought of our family, sometimes, as a tapestry: a perfect blending and weaving of colored threads that produced an enviable picture on our surface, while underneath we were a tangled maze of knots and stitches, colliding and separating in our own directions, united only in the mandate to keep the outward appearances lovely.

Whenever I could steal away, I went out with Lucille. We loved catching matinees at the cinema, our favorite being the grand Trocadero, with its curved screen and glossy white Wurlitzer. The Movietone reels' boring bits, like a review of Neville Chamberlain's first month as prime minister, were occasionally offset by good ones like the disappearance of Amelia Earhart. Father would ask me when I returned if they had shown any updates on the Gestapo or other concerns out of Germany, but Lucille and I usually used that time to take turns visiting the lavatory or purchasing a sweet. There was no way that we would miss a minute of Cary Grant, that celluloid enchanter whose magazine photos adorned each of our closet doors.

One afternoon we waited in a queue for two hours to buy tickets for the premiere of *Snow White and the Seven Dwarfs*. We snatched up some Mars bars and Coca-Colas, and dangled our legs over the side of our seats. Lucille and I had anticipated this opening for some time, wondering how the rather ghastly Brothers Grimm tale would be told to a young audience. But I did not have to think on it for long, because early in the film I was seized with a tightness in my stomach that had nothing to do with evil queens or floating mirrors.

The prince was the spitting image of Kyle.

All efforts to keep myself from thinking about him came screeching to a halt. I shifted in my seat and grasped the velvet armrests, daydreaming myself into a world where we had seven small children and lived in a forest. But I couldn't escape the fact that he was bound for something else, a loveless life. Even if that were not the case, he was forbidden to me in other ways, like a polished red apple, poisonous to the touch. He was a Catholic, a profound restriction in the eyes of my father, and a laborer, quite unsuitable in the eyes of my mother.

"What's wrong, Grumpy?" Lucille said later, attempting to pull me from my musings over an ice cream.

"What do you mean?"

"I mean that you've looked like you're in another world for weeks now, and that's not like you. What's going on?"

"Nothing. Just thinking about all we have to do for the festival." As if to prove the point, I pulled my notebook from my handbag and ran my finger down the agenda written in my mother's perfect, scrolled handwriting. Lucille eyed me suspiciously, but I kept my gaze on the paper. I never lied to my friend, and she was likely to see right through me. At last, she appeared to set aside any doubts as she pulled out her own set of notes.

Lucille had already proved to be of inestimable value, as her no-nonsense skills kept us all on task. She stayed over at my house for a few nights before the big event and helped me with the last-minute details. She was authoritative in the best of ways, so I nicknamed her "Doc." When I was ready to quit and go to bed, she called me "Sleepy" and coaxed me back to work.

"Julianne," she asked me at breakfast, list and pen in hand. "How many entries did we get for the bread-making contest?"

I cross-checked my own list. "Fourteen. Which may go up by one if Mrs. Clarke's daughter is able to make it into town. We can adjust the score sheets closer to the time if necessary."

"Right. Do you know if Alice White is making her lemon poppy seed bread again?"

"I certainly hope so—it's the best. But do you think I can get out of voting for her? I can just see the look on her face when she wins for the third time." I raised my chin and peered down my nose at her, but Lucille was all business and gave me no leeway for theatrics.

"We have twenty thousand things to do before the weekend," she said. "Did you ever find out from Mrs. Moore and Mrs. Ward what they decided in regards to the ring game?"

"I think Mrs. Moore won when Reverend Parker got involved. Her idea had been to toss the rings onto tall votive candles with a mock-up of the cathedral in the background."

"Yes, I'm sure it's impossible to defend a clown motif after that."

We carried on with the planning until Friday evening. Lucille declined to accept an official role, but she was an indispensable marvel. With her help, we mapped out the site, reminded everyone of their roles, took inventory of supplies, and sneaked more than one biscuit from the bake sale offerings when they came in.

"Now, the big question—what did you decide to wear for the auction?"

The auction. I was excited about it more than I wanted to let on. It had begun years ago as a parody of coming-out parties. But instead of introducing debutantes to the marriage market, the auction raised money for charity. The prize was the honor of escorting one of Liverpool's young ladies to a picnic at Reynolds Park a few weeks later. For the mothers, it held far less importance than the formals did, since you didn't have to be a real deb to participate. But for the would-be beaus, the competition was as frenzied as bees in a jar. What man passed up the chance to one-up his friends? It had developed into a beloved tradition, and brought in the most proceeds of any activity in the festival lineup.

This year was my turn, and Lucille had been looking forward to it almost as much as I had. Her January birthday prevented her from participating until next time, and she was poised to lavish me with all of her attention as I prepared for it.

"I was hoping that you would help me decide," I said.

We went upstairs to my wardrobe, where I had two dresses hanging apart from the others. I pulled out the first one, draped it on my arm with exaggerated flair, and introduced it in my best hoity-toity voice, which sounded a bit like an opera singer underwater.

"We have here a gown of ice-blue satin, with thin ermine fur trim around the V-neck collar. Sleeves are narrow at the shoulder, widening until gathered again at the wrist, again trimmed in the ermine."

Lucille pursed her lips and clapped her hands with a feigned propriety.

"And, to accessorize, silver sandals with heels, nude silk stockings, and matching ice-blue garters, not that anyone will see them."

"Stunning," Lucille effused with another round of soundless applause. "*Simply* stunning."

I laid that one down on the bed and pulled out dress number two. Displaying it on my other arm, I stroked it slowly as if it were a feather.

"Our next ensemble features a gown of smoky sage green with a curved neckline that hugs the collarbone and cuts dramatically down the back, which is adorned with three layers of pearls. The fabric gathers at the waist and becomes fuller towards the ankles. Again, the silver sandals and nude silk stockings round out this selection with the ice-blue garter, because the store didn't have one to match it."

Lucille rolled back on the floor, amused by both my presentation and my predicament.

"Well"—she drew out her word as she made a decision—"as *devastating* as it is to wear a dress without matching garters, you are *so* right in saying that no one will see them. Therefore, I deem you, Sage Dress, winner of the 1937 Maiden Auction for the Benefit of the Liverpool Anglican Cathedral and the Seaman's Orphanage."

She looked it up and down to confirm her choice.

"Really, Jul, you know that green is the best color for your eyes, and you want to earn as much money as you can, right?"

"Right."

"So, there you go. Now, what about jewelry?"

We raced each other across the house to Mother's wing, where we had been given permission to raid her vast collection and choose something to borrow.

The dressing room sat adjacent to her bedroom. If my parents had ever shared a bedroom, I wasn't aware of it. The décor of Father's rooms had a tastefully neutral palette, accentuated with massive mahogany furniture pieces and punches of navy blue. In contrast, Mother's rooms were delicate and feminine. Her dressing area looked like something out of a Hollywood movie, and was probably large enough to serve as a soundstage. Shades of pastels and various textures were used to create more interest. Ivory feather pillows lined a rosy velveteen settee. A creamy plush rug covered most of the floor. Ribbons of crystal dangled from the lamps. Any starlet would have been envious.

As a child, I was mesmerized by the myriad of prism-like bottles with oils imported from Egypt. They were lined up on her vanity, and in the afternoon the sun would hit them, casting half-moon rainbows on the carpet. When the mood struck her, Mother would draw out the lids one by one and let me inhale their foreign scents. Lotus. Jasmine. Hibiscus.

We opened her cherry wardrobe and found the jewelry cabinet just where we expected to, but discovered something else we didn't. Two bags, lined with the most exquisite lace, and trimmed with turquoise satin ribbons. Lying beside them was an envelope that read, "Julianne and Lucille." We looked at each other in awe, grabbed the bags, and plopped ourselves onto the floor.

Lucille reminded me to use my manners and read the card first. I released my grip on my bag and listened as she read.

"'Girls—I'd like to express my gratitude for all of your help.'"

"The card is read—let's open them!" Impatient as I was, I paused at the sight of Lucille sitting with her hands in her lap, one finger tracing the edge of the gift bag. Of course this would be more meaningful for her than it was for me. Lucille had lost her mother when she was just three years old, and any memories of receiving gifts had long since vanished. My own mother might not be a warm batch of scones and honey, but she was here, and nothing if not generous.

Lucille smiled at the bag, savoring every bit of this surprise, then looked up at me. "Gosh, Jul, your mother didn't have to do this. I didn't really do that much. And Saturday night is *your* night."

"Luce," I said, taking her hand, "you know that we could not have done this without your help. And Saturday night is *our* night. Mother wants it to be special for both of us."

She beamed at me and flashed an eager grin. "Let's open them!"

I let her go first. Gently, she pulled the black velvet box from the wrapping and opened it. She gasped, and put her hand to her chest. Inside was a gray pearl necklace with a garnet pendant framed by tiny diamonds. Garnet earrings and a gray pearl bracelet finished off the set. They were going to look stunning on her. Mother must have chosen the set for Lucille because garnet was her birthstone.

"I've never seen anything so beautiful in all my life! I can't believe that they're *mine*! Oh, Jul!" She threw her arms around me—as if I'd had anything to do with it—then wiped away a joyful tear and said, "Open yours!"

In design, mine was nearly the twin of hers. My pearls were white, and my stone was emerald. Not only the May birthstone, but my signature color. We tried on our dresses with full accessories—hats, gloves, jewelry, and all—and spent an hour twirling in front of the three-paneled mirror. We would have fallen asleep in an exuberant pile, save for the fear of wrinkling our gowns and the need to pin my hair.

I washed up while Lucille changed out of her clothes, and then we switched.

With my hair dry, we began to position the wave curlers and hairgrips. I grimaced at the ones that she did—always very tight on my scalp—but I knew from experience that they came out the best. Lucille didn't have to go through this torture. She was blessed with natural curls, long and dark, but as we are always unsatisfied with what we are given, she planned to iron hers out tomorrow.

No one spoke at first as our skillful fingers wrapped and twisted. We were exhausted after such a full day.

Lucille broke the silence. "Jul?"

"Yes?"

"I'm glad to have my friend back."

"What do you mean?"

"I mean that you've been moping about like something out of a Boris Karloff flick. I wasn't kidding when I called you Grumpy. But I think you're earning your way back up to happy now."

I was sorry that my melancholy had alienated her. Did anyone notice it besides Lucille? She knew me better than most and deserved to know the truth. Reluctantly I let her in on the whole story. She listened with rapt attention, her jaw dropping at all the appropriate times.

"A priest, Julianne? A priest? Oh, leave it to you—the one man that you finally fancy, you can't have!" Finding the irony amusing, she stifled a giggle at the whole impossible thing.

"Oh, let it out, Lucille! You know you want to laugh. But he's not a priest. Not *yet*, anyway. He still has six more years at the seminary." I said it as much to convince myself as her.

But there was no fooling her. "Jul, you know how King Edward abdicated to run off with that Wallis Simpson?"

"Of course. Who will ever forget?"

"What did we think of her?"

"That she was a lowlife bugger."

"Exactly. And why was that?"

"Well . . ." I hesitated. I didn't want to admit to what she was suggesting.

Lucille completed my sentence. "Because she brought scandal to the monarchy."

"Uh-huh."

"And you don't see the similarity?"

"You're not comparing me to an American divorcée, are you?"

"Of course not. Not entirely. You're a far better person than she was." She patted my hand. "But it's kind of the same thing. Isn't Kyle promised to God or something like that, even if he hasn't taken his vows yet? Isn't he supposed to belong to the people of the church, just like the king was supposed to belong to us?"

I was at a loss to disagree with her, but held out one desperate hope. "Well, with all the problems in the world, surely God wouldn't notice one stray seminarian leaving the fold."

She rolled her eyes at me. "And this is the theological brilliance of whom? The girl who goes to church, say, twice a year? When there's a good excuse to buy a new Christmas or Easter dress?"

"Why do you have to do that?" I sighed.

"Do what?"

"Be *right*!" I tried to act indignant, but could manage only an anemic huff as I threw a pillow at her. "I think we won in the end, though. King George is a doll, even if he does stutter, and it's quite fun to see the pictures of the princesses all dressed up."

"See, Jul? You'll win, too, if you just do what you should." She walked over to my four-poster bed, and I helped her pull back the enormous down blankets.

I admitted defeat. She was spot-on. It was pointless to wrap myself in knots over something so futile. I'd be heading to London soon, anyway. Full speed ahead.

I switched off the lamp and fluffed my pillow. I laid my slippers next to my bed, straightening them until they were lined up just so. I peeked at Lucille lying next to me, and her eyelids were already drooping. When she spoke it was with the low drawl of someone lingering between consciousness and the dream state, not that it dulled her witty tongue.

"Why Jul, what *is* that in your hair? *Holy rollers!*"

"Hardy har har. Good night, Lucille."

"Jul, do you think we'll have a *mass* amount of people at the festival tomorrow?"

I ignored her.

"Jul, do you think your father will *pope* his head in here if we're too loud?"

"Oh, that one was terrible."

"You're right. I just couldn't help myself. Sweet dreams."

"You, too."

We were quiet for ten minutes, and I thought she was asleep.

"Jul?"

"Yes?"

"You're not *incensed* with me, are you?"

"Good night, Lucille!"

Smiling as I closed my eyes, I sank into a refreshing calm, the kind that occurs when your mind is finally liberated from something troubling. I had no way of knowing that my afflictions would return stronger than ever by this time tomorrow.

Chapter Four

The weather was cooperating so far. Some rain clouds idled in the distance, but they didn't seem as if they would do anything more than threaten us. It was always a gamble to hold a festival outdoors, but if the sunshine prevailed, it was well worth it. The fresh air augmented charitable sentiments, and the grounds of the botanic gardens provided a stunning backdrop.

We remained home as long as possible before I had to take the curlers out, and Lucille spent the time reviewing last-minute details. She should have been the one inheriting my father's business.

When we could stay no longer, we took down my hair, ironed out Lucille's, and packed our gowns for the evening. The mislaid priorities of the earlier summer months needed to remain squarely behind me, according to Lucille's decisive counsel. I had to free myself from the preoccupation with Kyle McCarthy. The auction would be the perfect distraction.

Although Mother retained a chauffeur, Father and I shared an affinity for driving, and he let me have his new Bentley for the day. In its polished black exterior, we took a final look at our reflections. We drove the four miles to the grounds, whizzing by lesser automobiles and horse-drawn carriages whose owners defied progress. I hoped to park away from anything that could scratch the car, but people were already crowding into the limited spaces. I maneuvered it, finally, between a tangle of bicycles and a tree overrun with birds. I gave the birds a menacing stare, warning them against leaving any deposits, then took Lucille's arm.

We stopped first at the bake sale, where she priced the items and I sampled them before leaving things in her capable hands and going to check on the other tables.

The dunking booth was overflowing with water, and I called for a stack of towels to be placed behind it. Reverend Parker was the first to volunteer, and I wanted to make sure that he was well cared for when he got drenched. No doubt the booth would be the busiest when he provoked the crowd from the hinged seat.

The bread contest table had twelve of the entries in place already, including Alice's lemon poppy seed. It was iced with a sugary coating, and I knew from one look at the competitors that I would be pinning the ribbon on her yet again.

Tin cans were stacked in pyramids waiting to be pummeled, and lights were strung between lampposts. The band was rehearsing in a pavilion. All seemed to be in wonderful order. I reclaimed Lucille, and we set out to report to Mother. We found her talking with Mrs. Denton, and nearly knocked her over with our embrace as we thanked her for the jewelry.

"Now now, there's no need for that," she said, her arms stiffening at the contact. "Your help was invaluable." She slipped out of our hold and shooed us off. "Everything is under control. Go enjoy the festivities. I'll see you at the auction."

We set off to visit a caricature artist but didn't get far before hearing our names.

"Julianne! Lucille!"

Turning, we saw Lotte and Blythe waving us down. I hadn't seen much of them since leaving upper school, which, in Lotte's case, was a welcome interlude. Blythe was a jewel, though, and it was one of the world's great mysteries that they were friends.

"Everything looks aces, Julianne," said Lotte between breaths. "Really, you did a first-class job. Of course, I visited a carnival in Manchester once, where they had fire-eaters and unicyclists. And there was that fund-raiser for the university where they actually built an ice rink. In the summer, no less! But don't you worry. I'm sure you did the best you could."

Lucille grabbed my hand and squeezed it, lest I say anything I might regret.

"Where are you going first? May we join you?" Blythe chimed in, but Lotte charged on with the real reason that she had come over.

"Now, I have some news that'll really blow your wig!" She grabbed my arms, and I felt her nails press against my skin.

"What news?"

"John Parker proposed to Maude and she *accepted*!" Her hands flew in the air as she anticipated a response that would confirm her as queen of the tittle-tattle.

Although this was indeed news, I knew Lotte far too well to take the bait. I simply turned to Lucille, and she shook her head.

"Are you sure?" I asked Lotte.

"Of course, I'm sure," she said. "I just heard it from Maude's sister *herself*. We all saw it coming, but it's so exciting now that it's finally happened!" Lotte could have powered the strung lights with her enthusiasm. "Of course, how Maude could be content being a minister's wife, I don't know, but there are some things that defy all common sense. And it's not as if he even has a position yet—he's still a *student*, for mercy's sake. Still, one can't help but be bolstered by love in the air." She twirled her finger toward the sky.

Appearing to grudgingly accept the validity of Lotte's bulletin, Lucille added, "Well, if that's so, that means that Maude can't be in the auction now. You can't be in the auction if you are engaged or married. Couldn't they have waited until *after* the festival?"

"Oh, I asked her sister that very thing. I know how much she had been looking forward to the auction. But, she is *ever* so much *more* looking forward to showing off her ring, especially with so many people in one place!"

Something told me that it was Lotte who was *ever* so much *more* excited. Maude was not one to relish attention, a quality as foreign to Lotte as kangaroos and courtesy. In fact, I was sure that Maude was quite relieved to be out of the auction spotlight. Still, I was going to chide John for taking away such a valuable commodity at the last instant and call upon his honor to make up for it with a hefty donation.

Despite Blythe's request to join us, Lotte grabbed her companion by the sleeve and rushed off to break the news to her next unsuspecting target.

Romance flourished for more than John and Maude.

Boys of all descriptions were traveling in packs, whistling at the girls and making ardent attempts to pair off with some of them. I wasn't interested, since I was still smarting from the ridiculous infatuation that had swindled me out of my perfect summer. But for Lucille's sake, and that of the event, I finally acquiesced and let one boy buy a glass pendant for me. His friend won a stuffed puppy for Lucille. Bolstered by these cracks in our resolve, we had offers from others to win bigger prizes, but we declined and stole around to the food booths, where we split an undercooked Welsh cake with blackberry jam.

At five o'clock we made our way to the check-in at the lodge.

We were a few minutes late, and about forty girls had already gathered. Only sixteen were in the auction, but everyone liked to participate in the revelry. Some were reminiscing about their past auction years, and the rest, like Lucille, were giddy about their upcoming ones. We were engulfed in a sea of corsets and cosmetics.

After I'd washed my face, Lucille gently lowered my dress over my head and zipped the back. We powdered our noses, rouged our cheeks, smacked our lips, and darkened our eyelashes with mascara. She refreshed my curls and stepped back, looking at me with one finger over her mouth before smiling in approval.

The last touch was our jewelry. Earrings and bracelets on first. Lucille clasped my necklace for me, and I did likewise for her.

We waited our turn for a mirror.

"Julianne, you look like a starlet, straight from the screen," Lucille said.

"You sound like Lotte."

"Well, at least I mean it. And it's true. I pity the rest of the girls. They might as well concede now."

I was about to repay the compliment when Mother entered. I did a little pirouette for her, and she told me that my earrings were crooked. Then she spotted a friend and left with a pat on the cheek.

Lucille compensated me with a warm squeeze, and we walked out to the makeshift stage. We were again surrounded by fussing and flattery, girls complimenting one another lavishly while each covertly wondering how she measured up. The auction wasn't really a contest, but there was an undeniable cachet in being the one to raise the most money.

We drew numbers to settle the order of the auction, after which lists of all the contestants were distributed to the crowd outside so that they could make plans for their bids. Mine was number nine.

The emcee for the event was Lord Mayor William Denton, whose term was soon to expire. "Good evening, ladies and gentlemen." His booming voice must have sounded impressive in the halls of city government. Cheers erupted from all sides. "I hope that you have all been enjoying the festival so far."

More applause. Behind the stage sixteen girls fidgeted and adjusted their gowns.

Lord Mayor Denton gave a little speech on the importance of the auction's two causes tonight, drumming up enthusiasm and priming the crowd to loosen their purse strings.

"Remember," he thundered. "This is all in good fun for not one but two worthy causes. Tonight, you are bidding the opportunity to escort one of these lovely girls to the Ladies' Society Autumn Picnic. Let's remember that they are volunteering for this to help the cathedral building fund and the children of the Seaman's Orphanage. Remember as well that you may bid on a young lady *for* someone else. So, mothers out there, tonight is the night to win the girl that you've always had in mind for your sons!"

That got a chortle from the spectators, though it wasn't in the least facetious. Four years ago Mrs. Hawthorne won a bid on behalf of her visiting nephew, and he married Grace White a year later.

"And so, without further ado, let's bring out our ladies!"

The crowd applauded—mothers and fathers, sisters and brothers, friends, and potential suitors alike. As with all past auctions, this was sure to be talked about for the next few months.

"Lady Number One is Miss Penelope Cumberland. Miss Cumberland has been attending the University of Edinburgh, studying music. She enjoys playing the piano and helping her parents breed spaniels."

Penelope and I had been in school together for years. Plump and pretty, she was a sweetheart if there ever was one, and I hoped that her auction went well. She walked out onto the stage confidently, turning this way and that.

"Do I have ten shillings?"

"Ten shillings!"

"I have ten shillings. Do I have twelve?"

"Twelve shillings!"

And so on and so forth. Penelope went for a respectable one pound and two shillings, and was bought by her beau of seven months, Nigel Gray, who had worked overtime pumping petrol to make sure that no one else took his girl out. He hopped onstage after he'd won and planted a big kiss on her cheek. Together, they shuffled through the crowd toward the band, waiting for the auction to end and the dancing to begin.

"Lady Number Two is Miss Rose Smith. Miss Smith moved to Liverpool from Swansea only two years ago, and is employed as a seamstress. She enjoys seeing movies and going on picnics. Do I have ten shillings?"

Rose Smith went for one pound, seven to Mrs. Tabitha Brewer, her employer. I knew that Rose wanted to participate but *really* didn't want Charlie Franks to win her. He had asked her to step out with him several times, and obstinately didn't believe that her no was firm. When it appeared that he was going to be the winner, Mrs. Brewer threw out a mercy bid and won Rose herself. No doubt she intended to let Rose select her own escort for the picnic.

We were all crowded around in the back, hoping for glimpses of the progress of the auction. It provided juicy gossip, and everyone wanted to be the first to spread it.

I finally had my turn to peer through the curtain, just in time to see Lady Number Three, Miss Anne Murrish, daughter of a local solicitor, ready to take the stage.

"Do I have ten shillings?"

Thwarted by his last attempt, Charlie Franks was determined to win an evening with *any* girl, and was the first to acknowledge the ten shillings.

"Who will give me twelve?"

"Twelve!"

I looked to see who had bid next. I found the source of the voice, and nearly lost the contents of my stomach.

It was Kyle.

Dressed smartly in gray slacks and a herringbone jacket, he was even more handsome than I had remembered. And I had tried so hard *not* to remember. I must have been barmy to think I could. Why was he here tonight? Why was he bidding on a girl when he was heading back to the seminary? I thought he wasn't allowed to like them.

He didn't bid beyond the twelve, but that didn't make me feel any better.

I gave up my spot at the curtain and laid my head against a tree. My perfect day, my perfect evening. Ruined by the very person that I had tried so hard to forget.

I could hear that Anne went for a respectable two pounds. I tried to summon up happiness for her, but it was beyond my abilities.

Five more girls before it was my turn. I checked my wristwatch and ran back to the hall to put myself back together.

Lucille saw me leave and ran after me.

"Julianne! Jul! Wait for me!"

I slowed a little so that she could catch up, but I kept moving forward because I had to get out of there.

"Jul, what happened?" Her words came out with labored pauses as she caught her breath, but it didn't stop her from springing into action. She brushed my hair from my face and pulled out her powder to fix me up.

I hung my head and didn't want to tell her at first, but I knew she'd get it out of me anyway. "It's *him*, Lucille! He's here, and he just bid on Anne!" I pointed a shaky finger in the direction of the stage.

"Him, who? *Him* him? Your *priest*?"

"Cut it out, Luce. Yes, *him*. And no, he's not *my* priest. He's not *any* priest. I told you that he's not nearly done with school yet."

I sniffed, and she pulled a handkerchief out of my handbag.

I asked her all of the same questions that I had agonized over myself. "Why is he here? Why is he bidding on Anne?"

She put her arms around me, rocking me a little and shushing me like a mother to a baby. "There, there. Calm down. I don't know why he's here, but it's no concern of yours. Walk away from this. I've already told you that there's no good end in it."

"But *why* is he here?"

She sighed, resigning herself to my recklessness, and mustered the words to console me. "Maybe he's just a horse's ass."

"Lucille!" I'd never heard an improper word from her. But my darling friend knew what it would take to make me smile.

"Well, sometimes you have to just say what you're thinking. There's another possibility, though."

"I can't wait to hear this one."

"Maybe he plans to bid on you and he's just practicing."

I let this one sink in before dismissing it. "Practicing, huh? Not sure I buy that one."

"Well, dear, you have to believe something, because you're on shortly. There's twenty thousand people waiting for you, and you're a mess!"

Her urgency brought me back to the task at hand. Hastily, we reapplied the cosmetics and brushed my hair until it was shining. She grabbed my hand and led me back to the curtain, gave me a tight squeeze, and disappeared.

"Lady Number Seven is Miss Irene Bath . . ."

I paid no mind to the details, scanning the crowd for Kyle, and found him in the second row. My knees weakened at the sight of him.

"Do I have ten shillings?"

"Ten shillings." From the back.

"Do I have fourteen shillings?"

"Fourteen shillings!" From the right side.

"Fourteen shillings. Do I have sixteen shillings?"

"Sixteen shillings." It came from Kyle.

He didn't bid any higher than that, though, and Irene went for two pounds, five shillings.

Maybe Lucille was right. Maybe he was just preparing to bid on me.

Melody Carlyle came and went for two pounds, seven. Kyle had bid at sixteen shillings again, and no more.

My turn.

Primp. Plump. Straighten. Pucker. Toss. I was ready.

"Lady Number Nine, Miss Helen Westcott." I stepped through the curtains as he introduced me. "Miss Westcott will be attending a nursing college in London in September. She currently works with her father in Albert Dock. She enjoys reading, the movies, and fashion."

Before he could get to the bidding, I stepped close to him and whispered in his ear.

"Excuse me, Miss Westcott has informed me that she is usually addressed by her *middle* name, Julianne. So, do I hear ten shillings for Miss *Julianne* Westcott?"

Several bids for ten shillings were shouted out, and the Lord Mayor quickly increased the ante, knocking out a few men at a time. By the time I had reached two pounds, four ardent bidders had walked away.

I turned and turned again, summoning all of the coquettishness I could muster, all the time scanning the crowd for one face. But Kyle had vanished from his seat. When we reached two pounds, six shillings, I finally found him. Or rather, his back. He had left the crowd altogether, and was walking, hands in pocket, past the dance floor until I couldn't see him anymore.

I was infuriated. I had people in the crowd breaking previous records with their bids, and the *one person* that I had any interest in hadn't even offered two pence. Well, even if he wasn't around to see it, I was sure that he would hear how much I had gone for, so I waved and smiled, playing it up in the hopes of driving the bidding to unprecedented heights.

And I did. I garnered an astounding four pounds, six shillings, eliciting rousing cheers for several minutes. Whoops and handshakes came from the left corner of the crowd, and I was able to see that Roger Kline had won. I didn't know him well, but he was the son of a member of Parliament and was said to have a bright political future ahead of him. I was sure that an outing with him would be interesting, at least. I waved to him and blew him a kiss of thanks before slipping back through the curtain. With the pageantry behind me, my chest began heaving and I gasped for air.

Lucille and Mother and Father were waiting for me near the lodge. Lucille could barely contain herself, even jumping in place. She ran to me first and wrapped me in a giant, joyous hug. "Jul! Four pounds, six shillings! That's *amazing*! No one has ever gone for that much. And to Roger Kline! He's so good-looking."

I shot her dragon eyes, and she recoiled, recalling that I didn't care if Roger Kline or the Man on the Moon had been victorious. I wasn't going to play the charade for her, not when she knew the truth of it. But for Mother, who seemed immensely pleased with the prospects of the winning bidder, I bit my lip and smiled. And, of course, my father looked proud.

I excused myself to walk the grounds while the auction progressed, making a wide arc around the walled garden so that no one would find me, especially Roger. I was in no mood for adulation right now and didn't care to continue the pretense.

I found a tree stump to sit on and watched the gaiety from a distance. My mind was numb, and my legs were tired. I was looking forward to going home and celebrating a job well done tomorrow. Tonight only despondency would be my companion.

At the conclusion of the auction, Lucille found me and tried to pull me toward the dance floor—it seemed that there was no lack of gentlemen asking her for my whereabouts. I asked her to relay that I was feeling ill and told her to tell my parents that I would be walking home. I gave her the keys to the Bentley and hoped that she would find it unharmed.

The light from the moon was brilliant, and it made walking the familiar path easier. The people in the few cars that passed looked bewildered at the sight of the lone girl in the elegant dress, mascara painting trails of woe on her face. One bearing friends of my parents offered me a ride, and while it was tempting to give my aching feet a break, I stayed the course. Stubborn, like my brother.

A mile from home, the heel of my left shoe broke and I stumbled to the ground. Blood ran down my leg, and I felt shards of gravel piercing my skin. The throbbing was so intense that I could have sworn it was audible. I sat down and hugged my knees to my chest. *Great,* I thought. *It can't get any worse than this.*

Then thunder cracked through the sky, and I felt the first of what would surely be many raindrops.

Chapter Five

I looked around in what was quickly becoming a torrential downpour, and I saw in the distance a barn. I'd walked past it often and thought it was a blight on the landscape, with its peeling red paint and sagging doors. It was out of place in a city, one of those occasional plots where the family had owned it for centuries and had not given in to the development surging against its borders. But it was a welcome sanctuary at this moment. I pulled myself up and started to hobble toward it, unbalanced on my shoes.

"Here, let me help you!" a voice from behind me called out. A man stepped forward and wrapped his arm around my waist, helping me walk in the direction of the barn. I shuddered at the realization that I was alone in the dark with a stranger, but I did not have a choice unless I wanted to continue on in the storm. I couldn't see him because my eyes were closed against the heavy droplets, and I whispered a desperate prayer to a God I seldom spoke to.

Letting go of me, he opened the door with both hands. It made a piercingly shrill scream, and appeared to be off its tracks. He waved me inside, where the malodor of farm animals made my nose prickle, and their neighs and baas and groans were unnerving. I shivered in my dress and was once again aware of the pain in my leg. I waved my hands out in the pitch-blackness, utterly disoriented. He told me to wait, closed the barn door with a heave, and fumbled until he found a lantern along the wall. He stood in silhouette as he lit it before approaching me to put his jacket around my shoulders. I tugged the coat tight around me. It smelled good—like earth and cologne.

I wiped my hands across my hair and face as he took my hand and led me over a hay-scattered floor. My breath caught as I looked up. It was Kyle. What a way for him to see me, dripping with rain and tears. At least I had the rain to blame, disguising the tears. Or they could be attributed to my pain. The visible one on my leg. The deeper one was unseen.

I tightened my lips to prevent myself from saying the things that I *really* wanted to say, and let a meek "Thank you" escape instead.

He didn't answer but found a pail and overturned it so that I could sit. He rubbed his hands up and down my arms, shoulder to elbow, trying to warm me up. A month ago this gesture would have sent chills—*good* chills—through me, but right now I was only distracted by imagining how disheveled I must have looked to him.

In the dim light, he was as attractive as I had remembered, and my resentment softened against my better judgment.

He smiled at me briefly, and then moved his hands along his arms, back and forth, until he was warmer. They looked strong and masculine. I wondered what it would be like to hold them.

Foolish girl. There you go again. Was it Lucille's voice in my head or my own?

My teeth no longer chattering, I expressed my gratitude with more sincerity. He had made a habit of earning my goodwill. Kyle found a rickety milking stool, and scooted it next to me. He sat with elbows on his knees and hands together.

"My pleasure," he said. "We can't have young ladies wandering alone in the dark and rain by themselves."

"I was on my way home, and I didn't have much further to go."

"I know, but then you might have contracted pneumonia, and if your parents knew that I could have prevented it, they might just call up the Bootle Home and have me dismissed."

A grin had spread across his face, and just that quickly we were back bantering in the kitchen of Bootle Home. "Maybe I should tell them that you held me hostage in a desolate barn and see what they do then!"

"Oh, but at least you wouldn't be dying from the elements. I think I could talk them into pardoning me."

"It's my word against yours."

"Well, then I'll have to treat you like the lady that you are, and hope for the best."

I didn't have a response for that, so I asked him how he'd found me.

"I followed you," he said with candor. "I was on my way home after the festival when I saw you walking away. You looked upset, and I worried about you making it back safely. I kept my distance so that I didn't bother you, and I would have left as soon as you got in."

I couldn't let him know the true cause of my distress.

My knee ached and I looked down. The blood had seeped through the satin of my gown, as if it weren't already ruined from the fall. I gingerly lifted the dress away from the wound and, disregarding modesty, lifted the hem high above my knee and held it there while I went to work on the silk stocking. I rolled it down a bit at a time, wincing with every movement until it was finally off, and my bare skin felt the sting of the cold air.

When I looked up, I found Kyle's gaze fixed upon my leg. His eyes were slightly glazed and his jaw tense. I peeked down again and realized that the hem of my garter was showing. I stifled a smile, remembering the drama with which I had pronounced to Lucille that no one would, in fact, see my garter. I rolled the dress back down and smoothed out the wrinkles in vain.

His gaze met my eyes and he leaned in before abruptly sitting straight up. We stumbled out words at the same time.

"So, whose idea—" he started.

"What were you doing—"

"You first."

I nodded. "What were you doing at the festival? Aren't you a Catholic?" *Aren't you going to be a priest?* was what I really wanted to say, though I already knew the answer.

"Catholics can't raise money for good causes?"

"What about the cathedral? It's Anglican."

"Are you Anglican?"

"Well, no. My family's not very religious. I mean, we go to church once in a while."

"There you go, then. It's going to be a beautiful monument to God. I am happy to help make that happen."

He had me there. Damn him, I could never get in the last word.

We settled into awkward silence. When I shivered again, he got up to readjust his coat on me, then sat awkwardly again on the little stool.

"I wonder how long the storm is going to last." Weather was a neutral topic, and I wanted to keep talking. I feared that the rapid beat of my heart would give me away in the silence. Besides, I loved the sound of his deep and gentle voice.

"I don't know, but I'll walk you home when it's all over. If we get hungry, I can slaughter that cow over there and have a meal. Do you have a cleaver in that handbag?"

"Very funny." I smiled. "Lucille and I ate so much at the festival, though, I don't think that I could eat even a bird right now, much less a cow."

"All right, *Helen*." I could see his grin even in the dim light.

"Oh, you heard that?"

"Yes. So, what's the story?"

I stretched my legs a bit and removed the pail so that I could sit on the floor. Kyle did the same, and we sat side by side, leaning against the slats of a horse stall. All but touching.

"Well, my grandmother's name was Helen, and my father felt obligated to name his only daughter after his mother. But he allowed my mother to choose Julianne as my middle name, and to call me by that. I'm very glad that she did. My grandmother died when I was little, but I remember her and I didn't like her at all. She was old and crabby. I read once that *Helen* means 'torch.' But to me, it means 'old and crabby.'"

Kyle chuckled. "Well, that would explain how quickly you corrected the Lord Mayor. But it's ironic, you know. Your fictitious meaning for your name."

"How so?"

"Because I think *Julianne* comes from the Latin word for 'youthful.'"

I barely heard what he said, as my ears were ringing from the beautiful sound of my name on his lips. I wanted to hear it again. "I'm sorry, what did you say?"

"Your name—*Julianne*. It means 'youthful.'"

I loved it and wanted more. But I supposed that cajoling him into saying it a third time would have been too flagrant of me. I settled for saying, "Well, how about that?"

"Are you happy to have all that work behind you?" he asked.

"Yes and no. It's kept me very busy, especially in the last few weeks. But I enjoy it, and it's almost a competition with myself to see how much we can raise for a good cause."

"*Two* good causes," he reminded me. "Whose idea was it to split the proceeds this year?"

"My father's. He suggested the cathedral, because it's a popular project in town right now. I'm sure it has a good business angle to it. But the Ladies' Society still wanted to have a charity attached to it, so we added the orphanage."

"Speaking of which, how much did you go for at auction? I hope the winner checked your teeth and made sure that you were a good buy."

This was exactly the topic I wanted to avoid. I could still see his back as he walked away rather than bid for me. Smoothing back my hair and clutching my pride, I said, "I did *very* well, thank you. I brought in four pounds, six shillings, the highest amount ever garnered at the auction."

"Well, good for you! I'm not surprised. Who is the lucky man?"

Well, *he* certainly wasn't, and didn't even try to be.

"Roger Kline," I said. "And I'm *so* glad that he won. He's *so* handsome, and his father is a secretary at Parliament. I'm sure that he will be just *fascinating* to talk to." I couldn't help but follow this Scarlett O'Hara line of patter. The book was fresh in my memory.

"Roger Kline. Huh."

I wasn't sure if it was an interested "huh" or a mocking "ha."

"What do you have against Roger Kline?"

"I don't have anything against him. I was just remembering that I hit him once when we were younger. I broke his nose. You know, Irish temper."

I sat up straight. "You beat up Roger Kline? Why?"

"My father worked on his family's grounds. One time, he ran over and took my lunch. So I let him have it."

"He took your lunch? He doesn't seem like the type."

"Well, we all grow up and change, don't we?"

"Did you get your father in trouble?"

"Nearly. He and Roger's father worked it out. I had to be Roger's slave for about a month to make up for it. I shined his shoes and washed down his horse and helped him with his Latin homework."

"I wouldn't have thought that you have a hot temper."

"I used to, but I think a few weeks of servitude cured me of it. When you go out on your date with Roger, take a good look at his nose and think of me. I believe it is still a little crooked." He sat back with a smug expression on his face and crossed his arms.

"I will do that."

He watched me with an intense gaze, looked away, and returned with a more carefree expression in his eyes. "He's a good chap, though. Really. I hope that you get along well with him."

It sounded like the rain was stopping, but it only paused and then pounded again. The rafters of the barn seemed to shake, but nothing was leaking. I was beginning to feel a little warmer.

"So tell me about your brother," he said.

For an awful moment, I didn't know what he was talking about. The word *brother* was foreign to me on someone else's tongue, and barely an acquaintance on my own.

"Oh, Charles?"

"Do you have another brother?"

"No, no I don't. It's just that, well, I never get to talk about Charles to anyone."

"Why not? You don't seem to be ashamed of him. In fact, it's quite remarkable that you come to see him so often. You know, not many people come out to visit the residents."

I swallowed the guilt that gripped me, not wanting to admit that the most recent visits had little to do with Charles. "Well, you know how it is at those kinds of places. Even Bootle Home. The family is devastated when they realize that their child is not all that they expected. And they send them off to someplace that will take responsibility for them. It's like storing them in a cupboard, only to be dusted off when it's convenient. And sometimes it never is. Like with my family."

Kyle seemed taken aback. "With your family? I'm sorry. What do you mean?"

"Kyle—" I liked the feel of his name on my lips. The throaty groan that began in the back of my throat, finishing with the delicate sweep of my tongue across my teeth. If he noticed the hesitation in my voice, he didn't say anything, and I rushed my next words to make up for it. "Kyle—have you ever seen my parents? At Bootle, I mean?"

He paused, trying to remember. "I suppose I haven't. Maybe they come during the week."

"No, they don't. They never come. I don't know if they've ever been there since they dropped him off so many years ago."

"Wow." He frowned, the depth of my brother's isolation sinking in. "How old were you?"

"The same. He's my twin. One they discarded, and the other they're trying to hold to an impossible standard of perfection, as if to compensate."

I surprised myself with my own vehemence. I had not admitted these things to anyone, not even to Lucille. Perhaps not even to myself. Kyle had a way of making me feel as if I could confess anything.

But I wasn't finished. I was unable to stop now that I had unplugged the hole in the well-guarded dam. "And that's not all. Father became obsessed with his business, and I'm convinced that it drove Mother to drink. The perfect lady had an imperfect child. And the remaining one has been making up for it ever since."

I sniffed, holding back tears, and shook my head in determination. I would not cry in front of him. I had already said more than I ever planned to.

"How did you find out about Charles?" he asked.

"I was"—*oh, bollocks: Why not just let it all go?*—"I was in Mother's dressing room a couple of years ago rummaging through her drawers for some rouge. She said I wasn't old enough to wear it yet, but I just wanted to try it."

I knew I was procrastinating. "Anyway. The bottom flap of the drawer was loose, and I thought that she would appreciate it being set straight. But it moved easily and I saw that there were some papers underneath. I found a photograph of two babies, side by side. One was plump and smiling. The other looked somewhat lifeless, with slanted eyes and a blank stare. I turned it over and read, 'Charles and Julianne—July 1919.'"

"I can't imagine. What did you think?"

"I didn't have to think. The other paperwork contained a birth certificate and letters from Bootle. So the next week, I decided to take a look for myself. And I've been coming back ever since, making one excuse or another for my absence."

I was exhausted by the sudden release of this burden. Kyle sighed deeply, from what I couldn't say. Maybe he was thinking that this was what it was going to be like to be a priest. To hear a confession and choose between condemnation and forgiveness. The latter really seemed to fit him best, although I feared that I had strained the thin thread of friendship that we had begun. My family's secrets made me feel like a pariah in disguise as a princess.

He was a good listener, and it made me see him in a different way. The way I should see him. I could almost understand why he wanted to be a priest, and I knew that he'd be an exceptional one. That brought me some peace, and I almost found it easier to accept this die he'd cast. Almost.

"Is that why you want to be a nurse?"

We had scooted in closer to each other without realizing it, and I could have reached out to touch him if I'd dared.

"Partially. There's no doubt that my time at Bootle Home has been an inspiration. Or that it will be a useful skill if we end up in another war. But it's a good question. Why do I want to study nursing?" I looked up at the rafters. It was not an uncommon question. To my mother's friends, I answered, "So that I can give back, like Mother does," which was followed by airy approval, if not understanding. To my father's friends, I answered, "Oh, I don't have a head for business. But I need to do something useful." To which they responded with the smug acknowledgment that women, of course, were not cut out for a man's work. I supposed what I'd just suggested to Kyle was true—I'd first thought of it after meeting Charles. But to Kyle I could tell the darkest part of the truth, regardless of what he would think of me.

"To do something different than what is planned out for me."

There. That would seal the deal. I wasn't a selfless heroine, a Clara Barton for the ages.

He pursed his lips and nodded. "I can't say that I blame you."

I must have looked startled. I certainly felt it.

He continued. "It can be suffocating to live on a pedestal, to live according to someone else's expectations." His voice trailed off, and I wondered if we were even talking about me anymore. Just as well. I was tired of talking about me.

"So what's your story?" I asked.

"Mine?"

"Yes—you've heard all about me. It's my turn to ask the questions."

"Not much to say. I've helped my father in his work as long as I can remember. I'm here for the summers and in Durham during the school year. The end."

He made it sound so simple, but I had the sense that I was getting the brush-off. That wouldn't do.

I felt emboldened tonight. I'd been a success at the auction. I had revealed the secrets that troubled me. Surely I could delve into the questions that I most wanted answers to.

"But—a priest. How did that happen?" As if it had been an accident. *I tripped on a pavement crack and became a priest.*

"It's something that I've been drawn to for many years," he said. "The traditions, the rituals. I served as an acolyte, and I always thought that it could be a worthwhile life, saving people's souls."

"Won't you have to speak Latin and wear a dress?" *And give up women,* I wanted to add. But I couldn't bring myself to say that. So much for audacity.

"Well, I'm fairly proficient in Latin by now. And priests don't wear dresses, they wear cassocks. It's not the same thing."

"I just don't understand, though. It seems so—hmm—" I bit my lip, trying to think of the right word. "It seems like such a *drastic* thing to choose."

"God has blessed me with much. It's a small thing for me to give in return."

Again, he'd had the last word. How could I come up with a smart retort when he said things like that?

We continued to talk, and I was blissfully unaware of the time. He asked me more about my school plans, and I asked what Durham was like. I told him about Lucille, and he entertained me with some Irish jokes. I basked in the glow that I felt from being near him.

"Do you think we'll get in trouble for being here?" he asked.

"No, this is the Eckleys' barn. They're visiting family in Formby right now. Besides, they owe Father a favor, so I don't think they'd mind."

"What favor is that?"

"Some developers wanted the land, and Father petitioned his friends in the city government to let the Eckleys keep it. He says it's because there's too much development, but I think it's because they export a lot of wool from their sheep farm in Knowsley and store it in his warehouse until it's ready for shipment."

"That's a little cynical."

"That's business for you. Still, he does like his open spaces, so maybe there's a little truth in it. It's a good thing we live on the park."

"Oh, I completely agree. Ideally, I would love to live out in the country. Just me and the hills and the silence. What about you?"

I couldn't exactly tell him that I couldn't imagine living more than five blocks from a good dress shop. "Oh, absolutely," I said instead. "Hills and silence? What else could one want?"

The livestock had long since become used to our presence and stopped looking at us altogether. Although one of the cows eyed me with suspicion, as if she disapproved of my white lie.

I could see that we were each stifling yawns, but neither made a move to leave. At one point, he lay back against the stall and closed his eyes. I thought that he might be sleeping. I curled my knees up to my chin and put my arms around my legs, avoiding the painful area. Head on my arms, tilted to the side.

I looked at him, so still. Handsome. Good. Funny. He was so wonderful with Charles. He was unlike any other man that I knew, and I couldn't help but be drawn to him. Was this what love felt like? Or the beginning of it? I dismissed that thought, rationalizing that I had known him for too little a time.

I stayed in the same position, even as my joints stiffened. How I would have liked to sit next to him, to ask him the things that burned inside of me. To hear him tell me that he liked having me here.

Why didn't you bid on me? I can understand, with the priest thing, if you didn't bid on anyone, but you did. "Why didn't you bid on me?"

He shifted and I gasped—had I said that last part out loud? I hoped that he hadn't heard. It couldn't have been more than a whisper.

Still lying down, he said, "So you noticed that."

No turning back. I didn't try to hide the resentment in my voice. "Of course I noticed it. I saw you bid on Anne and Irene and Melody. I didn't even know that you *knew* them. But you didn't bid on *me*."

"I *didn't* know them."

"That's not an answer."

"That's the best one that I have."

"No, it's not. Why did you bid so low on them and then stop? Why did you leave when my name was called?"

"You really want to know?"

"Yes." We were almost yelling now. "Yes," I repeated in a whisper.

"I bid on them because I figured that raising the money was important to you. I didn't expect to win with those bids, but I wanted to drive up the price to help you—to help the cause."

He always surprised me with his answers.

"But that doesn't answer my other question."

"Which was?"

He knows perfectly well what my other question was, but he's going to make me repeat it.

"Why did you bid on them and not me." It was more of a statement, a small accusation, than it was a question.

He didn't answer immediately, and instead, sat up and folded his hands over his crisscrossed legs. He looked me straight in the eye, promising the truth. When he spoke, his voice had softened.

"I didn't bid on you because you are the *only* girl that I didn't want to go out with."

My eyes widened at this admission until he backtracked.

"Wait—my fault. That's not what I meant. It came out wrong. What I meant was, you're the only girl that I didn't trust myself with. I am going back to the seminary soon, and I couldn't risk—"

"Risk?"

He sighed and hesitated for a moment, juggling his thoughts. I felt electricity in the air, and we leaned toward each other slightly. I could kiss him now . . .

"I couldn't risk falling for you any more than I already have."

Abertillery

The baby nursed until she had her fill. It was unlikely that Mrs. Campbell would still be part of this world at the time of the next feeding, so I started to look for something that could substitute until a permanent solution was found. Perhaps they could put out an advertisement for a wet nurse. Everyone was trying to make an extra shilling here and there. Not that the Campbells could spare it, but what choice did they have?

I instructed Emily to find some cheesecloth. We'd try to create a make-shift bottle by dipping it into some goat's milk and letting the baby suckle it. As she left the bedroom, I could hear the murmurings of the men coming from the other room.

The baby suddenly let out a desperate scream, demanding my attention. My nipples tingled in response, startling me, and my arms encircled them out of instinct. My own milk had dried up over two decades ago, never used. My breasts, once a gateway to intimacy, had not been seen by anyone since then. And yet, I knew they were still the most beautiful part of me, smooth and plump, spared the scars that had entombed the face of my youth.

The newest Campbell wailed again, and I broke myself away from thoughts of long ago. I dipped her into the now-warm water that had been prepared, and gently, gently rubbed her wrinkled skin. How many times had I done this? At least a hundred. It was common knowledge that babies didn't need to be handled so delicately—they had just survived the trauma of the birth canal, so could certainly handle a decent scrubbing. But in my arms, this nearly motherless child felt especially fragile.

Behind me, the men entered the room—the dying woman's husband, and the mysterious Father McCarthy. I heard the priest open his kit and place bottles on the side of the bed. Oil and holy water, if I remembered correctly.

"Pax huic domui. Et omnibus habitantibus in ea."

A chill meandered down my spine, spreading through my body until I was covered in goose bumps. The name, the voice, the ritual—they stirred memories that I had thought to be permanently buried. Darkness surrounded me as I closed my eyes and recalled the explanation that the boy from my youth had given:

"This is called extreme unction. It helps to send the dying person along on their journey."

Those words sounded hollow, as if they were said in a tunnel, a long tunnel that spanned the distance of decades and was devoid of light. Holding the baby in my right arm, I put my good hand on my temples and squeezed hard, banishing the visions.

I glanced to my side just enough to see the priest wrap a flat purple stole around his neck, but he turned before I could see his face. "Miserere mei, Deus: secundum magnam misericordiam tuam. Gloria Patri, et Filii, et Spiritus Sancti." *The damned dead language taunted me. I hadn't set foot in a church since that Christmas morning when I became somebody else. The condemned don't have any need for religion.*

I returned to my task and laid the baby in a dry towel. Her cobalt eyes looked back at me through half-shut eyelids, still new to light. She relaxed in the comfort of my embrace as I rocked her gently. I was most at ease around babies. They didn't take a second look at me, for they had not yet been taught what is beautiful and what is not. They were born into Eden, only to eat from the Tree of Knowledge shortly thereafter.

I put her tiny hands through the arms of the sleeper, much too big for her, and rolled the sleeves until they seemed to swallow her. I did the same with the legs. Snap, snap, snap. She was bundled well, but as I laid her in a nearby basket, I covered her with a blanket for extra measure.

"Exaudi nos, Domine, sanctae Pater, omnipotens, aeterne Deus: et mittere digneris sanctum Angelum tuum de caelis, qui custodiat, foveat, protegat, visitet atque defendat omnes habitantes in hoc habitaculo."

The words were spoken with an excellent command. But maybe there was nothing special in that. Perhaps every priest could speak it as if it were his native tongue.

I heard him fiddle with the bottles of oils, and then whisper something to Mrs. Campbell. But the words that were audible to me were the ones from years ago. The scene not this remote farmhouse but a tiny flat near a train track. And the dying one is a man, the boy's father, victim of old age and tuberculosis.

"This is the part where the priest hears the confession, Julianne. It is the last chance to unburden themselves of their sins."

Julianne. No. I have no use for that name. Make it go away.

"Accipe, soror, Viaticum Corporis Domini nostri Jesu Christi, qui te custodiat ab hoste maligno, et perducat in vitam aeternam. Amen." *The priest behind me speaks. The boy in my head explains.*

"Now the priest is anointing him," Kyle says. *"A cross on his head and one on each hand." I recall a chipped teacup on the bureau.*

"Ego facultate mihi ab Apostolic Sede tributa, indulgentiam plenariam et remissionem omnium peccatorum tibi concedo. Et benedico te . . ."

"The holy water blesses him." I stand at the iron footboard and watch the ritual with awe. I do not know where I am. I clutch the baby and lean on a nearby table.

Go away. I do not want to remember this. Go away. I put my hand to my head.

Priest: "In nomine Patris . . ."

Boy: "He crosses his head, in the name of the Father, and of the Son, and of the Holy Ghost."

Priest: "Et Filii . . ."

Boy: "He's calling on the intercession of the Trinity."

Priest: "Et Spiritus Sancti."

Both: "Amen."

The words confuse me, and I cannot breathe. I do not know what is real, what is my imagination. The Latin. The English. The then. The now. The priest. The boy. The voice. They're the same. They're the same.

Chapter Six

The interior of the first-class cabin was unexpectedly shabby, and came with an apology from the porter, who said that this particular Pullman car was being taken out of service for refurbishment next month. Had Mother been sitting in my place, she might have threatened to write a letter to the president of the rail line. But I neither cared nor responded, and instead sunk into the green velvet seats with their unraveled gold embroidery, leaning my head against the window as I closed my eyes. The pane was cool against my flushed skin. This summer had been one of highs and lows, infatuation and disappointment. I was ready to leave that behind, and looked forward to starting school in London.

The train lurched, and I sat up straight. My seat faced the rear of the car, and no one had taken the one opposite me. I was relieved, as I was in no mood for making small talk. I watched the people who had come to see the passengers off. They trickled back in to the Lime Street station, and I thought I saw the back of Mother's hat as she left with Lucille. Father had said good-bye back at home before heading to a meeting with some flower importers from Amsterdam who wanted to store their bulbs in the warehouse.

The abandoned, chateau-like building that bordered the station came into view as the train gained momentum. It had once been the celebrated North Western Hotel, but was now four years closed. Its gray slate roof towered five stories above me, and its windows were darkened from disuse. I felt a pang of empathy with the old landmark. Its exterior preserved a stately deportment, while I could only imagine the secrets that the now-vacant rooms must hold.

There were appearances that had needed to be sustained for the remainder of the summer, but I, too, was empty inside. Kyle's admission had haunted my soul ever since he had spoken it. *I couldn't risk falling for you any more than I already have.*

We left the barn moments after that, the nighttime world around us gleaming in the renewed light of the moon now that the storm had swept past. We walked the rest of the way to my home in silence, with Kyle following me at a distance that deterred temptation. He spoke only when we'd reached the gate to the redbrick manor. "I'll stay to see that you get in safely. Look after that knee." After just a few steps I glanced back, but the shadows of the trees at the gate cast him into darkness, and I could no longer see him.

For days, I didn't come out of my room, telling everyone that I was ill. It was easy for them to believe. I'd come home, dripping, chilled from the rain. Mother had Betty make some chicken broth, and she also sent up tea with lemons. It was a common remedy for her complaints. Although she added bourbon to hers surreptitiously.

Little did she know that there was not a cure-all for my kind of ailment.

Father came to my room to check on me several times, but I feigned sleep. To add to my heartache, I was sorry that I'd been unfair in my description of him to Kyle. We might have seen things differently, but we were close, and he was good to me.

Do I or don't I? That was the question I wrestled with, hour by hour, as I recalled the evening—our easy way of conversing, how liberated

I'd felt with Kyle. My true self unveiled. Then I remembered those moments after he'd confessed his feelings, in which we had sat in silence, immobile, on the precipice of a scandalous decision. I felt shackled in my own body as I resisted my desire to lean in and kiss him, to show him what he would be missing. It wasn't too late, I told myself. Surely, there were hidden places on the grounds of Bootle Home where I could call him over and convince him to choose me.

Yet, if I truly cared about him, I couldn't be so selfish.

In the event I weakened, I could count on Lucille to keep me in line. She'd been eyeing me in an odd manner ever since the auction. Something was certainly awry, and knowing me as she did, she had probably figured it out.

And her inevitable, concerned admonishment would have been correct. *What was the punishment for stealing from God?* I didn't want to find out.

So, whether my motivations were altruistic or merely the fear of divine wrath, only one answer was possible. I had to let him go.

It wasn't so easy. Now that it had been in my grasp, I saw love all around me. Couples hand in hand in the park. Couples dining out together. Couples at the cinema, sharing popcorn. They were everywhere, and I just hadn't noticed before. Their happiness mocked my resolve, and I responded by avoiding Kyle at all costs.

I chose to visit Charles on weekdays, when I knew Kyle would be in Liverpool. Yet, as the days on the calendar dwindled and my departure for London grew imminent, I allowed myself one final Saturday visit. I couldn't bear to leave without seeing him one more time. But I wasn't going to let him see me. I took Father's Kodak from the closet in his library and hid it in the zippered compartment of my handbag.

"Yes, yes, Charles," I said and shooed his hand away as he tugged my sleeve. He murmured something that must have been an invitation to see his plants. I was immediately consumed by guilt. My brother was a victim of my distraction, and I promised myself to make it up to him by staying a little longer. Still, I couldn't focus on him. I peeked out of the window, desperate to avoid discovery. The curtains had a rough texture, like a brocade. Gold and red. I rubbed them in the palm of my hand. Funny, I hadn't noticed them before. But, patient in my surveillance, I saw details all around me with new eyes. The cobblestone path below was laid in an offset pattern and the iron gate was adorned with a scrolled *B* that was so elaborate, you could barely tell what it was.

At last Kyle appeared down in the gardens. His unkempt white shirt was unbuttoned at the top, and his forearms and neck glistened from the sweat of hard work. He had a melancholy look about him, and it only made my ache for him more pronounced. I wanted to run outside, to abandon every promise I'd made to myself. To tell him that I was here, that if he had fallen for me, he could have me. My knuckles whitened as I gripped the sill and debated my next move. But then, his mouth slanted slightly upward, forming a whistle. I wondered what tune was on his lips.

I pressed the lens of the Kodak right up against the glass to avoid a glare, wrapped the body of it in the curtain, and snapped the picture before he could see me. I hoped that it would turn out well, because I wasn't going to chance another one.

With my heart pounding, I took a breath and turned away from the window. I picked up one of the plants.

"My, my, Charles. Look how they've grown." I set it back and hugged him until he pushed me away. He didn't understand that I was leaving for a long time. Would he miss me? Or was each day the same to him? So often I wished I knew what went on in his head. I kissed his hands and fled the room, pulling out a handkerchief to wipe my eyes.

As I passed the reception desk, Miss Ellis came around and said good-bye to me with that tragic expression that had made a home on her face. "We'll miss you, deary. You write to us and let us know how you're doing."

"I will. And thank you. Thank you for everything."

I embraced her tightly, my partner in crime. She represented much of what had become special to me here.

"He'll miss you, too, you know."

I didn't know if she meant Charles or Kyle.

⤜✦⤛

After a couple of hours, the train slowed into the station at Crewe. I pulled a compact out of my handbag to powder my nose. My eyes were red, and I blinked several times to wet them. Stretching my arms, I reached for my bag and exited the cabin.

The porter took my hand to help me down the steps. "And where are you heading today, lass?" His voice had a Scottish lilt.

"London. Victoria station, please."

"Aye, that'll be Platform Four. Just go down a ways on your right. We'll have your trunks delivered." He glanced at his gold pocket watch and pointed to the left. "You've got just under an hour before it departs, and there's a café inside the hall over there."

I did not care to sit in a busy station, preferring to be alone with my thoughts. "May I just go straight to the train and board now?"

"Right you are, lass. It should be open. I think they've just cleaned it."

"Thank you. I do prefer that."

I handed him a few shillings, and he tipped his hat as I walked away.

The Crewe station was familiar to me, having made this transfer many times with Mother when we went to London to go shopping for a few days. Its large, angled ceiling was supported by a crisscross pattern of iron and glass, displaying none of the elegance of the Liverpool station, with its arched features that softened the industrial setting.

A train pulled into Platform Six as I continued on, sending billows of exhaust into my face. I turned away and coughed, and put my hand over my nose until I reached the Pullman that would bring me to my new home.

The porter at Platform Four was more perfunctory than the prior one, and I helped myself into the cabin. This one was immaculate. The velvet on the wide and comfortable seats looked as if it had been upholstered yesterday, and tables between the seats were reflective enough to see my face.

My stomach rumbled as I wandered to the adjacent dining car, which proved even more stunning than the first-class compartment. The starched ivory napkins were folded into perfect peaks, and the crystal goblets were spotless. The leather seats were adorned with beaded brass trim, and the lacquered wood paneling featured etchings of Greek gods. Mother would have loved this, and I let a little smile escape.

I slipped into a chair by a window and was met immediately by a steward who seemed to appear out of nowhere.

"Good afternoon, Miss. What may I get for you?"

"Some tea and roast with pudding, please."

"The kitchen will not be ready for hot food until a few minutes before we leave. But we may have some cold items already prepared."

"That will do. Whatever you have. Thank you."

He left as silently as he had entered, and then returned with a plate of egg salad sandwiches cut into triangles. I must have looked dejected, because he apologized.

"I'm sorry, Miss. I had hoped that the cucumbers would have been delivered by now, but as they were not, I brought these. If you are able to wait for half an hour, I will be able to bring something different."

"No, this is fine."

"Good, then. I'll have your tea out shortly."

I had not cared for egg salad sandwiches since I was about seven years old and had become sick after eating one at my grandmother's house. I'd successfully avoided them until just a few weeks ago at the picnic at Reynolds Park. I sighed and recalled the day for which my mother had harbored such high hopes.

Mother had been fidgety leading up to my outing with Roger Kline. She'd muss my hair as she walked by me, brush it back with her fingers, and frown. She took me to her jewelry cabinet and made me try several combinations of earrings and brooches until she was satisfied. When Roger arrived to pick me up, she stood and watched from the turret window, holding a handkerchief in front of her face to conceal the thin smile that I knew was there.

Mother had bought for me a blue dress with white polka dots, green buttons, and trim. My wide-rimmed white hat was banded with a matching blue fabric. As the day was warm and breezeless, there seemed no danger of it blowing away.

The drive was short, and my conversation with Roger was limited to the kinds of polite inquiries that flow like a report on the facts of a person's life. What do you think of the weather? Where did you go to school? What did you think of the festival? Do you have any siblings?

Thankfully, we arrived just as Roger asked that one, as it pained me every time I denied the existence of my brother. But neither could I think of including him in the secret that only Lucille and Kyle knew.

Once out of the Packard, I led us on to safer pleasantries. "My, it is already crowded."

Roger took a basket out of the backseat. "Yes. The weather is good for it. I hope you don't mind, but I told some fellows that we'd meet them in front of the mansion."

"That would be lovely." I forced a smile and took a blanket from the car.

We strolled past children playing ball and sweethearts getting close on benches. I turned my head to hide the tear that was trying to escape. At last, we passed the roundabout tulip garden and found most of the people who had been at the festival.

"Jules!"

"Anne!" It was good to see a familiar face. In fact, I recognized most of the girls, if not from personal acquaintance, then at least by the memory of the frantic primping that had preceded the auction.

"Golly, Jules—just everyone is talking about how much money you raised." She leaned in to me conspiratorially. "And what a catch—Roger Kline! We're all just swooning with jealousy! He's going to make something of himself someday, you just wait and see."

My smile was becoming more practiced, and I found it easier to put on. "Yes. How fortunate that it worked out that way."

"Well, you have a good time. I'm here with Ralph Henry. His pop's a milliner. Ha! Maybe I can get a discount on a new hat or two." She waved as a man with pinstriped trousers and red braces over his white shirt beckoned her on. "Ooh, I've got to go. We were going to try our hand at croquet, and I think they've just finished setting it up. See you around, Jules."

"Take care, Anne."

When I turned around, Roger caught my elbow and led me to a group of couples sitting near a small fountain. "I found a spot for us."

I sat down in the place where he had laid our blanket. Still standing above me, he turned to the side and started talking in an animated fashion to a fellow with greased hair. I adjusted my dress to cover my knees and waited for Roger to open the basket, but when his conversation showed no sign of letting up, I finally opened it myself to find that it contained a couple of plates of egg salad sandwiches and pea and mint soup. I dug deeper, looking for a tart, a chicken, anything, but it was otherwise empty.

I looked up, knee height to Roger, but he had turned to another friend. They shook hands and slapped each other on the back and displayed their perfectly white teeth. Another one joined the conversation, which I could not hear over, as the sound of water splashing in the fountain was right behind me. I looked at the sandwich like it was some kind of enemy to conquer and took my first bite.

It did taste good—it was flavored with a hint of paprika, which I found to be a nice touch—but it was not long before I began to feel decidedly queasy. I looked out through the forest of legs presented by the mingling crowd and then up at the sky, whose vastness made me dizzy. I dug around in the basket one last time in the hopes of finding something to drink, but there was nothing. At last, I clutched the rounded edge of the fountain and pulled myself to my feet, ignoring my wobbly legs.

"Excuse me, Roger," I said in a small voice. But he was letting out a hearty laugh and slapping the back of the man next to him once again. "Roger," I said, more loudly.

He turned his head and looked over his shoulder. "Hey, there. Are you OK? You don't look so good."

"I think I'd like to get some fresh air, please."

He looked around, understandably confused by what I meant, as we were in a park.

"I mean, maybe take a walk. Get away from the crowd."

"Hey, OK. We can do that." He turned back to the group that he'd been talking to. "We'll catch up later, then. David—call me on Tuesday. We can meet at my club and talk it over."

"Right, my friend. Looking forward to it."

Roger shook hands with everyone in the group before taking my arm. He looked down at the basket. "Did you get something to eat?"

"Yes, but I'm not sure it agreed with me."

"I'm sorry to hear that. That was a bit of stuff our cook made yesterday. I didn't have time to make it myself as I'd hoped."

"It was fine. It tasted fine. Could we go walk that way?" I pointed south near the end of the park, which was much less crowded.

"Absolutely. I'll just leave these here," he said, stepping on the blanket, "and we'll get them when we come back."

We walked to the end of the park until we reached Church Street, and just continued on. The passing cars were a welcome exchange for the glad-handing of a few minutes ago.

I finally spoke. "I'm sorry about that. I'm feeling a bit better now." I pulled my hair back and twisted it into a tight bun before releasing it.

"No, I'm sorry, Julianne. I wasn't paying any attention to you. I hadn't seen some of those fellows in a while, but we can get together another time."

"Really, I'm fine. It will help to talk about something else, though."

He nodded. "Liverpool beat Leeds United, did you catch that?"

"No, I don't really follow football."

"I don't imagine you do. It's quite the thing in our house. I played a bit in school myself. Mum's a sport. But she's not your typical girl."

"No?"

"No. She'll kick the ball around with me for fun, and she doesn't hesitate to light up a cigar with Pops, but you get her out to a party with him and she dazzles."

"I understand that your father is in Parliament."

Roger's eyes lit up. "Yes. He's been in for a while now. We don't see him much now, as he spends most of his time in London. He was a major promoter of Neville Chamberlain for PM, so that kept him fairly busy."

I bit my lip, but made a contribution. "I don't follow politics much, but I know that my father didn't really want Chamberlain to become prime minister. He thinks he's too focused on domestic policy, and he doesn't like the Non-Intention Committee, either."

Roger laughed. "I think you mean the Non-Intervention Committee."

"Yes. That's the one. You know, how Chamberlain wants to make friends with Mussolini and how he praised Nazi Germany in his first speech as PM."

"He didn't praise Nazi Germany."

"He didn't? My father ranted about it for days."

"No, he wasn't praising them, exactly. He was just congratulating them on their military restraint."

I wasn't sure I knew the difference. Roger explained.

"Look. Chamberlain knows that we're on the brink of war. We lost a million boys in the previous war. No one wants that to happen again. Warmongers like your father stand to make a lot of money if we fight, but the PM doesn't want to see us lose another generation."

I felt the heat rise to my face. I walked ahead of him with clenched hands and turned into the graveyard at the side of Saint Peter's Church. I sat on a bench that overlooked some moss-covered tombstones. Some names were so old that they had eroded into oblivion. I envied them at this moment.

Roger came to sit next to me. "Hey, I'm making a mess of this. I didn't mean anything against your father. It's just that there's a lot of tension right now, and no one seems to agree on how to best handle the threat on the continent. Germany is taking over territory like a hungry dog and making an ally of Italy, but Britain should stay out of it. I, for one, agree with Chamberlain. I don't want to go to war. I don't want the bodies of our boys strewn all over Europe. Do you want that?"

I hung my head. "Of course I don't. I didn't mean to get started on this."

He grinned. "I can get carried away. I want to be an MP as well someday, and I guess having an opinion comes with the territory."

I looked across at the graves and imagined a future where hundreds of thousands of British soldiers could die before their time. I turned to him. "The world just seems so troubled right now. I don't always understand it, nor do I have the answers. I mean, just a couple of weeks ago, the IRA tried to assassinate the king when he was in Belfast. It's mad! My father rants about Catholics and pacifists and tariffs. I just wish things would go back to how they were when I was a little girl."

Roger softened and patted my hand. "I know. We all wish times were different."

I stood up and smoothed my dress. "I think I'm ready to get back to the picnic now."

"Are you sure?"

I nodded, though in that instant I knew that was the last thing I wanted. "On the other hand"—I breathed in and out, beginning to steel myself for the upcoming conversation with my hopeful mother—"I think I'm ready to go home after all."

As he opened my front door upon our arrival at Newsham Park, I turned on the threshold to give him the obligatory "Thanks." I noticed that for all of his good looks and confident ways, Roger did have a crooked nose.

The steward appeared with the tea tray, and I pulled myself out of remembering that unfortunate day. The egg salad sandwiches lay untouched, but he made no mention of it.

"May I get anything else for you, Miss?"

"Just the tea, please. Chamomile."

He poured it deftly, despite the jostling of the people who had begun to enter the dining car, and as he did so, the steam rose with ghostly fingers from my cup. I watched the swirling of the light-golden brew and closed my eyes, inhaling its comforting scent. I sipped at it, knowing that it would scorch my lips but welcoming any sensation that would replace the numbness that had taken its residence in me. With each drink, it mellowed, and I settled back into that state where the line between memories and dreams are nearly indistinguishable.

The countryside blurred as we raced past it, and within a few hours we pulled into Victoria station. Through the steam, I could see the porters already unloading bags and trunks from underneath. Ladies were dressed more fashionably than in Liverpool, with stylish hats, and some were even wearing trousers. My mother would die before being seen in trousers. I wondered if I could get away with it.

When I stepped down, I inhaled the bustling sounds of whistles and the scents of the food vendors lining the terminal. I checked my papers and hailed a cab, giving the driver the address in central London. I felt anonymous among the bustle and crowds, a stranger even to myself. Here, I would be no one's daughter, no one's girl, and I had only my own ambitions to fulfill. Everything would be left behind, and I could start a new chapter in my life.

No, not a new chapter. A new book.

Well, almost. For one thing, I could never forget Charles and Lucille. Charles was my own flesh and blood, and Lucille was as much a sister to me as anyone could be. She had told me at the train station that there were "twenty thousand things" that she would miss about me, just as we both burst into tears. I would never find another Lucille among all of the millions of people in London.

And of course, there was Kyle. I'd resolved to forget him, to see my little fascination as nothing more than that. He was on the other side of the country, a world away, a mere page to be ripped out.

Chapter Seven

"What's that?"

"Nothing!" I snapped.

My one concession was the photograph of Kyle that I had shot from Charles's window, which I kept under my pillow. I didn't look at it, but somehow slept better knowing it was there. It had slipped out as I made my bed, practicing the rigid technique that we had learned in our first week of class.

"Mmm, handsome. Let's see."

My roommate had been trying relentlessly to pull personal information out of me, and I suppose I hadn't been very cooperative. She, on the other hand, was abundantly forthcoming. I already knew that the redheaded beauty had lived here for four years, and her father was a diplomat from the States. She liked strawberry ice cream and novels about politics, and she found it fascinating that anything built in the eighteenth century here was considered new. There was no corner of her life that was not up for discussion.

"It's nothing, Abigail." I put the photo back in its place.

"Well, you don't put *nothing* under your pillow. I'll bet he's your married lover. Or a convict!"

"Do all Americans have imaginations like yours?"

"You bet. That's how the West was won. Wild imaginations and a pioneering spirit."

"But you're from Virginia. Isn't that in the East?"

"It doesn't matter."

She tossed her copy of the *Materia Medica* aside. "The tiny print in all these books is making my head spin," she said as she lay on her bed and looked up at the ceiling. "And if I'm going to get dizzy, I'd rather do it dancing. You game?"

I couldn't argue that this sounded preferable to the evening of studying we'd planned, so I chose a pink dress and some matching shoes from the wardrobe. We knocked on the door next to ours and invited Dorothy to join us. She was already in her nightgown, and Abigail insisted that no one in her right mind was in bed on a Saturday night.

"I know just the place," Abigail pressed and turned to leave. As I followed her, Dorothy shrugged and told me that she would get dressed.

We agreed to split the cab fare to the Jitterbug Club and found one just as we stepped outside. Abigail sat opposite to me and leaned over to pull the top of my dress lower on my shoulders. She sat back to admire her handiwork and adjusted it once again, this time pulling the middle down to reveal a lower neckline than the one that had been designed. She crooked her finger over her lips and nodded.

"That's more like it," she said smugly. "We're going to have those men rocking on their heels."

I exchanged looks with Dorothy, who grinned, but who folded her arms over herself and refused to let Abigail fiddle with her.

"Phooey on you," the southern girl bemoaned. "Look like a prude for all I care. It's the cat that catches the mouse, they say, and I'm going to teach this one to be a cat." She slapped me on the knee.

Abigail's adjustments did, indeed, make me feel more like the old Julianne than I had since that day before the auction when I'd paraded around in newly purchased gowns, and Lucille made me giggle about the absurdity of falling in love with a seminarian. Now Liverpool was far away, and I lived in the horrid white frocks that we wore as uniforms. They had long sleeves, buttons that went all the way down the middle, black shoes and stockings on our feet, and awful, itchy hairnets for our heads. And if that wasn't enough, I'd learned how to take a pulse, interpret blood pressure, and bathe a patient. No wonder Mother didn't care for my chosen profession.

Our cab pulled up to a nondescript building, but the queue that stretched around the corner announced that we had arrived at the right place. Abigail said that everyone in the city came to the Jitterbug Club, from the students to the politicians, to the upper crust and the soldiers. On a dance floor, everyone was equal, and the threats we'd begun to hear of Hitler and fascism felt a world away.

When our turn finally came up, we stepped under the blue-and-white-striped awning. The three of us held each other's hands in excitement.

"If we . . . parated . . . ner . . . stand," Abigail said.

"What?" I shouted back at her.

She spoke right into my ear, loud and slow. "If we get separated, meet by the corner of the bandstand." The music was blaring; conversation was impossible.

I nodded in acknowledgment.

"Tell Dorothy," she mouthed.

The band was in full swing, and the people on the wooden dance floor spun in a dazzling display of color. A couple vacated their table just as we walked by, and Abigail slid into one of the chairs, elbowing aside a pair of competing girls.

Dorothy and I ordered champagne, and Abigail a dirty martini. Hers came with three olives, which she ate slowly and deliberately as three sailors watched. I became aware of my toe tapping to the beat.

As men came over to say hello, I noted that Abigail's accent became more and more southern. I had to hand it to her. The girl was a master coquette.

"Just look at all of the alligators out on that floor!" She looked hungry as the bright lights reflected in her eyes. She looked at me. "You're going to let down your hair a little, right? No pining for your Pillow Man?"

She was right. This is what I came for. I could be as forward as any American. I picked up my champagne flute and drank it in one gulp.

Pulling out the combs keeping my hair up, I let it cascade down my back. I ran my fingers through my blond tresses, and tossed my head from side to side. God, I hadn't felt this good since the beginning of the summer. I could do this. Maybe. I grabbed Abigail's martini and swung it back as well.

She looked shocked—no easy feat.

"I'll buy you another one. Don't worry," I shouted. But she already looked proud rather than piqued.

It wasn't two seconds before I had an offer to dance.

I tried my hand at the Lindy Hop, as it provided the most room for improvisation. I liked to dance as I felt the music, not according to a choreographed step, so it was ideal for me. However, it was mesmerizing to watch those who could do the American import, the Balboa. Two skilled partners were required to get this precisely right. Twirl. Spin. Step. The movements were captivating. The dancers held their bodies close most of the time and moved with intuition and sensuality. Jump. Jive. Hustle.

With two drinks in me, I imagined that I was good at the Balboa, too. I barely saw the faces of the men with whom I was dancing, and I couldn't say how many there were. I just swayed and moved as the music took me. My head began to feel heavy, and I kept my eyes closed whenever possible. I could have sworn that someone kissed me at one point.

Hop. Swish. Twist. My feet became a blur beneath me and moved faster than my head could react. I could feel my face grow damp under the hot lights, and I became thirsty. I sent my latest dance partner for another martini, promising to stay exactly in this spot until he came back. I lost count of how many I'd drunk through the evening, and I'd developed an unlikely appetite for olives.

"Let's go, Julianne." Dorothy was suddenly at my side, and she put her arm around my shoulders.

"I can't go yet. He's . . . um, I can't remember his name. But he's getting me another drink. And he's so good-looking!" The room spiraled around me as I leaned on Dorothy to keep my balance.

"He wasn't, Julianne. He had a huge head and pockmarks all over his cheeks." She shifted her weight as we walked toward the door. "Here, I brought you some water."

"What about Abigail?"

"She's waiting right over there. She already hailed a cab."

"I got kissed, you know."

"Yes, we saw. Let's get you home."

⋰⋰⋰

"What is that *noise*?"

"What noise?"

"That crackling sound. Can't you hear it? It's so *loud*!"

Dorothy looked around the room to see what I was talking about. "I don't hear anything. Wait. Could you mean the sausage? I just brought some up for you. Fresh from the pan."

I looked at the plate on my nightstand.

"I think I'm going to be sick." I ran into the lavatory and locked the door behind me. I leaned over the sink, gripping its cold white side. But the sensation passed, and I looked up at the mirror. I was aghast at my reflection. My hair was a bird's nest, and mascara had left murky smudges on my face. My head felt like a hammer had beaten it over and over, and the light made my eyes throb.

I could almost understand why Mother did this. Why she drank. It was to keep her from remembering Charles. Last night, if only for a few hours, I had erased Kyle McCarthy from my mind. I'd tried to numb myself to the hole that his absence in my life had created. It was difficult at first. Every time a man touched me, or brushed against me, or even tried to kiss me, I wanted it to be Kyle. It was his hands that I imagined around my waist, and his shoulder that I wanted to lay my head on during the slow numbers. It was the heat of his breath I wanted to feel on my neck. It wasn't until deep into the evening and some ungodly number of martinis that the discord of voices and touches blended together sufficiently to liberate me from the ache, if only temporarily. But I couldn't do it again. My body felt like it was split in two.

There had to be a better way to get over him.

I dragged myself back to our room and into my bed.

"Well, if it isn't the Swing Queen!"

"Abigail," I croaked. I was so thirsty. "I. Never. Want. To. Do. That. Again."

"Do what? Have all sorts of guys queuing up to dance with you? Getting kissed by a couple of good-looking soldiers? No, you're right. Let's never do that again."

"You know what I mean."

Dorothy came over to sit next to me on the bed and patted the space next to her. I curled up and laid my head on her lap. She took the hairbrush off my nightstand and started stroking the bird's nest. She started at the ends, very gently, and worked her way up.

"Abigail knows what you mean, don't you, Abigail? We shouldn't have let things get that far. You just looked like you were having such a good time."

I sighed. "Don't blame yourself. It's my own fault. I could have stopped and I didn't."

A banging sound pounded my ears. I looked up, and our dormitory monitor popped her head inside.

"Is anything wrong? It sounded like you girls were up awfully late last night."

Abigail spoke up. "Just some girl talk, Gertrude. We'll try to keep it down next time." In reality, I recalled hazily that they'd been trying to wrestle me into pajamas against my hysterical protestations.

The three of us looked at her, wearing the most cherubic expressions that we could muster. Her glare lingered on the always-obedient Dorothy, which must have allowed her to decide that we were speaking the truth.

"Well, just try to keep it down from now on. Anyway, I came in here because she has a call on the hall telephone. Some man." Gertrude pointed in my direction.

"For me? I'll be right there." I reached for my robe, laid out over my chair.

When Gertrude closed the door, Abigail turned so swiftly that she nearly knocked over the lamp. "A *man*, Julianne? Did you give out the house phone number last night? You're wilder than I gave you credit for."

"No. At least, I don't think I did. Wouldn't I remember that?"

"Who knows? Better see what it is he wants."

I tightened the sash around my waist and found my slippers next to my bed. The light in the hallway blared at me, so I closed my eyes and felt my way along the wall until I reached the phone. For a split second, my heart leapt in the faint hope that Kyle would be on the other end of the line. I picked it up and held my breath.

"Hello?"

"Hello, Miss Westcott?"

"Yes."

"It's me. Roger Kline. I'm in London."

Abertillery

The baby had loosed the blanket around her. I tightened it and tucked the corner under her arm, but she wasn't satisfied. I picked her up and rocked her, back and forth, over and over. It was a stiff movement for me, and not one that I liked. I delivered babies. I didn't cradle them. That was what mothers were for, and I made no claim on that title.

The priest's face was obscured to me as he held the hands of Mrs. Campbell and bent his head over her in prayer. Everything was silent.

My little crisis had passed. In that swooning moment I'd convinced myself that this Father McCarthy could be my Kyle—a priest! I was imagining things in my panic. Was I going mad? Or perhaps it was just another of the dizzy spells that I'd been getting lately.

Then it occurred to me: it was the pills I'd taken. Of course. They were confusing me. A glass of water to dilute them, and then another, and I felt like myself again.

If I ever let myself think of Kyle, I supposed that he'd died in the war, probably doing something heroic. Or if he'd survived, surely he had a cozy home somewhere, surrounded by loving children and a beautiful wife. Wasn't that why I'd done it?

Kyle would have said, "You worry too much, Julianne. You just have to let some things be, and pray that everything works out." Kyle's God was one of love and patience. My God was one who punished.

"Miss Bailey?" I looked up to see Connor Campbell in front of me. His eyes were damp, and he looked over at his wife, whose breathing had become markedly shallow. "I'd like to hold my daughter."

I looked down at the baby, having forgotten that I was even holding her. "Oh. Well, yes, of course."

He took her from my arms and rocked her the way that a parent should, with the gentle swinging motion that accompanied a lullaby. Then he handed the baby back to me. He walked into the adjacent room, and I wondered how many of the children were still awake. The priest stayed with his charge.

Agnes Campbell gasped, and I rushed to her side.

Chapter Eight

"Roger!" I cleared my throat, but still didn't sound like myself. I tried again. "How did you know where to call?"

"Your mother rang me up when she heard that I'd taken a position here, and she insisted that I call you."

"My mother?" I placed the receiver to my chest and rolled my eyes, lightly tapping the back of my head against the wall. When I put it back to my ear he was speaking.

". . . and please don't get the wrong impression. I'm glad she did. I was hoping to see you here and, well, apologize for being a prat the last time I saw you."

"Well . . ."

"I have no excuses other than I got caught up with seeing some old friends, and it was entirely unfair to you. Can we start over?"

I didn't think anything had really started in the first place, but what could the harm be? "That would be nice."

"You're a sport. You really are."

"So what are you doing in London?"

"I was hired as an assistant to Lord Baylon, over in Parliament. Best thing is, it had nothing to do with Pops. I used Mum's maiden name to apply and got it on my own merit. My flat is just across the river from Saint Thomas Hospital. I can see your school from my window."

"Is that so?" I wasn't trying to be rude, but I honestly didn't think my legs could support me much longer, and I just wanted to lie down: "Listen, Roger, I—"

"So, Julianne, when may I come and see you?"

I swallowed hard and considered how to answer. Did he want to see me because a familiar face from Liverpool would be a welcome thing in this vast place, or did he want to see me because he really believed that there could be something between us? And how involved was my mother in this?

I had to admit that seeing him would not be an altogether unpleasant thing. After the lunacy of last night, I felt inclined to grasp onto anything that felt real. And at least Roger represented a piece of home.

"What did you have in mind?"

"How about supper tonight? I found a great place near Charing Cross. Smashing beef Wellington. I think you'd like it."

"Tonight? I can't," I said, perhaps too hurriedly. All I could think of was going back to bed. I swallowed down the cotton-like feeling that I had in my mouth. "I mean, tonight is not good for me, but what about tomorrow?"

"Brilliant. Shall I come by for you at seven?"

Abigail assailed me with questions when I returned to the room, and was ecstatic to hear that I had made an appointment to get together with a man.

"It's not what you think, Abigail. He's just a friend from Liverpool."

"It's not—"

"No, it's not Pillow Man. So lower your eyebrows and don't get any ideas."

"Is he as good-looking?"

"What does it matter, if he's just a friend?"

Dorothy led Abigail out of the room then, telling her that she could bunk with her for the rest of the day so that I could get my beauty rest. I opened my bureau drawer and pulled out the most recent letter from Miss Ellis. Charles was letting his plants die, since Kyle and I were both away. But the weather had been good, so she'd been taking him outside on her breaks, and he seemed to like that. I held her letters to my heart, and those from Lucille. I missed home.

The next evening I met Roger at a restaurant overlooking the Thames. I had insisted on meeting him there rather than having him pick me up at the dormitory. In the first place, I didn't want to have to introduce him to Abigail, who would no doubt jump to all sorts of romantic conclusions. Second, I didn't want to give him an inaccurate perception of my intentions. We were just two friends from Liverpool, getting together to catch up.

I hadn't been away all that long, so he did not have much news from home to bring to my attention. If anything really important ever happened, Lucille or my parents would write or telephone. He did tell me that Maude and John had decided upon a Christmastime wedding, and I was happy that I would be home for that. The Liverpool Football Club was poised to win another league championship. A strike at the docks was averted, thanks in no small part to the swift work of my father. The IRA threats had subsided.

After dinner, we strolled along the riverbank. I stepped carefully over the uneven cobblestones, holding on to his arm to steady myself. I felt inconsequential next to the water that was bordered by centuries of history and the buildings that shaped the course of the world, even as I rambled on about itchy uniforms and bed-making foibles. Roger listened with amused, if perfunctory, attention before telling me that he was thinking about enrolling in some law classes at the University of London.

"That's the path to peace, Julianne. If we want to avoid a war, we need diplomacy and well-spoken leaders. Many of the MPs are barristers. So I'm going to follow suit. I want to be the youngest MP in recent history."

This was a city with a past. But I had the feeling that I was walking with a shaper of its future. The question was, how far did I want to walk with him?

In November, Roger surprised me with theater tickets. We saw *The Laughing Cavalier* at the Adelphi Theatre. It was a lively musical with heroes and villains, and love and abduction. Seeing how much I'd enjoyed it, Roger bought more tickets a couple of weeks later. This time, it was *Me and My Girl* at the Victoria Palace Theatre.

The title seemed apt. I had sensed, through our time together, that he increasingly hoped there could be something more between us. And to be honest, I was beginning to warm up to the idea. It was difficult to shut away the desire for love and intimacy, and I would have to acknowledge that someday. Why not now? Roger was what every girl would dream of—intelligent, considerate, success waiting to anoint him as its king. I couldn't muster up the intensity of feeling that I had experienced in the few times that I had talked with Kyle, but I believed I could ease into it.

We laughed through the first act, and Roger left at intermission when I asked him to fetch my wrap from the coat check. The crisp air in the theater had chilled us both.

"You make a handsome couple."

I looked to my right, where an elderly lady with a thick Italian accent smiled at me.

"Thank you." I fumbled with my program.

She persisted. "You would make beautiful babies."

My hand tightened around the page, wrinkling it beyond recognition. "Thank you, that's very kind. But he's not my beau."

"He's not? *Colpa mia.* I don't think he knows that, the way he looks at you."

"Well, maybe he will be. I don't know."

I looked back to see Roger, coming down the aisle. A smile came to his face when he caught my eye. He was here. Kyle was not. That had to count for something.

"Here you are," he said, placing my wrap across my shoulders.

"What about you?"

"There was a rush on the coat check, and I didn't have time to get mine. But I'll be fine. I'm just glad that yours was accessible."

"Thank you." I hugged it around myself just as the music of the entr'acte slowed down. The heavy red curtain parted.

My hands were cold and still, and when I rubbed them together Roger noticed and gently slipped his hands around mine. They were warm and comfortable there, and I let him keep them. My Italian seat-mate glanced our way and winked again. Roger looked over at me and smiled with a look akin to victory.

I felt none of the electricity that I had that evening in the barn with Kyle. But maybe if I played along, authentic feelings would follow. If I gave him an honest chance, *could* I like him as much? I thought that I could. I just needed to give myself time and opportunity, both of which I knew he would provide.

After my hands had warmed, Roger held one of them during the rest of the performance. He held it in the cab. He walked me to my dormitory door and, still squeezing my hand, said that he would call me soon.

"Well, well, well." Abigail looked like she had stayed up waiting for me. "Are we in love?"

I curled up on my bed and tossed a pillow at her, just missing her mask-covered face.

"I'll take that as a yes."

"Take that however you want. It's not a yes; it's not a no. We'll just have to see. Go to sleep and let your imagination have a rest!"

She threw the pillow back at me, and her aim was better than mine.

I'd been dodging Abigail's and Dorothy's entreaties for the chance to meet him with vague promises when the hall phone rang a few days later. Abigail answered it and shouted through the dormitory for me.

"There's a call for you, Julianne!"

Kyle, I thought, before I could stop myself. I laid the magazine I was reading on top of my textbook and wrapped a shawl around my shoulders. The hallway was always chilly.

Instead of leaving the telephone on the table, as we usually did, Abigail was speaking into it.

"Well, we can't have that now," she was saying. "We're just dying to meet Julianne's mysterious beau. Why don't you cancel your reservations and come dancing with us?" She listened to his response. "Then we're all set. I can't wait to check out the man that our girl has been droning on about."

"Abigail!" I hissed through my teeth.

She covered the receiver with her hand and whispered to me. "Oh, stop it. I'm just helping you out. A man needs to believe that he's the sun in your sky. If you won't do it, I'll do it for you."

She turned back to the conversation. "Then we're all set. Come meet us here around nine, and be ready to boogie!"

I stood in front of her and put my hand out for the telephone, tapping my foot.

"Mm-hmm," she said, and held up a finger to hold me off. "Bye-bye, then. See you tonight." She hung up the receiver.

I threw my arms up in the air. "Why did you do that?"

"Somebody had to save you from yourself," she said. She made silent smooching gestures into the air and turned back to our room.

Against her protestations, I wore something conservative and vowed to remain sober while we went dancing.

As in all things, Roger displayed unflappable self-assurance on the dance floor. In this one area, though, he proved to have no reason for confidence. His footwork was sloppy and his arms flailed about, as if there was a wind blowing through the club. But his body moved with an enthusiasm that one had to give him points for. Before long, a small circle of wide-eyed adorers had gathered around him, and I stepped back to find a refill for my drink.

The gyrations of the crowd diminished as the band played the first chords of a slower song. My eyes met Roger's across the room. He nodded and made his way over to me. I set my water on the nearest table and met his outstretched hand. I was a little nervous about this. Our occasional outings had remained innocent, but now we would move as one, bodies together, touching heads, sharing warmth and breath. Roger took my left hand in his right and put his arm around my waist. When he pulled me tightly to him, I could feel every contour of his body. His hand stroked the small of my back as his face descended to mine. Panicking, I turned, and his lips just brushed my cheek. I let my head fall on his shoulder, and I looked down at my shoes, counting the holes that punctured the white leather to create a scrolling pattern. Marking the time until the song was finished. *Was this what I wanted? Was this what I was supposed to do?*

"I'm thirsty," I said as the final notes faded. "I'm going to head back to our table."

Abigail was seated in my place and stood as we approached.

"Looks like I took your spot, and anyways, I see an alligator over there that I've been making eyes with. Time to go say hello."

I grabbed her by the arm. "Don't go. Stay."

"What, and horn in on you lovebirds?"

"I thought you wanted to get to know Roger better. I mean, seeing as you went to all that effort just to get him here."

Abigail looked at the "alligator" approaching us and waved him away, the abundant bangles decorating her arm creating a bell-like tinkling. "You're right," she said. "Let's see if the boy's good enough for my friend."

Roger joined us then, bringing two drinks. The condensation dripped onto his hands, and I gave him my napkin. Abigail took a swig from her dirty martini, her third of the evening, and patted her seat so he could sit next to her. Before she was halfway through her glass, they had already discovered four people they knew in common through their fathers' connections. Each new name brought a howl from her red-stained lips. They talked all the way home in the cab, and I closed my eyes while slouching in the seat.

In the morning, Roger sent over a note with a messenger saying that he had to travel with Lord Baylon and would be away for several weeks. There were important people that they needed to meet with. The messenger also carried pink roses. I found a bowl and trimmed their stems on the diagonal. I arranged them in the water, then lay down on my bed with a sigh. I slid my hand into my pillowcase and pulled out the slightly wrinkled picture of Kyle I had taken stealthily from Charles's window. Pressing it against my heart, I reluctantly retired it to a drawer in my bureau.

Chapter Nine

London, if it was possible, was even more beautiful in December. Christmas trees and garlands adorned store windows, beckoning the passersby to enter. Lampposts were embellished with burgundy streamers and bows. Carolers and cards, presents and Father Christmases enhanced the mood. Magic had descended upon the city.

Thanks in no small part to Dorothy's patient tutoring, I passed my finals with slightly better-than-average marks. So it was with great relief and exhilaration that we participated in the Ceremony of the Caps. We could now rid ourselves of the unsightly hairnets and wear the more attractive white caps of nurses. Of course we weren't nurses yet, but the cap ritual did mean that we would return next term for practical work in the hospital. I was very much looking forward to that.

Roger wrote before I left for the holiday. He was remaining in Belfast with Lord Baylon for the time being and wouldn't be able to see me at home in Liverpool. He included a postcard of Giant's Causeway and signed it, "Fondly, Roger."

I purchased two seats on the train ride home, since I had packages that I didn't want lost or damaged in the cargo car. Mother, Father, and Lucille were all recipients of an enthusiastic spree in Harrods. I had remembered Charles and Miss Ellis as well, selecting for them woolen scarves and gloves, his in black, hers in pale blue. Her latest note said that my brother seemed tired all the time, but she supposed that he just missed me. They were both looking forward to a visit.

Liverpool was chilly, but the welcome was warm. My parents and a gathering of friends were all there. From a distance, they were one blurred vision of coats, gloves, hats, and scarves. It wasn't until I approached that I could distinguish them. When I did get closer, I was smothered in a huddle of embraces.

Lucille's face reflected the same exuberance as the others, but every time we caught each other's eye, she pursed her lips and appeared anxious. It looked as if she wanted to tell me something, but it was impossible to get away and talk privately.

After assurances to everyone that we would get together often over the break, Father and Mother pulled the car up while a porter helped me with my bags.

Father got out to open my door and kissed my head. "It's good to have you home again, Princess."

It was odd to return to Liverpool after being in London for just a few months. It was like slipping on a pair of old comfortable shoes—but I also liked the shiny new heels. They each fit in their own way. I was looking forward to this time, though. No studying, and lots of well-prepared meals by Betty. Mother was pleased by my growing relationship with Roger, and I didn't disabuse her of her enthusiasm. But the separation of a few weeks was going to give me a chance to evaluate what, if anything, was going to happen between us.

Fate, that teasing nymph, was prepared to answer that question.

I had anticipated a barrage of questions about school, but Mother had her mind set on filling me in on recent happenings in Liverpool.

"Julianne, it's so distressing. We had the heaviest rains last week, and the cold turned some of it into ice. The trees are all sagging under the pressure, and the Merseyside Ladies' Auxiliary Benefit Lunch was canceled. We could barely drive anywhere. It was so inconvenient."

My father interjected. "Beatrice—the church!"

"I was getting to that, Richard. There's just so much to say, I don't know where to start. Julianne—Saint Mary's roof collapsed in all of the rain, and the church flooded."

"Oh no! What about John and Maude's wedding?"

"That's exactly the point. It's uncertain if the church will be cleaned up in time for Christmas, but definitely not by next week. They looked into other ones around the city, but they are already booked. So your father and I have offered for them to use Westcott Manor."

"Really? That's wonderful! I mean, that's terrible news about the church, but how exciting that it will be at our house!"

"Yes. They were so relieved when I—all right, Richard, *we*—suggested it. It is going to mean a lot of work, but I thought that you would enjoy helping out."

"Of course I will."

"Mrs. Parker already has so much to oversee at the church, so she has asked Maude and her mother to work out the details with me. The menu was already planned, so they will just be preparing it in our kitchen with Betty's help. However, they had already delivered some of the decorations to the church, and they got ruined in the flood."

"Oh, poor Maude!"

"Well, Lucille, Lotte, Blythe, and I have been working feverishly on that, and we have made a lot of progress. However, I think that it would be nice to bring a touch of Christmas to the house in time for the wedding. Plus, we need to add some flower arrangements. We've hired some men to take care of things. A father and son. The McConways or McCarols or something like that. I've asked the son to take you to the nursery and help you pick out some wreaths and sprigs and other things for the inside."

"The McCarthys?" Surely, it couldn't be.

"Yes, I believe that's it. They came highly recommended by Audrey Whitehall. They fixed up her gardens for her daughter's wedding in April. Of course, that was the springtime, and that's impossible now." She went on, but I didn't hear anything else.

Kyle was assisting with the wedding decorations? And Mother had assigned *us* to work together?

"Anyway, they've been such a help, especially the son. All that I asked him to do was to pick up flowers and evergreens, but he surprised me with a sketch of the different rooms with ideas for arrangements. They were really quite good. He should consider working in that field."

Casually, I said, "Mother, I think he's going to be a priest."

"What? You know him?"

I brushed off my mistake. I wasn't supposed to know about him. Or Bootle. "Oh, I think Elizabeth Whitehall told me something about it a few months ago—a father-and-son gardening team, I mean. It has to be the same two."

"Well, you're right. He is in the seminary. What a shame—such wasted talent."

I didn't like her talking about him that way. I had accepted his choice, and I thought that it should be defended. "Don't say that, Mother. You've never said that it was a waste that John Parker was following in his father's footsteps in becoming a minister."

"Yes, well, I think it's different with Catholics. Anyway, dear. We have a lot of things to go over. The McCarthy boy will be picking you up tomorrow morning at nine when he drops his father off. He said that the nursery plants were hit hard as well, so he's going to take you to a tree farm in Wallasey. Your father didn't like the idea of you two going out there alone, but I assured him he was worrying needlessly. The boy is studying for the priesthood, after all."

In her wildest dreams, she couldn't have imagined that Kyle might be someone that I could fall in love with. So of course I would be safe with him.

She prattled on about details that I should have been listening to. But I couldn't concentrate, thinking only of the fact that I would be seeing Kyle tomorrow. *And* spending the day with him. I couldn't deny that the thought stirred up feelings that I had spent months repressing. But I was happy in London now and had a new life. Kyle was the old life, a girlish attachment, and he had barely owned a whole scene on that stage. I was considering a future with Roger.

Lucille came over for dinner and to spend the night so that we could catch up. Betty prepared a feast worthy of Christmas itself with asparagus, gravy, cranberry sauce, and sausages wrapped in bacon. Scraping the last of the sweet pudding from the bowls, Lucille and I said our good nights to Mother and Father. Pajamas on, teeth scrubbed, and huddled by the fireplace in my bedroom, we were anxious to finally visit alone. But before we settled in, she clearly wanted to say something.

"Jul, I *tried* to warn you at the train station, but I just couldn't get a word in edgeways with everyone around. I didn't know how you'd feel about working with Kyle. I tried to bring it up with your mother—carefully, of course—and even volunteered to go out to the farm myself with him. But she wants me working on the menu with Betty."

"Thanks, Luce. I wish we *could* have talked then, but at least I found out during the ride home. It gave me a chance to prepare. Although I'm not even sure what there is to prepare for. I've moved on, and I hope that it's evident that I have done so."

"Evident to whom—you or Kyle?"

"Well, *certainly* evident to him. It would be humiliating if he knew that I had harbored those kinds of feelings for him. But I hope that it is also clear to me that everything is as it should be and that I have put it to rest once and for all. Besides, there's someone else to consider." Lucille had already received several letters from me about Roger and the tentative feelings that were developing.

"I hope so, too, for your sake." She didn't seem convinced and looked at me with worried eyes.

"I don't want to talk about that right now, though. I learned how to play backgammon at school, and I've been dying to teach you so that we could play together."

I taught her in which direction to move her checkers, how to get my singles out, and how to bear off from her inner board, but often she persisted in moving her pieces the wrong way. I laughed at her, and she threw a pillow at my face, which set off a full-scale battle. We fell into a fit of giggles so loud that Mother came in to see what all the commotion was about.

It was so good to be with Lucille again. I felt like I was twelve years old, with no cares in the world.

I can't say that I woke up at dawn, because I had barely slept. As much as I wanted to convince myself that today was meaningless, the possibilities of what the morning might bring kept me tossing and turning. It is no wonder that some people are afraid of the dark, fearing what might be hiding in the shadows. My own monsters were self-concocted fits of overthinking.

"I couldn't risk falling for you any more than I already have."

Kyle's last words in the barn provoked a hundred unanswerable questions. No resolution, no finality—only the whisper of what I longed to hear.

By full sunrise, I had a headache. It was a much more manageable injury than heartache, and I was planning to avoid *that* pain with all my might. I tried to burn Roger's image into my brain, but he quickly floated away and Kyle took his place. That was not a good sign.

Of one thing I was certain. It was going to be impossible to hide from Kyle during Christmas break, so I might as well face him head-on.

I nudged Lucille around eight. She waved me away, so I gave her an extra ten minutes. By then I could smell breakfast coming from downstairs, so I tried harder, and she opened her eyes.

"You are a bad influence on me, Julianne Westcott! I stayed up way too late!"

"And you hated every minute, didn't you?"

She flashed a grin. "I thought your mother was going to have us committed! I can't remember laughing so hard—ever!"

She threw one of my robes on over her pajamas, and we trudged down, letting our noses lead us to the scent, as our eyes were not yet fully functional.

I half-feared that Kyle would arrive early and see me in such disarray, but then again maybe that would have solved all of my problems. Although the last time he saw me, I was soaking wet, wearing his herringbone jacket, and tottering on a broken heel. This morning would likely be an improvement on that image.

Betty had outdone herself with breakfast, placing before us scrambled eggs, baked beans, mushrooms and tomatoes, and black pudding. Instead of the hot tea provided, I opted for a cup of coffee. Lucille lifted her eyebrows. Abigail had hooked me on it during late nights of studying. It was just the boost that I needed.

Father and Mother had breakfast with us, too, but only briefly. Father had an appointment with a contractor to repair part of one of the warehouses. It had sustained minor damage in the rain. Mother was already impatient to continue with the wedding planning, and her obvious anxiety made Lucille cringe.

"Jul," she whispered to me as we went back upstairs. "I love your mother, but *really*. You would think that this was *your* wedding."

"Oh Lord," I said, shaking my head. "I shudder to think what grand plans she'll dream up for *that* occasion."

"I think that tonight in my prayers, I will thank God that my family are simple folk. Besides, I have you for all the fancy stuff. Speaking of which," she said, "let's go see what you're going to wear for your big date today."

"Lucille, it's not a date!"

"I know, Grumpy. I'm only teasing."

We searched through my closet for just the right thing. Usually, it was easy to decide what to wear, since the purpose of an event was obvious. Today's outing with Kyle posed an unfamiliar challenge. Should I dress as I would on any other day, accentuating the positive? Or should I wear something unflattering so as to remind myself that this was, in fact, *not* romantic? What would be appropriate for traipsing around a tree farm? I had purchased a trouser suit in London, but it was just barely acceptable for women to wear trousers, and Lucille resoundingly ruled it out when I tried it on for her. Liverpool had not yet journeyed to the horizons of fashion.

We decided on something simple. A pleated dark-blue skirt, with a fitted gray sweater. A platter-shaped black hat with creamy silk flowers. Lucille selected small silver loops from my jewelry box and a silver brooch in the shape of a peacock—my little nod to vanity, since I had chosen such a basic and sensible outfit.

I brushed my hair, with perhaps just a few more strokes than were strictly necessary. Lucille's gaze pressed upon me as she noted the care with which I applied my makeup. Her expression was solemn as she pulled the curtains open and saturated the room with light. "Jul," she said, "I know you'll keep your head about you today. You know what's right." She must have read the worry in my face. Giving me a quick hug, she looked at the clock and said, "It's nine fifteen!"

Scrambling down the stairs, all of my senses were suddenly drawn to the parlor doorway where, waiting for me, was Kyle.

My body felt conflicted, like trying to press together the positive sides of two magnets. Every fiber in me was drawn to him. It took all of my willpower to not run toward him and instead walk gracefully across the room like the mature young lady I was at least pretending to be.

With the perceptive eyes of someone in love, I noticed that the muscles of his neck tightened and released, and he took in a sharp breath. In a second, our eyes told each other everything that we would guard our lips from saying. We each looked away quickly, only to return again with our masks on.

"Good morning, Miss Westcott," he said starchily. But he didn't fool me. I saw the corners of his mouth holding back a smile.

"Good morning, Mr. McCarthy." And my mouth fought the same battle. I looked at Mother and remembered that I wasn't supposed to know him. "It's nice to meet you."

"It's good of you to accompany me today. I'll appreciate your input on the flower and evergreen arrangements for your home."

"You're too generous. We appreciate all of your help with the wedding."

I hoped that all of this stiffness was for the benefit of my mother, who was standing next to him. I didn't think that I could manage a whole day of stilted conversation with someone who evoked such passionate reactions in me by his mere presence. Lucille stood behind her, arms folded, watching me like a guardian angel.

Mother broke in, clearly oblivious to the currents running beneath our exchange. "Well, you two run along. And, Kyle, when you get back, I'll make sure that Betty saves a plate of dinner for you. It is the least we can do to say thank you for your help."

"Thank you, Mrs. Westcott, but my father is feeling unwell today and I should sit with him tonight."

"Very well. Julianne, your brooch is upside down." Twisting it upright, she patted my back and sent us on our way. As soon as the door was closed, I could hear her calling, "Lucille, let's get to work!"

Poor Lucille. I was definitely getting the better end of the deal today.

Chapter Ten

Kyle's truck was faded and worn, but it looked like a fairy-tale carriage to me. He opened my door, but he needn't have because I could have floated in. As he walked around to the driver's side, I pinched my arm tightly in order to bring myself out of the clouds. This was going to be harder than I thought. *Mind over matter, head over heart.* I repeated it to myself, hoping I could believe it.

He slid in and slammed his door.

I was glad to see that he hadn't dressed up for the occasion. That made it easier to focus on the task at hand and not envision this as anything more than an extended errand. He wore cuffed canvas trousers, a white shirt, and a brown leather jacket. A winter cap covered his hair. While I missed his boyish, wavy locks, I could see his face more clearly now. He was still so handsome, with a strong jawline and the shadow of a beard. Not that three months away was going to change any of that. I had just tried to forget.

I was keenly attuned to his every movement. Igniting the engine. Shifting the gears. I had read that when a person loses a sense, the others overcompensate. I wondered which sense of mine was impaired, because my sight, hearing, and sense of smell were all very acute at this moment. There was something so essentially masculine about seeing him drive the truck, and at once I realized my preference for this over the suited, moneyed crowd of men that I was used to associating with.

We made our way down the winding path of the estate until we reached the edge of Newsham Park. A few dedicated souls were already out walking its grounds, bundled in their winter clothes. The twin lakes had not yet frozen over, but the geese had already left for the southern part of the continent. A vacuum of silence covered the land. I made a move to step out and open the iron gate that separated our home from the public grounds, but Kyle put his hand on my arm and stopped me. Our eyes met, and we lingered in the unspoken chasm that lay between us, lovers denied. At least, that was how I saw it.

"Please stay," he said. "I'll get the gate."

He stepped out to pull it back, and the creaking of the metal disrupted the magical feeling of the morning. Father said that as soon as electricity could be brought to the perimeter, he was going to install an automatic gate that would open on its own. I wished it were already in place. Then Kyle would not have had to leave my side even for a second.

He hopped back in and pulled through the gate, then ran back to close it after us. On his return he blew on his hands to warm them, then released the brake and sealed his eyes to the road. We drove in silence for a few minutes, passing shops darkened for another hour and homes lit as breakfast simmered. I wished I knew what was going on in his head. Either it didn't matter to him that I was achingly close, or he was very disciplined. I hoped it was the latter.

I got the small talk started. "I'm sorry that you're stuck with me today. Mother has these elaborate plans sometimes. I don't know that I'll be any more help than an extra set of arms to carry out what we buy."

"Don't apologize. And don't sell yourself short," he said, flashing a grin that made me feel even weaker, if it was possible. "Your arms will be useful. There will be lots to carry."

And with that, the wooden masquerade we'd maintained since leaving the house fell away.

"So why Wallasey?" I needed to keep to a topic that provided me better footing.

"There's a great farm there with a wide variety of Christmas trees. I thought it would add something special to decorate with different kinds of boughs."

"There is more than one kind of Christmas tree?"

"Yes, several. Firs, pine, spruces. And then, within those categories, there are other kinds. Douglas firs. Black spruce. Scotch pine, white pine. Norway spruce. I don't know how many kinds this farm has, but I knew that we'd have a better shot at it there than in the city. Wallasey fared better in the storm."

I was intrigued with the kinds of things he knew.

As we drove, he pointed out various sights—farms whose owners he and his father had had dealings with, features of the landscape—and offered bits of intriguing or amusing trivia about them. I had driven this way before, but without such an expert tour guide. The unwelcome image of him standing at a pulpit, sharing his knowledge with a congregation, entered my mind. I closed my eyes and thought instead of his nearness, his warmth.

"I'll tell you my favorite story about Wallasey."

My heartbeat coursed through my body. His audience of one. "What is that?"

"In the early eighteen hundreds, some roguish people in the town used to shine lights out to sea, and ship captains would mistake them for lighthouses. But they were really heading straight towards dangerous rocks, and the ships would crash. Then the bandits of Wallasey would raid the ship and store the cargo in underground tunnels."

"You're kidding!"

"No, it's true. You can still visit some of the tunnels today."

"I would love to do that."

"Maybe we can sometime."

Unintentionally, the puppet master pulled the strings of the marionette. When he said things like that, it sounded like an invitation for something more. But I knew that it wasn't. He was exactly what he presented himself to be, and I had to swallow away my hopes that anything more would come from our attraction.

We pulled into the tree farm shortly after that. I stepped out into the cold and pulled some gloves from my handbag. Kyle watched me as I did so, waiting for something.

When I started walking away from the truck, he stopped me. "Don't you have a hat?"

I put my hand on my head and patted the black felt hat. I could see where he was going with it, though. It was not exactly sparing me from the elements.

"You call that a hat?" He laughed. "Here, try mine."

He took mine off, tugging where the pins fought to keep it in place. He tossed it onto my seat in the truck, oblivious to how much it cost. Then he took off his own cap and ran his fingers through his hair, trying to put it all back in place. With two hands, he placed it on my head, pulling it over my ears. I felt a shiver run through me when he was that close. He lingered more than seemed absolutely necessary, and I breathed in the moment as our eyes locked.

"There." He stepped back to admire his handiwork. "It's not the latest in London fashion, but at least I'll return you home as healthy as I found you."

"What about you?"

"I don't need one. I am a strapping young man, and you are a damsel in distress. My hat is yours, m'lady."

I punched him in the arm playfully, and we turned toward the entrance.

The tree farm was expansive, and I could see why he thought it was worth the drive. There were hundreds and hundreds of Christmas trees of every variety. Kyle asked for my opinion as we sorted through boughs and measured the trees, but I knew who the expert was here and I tried to select my choice based on what I thought he would say. I chose differently only one time—I liked the evergreen better than the pine for the main fireplace, and he deferred to my suggestion.

This prompted another story, one regarding the original inhabitants of the United States, who evidently used evergreen boughs as body cleansers. I told him that I would stick with my lemon verbena soap, thank you very much.

We walked for about an hour through the rows of trees. Being next to Kyle made me feel absolutely weightless. I couldn't even hear the sound of my own feet on the ground. Early in the day, the mere sight of him had sent my head spinning and my heart heaving, but now I began to feel calm. The more I discovered about him, the more time I spent at his side, I knew that I was inching into something that felt like real love. And it was made up of so much more than childish daydreams.

After four trips to and from the truck, Kyle was satisfied with everything that we had selected. We paid the owner and hopped back into the cabin of the truck, smelling of winter and evergreen.

"Well, now. I'm sure that you've worked up an appetite. I know that I have. Would you like to have supper here in Wallasey before we head back?"

That sounded perfect. My stomach was growling at an embarrassingly audible level, and I wasn't ready to go home and have this all come to an end yet.

We drove along the water and found a little restaurant near the town hall. Several patrons were leaving, as we had arrived at the end of the supper hour, but a few lingered over their plates, the remnants of their meal sitting forgotten. The dimly lit candles and small tables made for close company, and music played from an unseen radio. In another circumstance, I would have said that it was romantic. But I reminded myself that we weren't in another circumstance.

Kyle lightly touched the small of my back, guiding me to a table by the window where we could see the water. He pulled out my chair and took my sweater from my shoulders. We were greeted by the elderly waiter, whose gaunt frame did not do much to endorse the food. But the menus suggested otherwise, and I found it difficult to decide between all of the offerings.

"Something for the young couple to drink?" *The young couple.* I felt my cheeks redden by several shades, and I avoided Kyle's eyes by focusing on taking off my gloves, drawing it out by loosening one finger at a time.

As Kyle ordered a Coca-Cola for me and a Newcastle Brown Ale for himself, my attention was turned to the radio. An Artie Wilson song was on, and his words seemed to mirror my thoughts:

> *Did I tell you that I adore you*
> *And you're all I think about at night?*
> *Did I tell you that I'm my best around you*
> *And how you make everything just right?*

It was impossible to hold on to my resolution with lyrics like that and a setting like this.

Kyle turned to me, hands folded on the table, and leaned in. "It smells so good in here. What are you in the mood for?"

I looked over the options. Leek soup sounded inviting on this cold day, but so did the shepherd's pie.

Our waiter came back holding a small black tray. He set my Coca-Cola down in front of me and placed an empty glass in front of Kyle. He poured the ale into Kyle's glass, stopping just as the foam grew to the rim, and left the bottle on the table to be finished later.

I decided at last on the lamb with mint sauce, my perpetual favorite, and Kyle asked for the tatws popty. I smiled at the thought that his selection suited him perfectly. Simple and straightforward meat-and-potato stew.

The foam in Kyle's glass had started to deflate into a thin tan line above the darker ale. He poured more from the bottle at a slight angle that he said kept it from rising again.

When the bottle was empty, he placed it on the table facing me.

"Do you know why there's a blue star on the label?"

"I don't."

"It stands for the five original brewing companies in Newcastle."

"You know a lot of little facts like that, don't you?"

He put his hand to his chest and feigned offense.

"They're not just 'little facts.' You never know when they might come in handy. You might fall into a ditch, and a passerby hears your cries. 'Help me,' you say. 'I will,' he responds, 'but only if you can tell me how many stars there are on the Paramount Pictures logo.'"

"How many stars *are* there on the Paramount Pictures logo?" I asked.

"Twenty-four, one for each of the stars that they had under contract at the time the studio was founded."

"And what other morsels of knowledge are swimming around up there?" I twirled my finger around his head.

"Did you know that the name of every continent ends with the same letter it begins with?"

I furled my brows and tried to remember all of them. "Wait—you're wrong," I said. I sat a little bit straighter.

"What do you mean?"

"North and South America. They don't begin and end with the same letters."

"Well, you have to take out the 'North' and the 'South.' It's the 'America' part that counts."

"That's cheating."

"Suit yourself. But it's not a very interesting fact if you look at it so precisely."

"No, I suppose it isn't."

He grinned at me and could have kept me captivated for hours with such trivial things.

"Well, I don't want to bore you now," he said, unfolding his napkin and placing it on his lap. "Tell me all about school."

I entertained him with stories about Abigail and Dorothy, the London sights we'd seen, the Jitterbug Club, and the horror of having to wear hairnets to class. I didn't mention anything about Roger, who I realized was rapidly fading from my memory. I couldn't even bring his image to mind, seeing only blurred features and outlines.

One thing was startlingly clear, however. After spending this much time with him, I could not continue to deny what I felt for Kyle, even if a future was impossible for us. But it also made me know that I wasn't willing to settle for anything less. My affection for Roger was no more than that. And he deserved to be with someone who felt that way for him. I didn't know how I would do it yet, but I was going to have to tell him.

But that was for a later day. Right now, I had such precious, limited time with Kyle.

The meal arrived just as I finished my narrative about the last three months. Betty made a much better mint sauce, but the lamb was tender enough, and I was starving. Kyle was clearly enjoying his stew, and he stopped his fork midair when he saw me looking at him.

"You have to try this," he said. I expected him to set some aside on the bread plate for me. But instead he stuck his fork into his meal and reached his arm across the table to feed it to me. My eyes widened with surprise. I had never shared a dish with a man before, and there was something about it that felt so intimate. Almost scandalous. I opened my mouth, though, and sampled the perfect trio of meat, sauce, and herbs. My lips closed around the cold metal, and Kyle slid the fork out, setting it back on his plate. I felt him watching me.

"Delicious, isn't it?"

I nodded, silenced by the taste and aroma of the stew, but more by the kind of connection that could be made from such an innocent gesture. "Winter Wonderland" came on the radio. I was relieved to have a break from the love song that seemed to take delight in taunting me.

I turned the questions to Kyle, and asked him about school.

He sat back. "Well, being in seminary in Durham isn't quite as exciting as swinging in London dance halls, but I am enjoying it. The town is well known as the final resting place of Saint Cuthbert and Bede the Venerable, so we get a lot of visitors. As I've assisted with Mass, I've met people traveling from all over Europe, making a pilgrimage. There's one old man who comes up once a month from Leeds to pray for the soul of his dead wife. He's been doing that for twenty-six years."

"Wow, that's dedication!"

"It is. I get to witness so much devotion in people. Last month, I met a woman who claims to have been cured of epilepsy after praying to Saint Cuthbert. We get a lot of people looking for miracles. There is so much sadness in the world. But pain and sadness have a way of drawing us closer to God if we let them."

I listened intently, not just because I loved the sound of his voice but because he had so much to say that was different from what I knew.

"I love meeting the people," he continued, "but most of my hours are spent in school or studying. It's still fairly introductory at this point. Some philosophy, early church history, and lots of Latin. I was put in upper-level Latin class."

"I'm sure your father is very proud of you."

"He is. It was my mother's dream to have at least one child enter the religious life."

"I've never heard you mention your mother."

"She died along with my two sisters during an influenza outbreak when we lived in Wicklow. Paula and Catherine, although I don't remember them. I was two years old. My sisters fell to the illness first, and from what I've been told, it tore my mother apart. I got sick next, and my parents prayed to John Vianney, a well-known priest from the last century. They told him that if he would spare my life, they would do all that they could to foster a vocation in me."

"And their prayers worked."

"Yes, but my mother died before I recovered, and she pleaded with my father to continue the prayers for me after her death."

"He obviously did."

"Oh, yes, and very ardently. He had not been a very spiritual man before that, but it became his sole mission to fulfill my mother's request. After her death, he moved us out of Wicklow because it held too many memories for him. Once we settled here, he started taking me to Mass on Sundays and on all of the feasts, and signed me up to be an altar boy."

"So your destiny was laid out for you long ago, and you didn't have a choice?"

"No, I had a choice. I don't want to make it sound like this was forced on me. If I were unwilling, I know that my father would understand. But it was so thoroughly encouraged that I suppose it was natural for me to pursue a vocation."

The Christmas program on the radio had ended, and the warbles of another crooner came on.

> *In the glow of the candlelight, by the light of the moon,*
> *All I can do is dream that we will be together soon.*

I tried to expel the lyrics from my thoughts.

Kyle glowed when he talked about this life that he had set upon, and I could see that he was, at least, content. I didn't understand it, though, and felt compelled to probe a little more.

"Kyle . . ." And I couldn't get the words out. How do you say the words that are so pivotal to your life?

"What is it?" he asked, concerned.

I took a breath. "Forgive me if I am being offensive, but please know that I just don't understand. Why can't Catholic priests be"—I almost said "married," but that would lay my hopes too bare—"in love?"

He put down the fork that had been idling on his plate and sat back. He sighed, as if he were looking for just the right words. My own words had set my face aflame, but I wasn't sorry to have asked the question. Without great risk, there is no great reward.

He leaned forward, and a serious expression came over his face. He took my hand in his and held it, looking at me with a gentle intensity. I quivered at his touch, as if we were on the precipice of something we couldn't turn back from. I didn't feel anything like this when Roger held my hand.

"Julianne," he said softly. "It's not that we can't fall in love. We are only human."

He continued, as if he were convincing himself as much as me. His thumb circled over my skin, and I felt every movement. "But how can I give myself entirely to God if I am also the head of a household? How can I lead my congregation if I have a wife and children who need me, too?"

"But other ministers are married, and they seem to do just fine!" Part of me wanted to fight for him, to take on a millennium of tradition.

"Their calling is different from that of a priest, even though it can look like the same thing."

"What do you mean?"

"Well, I guess the best way to put it is that a priest takes vows that are modeled after the life of Jesus. We take a vow of poverty, to live simply as he did. We take a vow of obedience, since he was obedient to his father. And, as he was unmarried, we take a vow of celibacy."

I had no response to that. It was so disparate from anything I'd known. I had been brought up to be a good person, and to follow good examples—just not so literally. I supposed you had to respect someone who could be that scrupulous about it.

"That's very—admirable," I said, restraining myself from so many other words I was thinking. "I don't know that I could do it."

Squeezing my hand, he said, "There are times when I don't know how I'm going to do it, either." And he let go.

It seemed to be the end of the conversation for him, and I wasn't going to push it. I bit my lower lip to prevent me from saying something I would regret, and I let my eyes wander over the triple molding that framed the ceiling of the restaurant.

The owner laid the bill on the table. As this evidently was not a romantic occasion, I reached for it—Kyle was on an errand for my mother, and it was only fair that we pay for supper. But he stopped me, insisted he be allowed to pay, and handed the money to our host.

As we prepared to leave, Kyle helped me with my coat, and his scent and closeness made me swoon. A new song assailed my ears.

I thought for sure that you were mine,
The way you made me feel so new.
But you've chosen another love.
And I don't know how I'll ever live without you.

That bloody radio was playing like a movie soundtrack to my life.

❧

I fell asleep on the way home, despite the truck's jostling. I was so tired after a night without sleep and drained from the daylong emotional tug-of-war. It was just as well, because I didn't know what I had left to say.

I dreamed, although in flashes instead of complete scenes. I saw glimpses of us together, but the settings were too unclear to make out. I woke up just as we approached Newsham Park, but kept my eyes closed, not wanting the moment to be over. "Kyle?" I was imagining us in a four-poster bed, with billowy white linens. My head lay on his bare chest, and we were sleeping.

"Hmm?" In my vision he looked down at me, and I saw that I had interrupted his own thoughts.

"Are we allowed to be friends?"

I opened my eyes then and saw that precious grin that I had missed for the last few hours.

"Of course we can be friends. I would really like that."

"Me, too."

He pulled up to the house, where Mother greeted us. Being more than a little deliberate, we stood at opposite sides of the truck bed as we began to pull the boughs out. She instructed us to put them in the cellar. Under her stare, we carried them, speaking only words of direction, belying the understanding that we had begun to touch upon. Whether it was due to her presence or an attempt to suppress the hint of desire in ourselves, I didn't know. But he did reveal the trace of a smile as I walked him back to the truck. And he promised he'd be by tomorrow.

Abertillery

Agnes Campbell gasped, and I lifted her head to dab water on her parched lips. She tried to speak.

"Ho—"

The whisper escaped, and the word disappeared. I dampened her lips again.

"I ho—" she tried again. A cough arose in her throat, and I felt her body go limp as I laid her head back on the pillow. Her head turned to the side, and the last of her breath wisped out. She was gone.

I was aware, suddenly, that I was alone in the room with the priest, whose voice had jarred me but whose face I had not yet seen. Silence descended upon us, and my heart beat rapidly in my chest.

The priest spoke from behind me, returning to English. "Did you hear her last words? Her husband may want to know them."

"I did not." I didn't recognize my own voice, entangled as it was in the strangeness of the feeling taking over me.

"I think she said, 'I hope.'" He sighed and spoke without looking at me. "Do you believe in hope?"

"I don't," I responded after a moment. "It's hard to believe in hope with so much sadness in the world. And what about you?"

"I used to believe in hope," he said. "But not any longer."

We reached forward at the same time to cover her eyes, and I flinched when our hands brushed each other, as if a flame had singed my skin. I felt the blood course through my fingers as I withdrew them. He placed his hand over her eyes, closing them for the last time and drawing a cross on each of them with his thumb. I caught a glimpse of gold on his left hand. That seemed odd to me, for a priest. Although it wasn't as if I'd known many of them in my lifetime. It was ordinary, just a plain gold band with a line of silver running through the middle. Like the one I'd slipped on Kyle's finger. But surely there were hundreds of rings just like it.

Chapter Eleven

I was only able to get away once to see Charles, on a Wednesday, as there were so many preparations to make for the wedding. He did indeed look tired but seemed greatly bolstered by my visit. The absence of Kyle at Bootle was agonizing to me, but the sting was mollified by the fact that he stopped by Westcott Manor on several occasions to oversee the hanging of the boughs, even though they looked perfect to my untrained eye. I deluded myself into thinking that he was there to see me, but the constant presence of my mother made conversation impossible.

The wedding of John and Maude was lovely, just like the couple. Even with Mother's grandiose schemes, it retained a restrained elegance. It was touching to see them recite their vows, led by John's father as the minister. To promise to love for better or worse. A string quartet played during the ceremony, while a live jazz trio alternated with holiday mummers afterward. I received a stream of offers to dance, but bowed out after a few and retreated to my bedroom until it was time to cut the cake.

Christmas afternoon was a quiet affair, with just the three of us sitting at one end of a dining table designed for eighteen. In deference to the women of the household, my father refrained from any talk about business, and Mother made a series of poorly veiled references to her high hopes for my association with Roger. I kept quiet by exaggerating my enthusiasm for Betty's plum pudding.

My salvation came on New Year's Eve when Lucille stayed over, and we talked through the midnight hour. I shared with her everything that had transpired with Kyle, and she listened with the heart of a friend who adopts your feelings as her own.

"Happy New Year, Jul," she said, when we realized that it was forty minutes past the magic hour. We had been too wrapped up in our conversation to notice. "Nineteen thirty-eight is going to be a great year for you—I know it."

"You, too." We clinked our mugs of apple cider and toasted what we hoped the year would bring.

I didn't see Kyle again before leaving for London. I heard that he went back to Durham right after Christmas. There was no good-bye, but I supposed I wasn't really entitled to one. Nor was there an occasion that would have brought us together again. I wished him well, but once again, I would be leaving Liverpool and trying to erase a memory.

I enjoyed an enthusiastic reunion with Dorothy, Abigail, and the other girls from our floor when we all returned to school, though the tone was clouded by a recent announcement from the government that all schoolchildren were required to carry gas masks. Classes were being held and home visits scheduled to educate parents in the use of the fearsome contraptions, as there were reports of babies nearly suffocating when they fell asleep wearing them. No significant harm had come to the country, but the government placed a high importance on preparedness.

It wasn't long before Roger telephoned. He wanted to take me to dinner, but I asked him if we could take a walk instead. So I bundled into my wool coat and met him at the dormitory door.

He was standing under a black umbrella, although the showers from earlier in the day had relaxed into a drizzle.

"Julianne," he said as he leaned in to kiss my cheek. "It's good to see you again."

"Likewise, Roger. I hope your holidays were good."

He slipped his hand into mine, and my cowardice didn't allow me to pull away. As we strolled along the weeping reflections of lights in the rain-soaked street, he recounted his meetings in Belfast in wearisome detail.

"We met with their PM, Lord Craigavon. He's a staunch loyalist to the king, as you know, and he's been instrumental in appointing only Protestants to key positions in government so as to counteract the traitorous notions of the southern Catholics. Lord Baylon came to help support that, especially with the upcoming general election there next month. He's asked me to write up the report that he will present to Parliament."

"How wonderful for you. Your parents must be proud."

"Oh, they are. Pops especially. I run into him in the halls sometimes, and he'll smile and introduce me to whichever colleague he's with."

"Well, I don't know much about politics, but I think I can safely say that on this subject, you and my father would be in agreement."

"That's good news. And perhaps in time I'll get to meet him and see if I can't convince him of Chamberlain's peace plan as well."

"I think you'd be well advised to leave that topic alone, I'm afraid. Over Christmas break, he seemed very hopeful over some of the opposition from Sir Winston Churchill. At least that was my impression."

"You just leave it up to us men, and we'll get it all sorted out. Don't worry your pretty head." He tousled my hair, which was hanging outside of my woolen hat.

When we paused to hear a flutist who had attracted a respectable crowd, Roger put his arm around me. I welcomed his warmth. But despite the romance of the surroundings, Roger was only a substitute for the one I truly wanted.

The double faces of Big Ben shone down on me like two eyes in the night, condemning me right there if I did not confess to him the insufficiency of my feelings.

"Roger, listen." I released myself from his arm and turned to face him, then took a deep breath before launching into the speech that had been delivered countless times by countless hopeless lovers: "You are wonderful. You are going places and making your mark on the world. Some girl is going to be very lucky to have you at her side. But I'm not that girl."

He moved in closer and put his arm around me, pulling me in to him. I put both of my hands against his chest and stepped back.

"No, please. I'm serious, Roger. I need to concentrate on my studies. I'm afraid that there's no room for anyone else in my life right now."

The umbrella cast a shadow over his face, but I could still see his look of chagrin. "You're making a mistake, Julianne," he said. "Just think about it. I'll be a young MP. You'll be at my side hosting parties, charming everyone. I'll start heading committees, and London will be at your feet."

My stomach lurched as I envisioned myself as a duplicate of my mother.

I shook my head. "I know it's hard to understand, but that's not the life I want for myself any longer." I started to walk away, and he followed after me. I let his words hit my back, and they became more faint as my steps hastened back to the school.

"The world is changing, Julianne," he shouted. "If we do go to war, I'll be exempt from service. You'll be protected."

If he said anything after that, I couldn't hear it. I hated to think I'd hurt him. But when he said my name, it carried none of the music that stirred me when the same word left Kyle's lips. Surely, in the end, Roger would see that this was right.

School resumed, a welcome distraction. The intensity of the studies and the demands of our hands-on work in the hospital left me too tired to think about Kyle or Roger or anything but making it through the day.

Our care for the patients involved giving sponge baths, cleaning bedsores, changing soiled linens, and the like—distasteful but necessary tasks that grew easier with practice. On the days we had hospital duty, we worked twelve-hour shifts. Dorothy, Abigail, and I sometimes just passed each other in the hall, one coming in, one going out, mere ghosts of the dancing girls that we had been just weeks before.

It felt good, despite the hours, to be gaining real experience. And I loved working with many of the patients. The sick children were, of course, heartbreaking, and the nurses with even an ounce of theatrical talent could perform little ditties in exchange for a smile.

Though most student nurses clamored for the activity in the labor and delivery wing, I preferred the nursery myself, as the mess of childbirth was woefully unappealing to me. Mothers were usually sedated during delivery, but there was a growing movement toward labor without medication. I witnessed both and wondered which path I would choose should I ever have a baby of my own. Both seemed appalling.

When it was possible, I continued to go out and enjoy the city of London. On one unusually sunny Sunday morning, late in February, I walked through South Kensington, with the intention of visiting the Victoria and Albert Museum.

Heading down Cromwell Street, I saw a courtyard, and beyond the courtyard, a church. Built with gray marble, its columns towered over me. The exterior was simple, but that wasn't what caught my attention. The doors of the church were open, no doubt to bring in the refreshing air, and emanating from them was the most exquisite music. A plaque near the entrance read: "Church of the Immaculate Heart of Mary."

I had never been inside a Catholic church and had not previously felt a desire to do so. But I didn't know Kyle then, and now I did. This was what possessed his attention, his very life. This was why he couldn't love me. My initial instinct was to be jealous, to see this ancient faith as a competitor, but I dismissed that temptation and found it replaced by a burning curiosity to know more.

My eyes were first drawn to the breathtaking stained glass windows pointing toward the dramatic Gothic arches. Color was everywhere—not only in the glass but also in the checked mosaics on the floor, the reds and blues of the frescoes, the height of the domes, and the many icons of saints that lined the church, framed in gold. Tall candles adorned the altar. From somewhere, I smelled the sweet, smoky scent of incense. The congregation was kneeling, heads bowed. I could see only the back of the priest, and his clothing was as ornate as the interior of the church. Purple, trimmed with gold braid, atop his black cassock.

At the same time, my ears were enveloped by the choir music that had caught my attention in the first place.

Sanctus, sanctus, sanctus. Dominus Deus Sabaoth.

I had no idea what it meant, but it was entrancing.

Pleni sunt caeli et terra Gloria tua.

I found a seat on the end of a pew in the middle of the church. An old woman holding beads in her hands scowled at me. I supposed it was because everyone else was kneeling, so I did the same. The kneeler was made of hard wood, and I covered my knees with my skirt so as not to tear my stockings.

After ten minutes, they shuffled out of their seats, row by row, and knelt again, this time at a railing in front of the altar. The priest paused in front of each person, mumbled words that I couldn't hear, and then dipped a host into a gold cup. It was not dissimilar to the Anglican services that our family occasionally attended, but I had never given the ritual such rapt attention. A boy who looked like a miniature clergyman held a golden plate under the chin of the person, and the priest fed the white host to him or her. As one person left the railing, the next one in the queue would take his or her place—a precise, solemn choreography.

The people in the rows just ahead of me stood to get into position, and I was keenly aware of my intrusion. I sat down and shifted my legs so that the family to my left could get past me. When they returned, I bowed my head to mirror their look of devotion. I had no conversation to make with God, so my eyes were distracted by the succession of shoes from the people in the rows behind me who were now walking past me on their way to the front. *Purple velvet buckles. Woman. In her twenties.* I peeked up to see if I was correct. I was. *Scuffed brown leather lace-ups, small. Boy, around six years old.*

The choir chanted a descant that consisted of four notes and sounded like an elegy. I gathered my handbag and slipped out of the pew before the song was over, avoiding eye contact with any soul who might glance up from their reverent pose.

Outside the church I squeezed my eyes shut and let the sunlight warm my face. As Lucille might say, twenty thousand questions entered my mind as I tried to make sense of what I had encountered. The music, the language, the trappings, the clothing—they were so unfamiliar to me, but it was the world that Kyle inhabited. Perhaps I could ask him about those things next time I saw him, whenever that might be.

My musings were interrupted as I took a step beneath the arched doorway at the school. A young boy on a motorbike pulled up. The engine sputtered and he lifted his driving goggles over his leather cap.

"Is this the girls' wing, Miss?" he said.

"Yes. How may I help you?"

"Might you be able to deliver a telegram for me? I'm not supposed to go in there, but I can't wait around. Too many deliveries today."

"Certainly. I'll take care of that."

He handed me a parchment-colored envelope and drove off with puffs of brown smoke following him. I turned it over in my hand. It read, *Julianne Westcott, King's College, Hampstead Residence, London.*

Who could be sending a telegram to me?

I ripped it open, not bothering with clean tears, and pulled out the card. It had been sent five days before.

Charles taken ill. Telephone Bootle when you can. Kyle

Chapter Twelve

Charles taken ill. Charles taken ill. The words repeated and repeated as I pushed through the heavy wooden door and raced up the stairs toward the second floor, brushing up against a first-year girl with whom I shared a couple of classes. She dropped her books as I continued on, and I yelled out a paltry "Sorry, emergency" when I reached the top.

The telephone was thankfully free, and I picked up the receiver.

"Long distance. Merseyside. Bootle Home," I whispered through staccato breaths.

The operator remained on the line for what seemed like an eternity before she said, "Connecting you to Bootle Home now."

The next voice, which I had expected to be Miss Ellis's, contained not a note of my friend's chipper welcome.

"Bootle Home."

"This is Julianne Westcott. I just received a telegram about my brother, Charles. Can you please put someone on the line who knows about his condition?"

"Let me look up that file."

I heard the receiver get set on the desk, and I slumped down to the floor. My head throbbed, and I rubbed my temples while I waited.

"Miss Westcott, I do not see you as being named in his file as someone to whom I can release information."

Of course I wouldn't be. My parents would not have included me in this permission.

"I understand. But I am his sister. Surely you can have someone tell me how he is doing. I just received a telegram saying that he had been taken ill."

"May I ask who sent that to you?"

"Kyle McCarthy. He's one of the gardeners during the summer."

"I'm sorry, Miss. I cannot release information on the authority of a gardener."

Heat rushed to my cheeks and I raised the receiver into the air, shaking it with frustration. Pulling it back down, I said, "Then Miss Ellis will know. Please put Miss Ellis on the line."

"Today is Miss Ellis's day off, but she will be back in tomorrow."

"This can't wait until tomorrow. I need to know what's wrong with my brother!"

"Again, I'm sorry, but I cannot help you without permission. Perhaps you could try to phone the gardener who sent the telegram to you."

"Thank you. I'll do that." I stood up and slammed down the receiver, muttering words that would have invited a reprimand from my mother.

Dorothy opened her door and looked out. "Julianne? Is everything all right?"

"I don't know. I don't know." She set down her textbook and walked out to me, encircling me in her arms and letting me sob into her shoulder. When I pulled back, I showed the telegram to her and told her about the telephone call.

"Well, it seems to me," she said, "that it makes sense to call this Kyle and find out more."

"I can't call him, Dorothy. He's . . ."

"He's what?"

"Come here." I took her by the hand and led her down the hall and into my room. She sat on Abigail's bed, and I pulled Kyle's picture out of my bureau. His whistling face looked out at me. I handed it to her and was about to tell her the details of our story, such as it was, when Abigail walked in and joined us.

When they had both heard what I had to say, Abigail looked impressed. "I didn't know you had it in you, girl. I mean, I thought I knew how to bend a few rules, but Pillow Man is a *priest*? Well, if you aren't just the most hard-boiled thing I've ever heard of."

"I don't even know what that means."

"Tough, Julianne. It means you're tough. You Brits really don't know how to speak English."

Dorothy spoke up. "You're not helping, Abigail."

"You're right," she conceded, then turned to me. "I suppose your little secret just shocked me. Look. I agree with that ninny at Bootle House."

"Home," I corrected.

"OK, then I agree with that ninny at Bootle *Home*. You need to call Kyle up and see what's wrong with your brother."

"Don't you think I want to do that? But how do you call a seminary? I hardly think he's allowed to take calls from girls." I sighed and dropped the telegram in my lap. "But I don't want to wait until tomorrow to talk to Miss Ellis, either."

"I think Abigail's right," Dorothy said. "You can say it's an emergency or something. You at least have to try."

But still my terror at calling a Catholic seminary overcame my desperation to hear about Charles.

Abigail offered a solution. "How about this? I'll make the call for you. At least to get through. You're in no state to think clearly. Would that help?"

I wiped my eye and nodded.

"Good, then. Let's do this."

The three of us walked back into the hall, and Abigail unleashed a stare like death to a girl who was just then walking forward to use the phone. The girl all but sprinted away.

Abigail spoke into the telephone. "Operator, please get me—"

"—Ushaw College in Durham," I whispered. Every word Miss Ellis had ever told me about Kyle was carefully stored in my memory.

"Durham. Ushaw College. Thank you."

We sat in silence as the call was connected. Abigail pressed on.

"Ushaw College? I need to speak with Kyle McCarthy. He's one of your seminarians. Well, could you please go get him from dinner? It is rather urgent. Yes, I understand that you are not accustomed to having women call this number, but I'm not accustomed to taking no for an answer, and if I have to crawl through this line and go find Mr. McCarthy myself, I will, because this is an emergency and I thought you're supposed to be a merciful man of God."

Dorothy and I looked at each other. Her eyes rolled, and my jaw dropped open.

"That's more like it. Yes. Please connect me to the dining hall, and tell them that a Miss Westcott is calling for him."

She looked my way and winked at me. My mouth had not yet closed.

"My work here is done." She handed the receiver to me. With unprecedented tact she led Dorothy away by the arm, and they went to their respective rooms and closed their doors. The sounds echoed into the now-empty hall. I slumped back down onto the floor and pulled at snags in my nails while wedging the receiver between my ear and shoulder.

I nearly jumped when a voice spoke on the other end. "Julianne?"

"Kyle? Is that you?"

"Yes. I'm sorry. Father Herbert said that some vulgar American girl was on the line, but then he gave your name, and it just didn't add up."

I smiled. "That was my roommate. It's a long story. I can explain another time."

"I'll hold you to that, you know." He was always saying things that made me feel as if there was hope when there was none.

"Kyle, I got your telegram, and I'm worried sick. I called Bootle Home, but Miss Ellis is out for the day, and the wench that answered wouldn't pass me through to anyone who could tell me about Charles."

"Gosh, I'm sorry to hear that. You must be really worried. Well, he's better now, so you can put your mind at ease, but I'll tell you what happened. I went back home last week on a break, and I was taking some of my father's hours at Bootle. I checked in on Charles, like I always do, and the orderly on duty told me that he had been experiencing chest pains and hadn't eaten in days."

"What?" I sat up straight and bumped my head on the table that the telephone sat on. I rubbed it while Kyle kept talking.

"Yes, and on top of that, he hadn't been sleeping. He didn't look well, Julianne, but I checked in on him every day between breaks, and he was doing better by the time I had to go back to school yesterday."

"What do they think is wrong?"

"They didn't really know, as far as I could tell, but the fact that he improved seemed to exceed their expectations."

"I've got to go up. I want to be with him. He doesn't understand why I haven't been there. I'll start making arrangements with my professors. Surely I can get away for a few days."

"I think that's rash, Julianne. He's on the mend, and I well know how easy it is to get behind when you miss classes. How about this? My father isn't doing so well himself, and I've been planning to come in for as many weekends as I can. I'll check on Charles, too, and ring you with an update. If he regresses, I'll be sure to let you know so that you can come up."

"What if I'm not in when you phone?"

"I'll leave a message with whomever answers and hope to at least be able to get word to you that way."

His kindness touched me, and I held my hand to my heart.

"Thank you. Again. And Kyle?"

"Yes?"

"I'm sorry that your father isn't doing well, either."

"Well, that's a story for another day as well. I can see Father Herbert coming around the corner, and I already have some excuses to make."

I placed the receiver down with care this time and smiled. Turning around, I went back to my room, where a thorough retelling of the conversation would surely be expected by my deserving roommate.

Abertillery

Agnes's white linens were soiled now with blood and sweat and afterbirth. It didn't seem like a fitting way for her children to see her. I found a large quilt and covered her body, leaving only her head and shoulders exposed. On second thought, I pulled her arms out and laid them on top. I folded her hands over themselves and interlaced them with the prayer beads that Mr. Campbell had set down. At the end, I arranged her hair in a way that looked almost normal.

Mr. Campbell was still with the children. At first Father McCarthy stayed, putting all his oils back into the black bag. My heart pounding, I knew that I could not put it off any longer. I needed to see him, to see if he looked like the Kyle whose voice I'd heard. But when I moved to the right side of the bed to catch a better glimpse of him, to see if the stirrings of my imagination had any grounding, he turned away. I only saw the back of him as he left the room to tell the family the news. I held my head. The dizzy spells were returning.

Chapter Thirteen

As my classes and hospital schedule had become unpredictable, I missed three phone calls from Kyle over the next six weeks. It was with joy and ache that I would find a page ripped from a school notebook and slipped under my door, imparting a hastily written message by an unknown girl who happened to be there when the telephone rang.

I no longer needed updates about Charles, as I had rung Miss Ellis several times until I was convinced that my brother had improved from whatever had caused his bout of illness.

The load lightened as we headed into two weeks of cadaver training.

On our orientation day of this session, we were seated in an auditorium-style classroom. Nervous chatter echoed in the cavernous space, and all eyes avoided the sheet-wrapped body on the table on the stage. Abigail slid into the seat next to me, and was uncharacteristically quiet, save for the sounds that accompanied her fidgeting. But I quickly learned that it was not the gruesome classroom matter that had her nervous.

"Julianne, I have something to tell you." She shifted in her seat and looked down at her pencil. It contained teeth marks near the end.

I placed my hand on her arm. "What is it?"

"You know me. I've been known to cross a line once or twice in my life, but it was an absolute rule of mine that I wouldn't go after another girl's beau. It's just not right."

"What are you saying?" I could only think of Kyle, but of course he couldn't possibly be who she was talking about.

"Jules," she said, scooting closer to me, "I ran into Roger Kline at an embassy dinner my father took me to. We got to talking, and, well, something just sparked. Do you know what I mean?"

I smiled and slumped into my hard-backed seat, letting out a sigh of relief. "Abigail, you dilly. I don't know why I didn't put that together before." I even laughed, which seemed to surprise her. "You. Roger. Your backgrounds. Ha! You will give each other a run for the money. I love it. This will be fun to watch."

"Then you're not angry with me?"

"Angry? Quite the opposite. Roger deserves happiness, and now I don't have to feel so bad about letting him go."

"Well, chap my fanny, you're a wonder. And here I was worried that I'd be rotting in hell for stealing your man, even if you had cast him off."

"No need to be coarse about it."

The tall professor, weirdly named Nurse Scrowl, shushed the room, and the girls immediately came to attention. The lights dimmed, and she began the demonstration that included photographs of the cadaver room, a warning that the formaldehyde and subject matter often caused students to faint, and the process we would use for skinning. It was sickening to think about, but I recalled hearing that our school was fortunate to have real specimens. Others used cats or pigs, which hardly replicated the human anatomy.

I can say with no small degree of pride that I made it through the two weeks without incident, but not without effort and a lot of Vicks VapoRub placed under my nose. As I trudged up the stairs to the dormitory after completing my test, I debated whether to answer the hall phone as it rang or go straight to my room and pass out on my bed.

Courtesy dictated the former, however, and it was with a yawn that I answered it.

"Operator placing a call from Durham for Miss Julianne Westcott. Is this Miss Westcott?"

"It is!" Immediately, every tired cell in my body was electrified, and I felt as if I could run a marathon if I were asked.

"Julianne?"

"Kyle?" I said it with more enthusiasm than I wanted to reveal.

"Aren't you the busy little bee? Did you get my messages before?"

"I did. I'm so sorry I missed the calls."

"Well, I just wanted to make sure that you knew that Charles was better."

"Yes, I'd spoken with Miss Ellis. It's such a relief. And how is your father?"

"Not as much good news on that front, I'm afraid. But nothing new, either. He's just a stubborn old man who won't see a doctor."

"I prayed for him, you know. As best as I knew how."

"You did?" I could almost imagine Kyle on the other line, standing straight up at these words.

I had, in fact, gone to Immaculate Heart of Mary two more times since my original visit, and I had finally gathered the courage to ask the priest after service how I could pray for someone who was ill. It was in these small gestures that I felt close to Kyle, that I tried to understand this vocation that separated us.

"Yes. I went to a church and lit a candle for your father. I think it was in front of Saint Joseph. I don't really know the names of the saints, but I picked a statue that was male. That made the most sense."

"I'm speechless, Julianne. I am. That means so much to me."

"Well, I wouldn't want you to think I'm a total heathen, right?" I smiled and wound the telephone cord back and forth around my arm.

"Not a *total* heathen."

"Ha! Shall I hang up now?" This felt like the flirting that I had seen other girls engage in. My cheeks flushed.

"No, no. Not when I was finally able to reach you. How is school going?"

"Busy. We just finished training on cadavers, and that's really all I want to say about *that* at the moment. That will haunt me for some time, I'm afraid. I do love the part where I get to visit with patients, though. I met an elderly woman the other day who was suffering from meningitis. Despite her pain, she had the most brilliant smile. I enjoyed listening to her stories. Sometimes, she thinks I'm her great-granddaughter and calls me Frances. I let her do it. It makes her happy."

"That's my favorite part of the seminary, too. The people. We have this woman, so old that I'm afraid to even breathe on her for fear she'd just disintegrate. But she comes to Mass daily to dress the altar. I admire anyone who can stick with a commitment like that, especially considering the challenge it must be for her to get there."

"Yes."

"But enough about all that. You and I spend enough time in those worlds. Tell me what you do in your free time. You must be living it up, being in London."

"I'm not quite as exciting as you imagine, I'm afraid. I do try to catch a movie with my friend, Dorothy, when we can."

"And boys? I picture a string of them lining up to take you out and show you a good time."

How could I answer that? In truth, when I did crawl out of the hole of a classroom and find myself at more social events, I never lacked for young men paying attention to me. But I was a cold fish. Never did I feel anything like what I felt sitting next to Kyle in that derelict barn, or driving in his truck, or even hearing his voice through these telephone lines. I had tried with Roger to give someone else a chance, but it was only Kyle who made my blood race and my mind wander. I was resolved to the fact that I could never be with him, but now that I had contracted that particular affliction, it didn't feel possible to settle for anything less. I couldn't tell him that, of course.

"Well, I suppose that those opportunities are there, but my classes are demanding, so I haven't allowed myself to be distracted."

"Mm-hmm," he responded. What were Kyle's own thoughts? I wondered.

"And other than that," I continued hastily, opening what seemed a less perilous topic, "it's getting quite worrisome to be here."

"What do you mean?"

"Would you believe that I'm buying myself a gas mask for my birthday?"

"A gas mask? It's so sad that it's actually come to that."

"More and more people are doing it. I hate to think about such things, but I'm seeing the need to be realistic, too."

"They're not taking such precautions out here, although I've been hearing murmurings that we'll go that way. Ever since Hitler invaded Austria, it seems that people are waking up to how much power he's trying to grab and what that will mean for England. There's a lot of debate here over whether or not we should join the war."

"Aren't you exempt from service, if our boys do get called up again? I mean, since you're going to be a priest?"

"Technically, yes, but I'm really not comfortable with that. If we go to war, I want to be in it."

I did not like to think of Kyle, even as my friend, donning a uniform and picking up a rifle and charging into certain death. The last war stole a whole generation, and the thought of Kyle lying on a battlefield was unbearable to me. I wanted to promote any means of keeping him out of harm's way.

"What about the fact that you're Irish? Doesn't that count for anything?"

"The only ties I have to Ireland are the fact that I'm a Catholic, but other than that England has been good to me, and something like that couldn't stop me from going."

"Well, I wouldn't want to go if it were me, so I can't say that I understand your enthusiasm."

"I'm not enthusiastic about war, Julianne." He sounded stern. "For goodness' sake, I'm going to be a man of the cloth. We're supposed to be men of peace. But I'm just being honest that if going to war meant that I could protect you and protect others, then I think there's something holy in that, too."

A tear escaped from the corner of my eye. I couldn't speak. Then I sniffled, and I knew he could hear it.

"Julianne? Are you OK? Did I upset you?"

I shook my head.

"Look," he sighed. "You are my . . ." He paused. "You are my friend. What I'm telling you is that no matter what else separates us, you will always be that. I will look out for you. I will pray for you, and I would fight to save you if it came to that. That's why boys go to war. We pretend it's for the glory and the pride and the victory of it all. But it's not. It's for those at home. It's for those we care about."

"You care about me?"

His voice softened to a whisper. "You know I do."

I could imagine that his body was next to mine. That we sat next to one another talking instead of being separated by the length of a whole country. That we kept a sliver of space between us, so as not to touch one another, so as not to violate everything that we each stood for. We used a guarded word like *care* as a substitute for a more authentic one like *love*, which hovered over the conversation like a thick dark cloud awaiting the slightest provocation to become a thunderstorm. I would not be the one to breach it. As Lucille would surely have said, I should not steal from God.

So I mirrored his restraint and said simply, "I care about you, too." Unable to bear a good-bye, I gently set the receiver in its place and returned to my room to cry.

Chapter Fourteen

The telephone was silent for the remainder of the school term, although a package arrived before we started our final exams. It contained a shiny, roughly carved peacock, with its tail framing its body, and a note that read:

> *I hope this takes away some of the gloominess of buying a gas mask. Here is something that I carved for you for your birthday. It reminds me of the brooch that you wore when we went to Wallasey.*
> *All my best, Kyle*

How was a girl to focus after something like that? The peacock fit in my hand, and I held it for hours every night until the lacquer started to wear.

I passed my finals and performed better than I had anticipated. Perhaps I had a knack for nursing after all. I made the rounds with all of my patients, as it was unlikely that I would ever see them again. By the time I returned, they would have either recovered and returned home or passed away.

I stayed on for an extra day to do some shopping and say good-bye to my friends. Abigail's father was a darling and arranged for a diplomatic car to take us to the train station.

The countryside raced past me as I got closer and closer to Liverpool.

It was heavenly to be home. Everything seemed more vibrant than when I had last left. Of course, that had been in the winter, so everything was dead. But now, my studies were behind me for months, and Lucille had written that she was in love. I couldn't wait to hear more about that. And, at some point, I would surely see Kyle.

Father was caught at work and couldn't get home right away. One of the warehouses had been vandalized. A homemade pipe bomb had been thrown through a window, and while it didn't explode, he'd had to call out the authorities and clean up the shattered glass. He insisted it was the work of "those vile IRA Catholics," despite a lack of proof and a general feeling in town that they weren't a current threat. I visited with Mother for a while and then went for a walk in Newsham Park. The crisp air felt liberating. I picked up a stick from the ground and mindlessly brushed it up against the spindles of the iron fence. I loved the sound that it made. Ping, clank. Ping, clank.

In the distance I heard the telltale noises of exhilarated children. As I rounded a bend, I saw that they were little boys, all rushing toward the lake, carrying model boats. I followed them, smiling, across the grassy lawn to a bench to watch their races.

The boys—and some girls, I discovered—were running about, thrilled that the summer break had arrived and their traditional pastime could resume once again. I had missed out on the particular delight of participating in the races—my mother thought it a silly boy's game and one that was beneath me. But I used to watch them from my window and envied the way they abandoned themselves to the fun. On nearly any summer day, you could find the children here sailing their boats. Many of the toys were homemade. The family's discarded trinkets would be raided for anything that could be used as parts for a boat and a sail.

How easy it was to be a child, your days spent in the sunshine playing with friends and constructing little playthings. Sitting on the bench, I realized that I was getting older. My studies were challenging. There were no simple answers to anything. It was no longer, "Will my boat hold up in the water?" It was "He loves me; he loves me not." At least for me. Abigail and Lucille both knew that they were loved.

Adjacent to the model boat pond was a wider lake. This one contained life-sized boats, with couples rowing in the idyllic setting, intoxicated by young love. I noticed that I was not the only girl sitting alone, looking down wistfully at the edge of the lake and hoping that her reflection would not forever be a solitary one.

What I did *not* see was someone coming up from behind me. Suddenly, a pair of large hands covered my eyes. I jumped, startled.

"Guess who?" The voice was unnaturally low, disguising the identity of its owner. But my body had its own suspicions as my heartbeat quickened.

"Father Christmas?"

"Wrong season."

"The man on the moon?"

"Wrong time of day."

"I give up, then."

He released his hands, and I tilted my head back. Even upside down, Kyle was unmistakable.

I leapt to my feet and nearly threw my arms around him, but stopped myself just in time from charging across the boundary of our friendship treaty. Not that my smile didn't give me away. I was secretly pleased to see in his expression a mirror of my own.

"Kyle!" Even my voice betrayed me.

"I didn't know if you were speaking to me anymore."

"How could you ever think that?"

"I didn't hear from you after that last call. I thought that I might have insulted you with the peacock."

"Insulted me? No, I *loved* it! In fact, it's sitting at my bedside. Lucille is going to get a kick out of it. She'll say that you must know me well. But I apologize. I got caught up in finals and didn't get a chance to write back."

"Don't worry about it. I'm glad you liked it." He put his hands in his pockets and tilted back on his heels. A lock of hair fell below his eye, and I wanted so much to smooth it back.

"I did. And thank you. I hope that you keep up woodworking, because you're very good at it."

"Well, now, if you were Catholic, I'd be sending you to the confessional!"

"At least I knew what it was! I'd say that's an accomplishment, and better than I could do. In fact, why don't I commission you to make me a model boat so that I can race it with the children?"

"That would be fun, wouldn't it?" His fingers brushed my arm as he invited me to sit. We both gazed at the smaller lake and smiled at the children, a useful distraction, but at last we turned to each other.

"So, what are you doing here?" I bit my lip, pondering. Did I dare hope that he was out looking for me?

"I suppose the same that you are. Just enjoying the day. My father is getting worse, so I'm going to work at your house today in his place. But I couldn't help wanting to take a walk here first."

"My house?"

"Didn't your mother tell you? I suppose she was pleased with our work at Christmas, and she hired us to help in her gardens on Mondays."

"No, she didn't tell me." I wasn't going to insult him by saying that issues of hired help were trivial to her, and it was unlikely that she would ever bring that up in letters. Nor did I tell him that Monday had just now become my favorite day of the week. "Anyway, I'm glad you decided to walk out here. And I'm sorry about your father."

"He has some good days, but he's definitely weaker than he used to be. Since I got home a few days ago, I've been cooking and cleaning for him. I even darned his socks!"

"Well, you're a regular housewife."

"Not exactly. Dinner was burned, I left streaks on the windows, and I poked myself with the needle."

I smiled at the images but could sense that he was just being humble.

My attention was drawn back to the happy couples in the boats. I longed to be sitting out there with Kyle, talking and courting, laughing, stealing a kiss. When I looked over to see him staring at the scene as well, I scooted in a little closer to him in the event that his thoughts matched my own. But he jolted to his feet abruptly and took a step back.

"Well, I told your mother that I would be there at ten."

"Yes, yes," I managed to say, covering my embarrassment. "She loathes tardiness."

"I can only imagine. So, with that, I'm not going to risk life and limb." He gave me a little wave and started back toward the house.

"Wait, Kyle!" I stood up.

"Yes?" he said, turning back to look at me.

"Um . . ." I said, stammering. "It was nice to see you again."

"You, too, Julianne. I'll see you around."

For the next couple of weeks, I kept myself occupied with friends—Lucille, Blythe, Rose, Lotte, Maude. Blythe's brother had opened a fish-and-chip stand next to the Mersey River, and we frequently gathered on its banks to watch the cargo ships go by. Much had happened since the last summer, and we struggled to keep the gloom of an impending war from dampening our conversations.

Perhaps my perspective was coming from my own pain, but it felt as if everyone we knew had either married or fallen in love. With the exception of Lotte. She hadn't found someone that she could stick with for more than a few weeks and was occupying herself with fictitious wedding plans for our friends. I thought that anyone who went out with Lotte purchased a one-way trip to boredom.

As I feared, this thread of conversation made its way to me. I told them that I enjoyed dancing in London but that my studies kept me from getting serious about anyone. They weren't satisfied, but they let me off the hook—for now. Only Lucille knew the truth, and she avoided making eye contact with me.

I stole away one afternoon to visit Charles. I hadn't seen him since getting that telegram from Kyle. Despite Miss Ellis's assertions to the contrary, he looked pale and was noticeably thinner. Only the eyes of someone who had been away for so long could be appalled by the subtle differences.

"Do you really think he's all right?" I whispered to her, as if he could hear us.

"I do see what you mean. All I've noticed is that he seems short of breath when he comes in from exercise, but I didn't think much of it until you said something. I'm not a doctor, though, dear, and I haven't heard that they've been worrying over him."

I wasn't convinced, but I received her assurances that she would keep a special eye on him and let me know if she could find out more.

I would have come more often to be with my brother, but my calendar found me mostly accompanying Mother on social calls. If she knew that Charles hadn't been well, if she ever received any updates from Bootle at all, there was never any sign of it. There was, however, ample evidence of her continued preoccupation with *my* well-being. The health of my future prospects seemed to be in dire need of repair after my ill-advised dismissal of Roger. Or so she insinuated. On two successive Mondays, she dragged me away from the house, dashing my hopes to casually visit with Kyle while he worked in our gardens. Instead, we visited Mrs. Sheldon, whose grandson was visiting for the summer. It became alarmingly apparent that she and my mother were conspiring to bring us together.

Now that I had been away at school, I planned to assert more control over my life. I was determined that on the next Monday I would stay home, even if I had to feign illness. Before Mother could hunt for me, I set out for the gazebo on the far side of the estate, wearing a white eyelet dress that had hung in my closet since last year. I carried with me a tray of cucumber sandwiches and a pot of tea I'd had Betty prepare. I placed a rose-colored doily on the small round table and completed the setting with the second cup I'd hidden in my handbag and some judiciously chosen daisies from Mother's flower beds.

As though on cue, I spotted Kyle approaching along the ivy-covered brick wall and pulled out a book of poetry to read. What a pretty picture it all made.

Yet Kyle only nodded politely as he walked by, shoulders drooped, exhaustion permeating his features. A pungent smell trailed him, and I recalled Mother saying that she hoped the winds blew away from the house, as he would be laying fertilizer on the lawn today.

I called after him, offering him something to eat, which he accepted hungrily. Barely a word passed his lips beyond a "Thank you" and a "Good to see you," and he returned to work before the tray was empty.

I stood up, indignant, and the lace-edged napkin fell from my skirt. I followed him across the grounds, hands clenched, disregarding the manure that caked up on my new shoes.

I confronted him as he bent over to pick up a rake. "What is wrong with you?"

He swooped up, surprised, and I had to step back to avoid the rake's sharp tines.

"Watch out, you could get hurt!"

"Hurt? Oh, I'm not worried about being hurt by a stupid old rake."

"Is everything OK, Julianne?"

"Why are you angry with me?" I blurted. Blood pulsed wildly through my body, and I had never wanted to kiss him more than at this moment.

He looked me up and down, out of breath, and then grinned when his eyes landed on my feet. "I don't think those will ever be the same."

I looked down at my shoes, which were covered in unimaginable filth, then met his eyes with a matching, though hesitant, smile. "I—I had to see what was wrong."

"Here, let me help you." He took a few steps to a tap and washed his hands, then he gestured for me to hand him my shoes. Bracing myself against the wall, I took them off one at a time, and he rinsed them for me. I didn't have the heart to tell him that the water would do nearly as much damage as the manure. They were silk.

After realizing the hopelessness of their condition, he handed them back to me. "Why would you think I was upset with you?"

"Back there." I pointed toward the gazebo behind us. "You hardly spoke to me."

He sighed and lowered his voice to a whisper. "Oh, Julianne . . ." He moved closer to me and traced the side of my hand with a touch so light that I could barely feel it. Our eyes locked and we stood paralyzed, his head tilted down toward mine. "I could never be angry with you."

"Then why are you upset? Why didn't you speak to me?" I turned my hand just slightly, linking one finger through his. Somehow I managed to remain calm despite the avalanche gathering inside me. His finger tightened around mine, and we lingered there until a distant car horn from the park snapped us back to the reality of our situation and we stepped apart.

"I'm sorry," he said. "It has nothing to do with you. In fact, seeing you here is the best part of my week. It's just—it's my father. I don't know what to do."

"What do you mean?"

"He coughs all the time, sometimes with blood, and he's losing weight. He won't see a doctor. He said that they couldn't save my mother and they can't save him. I brought one in anyway, but my father threw a paperweight at the poor man, and he ran off faster than the devil from holy water."

"Oh, Kyle. What can I do?"

"I'd tell you if I knew, but I don't think that anything can be done."

He leaned against the redbrick wall and slid down to a crouch. He ran his fingers through his mop of curls, then covered his face with his hand. I moved to him and placed my hand on his shoulder.

"Let me give it a try."

He looked up at me with only a whisper of hope. "What do you mean?"

"I'm a nurse, or at least I will be. But I'm not entirely inexperienced. Why don't we see if he'll let me in?"

A hesitant smile grew on his face. "I enjoy your friendship too much. I'm not going to lose that by exposing you to a cantankerous old man who hurls things at unwanted guests."

"I dodged that rake rather deftly, I think."

He glanced over at it and back to me. "You did now, didn't you?" He stood up and wiped his hands on his trousers. I touched his arm, and he stood still.

"Kyle, I'm serious. Why don't you let me see your father? That's what friends are for."

I could see the thoughts doing battle in his head until at last he said, "All right. You can go. Once." He held a finger up as if to drive home the point. "But if he's inconsiderate to you, that's it. I'll not have your pretty little head cracked if he launches something at you."

"I think my pretty little head can handle it."

"I think so, too." He reached out to stroke a strand of hair that lay on my shoulder, holding on to the end thoughtfully before turning away and walking back to work. He called back over his shoulder.

"If you're available tomorrow, I'll pick you up at nine, just outside your gate."

"It's a plan." To hell with whatever else was on my schedule. I was not going to let Kyle down.

⚜

The morning arrived cloudy and overcast, in direct contrast to my feelings, which were soaring at that prospect of seeing Kyle for a second day in a row. I met him at the edge of the estate. Not that it mattered. Father was already off to work, and Mother remained in bed, claiming a migraine. I don't think she even heard me leave.

He came around to the passenger's side to open my door. His actions were thoughtful but automatic. His own mood perfectly matched the weather, and I felt guilty for looking forward to spending the day with him under such unfortunate circumstances. I prepared myself for the task ahead, and in no time I was equally pensive.

We barely talked on the way there. It allowed me to pay attention to my surroundings. In all the time I'd spent thinking about Kyle, I had never thought about where he lived. He drove into town, and as we approached the railway station on Ranelagh he pulled over next to some flats and parked. When he'd come around to open my door, I stepped out hesitantly. The buildings were all made of gray concrete, with laundry hanging from lines stretched across the street. Children gathered on the narrow pavement to play with marbles, and I heard shouting coming from an upstairs window. It was so different from Newsham Park, and it made me sad that someone with such a lively spirit lived in such an unfortunate place. One after another, two trains screamed by, rattling my nerves and drowning out every other sound. No wonder he spent so much time working. I would prefer the sanctuary of beautiful gardens, too, even if they weren't my own.

Pulling a key from his pocket, he opened the front door of the building. The hallway was long and dark. We walked up three flights of steps, Kyle climbing ahead of me, still lost in thought. I supposed he was distracted by the purpose of our visit—which was no doubt true—but when he spoke, his words revealed something else.

With a shrug, he said, "Well, it's not Westcott Manor, is it?"

Suddenly I understood. Kyle was embarrassed for me to be here. Did he not understand? Did he not realize that my life had been turned inside out since I met him? Did he not see that it didn't matter to me where he lived?

"It doesn't need to be."

He smiled—just a hint, but it was there. Pulling out another key, we arrived at No. 33. He knocked first, then opened the door.

The interior was different from what I had expected. The few windows brought in a surprising amount of light, and bright paintings of green hills adorned the walls.

"My father's hobby," he said, answering the question that I didn't ask. Standing by the nearest window was an easel supporting a half-finished canvas, a layer of dust settling over its tray. "He remembers Ireland that way," he said when he caught me looking at it. "I'm not supposed to touch it."

Otherwise, the flat was as neat as a pin. He said, "I cleaned up last night, knowing that you were coming over. We can't have a lady seeing the squalor that two bachelors can sink into."

"It's very cozy," I said, returning his smile.

"Dadaí!" he called, and then whispered to me that this was an Irish word for "father."

A cough came from another room, then the squeak of springs as he adjusted himself in the bed. When we entered, I saw an emaciated old man struggle to push himself up on his arms and then rest against a pillow. He placed a ribboned bookmark inside the prayer book that he was holding.

"Dadaí," Kyle said, "I brought Julianne here, like we talked about."

"And I told you not to bother with that!" he said gruffly. "I'll be fit as a fiddle by tomorrow."

"You are not fit. You are ill. And, since you won't see a doctor, Julianne generously offered to come and talk to you."

"I don't need any help, boy. Take that young thing out of here, and leave me alone!"

"Mr. McCarthy," I said quietly, inching toward the head of the bed, "I won't stay if you don't want me to, but I would really love to visit with you." I slid into the chair at his bedside, took his hand, and turned upon him the most imploring expression that I could muster.

He flinched at first but then softened at my smile. "Well, since you came all the way out here . . ."

"Kyle," I said without taking my eyes from his father's, "why don't you make us some tea while we get acquainted?"

As though acknowledging that this would go better if I was alone with the elder man, Kyle slipped away and closed the door after him.

"Mr. McCarthy, while it's true that I'm here to help you get better, don't think that I'm just doing it to help you. My mother's rosebushes need work—and don't go repeating that to Kyle!"

I saw the first glimpse of a smile, which rolled into a slight chuckle. He shifted onto his side and the bedsprings cried out. "He does his best, *cailín*," he allowed, "but he's best suited to hauling the peat and trimming the hedges."

"Yes, so you see my dilemma. If we don't get you better, our garden will never look the same. I know that she's been quite happy with your work since you starting coming over." And with that, the manipulative charm I'd learned from my mother found a good purpose.

Distracting him with what my father would call prattle, I surreptitiously examined him. I held his hand and felt that it was clammy. When I wanted to check his temperature, I pulled a lock of hair from his face, brushing his forehead with my hand and feeling the heat coming from it. He coughed intermittently, covering his mouth with a brittle yellowed handkerchief and quickly stuffing it under the blankets. But I had a chance to notice that the cloth was stained with varying shades of red blotches. Even a novice like myself could easily diagnose his malady.

Kyle knocked gently and returned with three cups of tea in a delicate flower china pattern. I wondered if it had been his mother's.

He gingerly handed one to me, one to his father, and kept a chipped one for himself. I caught his eye and gave him a slight nod to indicate that I knew what was wrong. We didn't rush out of the room, though. He pulled up a chair, and the three of us talked while we drank our tea.

When we were finished, I stood up, smoothed out my skirt, and placed my teacup on the chest of drawers.

"Thank you, Mr. McCarthy, for letting me come visit. I plan to tell my mother that you will be by soon to tend to the garden. Don't forget what I told you!"

He winked at me, enjoying the conspiracy I'd created. "Don't you worry, darlin'. I will be there as sure as Saint Paddy can quiet a snake."

Kyle approached to place a kiss on his forehead, but the old man shooed him away. "Oh, go on," he huffed. "I'm sure you've got some work to get to."

As I stepped back from the bed, Kyle gestured for me to leave the room first, and then closed the door behind us. He put his teacup in the sink, and we sat down at the table in the kitchen. Seeing the distress in my face, he became alarmed.

"It's not good," I said. I hung my head, because I couldn't bear to look at him with this news. "It's tuberculosis, clear as day. I saw several cases in the hospital. He is very advanced. I'm so sorry, Kyle."

He sighed. "Yes, that's what I thought, too. I was just hoping that you would confirm it and I might be able to convince him then to get some help. When I came home that week during the spring, it was pretty bad. He improved a little at first, but his condition has worsened since I came home again. I didn't know what to do. You don't know how much it means to me that you came."

This was going to be hard to say. "Kyle, you must know he doesn't have much time, and you need to prepare yourself for that. At this stage, even if he allowed a doctor to see him, there is so little that could be done. Maybe nothing."

A tear rolled down my cheek and then another. The first one was for his father. The second was for Kyle, as I realized that he was about to lose the only family that he had ever known. He lifted his hand and wiped the droplets away from my face with the back of his finger. He stood a head taller than me, and I looked directly at the day-old stubble on his chin. My chest tightened at his nearness.

"Thank you for caring. He certainly warmed to you."

"Oh, you know, I used all of my feminine wiles on him." We spoke in careful whispers.

"They can be quite dangerous, I expect."

"Well, I only bring them out in emergencies."

We both grinned, a respite from the sadness in the adjacent room. But it overtook us again just as quickly. "I wish that I could bring a priest to anoint him," he lamented, "but he'll probably throw a bigger fit than he did when I brought the doctor."

"Why don't you let me work on him? He *did* like me. Maybe I can bring him around."

For two weeks, at every opportunity, I came to sit with Mr. McCarthy. I read the newspaper to him, made him tea. I drove myself when Father would allow it, having told him about the situation and how it would be good experience for me. But just as often, Kyle would pick me up. On a few occasions, Kyle cooked for me, and not surprisingly he was good at it. He seemed to do everything well.

Soon enough I gained the confidence of his father, and I was gently able to tell him the truth about his condition, though I was unable to convince him to see a doctor. It didn't come as a surprise. In fact, he even looked forward to death, since his faith promised that he would see his wife and daughters again. His only regret was leaving Kyle alone.

"He won't be alone, Mr. McCarthy," I said. "I'll always be his friend. And I'm sure he has many friends at school, too."

I thought I detected a look of appreciation.

Convinced that he had accepted the truth, I told him that it would mean a lot to Kyle to have him anointed. I didn't even understand what that meant, but if it was important to Kyle, then it was important to me to make it happen. Like butter on a hot pan, he melted to my request. I couldn't wait to tell Kyle the news on the way home.

Elated, and not satisfied with waiting, he drove us straightaway to his church so that we could see the priest.

Just as I had not thought of where Kyle lived, I had not thought of where Kyle worshipped. I was glad to be entering a more intimate part of his world.

The exterior of Saint Stephen's reminded me a little of the Church of the Immaculate Heart of Mary, but then again, I was not skilled in seeing the nuances of religious architecture. The interior was noticeably different, though. It had the same basic features—mosaic floors, stained glass windows, an altar—but it was not as ornate as the one that I had visited in London. I liked it better—it was more welcoming and less intimidating to me.

We walked over to the rectory, and although the hours posted had long since passed, Kyle knocked on the door. A housekeeper answered, a bitter-looking old sourpuss who lit up like a young girl when she saw who was on her doorstep.

"Kyle. It's good to see you. How is your father?"

"He's not getting any better, Mrs. Mawdsley. In fact, that's why we're here. I would like to have Father Sullivan give him extreme unction."

Extreme unction? I didn't know what that was, but it sounded so, well, *extreme*. I would have to ask him about that later.

"That's a shame, dear." Only then did she seem to notice me, standing just behind him. "And who is this?" Her tone changed to one of malice as she eyed me. I had no doubt that she knew Kyle was studying to join the ranks of this Father Sullivan. Who was this little blond girl with her recruit?

"How rude of me. This is Miss Julianne Westcott. She's a nursing student, and is the only one that has been able to get my father to face this reality. Julianne, this is Mrs. Mawdsley."

She continued to eye me as though I'd been sent by the devil himself to tempt Kyle from his vocation. "Well, come in, there's no use, you standing outside like this. Father Sullivan is in the dining room, but I'm sure that he'll want to talk to you. Have a seat over there, and I'll call for him." As she limped out of the room, I was reminded of Quasimodo and amused myself by imagining her crying, "Sanctuary!" I knew that it was wrong, but it helped leaven my discomfort in these surroundings.

We sat on the sofa in the parlor where Kyle looked as if he was at home within its creamy yellow walls, and it occurred to me that he must have spent a lot of time here. But his familiarity appeared to provide little comfort tonight. He put his elbows on his knees and folded his hands together. Not wanting him to catch me studying him, I looked around at the bookshelves that lined the walls and didn't recognize any of the titles. Several were in Latin.

Minutes later Father Sullivan came into the parlor, hurriedly dabbing at the corner of his mouth with the napkin in his hand. He was shorter than Kyle, with the beginnings of a paunch and a bald spot. Unlike his housekeeper, the presence of a young lady with Kyle appeared to neither scandalize nor infuriate him. In fact, I almost thought I saw a little amusement in his expression, which I did not understand. I followed Kyle's lead and stood up when the priest entered the room. He motioned that it was unnecessary and that we should sit, but I rather liked standing in the presence of this man. I was drawn immediately to his kindness, and I thought that this was the kind of priest that Kyle would be.

We explained the seriousness of Mr. McCarthy's condition, and Kyle said that it was time for him to be anointed. I gathered from their conversation a couple of things. First, *anointing* and *extreme unction* were interchangeable terms. (I liked *anointing* better. Far less severe.) And second, this was reserved for those who were very close to death.

Father Sullivan grabbed his long black coat, excused himself to retrieve his kit of oils, and followed us out the door. We squeezed into the cab of Kyle's truck. It was an odd feeling to sit between the two of them. Shoulder to shoulder with Kyle, my senses were on alert to his every movement and my body felt as if it were on fire where we touched; I had to press my hands together to keep them from involuntarily reaching out to him. On one side, then, an urgent reminder of what Kyle *could never* be. And on the other, an equally stark reminder of what Kyle was *destined* to become: a gentle and kind priest. I was thankful that the ride was brief, because jostling between the two was suffocating for me.

We walked down the now all-too-familiar, dark ground-floor hallway and up the three narrow flights of stairs. Mr. McCarthy could no longer sit up in his bed, but it was obvious that he was happy to see all three of us. Father Sullivan asked us to leave the room, and he closed the door behind him. Kyle explained that he was hearing his father's confession. I knew little about that and of the anointing in general, and Kyle patiently explained it all to me. This was considered one of their sacraments, and it was intended to help the dying person get his spiritual house in order to prepare for whatever was coming next. I found comfort in what he was describing, and I thought that it must be nice to have someone praying for you in your last days.

After the confession, Father Sullivan came for us. Although Kyle offered me a chair, I stood with my back against the wall, observing the rest of the ritual. Father Sullivan didn't look our way, and Mr. McCarthy had his eyes closed, with the most faint smile on his lips. Kyle explained things to me whenever I looked confused, translating from the Latin when necessary.

As Father Sullivan blessed the old man's eyes with oil, Kyle whispered the English translation to me. "Through this holy anointing, and through his most tender mercy, may the Lord pardon you what sins you have committed by sight."

Father Sullivan followed with gesturing crosses over his ears, and Kyle continued. "Through this holy anointing, and through his most tender mercy, may the Lord pardon you what sins you have committed by hearing."

The ritual continued with the nose, the lips, the hands, and the feet. Every avenue that might have caused offense in one's lifetime. Kyle looked at the scene, entranced, and I looked at Kyle. He hadn't shaved in days, and his shoulders curled in. My heart ached for his sadness.

Kyle stepped forward at the end and made the sign of the cross over himself. I gripped the footboard of the large iron bed and watched with fascination.

Kyle was quiet on the way back home, and I didn't pester him with idle conversation. I nearly fell asleep. I was both bewildered and moved by what I had witnessed, and my body was exhausted by the toll that had been taken during the weeks of helping his father.

"Here you are," he said as we drove up. The truck idled while he opened his door.

"Please don't get out," I said. "I can walk myself up, and you need to get back."

He sighed, a commonplace sound in these past weeks. "You're probably right." He pulled his door closed again. "Thank you for everything. And for being there tonight."

Silence lingered between us as our eyes met. I looked away first.

"Don't mention it," I said. "It was—well, different. I can't say I understood it all, but it was kind of beautiful."

"Now you see why the seminary takes eight years."

"Yes. So much to remember."

"Well, I'll see you tomorrow, then?"

I wanted to say yes. With all my heart. But I couldn't. "No, I've neglected much at home lately, and I should try to get up to Bootle later in the week. I've only seen my brother once since Christmas."

"I shouldn't have monopolized your time these past few weeks. I wasn't even thinking. I'm sorry."

"No—don't be sorry. I was glad to be there."

"We're glad you were." He paused. "I don't know what I would have done without you."

"Really, don't say that. He would have come around eventually."

"Why don't I come by in a couple of days and let you know how he's doing?"

"I'd like that. Now, go get some sleep. Your eyes are bloodshot, and your father needs you."

"You're right. Good night."

Our gaze lingered. If this had been a date, it would have been the moment where I'd be wondering if he would kiss me.

"Good night." I broke the spell abruptly and slid off the seat. The door made a rusty thud as I closed it. "I love you," I said into the cloud of exhaust left behind. I stayed until I could no longer see it.

I hoped that the next few days would fly by until I could see him again. I'd grown so accustomed to these daily visits.

But as it turned out, I saw Kyle much sooner than I expected.

Chapter Fifteen

I missed breakfast, but felt greatly renewed by the additional sleep. Mother peppered me with questions now that I had time to visit with her. They were suspiciously inquisitive more than conversational, but I think I finally convinced her that this time with Kyle's father had been an exercise in nursing and nothing more. I could see that she thought I was spending too much time with the younger gardener, and she didn't like it.

I caught a matinee with Lucille, whose company I had missed not only for the last few weeks, but ever since the days that we were inseparable. How distant was our childhood, where the dilemmas were no more difficult than deciding which dolls to invite to a tea party.

She let me pour my heart out about all that had occurred lately. There were so many emotions. I had really grown a soft spot for Mr. McCarthy, ill-tempered with the world but sweet to me. I had felt so alive being near Kyle for such an extended time, and the more I learned about him, the more I loved him. And so, the more I bemoaned what kept us apart.

I apologized to Lucille for being such a scattered mess, but she hugged me tight and listened as if every word I said made perfect sense.

Lucille's Ben met us for supper. I was pleased to have a chance to get to know him better, and I instantly liked him. He was so solicitous of my best friend, and I was gratified that she was in good hands. Lucille seemed to feel a little guilty for being so happy in front of me, but I made sure that I wore my biggest smile so that she could see that I was, indeed, sharing her joy. It was nice that, for once, she was receiving all of the attention. She certainly deserved it.

The clouds were looking dark and heavy as I headed home, and just as I arrived, they burst open with rain. I played backgammon with Father for an hour while he smoked his pipe. He had picked up my enthusiasm for the game over Christmas, and we made bets on the outcome for silly stakes. If he won tonight, I would have to clean his pipe collection. If I won, I didn't have to work at the warehouses for a week. Mother wasn't one for games, and she rolled her eyes when we were getting competitive. She went back to reading a magazine that had arrived in the post that day.

I lost our little tournament, five to three, and was ready to lick my wounds with the company of a good book. I kissed Father good night and went upstairs to put on my coziest pajamas. After lighting a fire, I opened *The Misfortunes of Mr. Teal* and settled into my warm bed. I loved nights like this.

Hours later, nodding my head in drowsiness, I heard a plinking sound on my window. I ignored it, thinking it was hail. It would have been unusual but not impossible. I had twelve pages to finish in the book, so I widened my eyes and refocused my attention. But I heard the sound again.

I walked over to open the window and was shocked to see a figure down below. "Julianne!" It was Kyle, shouting as quietly as he could. He was soaking wet. "Julianne! I need to talk to you!"

I held my finger up to my lips and nodded. "I'll be right down."

I went to my closet to grab something to wear but changed my mind when I considered the absurdity of the whole thing. If Kyle was here so late at night and in the rain, there must be an emergency. Instead, I put on a heavy, plush robe and a pair of slippers. I grabbed a towel for him, thinking that he must be cold. Tiptoeing downstairs, I slipped out the back door and adjusted my eyes to the darkness so that I could see him.

"Come on," he said, grabbing my hand. "Let's get out of the rain." We ran toward the gazebo in the distance.

When we arrived, he let go of my hand and I wrung the rain from my hair. I handed the towel to him. He patted himself down until only dampness was left.

He looked very serious and was about to say something. But when he had a chance to really look at me, the corners of his mouth turned up just a little. "You're wearing your pajamas!"

"You pulled me out of my house in the middle of the night, in the pouring rain, and you're talking about my pajamas? I thought you were in some kind of trouble, so I hurried down!"

"You're right . . . my fault. I guess that you just surprised me." He smiled a little wider, but I could sense sadness in his eyes. "It's a nice surprise."

I was suddenly aware that my pink terry cloth robe had loosened, and the rain had made the summer nightgown cling to my skin. I pulled the robe tight around me, embarrassed.

His voice was clenched when he spoke again. "No, there's no trouble. But I did want to let you know right away . . ."

"Yes?"

He looked down and ran his fingers through his hair. "My father. He died this evening."

Without thinking, I threw my arms around him. Against his chest, I felt him breathe a heavy sigh that sounded like the release of months of strain. I heard the quickened beat of his heart. He put his arms around me, too, and we held each other there, swaying slightly, comforting one another in our shared sadness. I had really become close to his father during this ordeal, and I felt the loss as well. At the same time, enveloped by the one I loved, I welcomed the physical closeness to him that I had craved for a year.

I started to sob from all of it, and he held me tighter.

I don't know how long we stood there, sheltered from the rain, leaning on each other in the dark.

Pulling me closer, if that was even possible, Kyle laid his head down on my shoulder, and I could hear him choking back a few of his own tears as he breathed. My hand moved to the back of his head as I stroked his hair slowly. I heard him shudder just a little, and before I knew it, I felt his lips press gently against my neck.

A chill ran through my body, and I froze in place, unsure of what to do. In another circumstance, I might have thought that it was a kiss. But this was not an ordinary situation by any means, and I didn't want to let my feelings take over the moment. It was excruciating to stand there, unresponsive.

I felt his lips on me again, a little more insistently, moving gradually up from my neck to my cheek. There was no mistaking what he was doing now, and I didn't want him to stop. I continued to stand still, not even breathing. He picked his head up and looked at me. While I could control my body, I couldn't control my expression, and I knew he could see the complete longing that I had for him. He moved his hands to my face, cradling it, and then slowly placed his lips on mine.

Gently, gently, he kissed me, several times, each time with a little more fervor. When I responded, suppressing nothing now, he gasped sharply and kissed me harder. We continued like that, two people desperately needing each other, a year of hesitation washed away in the rain.

He pulled back, looking at me again and brushing my cheek with his hand.

"Julianne," he whispered. And with that one word, he said a thousand.

He put his arms around me, holding me close to him, and I could feel the wild beating of his heart. It matched my own. We stood there again, laughing and crying all at once.

Taking my hand, he led me to the bench in the gazebo. He never released it but only held it tighter.

He whispered again, holding his head down. "You have no idea how long I've wanted to do that."

I couldn't get any words out and just looked at him. If he were to look up, I knew that my face would say it all.

"I've been in love with you since I first saw you," he said. "I suppose that it was only a matter of time before I gave up trying to deny it."

All I wanted was for him to kiss me again, but a part of me feared that this unexpected turn of events was the fault of the news he had come to share about his father. The morning might bring him regret. Which would mean heartache once again.

"Kyle," I said, putting both of my hands in his but pulling away from him. I couldn't believe what I was about to say. "What are you doing? You're losing everything you worked for. This isn't what you came here for tonight."

"No, it's not. Really, I surprised myself as much as I must have surprised you. But I'm not sorry. I'm not. *Please* trust me on this. You are all that I've wanted for a long time."

"But what about—"

"No—shh, hush." He pulled me back to him. "I realized in these last few months that I couldn't be a good priest if I knew my calling was elsewhere."

"Kyle—I don't know what to say." My mind was reeling.

"I think that I've been rejecting the notion for all this time because I didn't believe that you could ever feel the same way for me."

My eyes widened. "How can you say that?"

"Look at you. You've been surrounded by friends and admirers for so long, how could I expect you to see me through all that?"

"You are mad, you know that? I knew as soon as I saw you helping my brother that day there could be no one else."

He leaned in and kissed each of my eyelids tenderly. Then, pressing his forehead against mine, he twirled a strand of my hair in his finger, and we reveled in the closeness.

Oh, how alert my senses were! Without remorse, I could see him, touch him, hear him, breathe in his scent, taste the sweetness of his kiss. I savored the exhilaration of the moment.

I realized then that I had not asked him anything about his father, and that is what he had come for in the first place. I told him so.

He smiled, a look of complete contentment on his face. He continued to stroke my hair as if it were a precious possession. "You know, he is the one that brought us together. Not intentionally, that's not what I mean. But watching you care for him, seeing your devotion to helping him, I knew for certain that this is where I was meant to be all along. He was ready to go, and you helped make that happen. He is at peace, and I am too, because of you."

Kyle kissed the tip of my nose and then moved down to brush my lips again.

"I've tried . . . so hard . . ." I whispered, in between breaths.

"What is that, darling?" He was distracted by what he was doing, but I turned his face to look me in the eye so that he could really hear what I was saying.

"I tried so hard not to interrupt your plans and your ambitions. I even avoided you at times just so it wouldn't be difficult."

"You are an angel for that. But you have to realize that *you* are my dream. In fact, I even talked to Father Sullivan about you."

I stiffened at this and pushed him away. "You *did*?" I could only imagine what the kind priest could possibly think of me now. "How could you do that? He must hate me."

Kyle laughed and pulled me back to him. "Of course he doesn't hate you. Father Sullivan has been my confessor ever since I was a child.

He knows me better than anyone. This isn't news to him. In fact, I think he saw it coming even before I did."

"But surely he must want you to be a priest, like him."

"Father Sullivan wants me to be whatever I am led to be. And I know that is with you."

"And just when did you know that for sure?"

He grinned. "About ten minutes ago, when you threw yourself at me."

"Kyle, please, I was trying to *comfort* you!"

"Oh, is that what you were doing? My fault, then—I take it all back."

"Don't you dare!" I pulled him toward me and kissed him hard, leaving no doubt in his mind that I much preferred this course for us.

When I was confident that I left not a shred of doubt in him, I asked, "Where do we go from here?"

"Well, that is for another day. Because if your parents find you out here with me, there won't *be* another day."

I didn't want him to leave and have this enchantment end. I didn't want to sleep for fear I'd awake and find that I had been dreaming. But the brisk air biting my skin told me that this was real and that Kyle was right.

"Besides, I have to get back," he said. "The undertaker is coming first thing in the morning, and that's only a few hours away. I may not be able to come see you tomorrow, but please know that I will be thinking of nothing else."

"Can't I help with the arrangements?"

"There isn't much to do, honestly. My father was a private man and didn't know very many people. But there will be a burial shortly, and it would mean a lot to me if you were there. I know that he would have liked that."

"Of course I will."

He took my hand again and led me back to the house, staying in the shadows away from the moonlight. There was no sense in risking anyone seeing us.

Approaching the protection of the back porch, he put his arm around my waist and drew me to him. After kissing me deeply, he said, "Julianne . . . my love," and then ran off into the darkness.

It occurred to me as I dried myself off that it had been raining the last time Kyle and I had a momentous conversation, too. Maybe God was trying to warn me off. But I didn't want to listen.

Chapter Sixteen

I kept my eyes closed at the break of daylight, basking in remembered details, one by one. Every word and every touch had been absolutely perfect.

The only cloud in my newly sunlit world was the fear that Kyle might have second thoughts in the reality of the day. After all, a lifetime of expectation and effort was not going to be easy to release. Maybe he didn't really mean those things and had let his guard down temporarily. Certainly the emotions of losing a parent could distort one's intentions.

The nagging fear only grew worse and soon converted my previous elation into outright panic. To compound everything, I wasn't going to see Kyle today, so I couldn't be comforted by his reassurances. If there were any to come.

I became frantic with ways to occupy myself so that I wouldn't think of it. I organized my closet, then alphabetized the books on my shelves. I helped Betty in the kitchen. I read the *Daily Post*. Italy had beaten Hungary in the World Cup last night. That would surely be what everyone talked about today. But nothing worked. Maybe I needed a change of scenery.

It was Monday, so Father planned to go into the warehouses earlier than usual to get a start on the week. Maybe I could ride into town with him. But he beat me to it.

"Julianne."

"Yes?"

"If you can spare the time, I could use some help with the bills of lading. They need to be grouped into shipping lines and then calculated for invoicing. Remember, you lost our match, so no getting out of it."

He needn't have thrown in the reminder. It was the perfect chance to get out of the house. And it would be nice to spend the day with him.

"Of course I can spare the time!" I gave him a big hug and a kiss on the cheek. He looked at me as if I were a crazy woman. Sorting chin-high stacks of paper was not my, nor anyone's, idea of how to spend a day, but he had no way of knowing how desperate I was for a distraction.

"You're driving," he said. I grabbed my handbag, and he handed me the keys to the Aston.

Father talked about business all along the way, technicalities that I couldn't possibly keep straight. Shipping was his life, his mistress, his religion. Even over backgammon, he'd regale me with updates on cargo regulations. He'd been that way as long as I could remember, but I wondered if it had always been so. Was it who he was, or was it his escape from the devastation of Charles's birth, his public version of Mother's clandestine drinking?

Today, though, I was relieved that he wasn't attuned to the finer details of my life. Unlike Mother, whose sobriety seemed synchronized to my rides home with Kyle in the last few weeks. She'd tried cornering me several times already to register again her concern over the amount of time that I'd spent with him. Before last night, I had honest excuses.

"It's good practice for school, Mother."

"It will help me keep up my skills over the summer break."

"No, there's not anything between the McCarthy boy and me. He's a gardener, Mother, really!" I'd tell her anything she wanted to hear.

But now? Would I be forced to choose between my parents and Kyle, my obligations and my love? Could they ever accept the Irish Catholic boy who lived by the tracks?

We pulled up to the cavernous square of redbrick buildings that framed Albert Dock. The water gave off the putrid smell of low-tide fish and harbored sea vessels. But I knew that to my father, it smelled like money. A flock of gulls basked in a sunny spot that had escaped the shadow cast by the warehouse. But they scattered at the sound of the car door, save for one whose injured wing prevented him from flying off. I sympathized with him as together we watched the rest of them soar past a Cunard liner and disappear.

The monotonous project of sorting the bills of lading was heartily welcome today. I categorized them by imports and exports, and then by shipping companies—Maersk, Messageries, Intermodal, and so forth. Meticulously, I calculated their charges for temporary storage in our warehouses. It took me nearly six hours.

When I was finished, I peeked into Father's office and saw that he was still working. I debated between taking a bus home and waiting for a ride with him, and decided to help a little longer. Dusting the shelves and doing some filing, I stayed busy for another hour. He emerged then, jacket slung over his shoulder.

"Well done, Princess. You're a natural, you know. You could be great."

"Thanks, but I have other plans."

"I know, I know. But I hope you know that it's always here for you if the nursing thing doesn't work out."

"The 'nursing thing' is working out just fine. Maybe you should come see me in London sometime and I can show you."

"I'd like to. You know that. But I can't get away."

That was his excuse for everything. Why he hadn't come to my ballet recitals. Why he was late for my graduation ceremonies. I knew he loved me, but there was no doubt as to his priorities.

I tossed him the keys this time and sat in the passenger's seat before he could protest. I was tired and dusty after being in the warehouse, and I couldn't wait to shower off. My thoughts turned to Kyle again, to the impossibility of last night and the agonizing fear that he would think it was a mistake. It was too painful to contemplate. I had to think about something else, and I knew just the thing.

"Father?"

"Hmm?"

"Why didn't you have any more children? You know, it would have been nice to have a sister—or a brother."

Now, in a theatrical production, this would be his cue to pause, reflect, and tell me in choking words that I *did* have a sibling. And he was so sorry for keeping my brother from me. The turning point of the script.

But it wasn't like that. He didn't miss a beat.

"Oh, you know, Princess. The business was going through a major expansion when you were born, and there just wasn't any time. Besides, once you start with perfection, you can only go downhill from there." He squeezed my hand as if he were proud of the compliment he was paying me, but I pulled it away and looked out the window.

"That's too bad. It would have been nice."

"I'm sure it would have. At least you have Lucille. She's like a sister to you."

"Yes, at least I have Lucille."

Poor Charles. Was he entirely forgotten?

I closed my eyes and pretended to sleep all the way back.

He pulled up to the front door and told me that he had some documents to drop with a client.

"Tell your mother I won't be home until late. Mr. Laurent is in from Paris, and I need to meet with him about the opera shipment."

But Mother had something to tell me first. As I closed the door and walked toward the grand staircase, she called out to me.

"Julianne." She said it like a command.

I turned around. She was sitting in the parlor with her back toward me. In front of her lay pile upon pile of fabric swatches. Her finger landed on the top one, and she traced its scrolled pattern as though hypnotized.

"Yes?"

"I'm having the Victorian chairs reupholstered. What do you think of this?"

She gripped the corner of the nearest one, and still she didn't look at me. I stepped into the parlor and approached the table. The fabric was hideous, not something that I ever would have imagined her choosing.

"Didn't you just do those a couple of years ago?"

I knew very well she had. She'd had those chairs redone when I announced that I wanted to be a nurse. And when I was twelve, and she caught me trying to compete in the park's boat races. And at seven, when I fancied the idea of being a circus performer someday. They had become a time line of her disappointment in me, a curious thing to focus on, a needless thing to control.

"Yes," she murmured, "but I'm tired of that pattern."

She placed her hand flat on the swatch and turned to look at me. A look of restrained fury twisted the features of her face, normally so beautiful. She moved her hand to clutch an envelope sitting on the table and proceeded to wave it in front of my face.

"Kyle McCarthy stopped by asking for you today."

Kyle had been here? My heart skipped a beat.

"I told him that you were away, so he left you a note that he'd written. Julianne, you must know I cannot possibly—"

I cut her off and took the envelope from her hands, ripping the corner in the process. Surprisingly, it was still sealed. "It's probably just an update on his father." I wasn't going to tell her that I had found out about his death early this morning. Or how enthusiastically I had consoled him. I stifled a smile at the thought.

"I warned you, I *warned* you, Julianne Westcott, that his intentions were inappropriate, and you didn't listen to me."

"But—"

"I don't blame him if he's got some ridiculous notions about you. He can stand in line with ten dozen others. But if I were to think for a minute—a *second*, Julianne—that you returned those feelings, I'd disown you here and now."

"You can't mean that."

"Don't test me. No daughter of mine is going to carry on with someone so beneath her, so inferior—"

"So beneath me? Why? Because he works with his hands? Because he doesn't come from a proper family with loads of money? Is he beneath me because he turns to God instead of the drink, like some people I know?"

The slap that lashed my cheek burned like hell. I'd called her on it—her pettiness, her weakness. No one confronted Beatrice Westcott. But I had, finally.

Damn the consequences. I had a note from Kyle.

I ran to my room, but turned around at the landing and threw a punch of my own. "Oh, I forgot to tell you. Father won't be home for dinner. Again. No wonder. I'd rather eat with some boring old client than to have to sit there with you and your judgments and your secrets, night after night. At least I get to go away to school again. He's stuck with you here forever!"

I sank into my feather bed after locking my door more loudly than necessary. My heart raced, whether from the argument or the anticipation of the letter, I didn't know.

But at last I was alone with Kyle's words. Words that could either relieve the fears of my day or words that could break my heart. I held it to my forehead and closed my eyes, willing it to be the former. And then I opened it.

> *Darling Julianne—I am so happy to be able to say it openly and not just think it. I know that I said that I wouldn't be able to see you today, but I couldn't help it. I haven't been able to stop thinking about last night, and all I want to do is see you again. My father's burial is tomorrow at eleven. If it's all right with you, I can pick you up at 10:30. Despite the occasion, I can hardly wait.*
> *All my love, Kyle*

I read it again—three times, four times, pausing on certain words. Kyle had no regrets. Kyle had no regrets! The truth of it played over and over in my mind. How foolish I'd been to think otherwise. Of course he loved me. All that fretting for nothing.

I went to my closet to pick out something for tomorrow. I found a black crepe dress, short black gloves, an old but classic hat, and my best silk stockings. I laid them on my chair and went to turn on the showerhead so that the water could start to warm up. As I undressed, I caught my reflection in the mirror, seeing myself in a new way, seeing myself as a woman desired by the man I loved.

Turning right and left, I noticed the slenderness of my legs, the outward curve of my hips, contouring into a narrow waist. My breasts were of medium size, if I was to compare myself to other girls, and I wondered if that mattered as much as Abigail said it did.

My imagination got the better of me until the steam from the shower misted over the mirror and I could barely see myself. I stepped into the hot water and washed away the strangeness of the day.

I couldn't wait to get into bed. The sooner I slept, the sooner it would be tomorrow. But first things first. If I didn't defuse Mother, this would be a miserable summer indeed. At best, she would double up her efforts to pair me off with someone more to her liking. At worst, she would restrict my activities beyond comprehension. With confirmation that Kyle returned my love, I needed as much freedom to come and go as I could muster. So I acted preemptively. Preparing a most solemn expression, I headed into her dressing room, where she was putting on one of her many nightgowns.

"Mother, I shouldn't have spoken to you like that. I don't know what came over me. It was a long day at the office with Father, and I suppose I was just worn out. But it's no excuse. I apologize."

She didn't look at me as she slid her arms through a matching silk robe. Ice blue, and no wrinkle daring to make an appearance.

I continued. "And I suppose I was just anxious about news of the elder Mr. McCarthy. I can't help but be concerned, since he was sort of a patient of mine."

She looked at me then, pointed to her hair, and sat at her vanity table. I picked up the boar hairbrush and started at the bottom, gently smoothing out any knots. This was a sign that she was open to listening. "Kyle was only writing to tell me that his father died last night." I worked up to the middle, and then to the ends, just as she'd taught me when I was a child.

"I am sorry about that, Julianne. I know that you worked very hard to make him better." The words stumbled out of pursed lips, but I capitalized on the slight concession.

"Well, there wasn't much hope for him getting better. I was really there to tend to his needs. Good nursing experience. I might be able to earn some extra credit out of it." Part of me cringed for being so crass about what had been such a beloved time, but I couldn't share any of that. And besides, I needed to soften her up for tomorrow.

"Anyway, Kyle offered to take me to the funeral in the morning. I think that it would be both kind and useful to go. You know, kind of the final bit to the whole thing."

"Well, I don't suppose that I can say no to that. But Julianne . . ."

"Yes, Mother?" Our eyes met in the oval-shaped mirror.

"Be careful. Despite what you say, I think that Kyle has been pouring too much attention on you. Just keep your head and don't be naïve about it. After this, I don't see any reason why you should even see him again."

I nodded in feigned obedience.

She sat up straighter and looked at me with a chill in her eyes that belied the casual tone of her words. I felt the unspoken warning before she broke the stare and spoke again.

"And how silly of me to think that you would return any romantic notions where he is concerned. I raised you to be a smart girl." She slipped off her jewelry and went right into the next thing on her mind. "Anyway, your timing is good. Tomorrow afternoon Mrs. Sheldon is coming for tea, and her grandson, Simon, will be with her. He is a very nice young man, and he seems to have taken an interest in you. You know, he is reading law at Oxford."

"Yes, I heard something about that. I don't know how long the funeral will go, but I will try to be home in time for tea." The lies were coming more easily to me. If I were Catholic like Kyle, would that be something I'd have to confess? It felt completely justifiable right now, under the circumstances.

I brushed the crown of her hair, finishing again at the ends, and stepped back so that she could admire my work. She ran her hands down the length of it and smiled approvingly. I must be back in her good graces because she turned her cheek out to me.

"Good night, Mother." I kissed her perfunctorily.

"Good night, Julianne."

I went to the kitchen where I knew that Betty would have saved some supper for me. Breaking yet another rule, a minor one in comparison, I took the plate to my bedroom. Mother feared attracting rats by having food upstairs.

In the morning, at 10:30 sharp, I heard the welcome roar of Kyle's truck. Looking down from my window, I noticed that he was more dressed up than I had ever seen him before. He wore a black three-piece suit, white shirt, and gray tie. I hurried down just in time to see Mother taking in his new look. Her eyes were more approving than she wanted to be. Kyle's funeral attire made him look more like someone she would encounter socially. Unfortunately, I knew that the everyday Kyle, the one I loved, would never measure up.

"Good morning, Mrs. Westcott," he said, taking off his fedora.

"Good morning to you. I am sorry to hear about your father."

"Thank you, Mrs. Westcott. And thank you for allowing Miss Westcott to attend his burial. She was very helpful to us these past few weeks."

"Well, good. She might be earning some extra credit at school for it." I winced at her tactlessness.

Kyle looked my way, and I saw the tiredness in his eyes.

My mother turned. "Ah, here she is now. Julianne—don't forget about tea with Mrs. Sheldon and her grandson this afternoon." She gripped my hand with authority and cast a menacing glance at Kyle as she spoke to me. "Did you know that Simon's mother was a Dewhurst, from the Dewhurst Tea Company? I hear they have homes in Cardiff *and* in Paris. Such a catch."

"I will try my best to be here, Mother." I wrangled myself away, and we made our way to the truck. I would have offered the Aston, but I didn't want to deny Kyle the dignity of driving me in his own vehicle.

It wasn't until we'd driven the length of the winding drive and passed through the gate that I was able to shed the pretenses displayed for Mother and let myself delight at being alone with Kyle again. Even the gravity of the occasion couldn't dampen my spirits. He must have been thinking the same thing. At the first opportunity, he stopped the truck on the side of the road and slid over to me.

"Good morning, gorgeous!" He rested his head against mine, and we closed our eyes, tentative in the bittersweet emotions coursing through our bodies on this unusual morning. He moved forward for a slow and gentle kiss that rapidly became more hungry.

"Good morning, yourself," I said between breaths.

He pulled back, resting his head against mine once again. "I intend to do that every morning for the rest of our lives."

"I would like that. I think my mother might have some objections, though."

"Then I will have to convince her that her gardens need lots of attention to give myself a reason to be here all the time."

"And you'd have to move to London with me."

"I'll pack up tomorrow." He slid back to the wheel and started down the road.

Levity aside, I asked, "Where are we going?" I had expected to drive toward town to Saint Stephen's, but we were driving in the opposite direction, toward the country.

"We're going to a cemetery at All Souls in Charcross, past Knowsley Park."

"Not Saint Stephen's?"

"I was there this morning. We had a rosary and a funeral Mass for my father."

"Why didn't you tell me? I would have been there." I hated being left out of any corner of his life.

"Well, I know that you didn't feel comfortable last time that you were at Mass in London, and I didn't want to put you in a difficult situation this morning. There's a lot of standing and kneeling, and *Latin*." He knew that I would shudder at the last one, completely intimidated by the language that was so literally foreign to me.

"Well, that makes sense. This isn't the morning to jump right in. But Kyle, if we're going to be together, you're going to have to teach me how to participate there."

"What do you mean?"

"I mean, if I'm going to go to Mass with you."

His eyes widened. "You mean that you'd become Catholic for me?"

"I'd become *German* for you, if that's what you wanted."

"Hmm." He looked toward the road, lost in thought.

We arrived at a sprawling piece of land. Headstones dotted the horizon, with angels and crosses scattered among them, their height and detail indicating the wealth of the families that commissioned them. The arched iron gate reading "All Souls Cemetery" had seen better days. Flaking black paint revealed layers of color that had been applied in the fashion of long-ago years. Off in the distance I could see a tiny stone church with a steeple and bell tower. Next to it was another stone building, about the same size as the church. I asked Kyle about it.

"That's All Souls church, and next to it is the rectory. The priest lives on one side and the groundskeeper on the other. The congregation is very small, being all the way out here, but he's mostly here to conduct funerals and burials, and to counsel the grieving."

"How depressing!"

"Well, it depends on the priest. Some of them like this post because they're reclusive by nature, and this is about the loneliest church you could get appointed to. On the other hand, there are those priests who have a real gift for this work and see it as an important ministry. Either way, though, I've heard that the isolation gets to you after a while, so they rotate priests about every two or three years."

The cemetery was enormous, and Kyle told me that the oldest sections had been there for several centuries. The ones closest to us dated the farthest back. Their headstones were sunk into the ground at varying angles and their letters were weathered in places; the names and memories of the unfortunate ones below were slowly being erased. The newer ones ran up the hill and were arranged in ordered, symmetrical rows.

It would be impossible to find our way to the specific gravesite on our own, so we drove to the church. Kyle instructed me to wait in the truck while he asked for directions. I rolled the window down and looked at the church in more detail.

It was small. From the exterior, I doubted that it would fit more than a hundred people. It was constructed of stones in brown and gray, randomly laid, with white mortar seams that had discolored over time. The steeple seemed taller than it had from the road, and I saw two bells in the tower. I wondered what they would sound like—two solemn wails echoing and mourning in this vast resting place. The roof had a steep slant, and below it were simple windows, rectangular at the bottom until they came to a pointed arch at the top. The lone door mimicked the shapes of the windows.

In front of the church was a courtyard lined with the same kind of stones. An elderly couple walked out of the church, rosaries in hand, followed by Kyle. The woman pointed toward the rectory, and I couldn't hear what she said to him. Kyle knocked there and was greeted by what must have been the most recent priest sent to this beautiful desolation. I could see him nod as he put his arm around Kyle's shoulder, inviting him in. Kyle turned around to me, gesturing that he would be right back. When he returned, he had the plot location and a map of the grounds.

"We're all set," he said. "I'm glad we stopped. We could have been driving around forever!" He handed the map to me and asked me to navigate for him.

The newest part of the cemetery was about half a mile away, and it didn't take us long to find our destination.

Stopping the truck, he opened my door for me. I looked out and saw six other figures there already. Kyle leaned in toward my ear to tell me who they all were.

"You remember Father Sullivan and Mrs. Mawdsley. The others are Mr. Alden, our landlord since as long as I can remember, and two parishioners from Saint Stephen's. The other one is Mr. Paddock. He owns a bar near our flat and is also from Wicklow. My father always enjoyed grabbing a pint or two there and reliving the old days. Mr. Paddock is the only person who could ever make Dadaí laugh about the past."

"Do you think that he's laughing now, being with your mother and sisters?"

"I have no doubt of it."

I folded my hands together as though in reverence, but more because I didn't want Kyle to hold them. I was suddenly very intimidated that we were about to see people who were part of his life and who were, no doubt, aware of his previous vocation. I didn't know what he might have told them yet, and I wasn't sure that I wanted to.

But Kyle had different plans. Without knowing the uncertain anxiety that was racing through me, he worked one hand free of the other and grasped it tightly.

I tried to pull it away, but his grip was too strong. "Are you sure that you want to do that?" I whispered. "What are they going to think?"

"That I am a lucky man to be holding the hand of such a beautiful lady." I could tell that he had already considered the angles to this situation. And unlike me, he had chosen to be forthright. I felt ashamed at the contrast between my deception and his courage, and silently vowed to follow his lead in the future.

I couldn't help but be pleased that he was so confident in us.

Us. It had a nice ring to it.

I had trouble making eye contact with Father Sullivan, despite what Kyle had told me the other night. In any case, it was no matter that

Father Sullivan might be understanding of it—Mrs. Mawdsley glared at me as if she would throw me down in that two-yard-deep hole if she could.

My thoughts quickly turned to our purpose for being there, and I laid my hand affectionately on the simple coffin that held the body of the elder Mr. McCarthy.

"Requiem aeternam dona eis, Domine, et lux perpetua luceat eis," Father Sullivan began. Although I didn't understand the words, I prayed for Kyle's father in my own way and bowed my head like the others. I had brought a rose from Mother's garden, from the bushes that he had spent too brief a time tending, and I tossed it over the coffin, whispering a good-bye.

At the end of the service we lingered while everyone but Father Sullivan left. He shook Kyle's hand and then hugged me as if he had known me for a long time. I smiled at this gentle and generous man, grateful for his acceptance of me.

"Well, my son. This is a day of joy and sadness."

"Father Sullivan, maybe this is wrong, but I'm not feeling sad today. My father is at last with my mother and sisters, and with God. He's free from his pain. And I"—he looked at me with near adulation—"I am honored to have Miss Westcott here with me."

Father Sullivan beamed an approving smile. "Miss Westcott—may I call you Julianne? I feel like we know each other a little better now."

I nodded. I still didn't know the right words for this kind of situation.

"It is good to see the smile that you have put on our Kyle's face." He winked at him. "I've thought for some time that this is where he was heading!"

"I wish that *I* had known," I responded. "I could have saved myself a year of headaches!"

They both laughed at that. At another time it would have seemed odd to me to be laughing in a cemetery. But Kyle and Father Sullivan were both so good-natured that it was difficult to be anything but light-hearted around them, even given the surroundings.

As we started the drive home, I was pleased that someone very close to Kyle was so considerate of me. I was afraid that we weren't going to have it so easy.

"Kyle—what do we do about my parents?"

He looked over at me. "What do you mean, what do we do?"

"I mean, this—you—are not going to be very well received by them."

"Yes, I've thought of that." He sighed and turned his attention back to the road. "Look, it's not going to be easy. But whatever happens, we'll do it together."

"I know." I bit my lip, not knowing how to proceed.

"You do that a lot, you know."

"What?"

"You bite your lip when you're nervous, or when you're thinking too hard."

I liked that he had noticed such a detail about me. "I do, don't I? I'm sorry."

"Don't be sorry. It's adorable." He said it in such a way that indicated *everything* I did was adorable to him. That was going to be a hard one to live up to. He saw that I was still distracted, though, and held out a hand to reassure me.

"Julianne. We are good together. Since the first time we spoke, we fell into something that was so easy. We don't have to tell them right away—you can work out the best way to do that. But I'm not going anywhere, and sooner or later they will have to know that. Have faith."

"You're right. Thank you for that."

Kyle slowed down and gradually stopped a few blocks from our house. He had never stopped holding my hand, but he moved his up to my hair now and stroked it. Pulling me toward him, he kissed me reassuringly. "I want to be able to do that without hiding it."

"Me, too. Soon. I promise."

As I walked up to the house, I saw an unfamiliar car there and real-ized that I was in time for tea. I groaned and prepared myself for the none-too-subtle matchmaking session. I almost asked Kyle to drive me away, but he was right in telling me that I was going to need to face this. Maybe sooner *was* better than later so that I wouldn't have to waste so much energy keeping up a charade.

Kissing him on the cheek and hoping that no one was looking out of a window to see it, I hopped out and promised to meet him the next day at the lake.

Although I expected it, I felt as if I stepped into an ambush.

"Julianne, there you are; we were worried!" Mother had put on her best social voice. I knew that she was disappointed that I hadn't made this more of a priority, but she wasn't going to let on to her guests. Hugging me heartily as if it were an everyday affection, she continued. "Mrs. Sheldon has brought the most *delicious* little cakes, and Simon has been telling us stories about his rowing tournament in Oxford." She turned to the others. "Please excuse her attire. She had to attend a funeral this morning as part of a school project. She's a diligent one, she is!"

The chatter went on mind-numbingly for a solid hour. I was polite and executed every pleasantry that was expected of me. All the while, I was planning the picnic lunch that I would make for the lake date tomorrow. Would Kyle like chicken sandwiches? What was his favorite flavor of tea? I was thrilled at the chance to learn the minutiae.

Mrs. Sheldon and Simon stood up, thanked us for our time, and, evidently interpreting my manners as willingness, arranged for another tea within the week. Simon went so far as to ask me if I would like to join him for supper tomorrow night, but I declined cordially, saying that I already had plans with a friend. *A male friend,* I thought, but I didn't add that part.

Mother shut the door behind them and began flitting and swishing about. So eager was she to consider the afternoon a success, she chose to believe her own desires rather than what had actually transpired and put both hands on my shoulders.

"Isn't Simon just marvelous? So smart, such a brilliant career ahead of him. You *should* go out with him tomorrow night. He's quite a catch, Julianne; don't let him go."

"Mother, I told you that I already have plans."

"Well, cancel them, dear. You can always see Lucille another time. She'll understand."

I saw that I was going to have to do this now or I would never have any peace about it. I took a deep breath and took a step forward.

"It's not Lucille that I'm seeing tomorrow."

"Who is it, then? Lotte? Anne?" Her expression disintegrated as she began to fear the truth.

"It's Kyle, Mother."

Chapter Seventeen

Hell hath no fury . . . Suddenly I knew the meaning of this phrase, and Mother was the woman scorned. Her face turned so red that her rouged cheeks disappeared, and her hands clutched her hips.

"What do you mean, it's Kyle? His father is dead now. You don't have any more nursing duties there."

"I'm not seeing Kyle because of his father. I'm seeing Kyle because I'm in love with him. And he is with me."

There. I'd said it. Not even the Germans could drop a bomb like this one.

She raised her hands and shook her finger in my face. "Helen Julianne Westcott, that is *completely* unacceptable. I thought we had settled this already. It's entirely inappropriate!"

"How is this inappropriate? He has been a perfect gentleman to me."

"He is not a gentleman, he is a *gardener*—as you yourself said! And didn't you also say that he was going to be a priest? He's a *Catholic,* Julianne." She said it like it was a bad word. "He's Irish, and he has no money. Do you want me to go on?"

I was sure that she could if I let her. Clearly, she was ready to unleash her arsenal.

"I don't care what you think he is, Mother. I love him. I didn't want to love him, and I tried not to. But I do. And you can't change that!"

I stormed upstairs to lock my door and ignored the knocking that followed. Putting my pillow over my ears, I heard, "Just wait until I tell your father about this!"

An hour later I heard a gentler knock and the hesitant sound of my father's voice. "Julianne, may I come in?"

I blew my nose and uncurled my legs to go unlock the door. Turning around, I was back on my bed before he'd had the chance to turn the knob. Resignation on his face, he tried to sit down beside me, but I stretched out my legs so that there was no room. He pulled out the chair that sat next to my vanity. Had I been in the mood to appreciate it, his heavy frame would have looked comical in the wiry little seat with the pink-fringed cushion.

Neither of us spoke right away, each hoping that the other would. I wasn't going to give in. I wanted to hear what he had to say first.

"Princess. Your mother told me everything that happened."

"Did she tell it only from *her* point of view?"

"Naturally, and that's why I want to hear from you. Please understand that your mother is upset, too. She only wants what's best for you, and so do I."

"Simon Sheldon and all of the others that she plans for me are *not* what's best for me. I think that I am old enough to determine that."

"Of course you are, and I trust you. She will, too; just give her time. But please look at this from our point of view. You are our little girl. You live in London now, studying to do great things as a nurse."

I looked up quizzically. It was the first time that *nurse* and *great* had ever been used in the same sentence here.

He continued. "Yes, I realize that. It's what you want, which is why I'm paying your tuition for it. The point is, you have so many things ahead of you. Don't make big decisions right now. Not just about this young man. I'd say that about *any* young man." He paused and a more severe look came over his face. "But I will put my foot down about this particular one. Your mother says that he's Catholic."

"Yes, what about it?"

"You know how I feel about it. They are all damnable, unpatriotic papists, and their sympathies lie with the kind of people who would destroy the crown and commerce."

"That's a rather sweeping generalization, don't you think?"

"You haven't known as many as I have, and you're just going to have to trust me on it. This, I absolutely forbid."

"But—"

"I'm not hearing it, Julianne. Now you're going to get my full support on this nursing thing, and I'm going to ask your mother to back off with all of the rest of it. But you must obey me on this."

My face tingled with tears I fought to hold back. I had committed to being truthful. To try to help him understand and soften his prejudices. But in the face of such absolute disapproval, I had no choice if there was going to be any kind of future with Kyle.

"Yes, Father." I stumbled over the lie. "I'll—I'll try to see it your way."

"That's my girl. Now have some patience with your mother, and wait to get serious about any boy until you are finished with school."

I nodded, biting my lower lip, not wanting to speak any more words of deception.

"Good." He made his way out. "Now why don't you dry those pretty green eyes of yours and come downstairs."

"I don't think I'm ready to yet, but I will shortly."

He left my room, and I listened to his footsteps descending the stairs. Exhausted, I put my head down for a nap.

I only saw Kyle once that week, when I sneaked out for our picnic, and I was unsure when the next opportunity would arise. He worked every day, and my parents kept strict tabs on my evening activities. With Lucille out at the seashore with her family, I'd lost my usual excuse for going out. Mother didn't speak to me most of this time. When she was home, she sat fingering those blasted swatches and tapping at a drained glass of ice cubes at her side.

Being away from Kyle was agonizing, so I sent a note to his flat, suggesting a plan to meet up at least once a week at the lake at Newsham Park. Our routine became to sit on opposite sides of a particular park bench, lest a friend of my parents' should walk by and see us. We only spoke when we were out of earshot of passersby and kept our focus on the ducks and children.

"I miss you," I'd say, longing to lean over and nuzzle myself into his neck.

"I miss you, too, Julianne."

"You know, Mother and Father have a supper engagement on Tuesday evening. I want to see you and not here at the park bench."

"I can't. I need to go to Durham and pick up all my things."

"You didn't bring all of them back with you at the end of last term?"

"I thought I'd be returning. But I'll just be taking over my father's work, now that a little petite thing has bewitched me." He looked around to see that no one was near and reached across the bench to poke me in the side.

"Well, how about Thursday, then? They're meeting for supper with one of Father's clients from Amsterdam. I'm sure I could get away."

"I can't. I'm working on the Whiteheads' grounds then." All of a sudden his expression became very serious. "But it brings up what I wanted to talk to you about. You know I want to be with you every chance I can get. But we can't keep this up, and I don't like being deceitful. When are we going to tell your parents?"

"I don't know yet. Just give me time."

"How much time, Julianne? What are we waiting for? Be honest with me. Is this just some fling for you? Is this some rich-girl rite of passage?"

"Of course not. You know that!" I had never heard him say a cruel word before.

"Well, then you're going to have to tell me something I can believe. Do you think hiding your head in the sand is going to get you everything you want? Because it's time to make a decision. Now."

"I know," I cried, appalled at the sudden turn of the conversation. More so, embarrassed since I knew he was right. "But you're asking the impossible. And you don't have parents whose approval you need."

My hand flew to my mouth, regretting those words the second they left me.

He shot me a wounded look. This charade was wearing on us both.

"I didn't mean that, I'm sorry. Kyle, I'm sorry!" I glanced around. A couple was walking by, but they were pointing to the boys with their boats. I reached across the bench and rubbed his arm with my hand. "I just mean that it's complicated. Look. I'm all they have left. And despite our differences, they've tried in their own ways to give me a great life. This will ruin them. Personally. Socially. I don't know if my father would ever forgive me, and I couldn't live with that. Not to mention that we have to face the very real possibility that they will cut me off, and what are we going to live on then? Love? Even I know that there's no 'happily ever after' when the bills come due."

He sighed, and the silence between us made me feel crazy. Was it all over before it had begun?

At last, he looked at me and ran his fingers through my hair, seemingly unconcerned as to who might see us.

"Yes, it's complicated. Yes, there will be difficulties, and I will do whatever it takes to provide for you. But it's worth it. Anything worth having is worth sacrificing for." He looked at me sincerely. "I'd sacrifice anything for you, Julianne. I love you." It was the first time he'd spoken those words.

"I love you," I whispered back, my heart beating at this simple exchange. "You're right. I'll do something soon. I promise. But please be patient just a little longer."

I stood up as part of our rehearsed performance and opened my parasol, the largest one I could find. It was an old-fashioned accessory, but an ideal one for our purposes. Positioning it just so, he blocked us from anyone's view and gave me a kiss that was all too brief. And then another.

"Until then," he said, lingering just longer than was advisable.

"Until then."

I walked home with a weary smile on my face.

After weeks of good behavior, Mother must have been satisfied with my apparent acquiescence. She came into the kitchen nonchalantly one afternoon while I was slicing an apple.

"Julianne, darling."

I was startled to hear her voice. The knife slipped from my hands and nicked my finger. I dipped a towel in my glass of water and held it against my finger to stop the trickle of blood.

"Mrs. King had to leave for Birmingham because she received word that her mother is seriously ill. She may be with her for a long while."

I closed my eyes, trying to remember if that was supposed to mean something to me.

"So I have been asked to fill in for her on the festival committee."

"I thought that if you chaired it once, you wouldn't be asked again."

"Yes, that's true, but we must rise to the challenges that are presented to us, mustn't we?"

I nearly choked at these words. I couldn't help but think of Charles when she said things like this.

"Anyway, you did such a good job of running the booths last year that I would like for you to do it again."

Maybe this was her way to mend fences. These kinds of events were the one thing we did well together. Maybe this was my last chance to grow an affection between us, even a small one, in the hopes that I wouldn't lose that chance forever.

"I can do that. What do you need?"

Encouraged, she pulled out a chair, sat down, and showed me all of the notes that Mrs. King had left for her.

"Well, this year we are raising money for the Smithdown Hospital. They are building a new maternity wing, and the committee voted to send the money there. Mrs. Moore and Mrs. Ward are at it again, so I think that we should step in and decide on a theme for the ring toss on our own."

"You know, last year the candle theme was popular since we were raising money for the cathedral. This is a maternity wing, right? Hmm . . ." I thought for a minute and came up with an idea that I knew she would like. "What about baby bottles?"

It went on like that, the festival providing us fodder for neutral conversation. We reviewed the plans, made notes for improvements, and agreed that we needed to get Lucille involved. My time spent with Mother planning the festival booths bordered on enjoyable. True to her word to Father, she'd held off playing matchmaker.

I was so happy when Lucille returned. We fell into last year's routine as we planned for the event. But more than anything, it was good to have my best friend back. She reluctantly agreed to be my cover story whenever I wanted to see Kyle.

"I don't like the deception any more than he does, Jul."

"You think I like it? I'm just waiting for the right time."

"When will the right time ever come? When you've got twenty thousand children?"

She didn't continue the lecture, though, and we resumed the summertime joys that we'd shared for so many years. She became quite a threat in backgammon, and we pored through magazines with movie updates. We also made it out to several movies during that month, although the Movietone news clips shown beforehand were increasingly disheartening.

Germany had just ordered Jews to add the name "Israel" or "Sara" to their first names to make it easier to identify their ethnicity. Along with the rest of the country, I was increasingly alarmed at hearing these kinds of things, and I couldn't help but think of people our family knew—friends, neighbors—who might have to endure this injustice if Hitler gained power in Britain.

Listening to government radio addresses in the evening was becoming a favorite pastime of Father's. Although he clearly didn't want war to break out, he also had to position his business for what would certainly be an increased demand for his services during wartime. His warehouses would be very valuable, with their proximity to the Liverpool port. But they could also be targets.

At least his anti-German rants had distracted him from his Catholic ones, and I no longer heard about the IRA.

Kyle tried to talk to me about war—men seemed to be electrified by the topic—but he would stop when he saw how much it upset me. I remembered my father talking about the countless boys lost in the last war. It was not only for Kyle that the dread of the topic unsettled me, but the thought of another generation of our young men fighting once again.

It was the British way to grin and bear it, though, and I was not going to let faraway hostilities dampen our enthusiasm for the charity event ahead. I stayed over at Lucille's house the night before the festival, and she let me experiment with hairstyles. It was her turn to participate in the auction, but she wasn't looking forward to it as much as she had expected to. Ben was now in her life, and although he had promised to bid on her, she was worried about someone else winning. Even if it was only for an afternoon, she didn't like the idea of being paired off with anyone other than him. She thought about dropping out of it, but he called her a silly goose and told her not to worry. Lucille capitulated when we found her a stunning red gown to match the garnet necklace from last year and started to enjoy the idea of dressing up and taking part.

Festival day started much the same way as last year. Lucille and I checked on the booths early on and ran off to enjoy it all with our beaus. I ached to hold Kyle's hand as he walked two steps away from me, but although Father was in Paris for the global freight conference, Mother was flitting about. Kyle and I had argued once again about talking to my parents, but he'd agreed for me to put it off until after this event, as I'd just begun to rebuild goodwill between my mother and myself.

But for tonight Ben and Kyle were in high form and kept throwing each other conspiratorial glances. They looked innocent and bewildered whenever we asked them what they were up to.

Leaving them behind, we made our way to the church hall before dusk, but not before seeing Maude Parker, round with pregnancy, dethrone Alice with her banana bread in the contest. Domesticity suited her, and I smiled to recall the days that Kyle and I had spent working together on her wedding.

Lucille looked beautiful in her gown and upswept hair, with wispy tendrils cascading to her chin. Like last year, we secured each other's jewelry. My attire was far simpler, since I wasn't in the auction, but Kyle couldn't take his eyes off me all night. It must have been all the decorative lanterns. The dim lighting worked wonders on one's complexion.

After kissing Lucille's cheek and betting her that she would surely raise the most money tonight, I ran off to join Kyle and Ben and watch the proceedings.

This year there were fourteen girls, and Lucille was number four.

The now ex–Lord Mayor Denton emceed the event again this year, back by popular demand, and he overpowered us with his thundering voice. The first offerings were modest, with Ruby Haught fetching the most of the three.

"And now we have Lady Number Four, Miss Lucille Morris. She enjoys backgammon and movies, and will be attending Edge Hill Training College to study teaching in January."

A polite clap from the crowd.

"Do I hear twelve shillings?" He had upped his ante since last year.

I saw Kyle slip an envelope to Ben, and when I looked at him with inquisitive eyes, he shrugged, placating me with a kiss to the forehead. The bidding went back and forth between several young men, but none of them were Ben. Just as the bidding was about to end at two pounds, four shillings, Ben waved his hand. "Six pounds, two shillings!" We all looked at him in disbelief, except for Kyle. Lucille froze in place on the stage, and Denton asked him to repeat his bid, thinking that he had heard incorrectly.

"Six pounds, two shillings," he shouted again.

A cheer rolled around the stage, and Denton pounded the gavel like a judge keeping order in a court. Encouraged by the crowd, Ben leapt to the stage to claim his girl.

Kyle was grinning. I glared at him for still not explaining all of this to me beforehand. However, I only pretended because, for one thing, I could never be angry with him. And for another thing, I was deliriously excited for Lucille to be gaining the highest amount ever in the history of the auction.

After some time the roar died down. Lucille and Ben left the stage, and Denton started with Lady Number Five. I felt sorry for her. That would be a tough act to follow. Kyle took my hand and led me from the crowd over to the woods behind where the band was playing.

Putting his arm around me firmly and taking my hand in his for the dance, we moved slowly, and I longed for the day when we could be on the floor with the other couples. I still shivered when he touched me, and I took a breath of anticipation whenever he leaned his face close to mine. We swayed there, not talking at first, enjoying this intimacy. No doubt, we were both thinking how different this year was from the last one.

In a gesture reminiscent of our time in the gazebo, he leaned over to kiss my neck softly and moved his way up to my ear. "I have something to tell you," he whispered. He didn't say anything else, making his way down to my neck again. He knew that he was torturing me, and he loved it.

"What?" I asked weakly. I didn't want him to stop kissing me, but on the other hand I wanted to know what he was going to say.

Switching to the other side of my neck, he did the same thing. Making his way up to my ear, he taunted, "You're going to like it." And back down to my neck.

I couldn't take the suspense, nor could I let him continue kissing me without crossing some major social boundary.

"Kyle, what?" I pulled him away to look in his face. "You have been full of secrets lately."

"Oh, tonight is full of secrets. And I'll let you have three guesses."

Abertillery

The children quieted when Father McCarthy entered the room. I could only hear the muffled sounds of his voice from where he'd left me at their dead mother's bedside, but he seemed to calm them with his words.

I would have liked to go home now, but the only exit was through that crowded room. I felt claustrophobic and blamed it on the house. But truly it was my own mind closing in on me. As though the static from a radio program was fragmenting the voices trying to come through:

". . . don't like the deception . . ."

". . . twenty thousand things . . ."

". . . I forbid . . ."

". . . secrets . . ."

". . . I'm enlisting . . ."

". . . be safe here . . ."

The memories these words carried were unwelcome, but they assaulted me anyway. Like artillery, they pounded the remains of my fortress, leaving holes that let the past escape piece by piece.

The people I'd loved, the people I'd left, their voices came back to me in a rising tide until, overwhelmed, I crumbled down onto the floor and wept with abandon. The tears burned my skin, and I made no attempt to wipe them away. I was supposed to suffer—my eternal punishment—because of what I'd done. Maybe this was just the beginning.

I heard the priest return to the room. I didn't need to see his face to finally acknowledge the evidence. The voice. The ring on his finger. His reassuring presence. My Kyle was in front of me. What was I going to do about it?

Chapter Eighteen

Three secrets, three guesses.

Did he think it was funny to drive me mad like this? Obviously, he did.

I could play that game.

We stopped dancing, and he took my hand to lead me farther off among the trees. We sat on a large fallen trunk and enjoyed the privacy that it offered.

"Three guesses, right?"

He nodded.

"You found out that I'm running away with Reverend Parker because I'm determined to be with someone in the clergy after all."

"Very funny. I happen to know that he's already married and way too old for you. Try again."

"All right. You made the winning banana bread and let Maude take the credit for it."

"Did she tell you?" He put his hand on his mouth in feigned surprise, then dropped it. "I'm glad it's out. Chopping all those walnuts, mashing the bananas—I deserve the credit!"

"Ha, ha. OK, number three. But if I get it wrong, are you going to tell me?"

"I promise."

"You and Ben are spending your evenings luring ships to their doom in Wallasey and pirating them."

"A fellow has to make a living."

"I'm out of guesses. What are you up to?" I scooted in closer to him and feigned a menacing look.

"You win. Secret Number One. I have been drawing up land-scape plans and submitting them to firms in London. One of them has accepted my work and hired me. I'm moving to London with you."

My mouth hung open, as he had answered the very question that had been pestering me. What was going to happen when the new term started? I hugged him tightly, teeming with elation and kissing him all over his face.

"Kyle, Kyle, oh, that's *wonderful* news. I can't believe it! Oh, it's *wonderful!*"

He pulled me back before I mauled him and held me by the wrists. "Easy there, gorgeous. It's just an entry-level position, and I'll have to work for years before I design anything on my own. But it's a start, and it means we can be together."

"I don't care if you move to London to clean the king's toilets! I'm just happy that you'll be there. I didn't know what I was going to do without you."

Kyle sat back and grinned at my exuberance.

When I had at last calmed down, I said, "I don't know how any-thing can be better than that, but what is Secret Number Two?"

"Secret Number Two, coming up!" He paused, letting the drama set in. "Did you see the envelope that I passed to Ben at the auction?"

"Yes I did, but I had forgotten about it. What was that all about?"

"Ben saved hard to bid on Lucille in the auction, but he was worried that it wouldn't be enough, so I contributed four pounds, seven shillings."

He waited for that to sink in, but I knew I was missing something.

"That's how much I should have spent to win *you* last year, sweet girl, but I didn't. So I figured that I owed some money to a good cause and I helped out a friend at the same time."

I blushed and thought of how much easier everything could have been if last year had been different. But then again, a year of longing never hurt anyone.

"I love it! That was so considerate of you. And how fantastic for Lucille to receive so much attention for once. No one deserves it more. Thank you. You're the best."

"That's not the rest of Secret Number Two."

"There's more?"

"Yes, but you can't tell anyone."

"Isn't that the very definition of a secret?"

"I suppose so." He hunched in, as if he was going to pass along treasonous information. I felt the heat of his breath on my ear, and it dizzied me. But he didn't say anything.

"What?" I sat back and looked right at him. "Kyle, *what?* You're killing me here!"

"At the picnic Ben's going to propose to Lucille."

I let out a scream that made people on the dance floor look off into the trees.

"He *is?* Oh my goodness, Lucille is going to be so happy!"

Kyle folded his arms and listened bemusedly, watching me as if I were some kind of sideshow. I think so many weeks of forced reserve were getting the better of me. Realizing I was beginning to sound like Lotte—*bletch*—I again forced myself to relax.

"OK," I said. "Secret Number Three. Let's have it."

"Nope," he said resolutely.

"But you *promised*!"

"Based on how you reacted to the first two, I'm afraid you'll drop dead of a heart attack if I tell you any more."

I assured him that I'd keep myself in check, over and over, until he gave in. I knew what he was going to tell me all along, and he knew it, too. He was just going to drag this out for fun.

"You win. Secret Number Three." He leaned in and held my hands. "So Ben is going to propose to Lucille, right?" Sliding down to his knee before I even realized it, he said, "And I am proposing to you now."

Putting my hands over my mouth, I stared at him in disbelief. It shouldn't really have been surprising to me. It was something that I thought about all the time, and it was the only natural path for us. But I hadn't expected it tonight, and I couldn't find the words.

Still kneeling, Kyle took my hands away from my face and kissed each fingertip before looking at me with those malt-colored eyes.

"Julianne," he said softly, "before I met you, the path for my life was set. And it was a good one. Then you came along, with your charming ways and your love for your brother and your regard for my father, and a hole appeared that I didn't even know existed. It grew wider and deeper every time we talked until it hurt so much that I couldn't study, I couldn't focus. I knew that it would never be filled, and I could never be fully at peace, until I was with you. *You* are my vocation. I was made to love you, protect you, through the good and bad, and through every vow that will be asked of me. Will you, then, make me a whole man and marry me?"

I don't know how long I looked at him, speechless. I just stared at him, barely breathing, finding it hard to believe that someone loved me enough to say such things.

Arching his eyebrow in the way that always made me laugh, he said, "And your answer is . . ."

I shook off my daze and smiled and hugged him. "Of course! Of *course*!"

From his jacket pocket he pulled out a tiny black bag and dropped a ring from it into his hand. He took my left hand and slid it on my finger. It was a small, round diamond set in gold.

It was the most beautiful thing I'd ever seen, but he apologized. "I promise, when I can I'll buy you something bigger, something you deserve. But I wanted you to have a ring now."

Tilting his chin up, I looked at him in earnest. "I don't want something bigger. This is exactly what I want." I kissed him slowly, and he came to sit next to me on the trunk again.

We stayed there until the sun began to fall, in the haze of new love, thinking that nothing could ever be better than this moment. We agreed to save the wedding details for another day.

❦

On Tuesday we took a walk to one of the lakes in the park and rented a boat for the afternoon. I remembered looking at the couples here only a few months ago, envious of their bliss. And now I was one of them. I loved this summer. Lucille had been right on New Year's—1938 was turning out to be just about perfect. Save for the fact that everything perfect about it was being done behind my parents' backs.

We talked about all that had to be done. We decided that we wouldn't tell Lucille about our engagement until Ben had a chance to ask her. That was only days away, and I was confident that I could hold it in, difficult as it was. Kyle would keep my ring until everything was out in the open. I missed it on my finger already.

I agreed, quite apprehensively, that Kyle would ask my father for my hand. I think we both knew what the answer would be, but Kyle said that it was the right thing to do, and he wasn't going to shirk his part of it. He declined my offer to accompany him. I was hoping for a miracle, but we'd agreed that we were going to be married, blessing or not.

We set a date for that Wednesday evening, since I wanted a few days to prepare. Kyle's question to my father was sure to change things forever, for better or worse, and I needed a little time to collect myself. It didn't hurt that the *Richard Robbins Comedy Hour* was on Wednesdays, and it might put Father in a good mood. I suggested that Kyle arrive after the show. When the appointment time arrived, my nerves were no less edgy.

"Why, Julianne, you're wearing the scarf I bought for you." It wasn't really one of my favorites, but Father had picked it out for me in Paris. Anything to be in his good graces.

"Of course! I just love it." I even did a little twirl before joining him on the couch. Like when I would show him a pirouette after ballet class.

"Did you catch the bit that Richard Robbins did last week about the elephant and the motorcar salesman?"

"I didn't. Lucille and I were working on the festival details."

"Oh, that's right. It was a stitch. You should listen more often, like we used to."

"I'd like that."

He patted the spot right next to him. I scooted over, tucking my legs up next to me, and laid my head on his shoulder. He smelled like peppermint and pipe tobacco. I closed my eyes and breathed in deeply, memorizing his scent just in case this was the last time we'd sit like that.

"Is something the matter, Princess? You're very fidgety tonight."

He was right. My hands were clenched and my feet were tapping up and down on the sofa. I wanted to tell him right there, to let him hear it from me first. To believe that my father would love me enough to trust my heart. But if things went poorly, Kyle would be stepping into a disaster, and I couldn't let that happen.

"Oh, you know, just winding down from all of the activities of the weekend."

"Well, I'm glad that's all behind you now. I was starting to feel like a bachelor with you and your mother away so much."

He kissed the top of my head, and I fought back a tear.

"Hey, why don't you help your old man out a bit and turn up the volume? It's starting in just a minute."

"What old man?" I said as I walked over to the radio.

"That's my girl," he laughed.

"We interrupt our normal programming for a special report from Downing Street. The *Richard Robbins Comedy Hour* will return next Wednesday at its regularly scheduled time."

Oh, no, I thought. *Not tonight. Of all nights, not tonight.* This wouldn't help his mood at all.

I was right. Prime Minister Chamberlain came on, followed by a panel of commentators. Germany seemed to be positioning itself to invade the Sudetenland region of Czechoslovakia, and in an effort to appease them, Britain was considering an approval of that move.

"The bloody bastards!" Father shouted. I didn't know if he meant the Germans or Parliament, whose reluctance to enter the war enraged him. His strong views on this, and his support for Winston Churchill, were well known in Liverpool, causing an ongoing commentary in the newspapers. A recent article had accused him of being a warmonger, because he was surely poised to make a lot of money from it, as the military would no doubt make use of his warehouses.

As for myself, I didn't like to hear the words *Britain* and *war* together, especially right at this moment. I distracted myself with a magazine and tried to keep the pages from rattling as I counted down the minutes to Kyle's arrival. I looked at my wristwatch and hoped that the news program wouldn't overrun the hour.

Mother came downstairs, dressed smartly, and said that she was meeting with the committee from the festival to tally the receipts. Father tapped his pipe and nodded as she left. On another occasion, he might have said, "You do too much, Beatrice." But tonight he sat forward with his arms on his knees, looking like he could bore holes into the radio with his eyes.

This did not bode well for Kyle.

I saw the lights from Kyle's truck through the window and heard the door as he closed it behind him. Father didn't flinch, even as the doorbell rang.

I was about to go answer it until I remembered that Mother had hired a butler last week because "there is just so much to do around here." I knew it was because Mrs. Parkington had hired one, and Mother wasn't going to be outdone.

The protocol was still new to me, so I sat in my seat and waited for Kyle to be announced. A minute later, there was a knock on the parlor door.

"A gentleman is here to see you, sir." The butler's voice was steady and polished. I knew that Mother would have employed only the best.

"Show him into the study," he responded without inquiring who it might be. I gripped the magazine as I felt my whole body tighten. I wouldn't even be able to see Kyle before he went in. I was not one to turn to prayer, but I felt as if my life was on the line, and it was as good a time as any to befriend a higher power.

Father stuffed a little more tobacco into his pipe. He stood up, leaving the parlor door open, and walked into the study. I peered around just in time to see the back of Kyle's head before the large doors were closed behind them.

I held my breath, waiting for the tirade to begin, but I couldn't hear a thing. I turned off the radio and went into the hallway. I slipped off my shoes so that I wouldn't make any sound. The marble was cold underneath my stockinged feet, but I didn't let it bother me. I had to be as close to Kyle as I could.

The silence was thick as a muggy London morning, save for the ominous ticking of the grandfather clock in our parlor.

I paced back and forth, tracing the veins of the marble with my eyes, imagining them as little rivers that went to nowhere. I wondered how they were formed, these thin lines. Did they meander so casually because they were carefree? Or were they trying to escape the confines of the sediment, only to be quarried and immortalized forever on our hallway floor?

After some time I heard the door click, and I tiptoed up to the first landing of the stairs, hiding myself from view. The clock chose just that time to announce itself in nine long, dirgelike tones, and I couldn't hear what my father and Kyle were saying to each other. By the time it was done, the front door had closed and Father had made his way back to the parlor.

Before he could see that it was empty and come looking for me, I raced to my room, put on a sweater and shoes, and escaped down a side staircase leading to the kitchen. Kyle's taillights were already two distant dots on the horizon. They were just about to disappear when they stopped. I quickened my pace to catch up. I slowed down just a few yards away, pausing to catch my breath. I walked more deliberately, running my fingers through my hair and composing myself before I saw him.

Kyle stepped out of the truck as I approached. In the glow of the taillights, he was silhouetted, but as I approached, he was quite a sight. He was wearing the suit that he'd worn for his father's funeral and looked as handsome as I'd ever seen him. He didn't smile when he saw me, though, and he was immobile when I threw my arms around him. I didn't know if my heart or his was beating more quickly. Without speaking, he led me to the other side of the truck, opened my door, and helped me in.

He came back around to his side and closed the door. I moved to slide in closer, but he took my hand firmly and kept me just where I was. He looked at me but turned away when he caught my eye.

"What is it, Kyle?" I didn't like what I was seeing.

He finally spoke, still looking forward. "Why do you want to marry me, Julianne?" His shoulders sagged and his voice was passionless.

"What do you mean, why do I want to marry you?"

"I mean, you can do a lot better. *Quite* a lot better."

"You know that's not true. What happened in there?"

He finally looked my direction, but still thwarted any efforts on my part to move in closer. "Your father looked surprised to see me, no doubt, and told me that he thought he'd already made his feelings known to you. But to his credit, he kept his composure and offered me a seat."

"Did he sit next to you or behind the desk?"

"Behind the desk."

"Oh, that's not a good sign."

"Why do you say that?"

"When I was little, I could tell if I was in trouble for something when I was called in to his study and I saw where he was sitting. If he was in the chair beside the other one, he just wanted to have a chat. But if he was in that oversized chair behind the desk, I knew I'd done something wrong. He means business when he sits there."

"Well, that would be in line with how it went."

"Was it that bad?"

"Neither good nor bad, I guess." He turned to the front window again.

"What is that supposed to mean?"

"Just that we had a conversation, man to man, that made me realize a few things. He didn't get angry like I might have expected. In fact, I think on some level, he respected that I was coming to him. But he was adamant, Julianne, about the one thing I'd been struggling with myself. It's not good for you to be with me."

He wasn't going to keep me away after saying something like that. I moved in next to him, grabbed his arm, and forced him to look at me.

"Don't listen to him! There isn't any truth in that. Don't you under-stand? He has a way of making people see his side of things! He is a master of manipulating things to his advantage. How do you think he became as successful as he did?"

"I don't know about all that. I just know that he wants what's best for you, and so do I. And he made me see that you'd be better off with someone else."

"That's mad. Please stop saying things like that. Don't you look away again; look at me!"

His voice became frantic. "I *am* looking at you. And I'm seeing the truth. But surely you see it, too. You can have anyone. You have the world at your fingertips. I am nothing. I have no way to provide for you in the way that you're used to. I have no parents. Not to mention that my religion makes me some kind of enemy to you."

"I don't give two pence about that, and you know it! He's got to you, Kyle. Please don't let it happen. Please." My face fell to my chest, and my nails dug into my clenched fists.

"No, he hasn't got to me. He just made me see what I would have already known if I hadn't been so selfish. And what you'll see after it's too late. What if you don't really love me, Julianne? What if you only think that you love me, but I'm just an escape to you? You told me yourself that you chose nursing, in part, because it would put you on your own path and was the opposite of what they wanted."

If he had hit me, it wouldn't have stung any more than him throwing my own words back at me. "How dare you compare that! That's entirely different, and it's not even like that anymore. I like what I'm doing, you know that."

"That doesn't matter. What matters is that this is wrong on so many levels, and as much as it kills me to say it, we can't let this go on."

I turned away and stared into the night sky. Was this what it meant to be star-crossed?

"Kyle, look. I don't know what it will take to make you believe in what I feel for you. But if you don't want to be with *me* anymore, then I won't make you." My words were slow and deliberate, and each one burned in my mouth as I said them.

"Darling." His voice sounded so sad. "Look at me."

I wiped away the mascara that was undoubtedly winding its way down my cheeks. His finger met mine there, then left it behind and traced a tender course down the side of my face.

"I want to be with you more than anything," he whispered. "I've given up everything I've ever known to be with you. But there is only one thing that I want more, and that is your happiness. I couldn't bear it if someday you woke up and regretted everything that you'd given up for me."

"Isn't that what love is? Isn't it, Kyle? Giving everything to each other?"

"You're right, it is. But it also means looking out for the good of the other."

"If you end this, if you leave me, I would rather wither away and die. You can't tell me that that's any good for me."

"You won't. You'll meet someone else in time, and go on to think of this as a lovely summer and a dear friendship. But you will be glad that everything else is intact."

"Nothing is intact if I don't have you." I pulled him toward me so that the steering wheel wouldn't be in the way, and I kissed him hard, so hard that it could bruise. I was angry and hurt, but I knew that he was doing this because he loved me. He had to know that I loved him back. That I would give him everything, right now, right here in the cab of this truck. He'd have to marry me then. He'd have to know that I was serious.

He started to draw away from me, but only half-heartedly. I pinned him in place, sliding my legs on either side of him, and he stopped resisting me. He kissed me back, deeply, until I couldn't breathe. I moved my lips to his neck, traced it with the tip of my tongue up to his earlobe. I tugged at it gently, and he let out a quick gasp.

He tightened his arms around me and loosened the back of my blouse from my skirt. His hands slipped underneath to my skin. I stopped kissing him and held my breath as I felt his hands moving up and down my bare back and then around until his thumbs were tracing the outlines of my breasts. Crazed with wanting more, I had started to unbutton the front of my blouse when his hands abruptly moved to my hips and he pushed me back onto the seat of the truck. I hadn't even finished the second button yet.

"We can't do this. Not here."

"You're right. Someone is bound to drive by. Let's go back to your flat." I looked out the window to check for passersby.

"That's not what I mean. We can't do it like this. I want you, Julianne," he said in a throaty, frayed voice. "Believe me, I do." He dragged his fingers hard through his hair, which was matted down with sweat. "But not this way. You'll always regret it. We should be married first."

"You mean it?" Now he was making sense. "You still want to get married?"

"Of course I do. It's all I've wanted. I guess you convinced me that you do, too."

"Are you sure you don't need *more* persuasion?" I moved in to continue where we'd left off, but he held me firmly in place.

"Any more persuasion, and someone's going to call the coppers."

He turned the key and started the ignition.

"I'm sorry," he said. "I shouldn't have doubted us. I just love you and want you to be happy. I want you to be sure. Always."

"I *am* happy. Deliriously happy. But I appreciate you looking out for me. I really do."

"Here's a handkerchief. Why don't you wipe your eyes, and I'll drive you back home."

"All right. But Kyle?"

"Yes?"

"What do we do now? I mean, what is the next step?"

He took a deep breath. "The next step is for me to go back to your father—tonight, now—and tell him the truth about our plans."

I considered this for a moment. I didn't want to start a marriage on a bed of deception. But I knew how formidable my father was and what strings he would pull out of love for me. I did not want to take the risk that he could come up with some obstacle to keep this from happening. I told Kyle as much.

"You're probably right," he sighed. "There really isn't any other choice. I will have to talk to Father Sullivan, though, to get the process started. I'll go first thing in the morning."

"Hurry, then. As long as I'm not going to have the big family wedding, I'd rather do this sooner than later."

He looked somber for a moment. "And you're absolutely sure about this? No big wedding? No newspaper write-up?" He grinned. Surely he knew by now that those things were not important to me.

"Oh, you're right. No months spent deliberating over a dress and menu, or finding musicians, or booking the church, or making seating arrangements or—"

"I get it, I get it. Maybe I'm helping you more than I thought."

"You are, love. A wedding is just a day. Our marriage is going to be forever." I pecked his cheek and faced forward as he drove me the very short distance home.

I slipped in through the side entrance and took the back stairs up to my bedroom. I heard my father calling for me around the house. I didn't even bother taking my clothes off, as I wanted to get straight into bed in case he came up here. I pulled the covers up to my face just before I heard my father walk past my door. I closed my eyes tightly and willed my heart to still and my breath to slow as he paused. *Please don't knock.* And he didn't.

The next morning I got up very early and sped off in the Aston Martin before my parents were up. I had woefully neglected Charles, and it was high time that I saw him.

Bootle Home wasn't even open to visitors when I got there, so I parked and waited for an hour until its doors were unlocked. I stepped up just in time to see Miss Ellis ascending the stairs on her way in.

"Why, Miss Westcott, sweetheart! You are a sight! We've missed you around here." She gave me a big hug, the kind a girl might expect to receive from her mother. "You've been too much of a stranger."

"I know. I'm so sorry. Has Charles missed me?"

"Well, my girl, you know how it is with him. It's hard to tell what he thinks. But I'm sure that he'll be happy to know that you're here."

We reached the top of the steps and I opened the door for her.

"Now I have a few more minutes before I have to turn the telephone on. Why don't I come sit with you and you tell me everything that's been going on with you."

She opened the door to the reception area and joined me on the couch.

"Well, for starters, Miss Ellis, I'm not going to be Miss Westcott for much longer."

"Oh, now is that a fact, young missy? Do tell all."

"I'm going to be Mrs. McCarthy quite soon."

Her squeal could certainly be heard down the hallway, and she clapped her hands in delight. It was so nice to tell someone, especially someone who would be so excited about it. But more than that, it felt good to say Mrs. McCarthy. Julianne McCarthy. Mrs. Julianne McCarthy. Mrs. McCarthy. That was it. I liked that one.

She peppered me for details, grinning and frowning as the story called for but ending with a warning.

"You tread carefully now, dear. Upsetting your parents is not something to trifle with, and you might end up regretting it."

"I know." I did feel sorry for them, in a way. Their son, here at Bootle, all but forgotten by them. Their daughter, disappointing them beyond measure. For two people to whom status and reputation meant so much, their children had certainly let them down.

"May I see Charles now?"

My brother was being bathed before breakfast. They allowed me to wait in his room until he was back. Before long, Charles shuffled in on the arm of a new and perfunctory orderly, who seemed happy to leave him to my care while he went on to see to his other patients.

I took my brother by the hand and led him over to the window where some of the plants had grown quite impressively. He smiled as soon as we were touching them together.

I pulled a little wooden train out of my handbag and helped him feel it rolling on the table. He smiled again.

"I'm going to have to say good-bye once more," I told him. "I know it's not fair, since I was barely here all summer anyway. But I'm going back to school. And I'm getting married. To Kyle. I know that you know Kyle, the one who gave you the plant. You brought us together, Charles, do you realize that? Thank you."

Of course, he couldn't hear me. But when I left, I gave him the biggest hug, one that I hoped would communicate everything to him.

"I don't know when I'm going to see you again, but I love you. And I'll write more this time. I promise."

I made my way home to what I expected would be a less than warm reception.

The house was quiet. I didn't know if Mother was out or upstairs, but I did see the light on in Father's study. I knocked lightly, in case he was in with someone.

"Come in."

I opened the door with hesitation and bit my lip before making my way in. He was reviewing paperwork and didn't immediately look up. I slouched into my usual seat in front of his desk and waited. My parents' wedding photo sat on the bookshelf, faded from the way the sunlight hit it. Surrounding it were pictures of me—in my dance clothes, at my birthday parties, on our travels. They made me want to smile and cry, at least until Father cleared his throat and finally looked at me.

He didn't say anything at first but laid his hands on the mahogany desk, palms down. He looked like he was trying to decide something. He pushed himself up and walked around the desk to sit in the chair beside mine.

Even then he towered over me, but it was a good sign. He folded his fingers together and spoke. "So I had quite the conversation with your young man."

"Yes, Father. We—we would like to get married."

"That's what he said. But I explained to him, as I will to you now, that I can't allow that."

"But—"

He held a hand up and I immediately shut my mouth.

"You're a smart girl, Julianne. But you're just a girl, barely a woman. I can forgive you for romantic notions. But I can't let you throw your life away. You need to finish school and then find a young man who is more worthy of you. He is entirely unsuitable, and by the time he left he agreed with me."

"Yes, Father." It was easier to agree than to try pointlessly to win an argument. Besides, I was lucky to be getting off without a tongue-lashing. At this point, my goal was just to get through the next few weeks in peace and make sure nothing stopped our plans. I hoped that after we were married—after it was too late for them to do anything—we could have the kind of honest conversation that I longed to.

"You will not need to see him again. I effectively broke things off on your behalf. There will be no more communication with him, do you understand?"

"Yes, Father."

"I know that you are feeling hurt, and I'm sorry about that. But, Julianne, wait until you have a daughter. Wanting what is best for her sometimes means making tough decisions."

"I understand."

"By the way, I have not told your mother about this latest development, and I expect you not to, either. She doesn't need to be upset, and since this is over anyway, there is no harm done."

That was a relief. I wouldn't have wanted to talk to her about this.

"I'm tired. I'd like to go upstairs now."

"That's fine. I think Betty left some shortbread in the kitchen. So go on upstairs, and if you want to bring some with you, I won't tell your mother about that, either."

"Do you want me to bring you any?"

He patted his stomach. "I've already had some, but thank you."

"All right. I'll see you for supper."

He was already returning to his paperwork on the desk. Before I stepped into the hallway, though, he stopped me.

"There's one more thing."

I paused and looked back at him.

"I told you that I can't blame you for having romantic notions. But there is no excuse for your behavior. You were forbidden to see him, and you did so behind my back. From now until you leave for school, there will be no telephone, no going out with Lucille, no walks to the park. You will be home helping your mother, or you will be with me at the office. But you will not be seeing him again. Am I understood?"

He had just choked off any chance that I had to get out. I'd have to get creative.

"Yes, Father."

"Good. Now go on upstairs."

Lucille came by two days later. The new butler—his name was Collins, I'd learned—let her in.

"Julianne, what is wrong? I've been phoning, but no one will let me through. I finally just decided to come over."

"You know, my parents have needed a lot of help with things."

"I've known you since you were seven years old, Jul. I can see right through you. But if you're not going to tell me, you must have your reasons. And, besides, I'm on a happier errand."

I'd nearly forgotten that she was going to have good news to share with me. I was a terrible friend. "What is it?"

"OK, I can't wait any longer. Ben asked me to marry him!"

We ran up to my room where we could talk in private. She was deliciously happy, and it put the first smile on my face in days. I didn't tell her anything about Kyle. I didn't want to dampen her news, nor did I want to make her an accomplice. I let her chatter on.

But my mind kept wandering to my own problems.

My immediate dilemma was how to get in touch with Kyle. Father wasn't going to allow any communication, nor was I allowed to go out. He had me spend days with him at work and kept an eye on me in the evening. My chance came a week later when he was making some rounds with clients, and he instructed me to help my mother with anything that she might need.

An idea struck me. It was a rather appalling idea. But I was desperate.

I made her a cup of tea in the afternoon and added two of her sleeping pills. I convinced myself that since she nearly always took an afternoon nap anyway, it wasn't such a terrible thing.

Within an hour, she wouldn't have heard a tornado if it passed through the house.

I didn't know how much time I had, so I raced the car into town to Kyle's flat. He wasn't home, so I slipped a note under the door and hurried back home.

That evening after supper, I was especially attentive to my mother, who'd mostly recovered from her unexpected nap, played backgammon with Father, let him win convincingly, and gave them both kisses good night before retiring upstairs. A model daughter. At precisely ten o'clock, I tiptoed out the side door and ran to the gazebo.

"Kyle?" I whispered. "Are you here?"

A figure moved out from behind a tree.

"Is that you?"

He stepped just to the edge of the path lit by the moonlight. "It's me."

I fell into his arms and held him without words. It seemed like an eternity since I'd seen him.

"I got your note. I was going crazy. I didn't know what had happened to you."

"I know. It's been like a prison here. Please tell me that it was worth it, that you have good news."

"I do." He pulled out a paper from his pocket. "Here is the paperwork for our marriage license. You're going to have to go in and give your signature in person."

"I'll figure something out."

"And I talked to Father Sullivan. I thought that there might be a problem since you're not Catholic, but he's asked the bishop for a dispensation, and he doesn't think it will be an issue. He vouched for us personally. He'll be able to marry us at Saint Stephen's two weeks from today."

"Two whole weeks?"

"Yes, it will take that long to get the paperwork from the bishop."

Marrying outside of the Catholic Church was not an option for Kyle, and I supported that. I was lucky enough to be marrying him at all—if it took longer than we hoped, then so be it. He had probably lost a portion of his salvation already by stepping away from a vocation, and I wasn't going to be responsible for any more.

"Father Sullivan wanted to spend that time working with us, talking to us about marriage, but under the circumstances, I don't think that's going to be possible."

"You're right. It's going to be tough enough to get away for the license."

"He'll understand. He's a good man."

"Yes, he is."

"Julianne—before we go forward. Are you sure you don't want us to try one more time to talk to your parents? Maybe if they know we have a date set, that you're serious, they'll come around."

This is why I loved this man. The things he was willing to do for the sake of what was right.

"If I had any hope that it would help, I would." I rested my head against his chest, as I hoped to do for the rest of my life. "But they've cast their lot and so have I. Any mention of it would almost certainly bring on an attempt to stop it by any means necessary. It has to be this way."

"You know them best. I'm just sorry it came to this. I love you." He kissed the top of my head before stepping away. "You'd better get back. I don't want you getting into any more trouble. I'll tell you what, in case we can't talk, let's leave notes here, under this rock. I'll keep you posted on what is going on."

"That's a good idea."

He kissed my forehead and held me tight. "Two more weeks, darling, and we'll be together always."

"I can't wait." I avoided the moonlight on my way back in.

My behavior was exemplary for the rest of the week, and Father even commented that I was taking things very well.

"Well, I've been thinking about it, and you're probably right." I could feel the hellfire kindling already. These lies were getting easier as time went on. "Is that the package that needs to be brought to the train station?"

He looked at his pocket watch. "Yes, and the courier is late."

"Why don't I take it for you?" I noticed that the address was near the licensing office. This could be my only chance.

I had turned my attention to some files, but felt his eyes upon me. If he was regarding me with suspicion, he pushed past it. "I suppose that would be fine," he said. "Thank you."

I left a note for Kyle that night giving him the update. There was one the following evening.

Hello, Gorgeous. Good news—the dispensation came through, we're all set, and we should be able to get out early. How about Thursday? Be at our bench in the park at seven in the morning. Bring a suitcase with enough clothes for a few days. I'm taking you somewhere. It's a surprise.

All my love, Kyle

Thursday! It was only three days away. Three days, and I would be married to Kyle. I used the back of his note to leave my own, saying that I'd be there.

Father must have been softening, because when I asked him if I could go shopping with Lucille to Lewis's on Ranelagh the next day to look at wedding dresses with her aunt, he didn't immediately say no.

"Wedding dresses? Isn't that going to be a little tough on you, Princess?"

"Maybe. But it's Lucille. I can't miss out on doing this with my best friend. A wedding is a once-in-a-lifetime thing."

"You're right. And maybe I've been a little hard on you. It's all right with me, since her aunt will be with you."

"She will."

"Have a good time."

"Thanks!"

It was so good to be out with Lucille. Her usual efficiency had unraveled, and for once I was the steadying influence.

"Oh, Jul," she cried, "there's twenty thousand things to do. I never imagined! And we're having a *small* wedding!"

She was drawn to dresses with flowing skirts, but I finally talked her into the more slender sort that lay like a sheath.

"See, if the dress is simple, then we can do something fancy with your hair, like this." I pulled it up into a loose bun, leaving strands running down her cheeks. "And we can put some flowers around here." I traced the perimeter of her hair.

"Oh, you always have the best taste, Jul. You're absolutely right."

I ran my hands along some of the more beautiful gowns, just a bit sad that I would never wear one of them. I was going to wear a simple ivory suit that was already hanging in my closet.

Her aunt left us after that, as she had other errands to run downtown. Lucille and I paused as we passed the lingerie section.

"Should we?" She giggled and just stood there, as though waiting for my permission.

"We definitely should!"

We had snuck into this part of the store once when we were twelve and my mother was in the cosmetics section. We'd held things up to ourselves in the mirror and wrapped the whalebone corsets around our slender bodies.

"Look at my bosom, Lucille!" I'd said, spinning around. It was just then that the sales clerk came over, waving her skinny finger at us. We dropped the corsets to the floor and ran off to another department.

I looked at my friend now, remembering so many of our happy times. Now we were real women with real bosoms.

"How about this one?" I held up a black one with some delicate red lace trim and handed it to her.

"That is positively *burlesque*, Julianne! You are naughty." But I noticed that she kept it tucked under her arm.

I looked at a few items myself. I was especially drawn to a rose pink negligee with a diamond-patterned bodice, and a Fischer silk nightgown in an ecru tone. The capped sleeves and hemline were made of lace. I hooked the hangers on my finger. The Fischer gown had a matching robe. I picked that up, too. One can never have enough robes. And my parents would have spent far more on a traditional wedding.

"Are those for you, Jul?"

"Um, yes."

"Kind of fancy, don't you think?"

"Well, I'll be getting married someday, too. Why not stock up now?"

"You're right. It's fun doing this together. I like this one." She held up a white one with a neckline that swooped down to the belly.

"You're the naughty one now, Lu."

She giggled. "I know. But, hey, you only have a honeymoon once. The price tag is maddening, though. It's too much to spend, especially when you won't be wearing it for long!"

I looked at the tag. She was right—it would take most people a couple of weeks to pay for a gown like this.

"But you know, it suits you. And you're right. You only have one honeymoon. It's my gift to you." I added it to my pile and picked up a second one for myself.

I selected some new silver cuff links for Father before we left, as a thank-you for letting me go today.

I slipped my bags upstairs without anyone seeing and tossed a suitcase onto the bed. I packed everything I thought I'd need for a few days, putting the lingerie on top and smoothing it out so that it wouldn't wrinkle much. I packed two trunks with nearly everything I owned and just missed needing a third one. I called for a mover to come by on Wednesday at ten, when Father would be at work and Mother would be at her monthly Ladies' Auxiliary brunch.

By Wednesday evening, I was all set to go.

I had put off the last task, but couldn't procrastinate any longer. There were two letters that I felt compelled to write.

I decided to tackle the easier one first.

17 August 1938

Dearest Lucille,

First, I am so happy about your engagement to Ben. He is such a decent and wonderful man, and you are lucky to have each other. I look forward to seeing lots of blue-eyed, dimpled babies in your future!

Secondly, I am leaving in a few days. Of course I'm leaving next week for school, anyway, but I am leaving tomorrow. With Kyle.

Don't be shocked. Well, maybe that can't be helped. We are getting married tomorrow. Of course, by the time you read this, tomorrow will have passed and I will be Mrs. Kyle McCarthy. (I love writing that!) We became engaged on the night of the auction.

It has been very difficult not to share this with you, especially with all of the wedding talk. I almost broke down several times but stopped. And only because it's for your own good.

You see, we approached Father about it, and he refused us, for all the reasons that I know you can imagine. But I'm not going to let that stop me.

Anyway, I didn't want to ask you to lie or conceal anything for us, and that is why I had to make sure that we were married and out of town before you knew. I will be back in a few days, and I hope very much that, if you're speaking to me, we can celebrate together.

I love you, Lucille. I already know that you will understand, and you're an angel for it. There are some difficult roads ahead. But at least Kyle and I will be facing them together.

Love, Jul

The next one was much more challenging and required many more drafts.

17 August 1938

Dear Mother and Father,
This is the hardest thing that I have ever had to do. But there is really no way to lead up to it, so I am going to get right to the point.

By the time you read this, I will have married Kyle.

There must be a million thoughts swirling around in your heads now, not the least of which I'm sure is some shock and anger. And you are justified in that. This is not what any of us planned.

You see, I have loved Kyle for over a year now, and I've known that if by some miracle he loved me back, that this would always be.

We wanted to do this with your blessing but were willing to proceed without it. We are not being impetuous, although it may seem so with its sudden timing. But it was in fact carefully thought out. We are both moving to London and find it appropriate on a number of levels to arrive there married. Kyle has inquired about a studio flat that is not far from school and not too far from his new job.

I beg of you to consider opening your heart to him. He is a good, good man who loves me. He wants to take care of me. He has been a gentleman with me, and it pains him as much as it does me to hurt you and to go behind your backs. Perhaps even more. I know that he will be an exemplary son-in-law, and I hope very much that you will get to know him like I do and see him in this way.

I will be back on Sunday afternoon. I can't tell you where I'll be because, frankly, I don't know myself. Kyle has planned a little surprise honeymoon for us as a wedding gift. When I return, and the shock has worn off, let's have a real discussion about this and about the future for all of us.

I love you both. I love Kyle. And you all love me. Keeping this in mind, let's make this all work out.

Love, Julianne

It wasn't perfect, but my hand was cramped, and it was the best I could do at this point.

I placed it on my bed in the morning, put Lucille's letter in the post stack, and left with my suitcase. I closed the door behind me, not knowing what I would return to should I ever open it again.

Chapter Nineteen

Kyle's truck was parked in its usual spot down the road. He took my suitcase and put it in the back.

"Good morning, gorgeous." He kissed me on the cheek and couldn't stop grinning. "This is it. Are you ready?"

"I have never wanted something more."

"May I ask a favor?"

"Anything."

"We have some time before Father Sullivan is expecting us. Would you mind if we drive out to Charcross to visit my father's grave?"

"Of course, I wouldn't mind."

We drove out once again to the vast cemetery. This time, we knew just where we were going and didn't stop at the church. Kyle had a pile of flowers sitting between us, and he took a handful of them with us when we walked over and knelt at the site.

I asked, "Do you think he would have approved of us? Of today?"

"I do."

"I mean, wasn't it his dream to see you become a priest?"

"I think it was. But he really grew to love you as you spent the last weeks with him. He even told me that you reminded him of my mother."

"He did? You didn't tell me that."

"He said that you were a *cailín maith*—a good girl—and that my mother would have liked you. That's as good a compliment as he could ever give."

"That's a nice thought. I loved him, too, you know, crustiness and all."

We walked hand in hand back to the truck and made our way to Saint Stephen's.

Before we got out, he gave me the remaining armful of flowers. They were all my favorites—tulips, calla lilies, and daffodils.

"I've been growing these especially for you. I was going to give them to you as they bloomed, but I decided that I'd save them for my beautiful bride should have a bouquet that equaled her."

"I'm speechless, Kyle."

"Well, that's a first."

"Oh, shush." I punched him lightly in the side. "But really, they're stunning. Wherever did you grow them? You don't have a garden at your flat."

"Oh, Miss Ellis was able to find a little corner of earth for me."

I brightened up at her name.

"I have something else for you," he said, pulling from his coat pocket a little velvet bag, which he emptied into his hand. Three rings fell out.

"Hold out your hand." He picked up the one with the diamond. "Here is your engagement ring back. Now you can wear it always." He slipped it on my finger, and I held out my hand to admire it.

"Here's a small wedding band to match it," he said, giving it a nudge on his palm with his fingertip. "We should wait for you to put that one on, don't you think?"

"I suppose," I conceded.

"And this one," he said, picking up the remaining ring, a larger gold band with a line of silver running along its middle, "this was my father's wedding ring. I thought it would be appropriate."

I stood on my tiptoes to kiss him. "I can't believe this is really happening." I took the rings from him and returned them to their little velvet bag, which I tucked into my handbag to be used later in the ceremony.

The wedding was just what it needed to be. Plain and uncomplicated, nothing like what my mother would have liked to plan. Once I might have wanted the same thing that she did. But that was back when I thought that the spectacle of the event was actually necessary. Now I understood love, and I knew that what mattered was Kyle and me and our commitment. I held the flowers in my left arm and kept my right one linked through his.

The vows rolled off my tongue with ease as I promised to love Kyle until death, for better or worse. Even more, I loved hearing the words "I do" as he professed them back to me. He rocked back on his heels after he said that, his joy barely contained.

My favorite words came from Father Sullivan. "I now pronounce you husband and wife." Husband. Wife. New roles for us. I said the words a few times, and in their newness they tasted sweet like a confectionary. I'm sure that I was not the first newlywed to savor them.

Mr. Alden, the landlord, and Mrs. Mawdsley were our witnesses, the first beaming at us with a proud smile, and the second looking like she wanted to pull my hair out. Our marriage was now unwelcome to three people, and we were hopeful that there weren't any more.

Kyle asked Mr. Alden to take our picture and handed him his camera. We took some of just the two of us, then some with Father Sullivan. Mrs. Mawdsley was invited to join us, but not surprisingly she declined.

With the most sincerity that I may have ever expressed, we thanked Father Sullivan for his support and his belief in us. Kyle and I were well aware of what he had done to make this happen. We invited him to join us for a late breakfast, but he insisted that the "young couple go off and get their honeymoon started."

Not needing to be told twice, we raced out of the church at the most respectable pace we could manage.

Kyle headed east out of Liverpool. Before long we passed through Wallasey, and we recalled our day there back in December. It seemed like so long ago.

"You know," Kyle confessed, "I almost kissed you, right in the middle of all those Christmas trees. You looked so adorable with my wool cap pulled over your ears."

"I wish you *had* kissed me then, and I expect you to make it up to me."

"I intend to, Mrs. McCarthy." And we bantered on like the hour-old married couple that we were. This kind of silly love talk once made me roll my eyes when I heard it. But now that I was in the middle of it, I couldn't get enough.

Continuing west, we passed Abergele, Conwy, Llanfairfechan, then Bangor. I thought that this might be our destination at last, as I had heard much about the university town, but Kyle kept driving.

The next town of note was the seaside town of Caernarfon, and it was here that he told me we would be spending the next three nights. But before we checked into our hotel, he wanted to take me somewhere else.

He approached the pier and waited in the queue while other cars entered the ferry ahead of us. Parking the truck on the bottom level, we walked up two flights to the outside deck. Most people stayed on the interior deck, so we were happy to find a spot where we could sit alone. The movement along the water created wind, and he chuckled at my attempts to keep my hair from flying into my eyes and mouth. He asked if I would like to go downstairs, but I declined, preferring this secluded spot.

We didn't talk much as we crossed the Menai Strait, just enjoying the rhythm of the water. I swayed to the lullaby. When I grew cold and wrapped my arms around myself, Kyle layered them with his own.

We landed at Anglesey Island. After waiting a few minutes to let the stairs empty, we returned to the motorcar level and sat in the truck until it was our turn to disembark. The truck sputtered and whined as Kyle turned the ignition, but soon we were making our way around the other side of the strait.

Verdant and rocky, Anglesey was not heavily populated. Before long we were in an area that was even more remote. The seaside road forked, and Kyle consulted a map before turning left onto a long and skinny peninsula. As we drove through the middle of it, there were times when I could see the water on either side of me in the distance. It seemed as though we were moving along the narrow finger of a woman beckoning us toward her to learn her hidden secrets. Kyle told me that it was called Llanddwyn Island, as sometimes, depending on the tide, the thin strip of land seemed to be disconnected from Anglesey.

We passed the random lighthouse and cottage, but Kyle didn't slow down until we reached a rolling, stony field. In the middle sat the ruins of what was once a small building. Only three sides remained standing, if you could even call them sides, as they weren't nearly as tall as they once had to have been. One side had an open, arched space that probably used to serve as a window. The rest looked like nothing more than neatly laid rows of piled stones, haunting echoes of their former selves.

Kyle stopped the car, and I couldn't imagine why we had come all the way for this. When I saw him pick up his camera, I searched my handbag for a little lipstick and rouge. If he was planning to take my picture, I wanted to look my best. When I'd finished touching myself up, he told me to bring my scarf, and I could only assume that he thought it might get a little windy again.

I put my arm in his and let him lead me to the ruins through paths of mosslike grass. "Where are we, Kyle?"

"This is, or it *was*, the Church of Saint Dwynwen."

"Of who? I've never heard of him."

"Of *her*. Saint Dwynwen lived in the fifth century. She fell in love with a young man named Maelon, but her father wanted her to marry someone else. She begged God to spare her from this unwanted marriage, and an angel appeared to give her a potion that would erase all of her memories of Maelon. Instead, it turned him into a block of ice. She promised to retreat from the world if God would thaw him, and her wish was granted. She founded a convent on this very spot, and her fervent prayer for the rest of her days was that all lovers would find happiness, since she did not."

"How sad! How *lonely* for her."

"Yes, it must have been. But years later, in the Middle Ages, this became a site of pilgrimage for lovers seeking her intercession. Legend says that there was once a pool of water here, populated by eels. Couples would throw bread crumbs in the water and cover them with a scarf. If the eels ate the bread and disturbed the scarf, it was a sign that the lover would remain faithful."

"How peculiar. But I suppose it's romantic in its own way."

He laughed at that. "Well, have no fear, there are no eels here. Not anymore, at least. But I did want to bring you here, since Saint Dwynwen is the patron saint of lovers. I thought it would be an appropriate place to begin this weekend."

Kyle's gifts were from the heart, dearer to me than anything that could have been bought at Harrods. Who else would have thought of something like this?

"I also wanted to take a picture of you here, because you have never looked more beautiful than today."

I arched my eyebrow, trying to imitate the way that he did it when he was trying to be funny, but I failed to pull it off. I knew that my face had to be red and my hair windblown. Surely I was miles from beautiful. But he insisted. I put my scarf around my neck, thankful that it wasn't destined to be eel food, and sat in the opening of the ancient window. Taking his time to frame the picture correctly, Kyle snapped away once he was happy with the position. I posed nicely, but when I thought he had taken enough shots for at least one to turn out well, I made silly faces until he laughed and joined me in the window.

Sliding his arm around my waist and pulling me closer with my scarf, he kissed me tenderly.

We couldn't stay any longer, as there was only one ferry going back today. As romantic as it might have been to have our honeymoon right then and there, it would likely get very cold and the warmth of a hotel bed sounded much more inviting.

I took off my scarf, found a jagged rock, and tied it around twice so that it wouldn't loosen and blow away. I whispered into the ruins, "Look after us, Saint Dwynwen, that these lovers will be faithful until the day we die."

The ferry back was even colder, and I begrudgingly agreed with Kyle that we should sit downstairs this time. I rested my head on his shoulder and nodded off as the water rocked me once again.

I dreamed of Saint Dwynwen, beautiful maiden of long ago. Her long red hair became part of the breeze, and she seemed to be shouting to me. I couldn't hear her, so her cries became more desperate. But I couldn't understand her warning over the sound of the waves.

It was dusk when we arrived in Caernarfon. Kyle had booked a room at the tiny Menai Bank Hotel—a charming, peach-colored bed-and-breakfast overlooking the straits. With its bay windows and pointed dormers, it looked like something out of a storybook. Being a Thursday, it looked like we were the only guests for the night, although they expected to be full tomorrow and through the weekend.

But tonight, we were told, it was all ours.

We took the key and raced up the stairs.

Chapter Twenty

The counter of the reception desk at the Menai Bank Hotel was arrayed with colorful pages advertising local sites. The brochure for Caernarfon showed pictures of the immense historic castle that was a short drive from our hotel. Roman ruins could be found nearby at Segontium. Viking ruins were in Beaumaris. We saw none of these.

When we finally emerged from the hotel into the bustling town, it was late afternoon on our last full day. The sky was the kind of gray that heralded an impending dusk, and the sun began its descent by sending out orange cascades to line the clouds. We walked hand in hand to the bank of the Afon Seiont and found the rowboat rental that had been recommended by the hotel owner.

"Are you Brecon?" Kyle said to the grizzled man who sat on a white-washed pier.

"*Ie,*" he said.

"Good, then. We'd like to take a row on the river before it gets dark."

"That's the only one I have right now," he said, pointing to a small white vessel to his right. The rowboat needed a coat of paint but looked to be waterworthy. In blue letters on the back, the name *Aberfa* was printed. "But she's a good girl."

Kyle handed over the named amount and held my hands as I stepped in. Brecon gave her a shove and we glided out, barely missing some fishing boats on either side. Kyle didn't speak while he looked over his shoulder and navigated the narrow passage. I was impressed that my husband could maneuver it so ably.

When we had cleared the banks and entered the wider body of the river, he relaxed.

"Stretch out your legs, Julianne," he said.

"Won't they be in your way?"

"Has any man ever minded the legs of a beautiful woman being next to him?"

I blushed. "Kyle McCarthy, you say such things."

"And I will say them forever, Mrs. McCarthy."

I grinned at the delight of my new name.

We rowed past attached homes painted a myriad of colors to distinguish their borders. Their roofs displayed various shades of red, which were really the reflection of the sun's setting rays. We passed fishing boats and recreational boats, lingering picnickers on the banks, and in the distance we could see Caernarfon Castle and the hills behind it. It was beautiful, but Kyle and I still existed in that newlywed state where the wonders surrounding us couldn't begin to compete with the gaze of the person in front of me.

"I found a place to go to Mass in the morning," he said. "Saint Monica's. I can slip out early and let you sleep. Then we can eat breakfast and head back home."

I turned my head and couldn't speak.

"What's the matter, Julianne?" He stopped rowing.

I tilted my chin down to my chest. Kyle leaned forward and we both shifted to maintain our balance. He reached out his hand.

"You don't want to think about tomorrow, do you?"

I pursed my lips and shook my head.

"My darling, you don't have to worry about anything. We're a team now. There's nothing you'll have to go through alone."

I looked up at him. "I don't know what I'm going to say to my parents. I don't have any idea how they're going to receive me. I wish we could just forget Liverpool and go straight to London."

He squeezed my hand. "I know this is going to be difficult for you. But don't let it spoil these last few hours." He put his hand around my face and drew it nearer. He placed a delicate kiss on my lips and said, "I love you. No matter what, you can count on that. Nothing can change how I feel."

I nodded and smiled, and the tears that had come to my eyes refracted the light of the setting sun. We didn't speak again as he turned the *Aberfa* around and returned her to her owner.

The next morning I woke up after only a couple hours of sleep. I had taken Kyle's advice not to let thoughts of today detract from the time we had and seen to it that we didn't let it go to waste. I was hungry, but I noticed that Kyle was already awake and lacing his shoes.

"Where are you going?"

"I'm heading out to Saint Monica's for Mass, remember? I wanted to let you sleep." He came over and placed a kiss on my forehead.

"I'll go with you if you can give me a minute. But can we have breakfast first?"

"I can't, love. Fasting."

I sat up, pulled the sheet over me, and started brushing my hair with my fingers. "What do you mean?"

"It means that I can't eat before going to Mass."

"Why not?"

"It's one of the rules. The physical hunger we feel is supposed to call to mind the spiritual hunger we should have for our Communion."

"OK. I'll just take your word for that. There's a lot I don't understand, Kyle."

"You don't have to. You have a lifetime to learn about it. And only if you want to. I'm not making any demands or asking anything of you."

"I know. You've been good about that. But I want to understand, so I hope you don't mind if I ask questions."

"Of course not. Come on." He put his hands out to mine and pulled me up. The sheet fell from me, and my nakedness was revealed. I walked my fingers up his chest to his shoulder.

"Are you *sure* you want to leave so early?"

He kissed the palms of my hands. "My love, there is nothing I would like more than to stay right where we are, for today and forever. But," he said, as he let go and turned around, "we do, in fact, need to get back to Liverpool today, so I am going to have to decline. *Very* regretfully decline."

I jumped up. "Then I'm going with you."

"Would you like for me to grab a roll for you from the kitchen? You're not fasting."

"Thanks, but no. Whatever you do, I'll do. We're in this together."

The church was far less ornate than both the Immaculate Heart of Mary and Saint Stephen's. The people mainly worked in the fishing trade, and they were adorned as simply as their church. The heads of the women were covered with long lace veils, and I felt self-conscious at not having one. I made a note to ask Kyle to get me one for the future so that I wouldn't embarrass him.

I was getting used to the Latin, and for the first time I followed along with a missal. It wasn't as intimidating once the translations were in front of me. The English reminded me of something Shakespearean, with its many *thee*s and *thou*s. The hardest part for me to catch on to was all of the standing, sitting, and kneeling. I tried to follow whatever Kyle was doing but was always, noticeably, a second behind. He told me later that posture was part of prayer—just one more thing that I would have to learn.

We arrived back at the hotel for breakfast, packed our suitcases into the truck, and headed west. With each mile, I found it harder to breathe, anticipating what scene might be waiting for me when I arrived home.

We had the first argument of our marriage, and I hoped our last. Kyle had every intention of going in to speak with the parents of his wife. He felt that they deserved that respect and that I deserved to have my husband by my side through what was undoubtedly going to be a challenging conversation. I knew that he was right. I knew it, but I adamantly refused his assistance. It was a conversation long overdue, and I needed to do it on my own.

Quite reluctantly, he gave in and agreed to meet me by the lake.

As he drove off, it felt as if my heart beat louder than the rumble of the truck. I turned to face our house. The stately brick manor had never looked so intimidating. It had always been home, and yet I realized suddenly that it was no longer my home. I was a married woman, and home for the foreseeable future was going to be our studio flat in London.

I felt guilty but only for the disappointment that I had caused my parents. Not at all for marrying Kyle. If I went in with my head hung, it would look as if I had something for which to be ashamed. Then again, if I held it high, I would appear aloof and uncaring of my parents' wishes. I decided to carry myself in a way that best relayed what I was feeling and hoped that it would make my intentions apparent. I was neither ashamed nor arrogant. I was a happy bride, and I wanted my parents to share that joy with me.

Taking the key out of my pocket, I opened the latch loudly, hoping to give them notice of my arrival. The door creaked on cue, and I closed it without finesse behind me. Surely, they knew I was here, but no one came out to greet me. I walked around the parlor and through a few other rooms, but they were empty. At last, I looked at the closed doors of my father's study, with light shining through the seams. He never left lights on unless he was in there.

I knocked gently.

"Come in," he said, releasing in me a strong wave of déjà vu.

I took a deep, shuddering breath and suddenly wished that Kyle were here after all to steady me. Why hadn't I listened? Four days in, and I was already failing at marriage.

I opened the heavy wooden door and closed it behind me without yet looking at the figure behind the desk.

Turning around hesitantly, my first impression was that Father had aged ten years in four days. I had expected him to be angry with me, but his expression as he regarded me was one of pure desolation. This would have almost been easier if he had showed some outrage. A part of me felt as if I deserved it.

I walked to one of the chairs across from him and perched upon its edge. This time, he didn't walk around to join me.

"Papa . . ." I said, using a term that I hadn't spoken in a decade but feeling suddenly like I wanted nothing more than to climb into his lap and embrace him.

"Julianne." He used the same tone that I'd heard him use with errant employees.

We sat for a moment at a stalemate, assessing one another and not knowing what to say next. My face tingled as tears formed and rose to the surface. "Papa," I said again, rising and beginning to move around the massive desk, putting my arms out.

"Have a seat, please." He pointed to the chair I'd just vacated.

I returned to it and sat with my hands folded in my lap. I twisted my wedding band around and around my finger.

"Where is Mother?" Surely, she knew that I was coming back, as I had stated in my letter that I would be returning this afternoon.

He looked at me, surprised that I even had to ask. "Your mother has decided to visit your aunt in Hereford for a few weeks."

Without saying it, he was telling me that she did not wish to see me now nor see me off to London in a few days. It was obvious how she felt about this. I clung to the fact that my father had remained. If he had wanted to avoid me, there were many trips he might've taken. But he was here, and that had to count for something. I was grateful for this shred of hope.

"You got my letter?" I asked, although that answer, too, was obvious.

"Of course. We found it Thursday afternoon, and I spent the rest of the day driving everywhere I could think of, looking for you. I suppose it was too late by then, though."

"Yes, Father. We got married at nine, and drove to Anglesey from there."

He didn't respond, so I gave him some details about the wedding and the places that we had visited in the last few days. My nervous chatter filled the silence, an empty space that I wanted to avoid at all costs.

Finally, I said, "Father, I'm sorry. At least, I'm so very sorry that I hurt you and Mother. You have to know that it is not what I wanted. But I am not sorry, not even a little, that I married Kyle."

"And where is Kyle? Don't you think that at least the young man could come and face me on his own?"

"He wanted to. In fact, he was quite angry with me when I insisted that he let me come here on my own. Please don't blame him for that. I didn't give him any choice."

"He was right to be angry, Julianne. If you think that you are mature enough to get married, then you have to have the maturity to accept what comes with that. Whether I like it or not, Kyle is your husband, and he should be here."

"You're right. He was right. I was wrong to send him away."

"Let me ask you a question. Are you with child? Is that why you did this?"

"Am I *what*? Of course not! What a thing to say."

"Well, it would just explain this whole thing."

"No, it wouldn't. I've already told you the explanation. I love Kyle, he loves me, he's coming to London with me, and we wanted to be married."

"Well, I hope you enjoy starving, because that's what will happen there. I'm not going to support you any longer."

"That's just fine with me. I know it will be a struggle, but we have plans, and we have each other."

"Julianne." He leaned forward. "Look. I am disappointed that you disobeyed me. I am appalled that you married someone that I explicitly disapproved of. But more than that, I am angry. I am angry that you lied to me and did this behind my back."

"We tried to include you. Kyle came to speak to you. But you didn't listen."

"That's like a wolf telling the hen that he's going to raid the coop just before he does. Some man you married. He sat in this very room and listened to what I had to say and even seemed to agree, and then has the *audacity* to turn around to do exactly what I forbade. Is that what is passing for a Catholic today? Deception? Manipulation? A fine priest he would have made." He pounded his fist on the desk so forcefully that the pens rattled in their canister. "But he is no longer the issue. I have always prided myself on our open and honest relationship, and I don't see how I can trust that anymore."

No. He could not have just said those words. I was ready for the fight.

"I agree, Father. Open and honest. Which is why you told me about Charles, right?"

His eyes widened just a bit at that name, but his face remained set. "I don't know what you're talking about."

"Open and honest. That's why you have been so forthright in telling me that I have a twin brother."

His jaw quivered and finally dropped open. "How did you—"

"It doesn't matter how I know. I just do. It would have been a nice thing to know, growing up. That I wasn't the only one. It could have been a lot less lonely."

"You don't understand. He's not like you. He's a very unfortunate boy."

"No, I *do* understand. I understand that he likes chocolate. I understand that he loves growing things. I understand that he likes to take walks. I understand that he can't hear me or see me, but that he knows I'm there."

He slumped into his chair like a defeated schoolboy. "How . . . how do you know these things?"

"Because I've been to see him. Many times over the years. Oh, you picked a *lovely* place for him, and I'm glad for that, but the problem is, he can't *see* the marble floors or the brocade curtains. But he can feel the presence of another person, and it makes him feel loved. He might have liked to know his parents."

He leaned forward and placed his elbows on the desk and his head in his hands. He looked up at me with red eyes.

"You don't know what it's like to be in my position and to have a son, only for him to turn out, well, the way that he turned out. You don't know what it did to your mother."

I felt certain I had a very good idea of what it did to her, but chose to keep that to myself and let him talk, now that he seemed of a mind to. He sighed and gripped a youthful photograph of her from the side of his desk.

"She used to be so vibrant, so joyful. I met her at a concert out at Newsham Park. Everyone was so elegant in all of their finery, sitting properly and clapping politely as each piece finished. But not your mother. Her shoes peeked out of her skirts, and they moved with the music. The rest of her body was still, but underneath, she was dancing."

I listened expectantly, caring more than I wanted to. They'd always said that they'd met at a charity ball. I didn't know this part of it.

"I caught her eye, and I expected her to turn away. But she didn't. She looked straight at me, almost like she was daring me. So I started moving my feet, too. Just a little, but she saw it. I didn't have the rhythm that she did, though. We went on like that for the rest of the concert, ten seats away from one another, moving our feet discreetly and stealing glances. When it was over, she disappeared, and I drove myself mad looking for her. That's why, when I saw her at the ball a couple of weeks later, I headed straight toward her, asked her to dance, and put my name on every slot of her dance card."

He looked back at me and set the picture down. He leaned in and folded his hands together over the desk.

"She was so *alive*. Nothing frightened her. There was nothing that she couldn't do. Then you and Charles were born. She wanted a son so badly, because she knew I wanted one. When he came out, well, so *wrong*, something broke in her. She wouldn't look at him. She wouldn't even try to nurse him."

He hung his head down and shook it. He continued, almost in a whisper. "She's never really come back to me, my Beatrice. Sometimes she's like a stranger."

A part of me was moved by this sad, arid portrait he'd painted of their marriage. But I couldn't help thinking of what he'd said about my husband, words he had yet to retract.

"But why didn't you go see him? All this time, you have a son and you've never gone to see him."

"It's easier just to forget. But I suppose one can never forget. It's easier just to pretend and to move on."

"That may be so, but you've *robbed* me. You've robbed yourself, and you've definitely robbed him. How's that for being open and honest?"

He sat straight up again and pounded his fist on the desk. "Don't try to distract me from the real issue here. Perhaps I've made my own mistakes, Julianne. But that doesn't excuse your behavior. This conversation is still about you and that Catholic boy."

"That Catholic boy has a name, Father. It's Kyle. He's my husband now. And do you want to know how *we* met?"

"Frankly, I don't. In fact, I'm going to ring my barrister and see what can be done about this."

"No, you're going to listen to *me*. I met Kyle at Bootle Home, where he was taking care of Charles. He was taking care of *your son*, out of the goodness of his heart, while you sat here, far away, denying his existence. You might donate to the cathedral, and Mother might raise a king's ransom for the less fortunate, but so much for your values. They're empty. All this time, it's a *Catholic* who's been doing what you should have been doing all along."

He looked as if I'd struck him, as if we both saw our long-cherished rapport crumbling before our eyes.

I stood up. "I'm sorry that you can't see it that way, Father, but you have a choice here. And if you make the one that I think you will, it is your loss. Here's some honesty for you, since it seems to be so precious. You've lost a son. You're going to lose your daughter. And you're going to lose out on knowing the best son-in-law that one could hope for. You are a wealthy man, Father, but you are a poor, poor excuse for one."

I marched out the front door and ran off into the park to find Kyle.

We left for London on Thursday, on a nine o'clock train, a week to the hour from our wedding. It was amazing how seven days could change everything. Kyle had sold his truck to the man who replaced his father at Bootle Home. I'd planned to make it out there with him, to say my good-byes to Miss Ellis and to Charles, but a terrible cold kept me in the flat, so I asked him to extend my love to both of them.

Before we left, I had seen Lucille, who peppered me with questions. They ranged from "How are your parents going to explain this to their friends?" to "What is it like to make love—really, do tell me, because I am so nervous!" and everything in between. To the first, I answered that I didn't give a whit what they would tell their friends. To the second, I answered that she would have to find out for herself, but I promised with a wink that it was *wonderful*.

My parents were noticeably absent at the train station, but Lucille was there, as well as Father Sullivan.

The train ride was our second trip together in a week, and I was glad that Kyle wasn't driving so that I could sit closer to him. When I was hungry, he pulled out cucumber sandwiches that he had packed. Third class was so different from the luxury I had traveled in only a year ago. Gone were the etched carvings, the embroidered upholstery, the doting service. But I paid no mind to all of that. Kyle was an excellent substitute for all of that posh. I believed I was living in absolute bliss.

Well, almost.

The flat that Kyle had inquired about from an advertisement was still vacant, which we originally thought to be a stroke of luck. But when we saw it, we realized that the description had been woefully optimistic. *Cozy, cottage-like flat above charming neighborhood café* should have read: *Dingy closet situated above obnoxiously noisy pub; rats available at no extra charge.* We left as quickly as we could, grateful that we had not sent in a deposit or signed any papers. We stayed for the first few nights in a boardinghouse and scanned the newspaper for another option.

We were just about to give up hope when I had dinner with Abigail. Kyle was meeting with his new employer, and Dorothy hadn't arrived back in town yet.

"A runaway marriage, now? And you thought *I* was a bold American. You're an honorary member of the club." Abigail had hung on to every word of our story. "What are you going to do now?"

"Well, Kyle has a job with a landscaper, and I'm going to ask the hospital for some kind of employment to offset my tuition. I don't think

I can afford to come back full-time, but I'll still work away at it. Maybe they have some kind of housing for married people."

"Oh, nix that. There's a waiting list and it could be another year before you get one of those. I think I have a better idea."

"What's that?"

"My father's assistant just got transferred to the embassy in Rome. She had a lovely little flat not too far from the school, and she has to sublet it. It can't possibly cost very much, not on a secretary's salary. Maybe something can be worked out."

"You're a peach, Abigail."

"Hey, it's the least I could do for stealing your boyfriend."

"Oh, Roger? He was never really my boyfriend. And you're much better suited for him."

"Ha! I don't know about that. I often wonder what some of his stuffy colleagues think of me. I mean, I know how to act correctly at these functions we go to. I'm not the daughter of a diplomat for nothing. But my mouth can't help but get the better of me once in a while. Still, he seems to like my crazy hide. Especially when I let him touch it."

"Abigail!"

"Oh, don't pretend that I shock you. You know me better than that. But our proper parliamentarian friend, I'm telling you—he has a wilder side." She pressed her finger into the table squarely to drive home the statement.

"I have a hard time believing that."

"Oh, but it's true. There was this one time—"

"I do not want to hear this."

"OK, I wouldn't want to damage your innocent ears. On the other hand, you're married now—you should know what I'm talking about."

"Another subject, Abigail."

"Fine, then. When do you want to see the flat?"

We were able to get in the next day, and it was ideal. It was closer to the school than to Kyle's office, but he didn't mind the commute.

It was in Lambeth, on Black Prince Road, above a pub called the Jolly Gardeners. We occupied the middle floor of the three-story, red-and-white-bricked building. The rumbling of the train just a block away became such a routine noise that we no longer heard it. It was also a little more expensive than we had budgeted for, but it was furnished, so we made up for it out of some money that we had earmarked for that. The icing on the cake was a place on the roof where Kyle could place several wooden boxes for growing herbs and small vegetables. It reminded me of Charles and how he liked to put his hands in soil.

The flat situation was just my first awakening to living within my means. I'd never realized how expensive things were. Last year I had a healthy allowance, and although I wasn't particularly reckless, it never ran out. Anything I needed was available. If I was hungry, I'd pop into a café and get a sandwich and soda. If I was bored, I'd buy a magazine. If I was cold, I'd stop into a fashionable shop and buy a sweater without even looking at the tag. All too soon came the crashing reality that my former carefree lifestyle was over. I discovered that I could make my own sandwiches for far less, a Coke wasn't necessary, a magazine could be borrowed from a friend, and my goodness, the price of a quality sweater could feed a small army.

Kyle wasn't bothered by this, of course. He'd been frugal his whole life. He was proud of the efforts that I was making, but he couldn't pass up an opportunity to tease me.

"What are you doing, darling?" He looked up at me earnestly as I was disposing of the scraps from supper into the waste bin. There was quite a bit to toss, unfortunately, as I was in the beginning stages of learning to cook for myself.

"I'm scraping the plates."

"You mean, you don't save the bones for the secondhand market?"

"What on earth are you talking about?"

"The bones. Didn't you know that you can wash them off and resell them to cobblers? They grind them up into a powder and use it for shoeshine."

"I had no idea."

"Oh yes. Of course, they'll deny it when you first approach them, but that's only because they want to talk you down from your price. Don't fall for it, though. If you're persistent and tell them that it's fifty pence or you're walking, they'll meet your price."

"That is very clever! I never would have thought of that."

"It's not such a secret. Growing up, I'd save up for Dadaí's Christmas present with the bones I'd sell throughout the year."

I didn't think we were quite that desperate for money, but I wanted Kyle to be proud of me. It only took three visits to befuddled cobblers and one threat to "ring the bobbies" if I didn't leave to realize the full scope of my gullibility.

Kyle had a tremendous laugh at my expense, egged on by Abigail, who thought it was a brilliant prank. But a night of sleeping on the sofa brought a sincere apology and a promise never to do anything like it again. Not that I could stay mad, though. He looked so desolate all alone in the other room, and the bed was too empty without him. I put on one of my new nightgowns and called him into our room.

Who said that you needed money to have fun?

Chapter Twenty-One

Word of continued Nazi aggression dampened the revelry of our first few months together. In late November, word spread about what was being called *Kristallnacht*, or "Night of Broken Glass." Newspapers posted staggering numbers, reporting that thirty thousand Jews had been sent to concentration camps, a thousand synagogues had been burned, seven thousand Jewish businesses had been damaged. People were committing suicide by the hundreds rather than face the terrors that might come. The Movietone reels, which we saw when we scraped together enough money to catch a show, showed glass flooding the streets of Germany and Austria as the destruction continued.

I feared Britain's involvement in a potential war for the selfish reason that Kyle no longer had the exemption of the seminary to fall upon. If anything happened to him, it would be my fault. And the possibility of violence in our own streets was daunting.

So far, professors at the school had managed to maintain a sense of normalcy, and I was too busy to think any more on it. Our studies were delving deeper into anatomy and physiology, and our hospital hours remained taxing. We were being encouraged to start choosing a specialty, and I was debating between elder care and midwifery.

I decorated our little flat as December rolled in, with candles in the windows and tinsel around their frames. Kyle had brought scraps of boughs and an anemic little tree from one of his sources through work.

Two weeks from Christmas, I had fallen asleep upon an open textbook when I heard a knock at my door.

"Father!" I cried, as I saw the tall man in the woolen overcoat standing at my threshold. Despite how we'd parted, I couldn't help but throw my arms around him. He responded, somewhat stiffly, but I considered it a good sign that he was even here.

"Julianne," he said, as I waved him in. He took off his hat and patted the thin layer of snow into the sink. Quickly, I closed my books and piled them with my pages of notes into a corner of the table. I wiped the chair clean of some crumbs that had fallen from an afternoon snack.

"Have a seat. Please."

He looked around him and pursed his lips. "Do you have a coat? There is a restaurant I passed a few blocks away. We could talk there."

"Yes, let's do that." I bundled up, and we walked to Princes Arms, a small place with geometric black-and-teal floor tiles and brass lamps lighting each table. I had peeked through its windows in the past but couldn't afford to go in.

We slid into a green leather booth, and I braced myself for whatever my father must have felt it important enough to come say.

I knew immediately that a beef stew sounded perfect on a cold day like this, so I spoke first while he studied the menu. "It's good to see you. What a wonderful surprise."

He shut the menu and placed his folded hands over it. "It's good to see you, too. I'm in town for a freight conference. I also had a meeting with a shoe manufacturer who was going to talk to me about shipping through our Liverpool port, but he had to cancel. So I thought I would drop in on you and see how you are getting along."

I wondered if I had, in fact, been a mere afterthought to a business meeting that never happened or if, in his pride, he could not admit that he might really have wanted to come see me.

"We're getting along well, Father. Kyle is working extra jobs so that I can go to school full-time, and I'm taking on extra work at the hospital. He's good to me. We're happy. We really are."

The tuxedoed waiter arrived just at that time. Father ordered a roast with Yorkshire pudding, and I chose mint tea with my stew.

I fiddled with the necklace I was wearing. "And how is Mother?"

"She's well. Keeping busy. You broke her heart, you know."

I remained silent at that.

"But still, she saw fit to send along a Christmas gift for you." He pulled from his pocket a small box and encouraged me to open it. I pulled at the long silk ribbon and opened the paper as carefully as it seemed to have been wrapped. Inside was a silver bracelet with an anchor charm.

So I hadn't merely been a substitute for a shoe exporter.

"Your mother saw that in a store on Lord Street, and she thought it might be a way to show you that if working was your little rebellion against the other plans she might have had for you, then you have her forgiveness and her blessing to come work with me at the docks and learn more about the shipping business." He leaned in. "We have been talking, Julianne, about your little stunt. Perhaps we were harsh in taking it so seriously and not realizing that you had got caught up the way young people do when they try to rebel and make their own way. We thought that perhaps by now you would have realized that your marriage was a mistake, and we are prepared to bring you back home if you would like."

I breathed deeply in and out, holding back the things I wanted to say. I tried to find it in my heart to pity that woman, but years of resentment interfered.

He continued. "It's not too late. It's not as if there's a baby in all of this mess or anything that will hold you back from just making a clean break of it."

I stood up. "If this is going to be the nature of this conversation, then I think that I will go home. Everything I said in August is still true today. Kyle is my husband. We are happy. I am not coming back to Liverpool unless we are both welcome."

"Sit back down, Julianne."

The little girl in me, the one who once crawled on his lap so he could sneak a peppermint to me before dinner, obeyed.

"Look. Let's put this talk of your marriage to that Catholic boy aside for a minute. I'm convinced you'll see our way of thinking before long, so I'm not going to bother over that. But the truth is, you need to know that London is not going to be a safe place to live in for much longer. You keep up with the reports from Germany, I assume?"

"Of course I do. It's all anyone talks about. In fact, the hospital is preparing us for an influx of Jewish children over the next few weeks. Most of them are the only ones in their family to have survived, and we may need to take some of them in, depending on what their health conditions are."

"Yes, I've heard about that. Ten thousand over the next few months. The Liverpool Ladies' Society is working to find homes to place them in up north. See, you could continue that work back at home."

"I understand what you are both trying to do, and that you think this is helping. I appreciate that. But this is home. Kyle is home. I have no plans to return to Liverpool."

"Well, then, I don't see that we have anything to talk about." He called the waiter over and pulled out a wad of notes. "Please package up the food we ordered and send it with this young lady. I have been called away."

He placed a few more notes in front of me and stood up. "Have your fun while it lasts, Julianne. We'll see you when things have changed." I didn't turn around as he left, just stared at the ten pounds he had left for me. On principle, I wanted to leave them there. Maybe give the waiter the best Christmas of his life. But if that money would allow Kyle to work fewer hours, then I could swallow my pride and take it. I waited for the waiter to bring the food and carried it all home.

While I had originally chosen to work at the hospital on Christmas Day, the money from my father allowed me to give the higher-paying shift to another nurse. Kyle and I chose to spend our first Christmas together at midnight Mass, and it seemed fitting to go to Immaculate Heart of Mary. We learned from the cabbie we'd hired to take us that it was more commonly referred to as the Brompton Oratory. The cab ride itself was a splurge, but the thought of riding the Tube so late at night was a little frightening.

When we got home, we huddled next to our little tree, with the window candles casting flickering light into the darkness.

"Happy Christmas, Julianne."

"Happy Christmas, Kyle."

We brushed our lips together lightly and laughed as our cold noses touched.

"Here, I have a present for you." Kyle handed a package to me. It felt like a book, and was, in fact, *Rebecca*, by Daphne du Maurier.

"Oh, thank you! I've heard of this one and I've been dying to read it." I threw my arms around his neck.

"I went to W. H. Smith, and they told me that this one is all the rage right now."

"It is." I opened it up to read the first pages. "'Last night I dreamt I went to Manderley again . . .'" I snapped the cover shut. "I can't start now. I'll never want to stop. And, besides, I have to give you your present."

"OK, I'm ready."

"I'll give you a hint. It's small."

"Um, a pocket watch?"

"Smaller."

"A money clip."

"Smaller. Think tiny. Infinitesimal."

He was silent. I grabbed his hand and put it on my belly.

"Kyle, we're having a baby!"

❧

It was at this time that I mourned the relationship with my mother more than any other. How comforting it would have been to have someone besides a doctor tell me what to expect. The midwifery courses I'd been taking dealt more with the birthing process than with everything leading up to it. Kyle did everything he could to tend to my needs—cravings, nausea, fatigue—but as wonderful as he was, a girl just needs a girl. I was eager to share the news and complain about the misery with Dorothy and Abigail, but no one could know before Lucille.

For weeks, I tried to reach her, but between my party line and hers, my schedule and hers, I was beginning to think that my child would graduate from primary school before I got to share the news with her. We kept in touch with letters, of course, where I learned that she and Ben had set their wedding date for 10 June, and she had started classes to become a teacher. But I longed to hear her voice.

At last, the miracle happened, and the operator passed me through to a free line at Lucille's house. Her squeals at my news must have deafened any busybodies who might've been listening in on the party line.

"I'm going to be an aunt! Well, kind of. But still! I can hardly believe it. Kyle must be so excited."

"Oh, he is. Probably more than I am, I think! He's already getting to work carving pieces for a cradle, and it's not looking half-bad. In between rubbing my feet and fetching crazy things for me, you know."

"Golly, you picked a good one, Jul."

"I know it, Lucille. I just wish my parents could see that."

"No improvement on that front, huh?"

"No. My father came down in December, and they did send me a Christmas card. But it was only addressed to me. I just can't reconcile with them until they accept Kyle as my husband."

"Well, don't you think they'll have to with a baby on the way?"

"One would hope, right? But I'm just not sure what to expect."

"When are you going to tell them?"

"Well, this might sound silly, but I thought I'd come up for your wedding in June and tell them then."

"Won't you be just huge by then? Are you sure you want to wait that long?"

I paused for a minute to breathe through a cramp, one of many I'd been experiencing lately.

"Jul? Are you there?"

"Yes," I answered, rubbing my abdomen. "Whew. It's tough growing a little one."

"I can't imagine. Although, I hope to be in your shoes someday. Maybe sooner than later."

"Lucille!"

"Ha! That's not what I meant. Funny girl. No, I just mean that after Chamberlain's speech the other day, we seem closer to entering this war than we've ever been. Ben's certain that we're going to enter the war and he's going to be called up. So we've been talking about moving up the wedding. In fact, it's going to be in April, just a few weeks from now."

"April? Oh, Lucille, I can't make it to Liverpool then. I'll still have classes and I'm supposed to attend the opening of a hotel with Kyle. His landscaping team designed the grounds of a place out in Kensington."

Camille Di Maio

"I figured as much. I never imagined that we wouldn't be there for each other's wedding days. But that's the way things work out sometimes, I suppose. Drat! There I go again. Ben's been telling me I'm too gloomy over the war stuff. Boys, right? So. There must be twenty thousand other things to talk about. Go!"

We distracted each other with titbits. Miss Ellis and I corresponded regularly, and Charles was the same as ever. Abigail and Roger had got engaged. I'd learned to make cinnamon rolls, and Kyle loved the drops of lemon juice that I'd add to the icing to make it tart. Lucille told me that Blythe had taken the bookkeeping job at my father's docks when Mavis retired.

Another cramp rolled through my belly, and I told Lucille reluctantly that I had to get back to studying. What I didn't tell her was that the pain was so bad that I needed to lie down. I didn't want her to worry needlessly nor hear the fear in my voice.

Chapter
Twenty-Two

Sadly, it was the day after Kyle finished the beautiful cradle that I started bleeding.

I had been told that a little spotting wasn't unusual, but it became heavier and wouldn't stop. Kyle insisted that we go to the hospital. Although it was a familiar setting to me, it was unnerving to be on the other side of things. To have a stranger tell me the worst news that a woman would ever want to hear. To arrive as a family and leave as a couple.

When we returned home, I didn't leave my bed for two weeks. Physically, I felt fine, but as the shock wore off and the grief set in, it just overwhelmed me and I could barely breathe. It surprised me that I could ache like this for someone whom I had not known. Cries rose up inside me, but wouldn't escape. I even wondered, more than once, if the penalty for having married Kyle had finally come due. But I kept that particular thought to myself out of fear that the account might not yet be settled.

Kyle came home every evening, made my dinner, and helped me change into fresh pajamas because I had not changed from those of the previous night. I caught him looking at me with worried glances when he thought that I was asleep, and it broke my heart to think that I was hurting him. I knew that I had to let him in, but I didn't know how. It was as if I was at the bottom of a dark well, struggling to get out but without a rope to climb with.

Lucille begged to come down and take care of me, but I refused to see her. She was about to be a bride, the happiest time in a girl's life. If I had brought this retribution upon myself, especially for something she had warned me against, I couldn't bear to bring her down into it.

I found out later that Kyle corresponded with my friends and professors, keeping them apprised of my condition. In hindsight, I don't know how he managed to pay the bills without my income.

He slept on the sofa, thinking that I wanted to be alone. But he *didn't* want to be alone. In the third week, he came to our bed hesitantly, gently pulled the quilts up, and crawled in behind me. The warmth of his body flooded me. Having him next to me filled the void more than I would have expected. I pulled his arm around me tighter and wailed. Turning to look at his face, I saw that his eyes, too, were red and impossibly weary. He took my hand, pressed his lips to it, and closed his eyes tightly. Saying nothing, we lay there all night.

We fell asleep just before dawn and woke up in the late morning. The sun had forced its way inside, inviting us to rediscover the world that was awaiting us. Kyle got out of bed first, and he pulled out a soft pink blouse and pleated white skirt for me to wear for the day. I looked at the clothes as if they were brand-new. While he made breakfast, I showered, feeling the water wash away the hurting inside me. He had thrown me a rope in that well, and as I climbed, I saw light in the distance. It was the beginning of feeling normal again.

On a chilly March morning Kyle walked in with bags in his arms and frost on his cap. "I've come back from the market, Julianne," he called. He set them down on the table and rubbed his hands together.

"Did you bring the headache pills?"

"Yes, and some chicken and carrots for dinner."

"Sounds grand. I'll help."

"Nope," he said, as he came and kissed me on the head. "I have another project for you."

I eyed him with suspicion. "You've got something up your sleeve, Kyle McCarthy."

"I do, and I don't think you're going to like it."

"What kind of surprise is that?"

"It's not a surprise. It's a task I have for you."

He came around to sit with me on the couch. "I brought you some writing paper. I want you to write to your mother."

"I'm sorry, did I lose my hearing these past few months? Did you say that you want me to write to my mother?"

"Think about it, Jul." He held my hand. "There will never be a better time to reconcile with her. Whatever you can say about her, she did bring you into the world, and you can see yourself now that it's no easy task. You don't have to tell her anything about the baby. But maybe you can find a few nice words to say. After all, Mothering Sunday is coming up next week."

I sat quietly for a moment. "I know you're right. It's one of the things that would have made you a great priest, Kyle. You won't let anything stand in the way of family and forgiveness. But I just don't have the words."

"I thought of that, too, just in case. Look." He pulled a card and an envelope from the bag. Its lithographic print depicted a floral scene, and the interior had a benign message that could have been sent to nearly anyone. "Someone already wrote the words for you. You can just sign it, *Love, Julianne*, and I'll post it for you."

"*Love, Julianne?* This is Beatrice Westcott we're talking about."

"How about *Affectionately, Julianne?*"

"How about *Warmest regards?*"

"We have a winner! I'll bring you a pen."

Kyle posted it as he'd promised, and I marveled once again at this man that I married. He had been dismissed, ignored by my parents. They had tried to bribe me out of my marriage to him. And still he sought to create a truce to our estrangement.

For whatever it was worth, his plan worked. I received a birthday card from my parents signed by each of them and containing another ten-pound banknote. Kyle was not mentioned, of course, and my instinct was to consider it nothing more than another attempt to lure me home. As if they were showing how easily I could have all the things they thought I wanted. But I decided to follow Kyle's lead and assume the best of them.

As I continued to emerge from the fog and return to routine, I looked at everything with new eyes. I was not the same person that I was before, and I felt like a more grown-up version of myself. It was easier to be gay and lively when the realities of life hadn't set in yet. In just a year, I had gone from a girl who pined over love, danced at every opportunity, and shopped at all the best stores, to a wife, a mother of a lost child, and a citizen of a country on the precipice of war. Leaflets prepared us for rationing, recruitment for air wardens had begun among civilians, and an engineer came to our building to assess its potential for a basement shelter. One had no choice but to grow up.

Oddly, I didn't miss my former self. She felt like a shell that was now being filled with memories and experiences. We already had so much to look back on and treasure, with even more to come. But I discovered that even painful experiences could help fill the shell. I had been a girl last year, and now I was a woman. That didn't come without some bruises.

We felt the grief through the beginning of the summer, and we coped together by taking walks in the evening and going out on the weekends. Kyle treated me like I was a porcelain doll capable of breaking at any moment. Sometimes it irritated me, but I knew that he was just concerned for my well-being. It occurred to me what a wonderful and understanding priest he would have been, and I felt more than a little guilty for taking him from that. I voiced that once, and never again, when I saw how vehemently he stated that he was exactly where he wanted to be.

Gradually, as the weeks went on, it became easier to be at home, and I no longer spent *every* moment recalling that there was someone missing.

The whole experience left me thankful that I had chosen nursing and caused me to reflect on how I could empathize with other women in the future. I had made the decision months earlier to follow the midwifery course, and I was especially glad now. It seemed as if it would be painful to deliver babies after the loss of my own, but I knew that there would be women coming in just like me, and they would need my support just as I had received it.

Besides, I was confident that one day Kyle and I would successfully bring a child into the world and I could share that experience with my patients, too.

The end of the summer also brought our first anniversary, and it was a welcome celebration. We spent the evening on a dinner boat that cruised up the Thames and back for a couple of hours. There was music, mostly slow, and we swayed while holding one another. I didn't know how I could possibly love him any more than I did at that moment.

I thought that the dinner *was* our anniversary gift, but Kyle told me that he had something else planned, something that I couldn't have for another week or so. When I pleaded with him to tell me, he looked at me with the laughing eyes that I had missed for the past couple of months. Tapping my nose with his fingertip, he told me that I would have to wait, and that there was nothing that could be done about it.

I busied myself in these last days before school started by freshening up the paint in the flat, thoroughly scrubbing every surface, and having hot meals prepared when Kyle came home from work. I was eager to slip back into normalcy.

One evening I decided to surprise Kyle with cinnamon rolls. It was my first batch since the miscarriage and the last that I could make before classes. I wanted to show him my appreciation for all that he had done for me over those troubled months.

Concentrating on a measurement, I didn't hear him come in, so I squealed in shock when I felt him put his arms around my waist.

"Hello, gorgeous," he said into my ear, nibbling the tip just a bit. Despite the doctor's orders being lifted weeks before, Kyle was still reluctant to make love to me for fear of hurting me, and that absence made me especially sensitive to his touch.

"Hello, yourself," I said, turning around and kissing him quickly on the lips.

He laughed at me and brushed my cheek with his finger, where I had apparently splattered myself with icing sugar. I put my hand to my cheek, only to leave a dollop of dough where the sugar had been. Mortified, I turned back to face my bowl and gently scolded Kyle for ruining my surprise.

Turning me back around, gently but firmly, he reached behind me and scooped up some icing onto his finger. Tracing my lips with it, he proceeded to taste the icing slowly, repeating the step again. This time, I kissed him back steadily, eager to connect with him again in every way. I think that I surprised him with my enthusiasm, and he pulled back briefly to ask if I was all right with this. I set my wooden spoon on the counter and put my hands behind me to untie my apron.

Kyle stopped me and put his own arms around me to untie the strings. He lifted the apron over my head, and then my blouse. He leaned in to kiss my cheek, my jaw, my neck, less careful now with his porcelain doll.

We didn't even make it to the bedroom.

❧

I don't know what time I woke up, but I was in our bed and it was still dark outside. Kyle was asleep next to me, and he stirred when I moved. Reaching over me to turn on the lamp, I smiled with utter contentment and ran my hand down his arm.

"Good morning," he murmured, eyes blinking as he adjusted to the light.

"Good morning." I stretched and felt that every nerve had been reawakened from a dormant sleep.

We turned on our sides, facing each other, and he drew little circles on my hand with his finger.

"Are you ready for your present?" he asked.

"My present? Didn't you give that to me last night?"

"Mmm, you can have *that* present today, tomorrow, and anytime that you want."

"Then can today be my birthday?"

"You're skipping holidays. You still have to go through Christmas, Boxing Day, New Year's Day . . ."

"OK, stop it. Just tell me what you're talking about."

"Our anniversary present. I *was* going to give it to you last night, but you made me forget all about it."

I leaned up on my elbow. "Well, I'll be certain *not* to let you forget if you don't tell me what it is!"

"Ouch! Blackmail! You win. Here you go."

He handed me a plain white envelope. I opened it and found tickets to *The Dancing Years* at the Theatre Royal on Drury Lane for the next day.

"Kyle! You remembered! How did you get tickets? They're impossible to get now that the show is closing for the war!"

"I had a little help from Abigail's father. He knows everyone, apparently, even theater managers."

"Yes, he does, doesn't he? Oh, I don't care *how* you got them. I'm just so excited!"

Kyle had arranged to take the day off, the first in as long as I could remember. We got up for breakfast and went back to bed, but not in order to sleep.

The tickets were for a matinee. There was a time not long ago when it would have thrilled me to be able to say that I was seeing such a popular show. But such empty thrills were behind me now. In their place was the joy of being married and of being loved.

⁓⁂⁓

I learned quickly that I needed to hold on to that joy with all my might. Not only had my own private world changed, but the world at large was about to look very different.

On 3 September, Britain declared war on Germany.

What had seemed inevitable was now definite.

The announcement was not sudden. For weeks leading up to it, London had started to make noticeable preparations, and the late-morning radio speech by the prime minister only made it official. Just ten minutes later, the air-raid sirens started. The pitch of the sirens rose and fell in step with our anticipation. They were only for practice, but they were nonetheless chilling—a prelude to what was likely going to be a devastating reality. I pulled out the gas mask that I had bought last year. I'd got out of the habit of carrying it but would start doing so again. Kyle received one at his office. We kept them by the front door so that we could bring them with us whenever we went out. The cheap cardboard boxes that they came in reminded me of the frailty of this new existence.

The evenings brought blackouts. At first, we used blankets to cover the windows and listened to the radio by candlelight. Later, specific blackout material was made available at two shillings a yard. Some people were cautious about even lighting a match. As I saw children leave on trains to stay with faraway relatives, I felt the heartbreak of the mothers who were losing their children. Was it more difficult to have never known my child or to send a beloved one into the large world with its uncertain future? I didn't think that there was a difference. Surely, any separation was agonizing.

It was easy to spot the mothers who had sent their children off. They had a listless look in their eyes, and their existence was fixated around the telegrams with updates of the whereabouts of their sons and daughters.

London was visibly, strikingly different. The pavements were painted white so that cars could avoid them during the blackout. The ground was filled with sandbags, hoisted against buildings, the most important of them fortified first. The air was dotted with barrage balloons to thwart enemy planes. Our area in Lambeth was particularly secured due to its proximity to Waterloo station, and the tunnel behind our flat was routinely checked for explosives. Airplanes carrying bombs and troops flew overhead constantly, and we listened with acute attention to updates on the radio telling us where they were heading. More than once, I wondered if Lucille's Ben was aboard one, as his training was now being called into use.

Many people heeded the call of the government to evacuate London. Two-way roads were now running one direction as people fled to the countryside.

We considered leaving, too, maybe to Liverpool, but the school remained open and nursing had never seemed more vital. I found myself clinging to my studies even more determinedly, both as a distraction and necessity. Kyle's office was quickly shut down, as no one was hiring landscapers when it was unknown what the landscape might look like from one day to the next. But he had no trouble finding odd jobs, since so many people had left the city. One week he might be delivering milk, and another week he might be stacking sandbags. He never complained of more than a sore back.

I delighted in the role reversal of taking care of him after my period of convalescence. In the evenings I would rub his neck and shoulders, pressing my thumbs deeply into the tight spots. He groaned when I would find an especially tender spot, and I lightened my touch into no more than a caress.

I studied by day and worked some nights in the hospital. We were too tired to cook as we once had, eating out of necessity more than enjoyment. This became a reality for everyone in the early part of the new year, as food became rationed. At first, it was meat, butter, and sugar. Even paper was rationed. We coped with blandness and savored Sundays, when we allowed ourselves the use of the majority of our coupons. What wasn't rationed was still scarce, and what wasn't scarce lacked variety. Fruit and fish and bread and such were limited to what-ever could be imported into the city. The queues to purchase even those things sometimes took over an hour. Most people were impatient with this, but I always made sure to bring a book. I avoided all of those murder mysteries that Lucille so loved. There was enough talk about death around us as it was.

As a treat, we would sometimes eat at a Corner House since res-taurants were considered off ration. The atmosphere there was one of escape, as people from across the social spectrum could gather and imagine that life was, for an evening, what it had once been.

Mother and I communicated more regularly now, keeping details newsy and impersonal for the time being. She never inquired about Kyle, and I never told her about the baby we almost had. It was a tenuous start, but one for which I was grateful. I just wish she had known that it was Kyle who was encouraging the mending of our relationship.

The draft continued to call young men to service. I could see that my husband was impatient to trudge off to the continent and serve his adopted country. But I knew he also felt reluctant to leave me, whom he still viewed as delicate, just months after the strenuous summer. I didn't want him to go, rationalizing that if the country needed him, he would get the summons.

The sinking of the British vessel HMS *Exmouth*, and the subsequent death of its crew of 175 men, had a strong effect on him, though. He became more focused than ever on joining the war effort, and I gave in to his desire to enlist. It was only a matter of time, anyway, and who was I to keep my husband from the war when so many others had already gone?

His draft papers arrived by post just an hour after he left for the recruiting office.

Kyle passed the physical exam and was assigned to the Seventh Armoured Division. He was set to leave for training soon and was expected to be sent to the front lines in Egypt.

Egypt. I used to think that Durham was a world away, when I was aching for a love that I couldn't have. Now I had my love, and I was sending him off to a faraway desert, farther away than I could comprehend. He was enthusiastic about it, albeit restrained for my sake. As was his habit, he drew an analogy to his faith. Like the flight of Joseph and Mary into Egypt to protect their son, he saw this as a providential journey to protect us all from evil.

We spent our last two weeks pretending as if there was no war, that life was grand, that there were no cares. Spending some of our carefully earned savings, we went to the cinema several times. The cares of the outside would be remote for an hour or two. *Pinocchio* was released, and Kyle saw it with me two days in a row. We dined at restaurants, affordable ones, and made love in the evenings as if there were no tomorrow. Because there might not be one.

Kyle was due to meet his unit at 7:00 a.m. on the morning of 23 March. I woke up a few hours earlier after a night of restless dreams filled with obscure scenes that frightened me. Kyle slept peacefully, the man on a mission. I turned around to face him and scooted in so close that our bodies were indistinguishable. I framed his face with my hands as if to burn the image in my head. He smiled without opening his eyes and said, "Good morning, gorgeous," like he did every day. It never sounded rote, though. How long would it be before I would hear those words again?

I whispered desperately, "Don't go," even as I knew there wasn't a choice.

He pressed my palm to his lips and said, "I must."

We lay there without talking, a million things racing through my mind while *his* still seemed peaceful. I wished that I could feel as confident as he did, but I felt instead as if my world was crumbling. Again.

One question came to mind more strongly than anything else. Something that I had never asked, but had always wondered: What if this was my only chance?

"Kyle?"

"Hmm?"

"Why did you fall in love with me?"

It's funny that I had never asked. Maybe it was because I was afraid of the answer. To me, Kyle was hardworking, funny, handsome, tender, so many other things. In his shadow, I felt like something pretty to look at, with some respectable characteristics, but not much more. Here he was, bravely heading off to war, and I was cowering in the corner like a mouse. I wished for the first time that he had not become a British citizen so many years ago; otherwise, he could have fled to Ireland, which had remained neutral. He once had in front of him the venerable life of a man of God. As a seminarian, he would have been exempt from military service. Now, married to me, he suffered through odd jobs and had to put his life on the line. Why was I worth it? I couldn't see it, and if I knew nothing else before he left, I had to know this.

His eyes opened fully, and he looked at me incredulously. "You really don't know?"

"No. Tell me."

Leaning up on his elbow, he smiled at me as if I were a child about to hear a story. How I was going to miss that smile.

"Do you remember years ago when you had your birthday party outside?"

"Yes. That was my sixteenth. How did you know about that?"

"Well, apparently, it was a big ordeal for your mother, because she brought on extra help. She had a different gardener then, but he brought in Dadaí to help manage all the work. I was about to graduate, so he needed me to start helping him. I had a lot of studying to do that weekend, and I'll admit that I wasn't in the best of moods about coming out. But then I saw you."

"I was wearing green chiffon that day. I loved that dress."

"You weren't wearing that yet when I saw you. You were out early, taking a walk near the garden. You were lost in thought, twirling a curl in your finger and biting your lip the way that you always do."

"I don't remember that."

"I do. It's very vivid to me. You didn't look like a girl about to celebrate her birthday. You looked like you were . . . uncertain. And a little nervous."

"Oh, I remember feeling that. I *was* a little nervous. Mother saw it as a coming-out party of sorts, a precursor to being a debutante, and she had invited so many people that I didn't even know. I wanted to be sure that I was going to say and do the right things."

"That's what I mean. You looked very vulnerable, and I wanted to protect you from whatever was making you sad. But of course I couldn't. Then you came out a few hours later, looking like a vision, the most beautiful thing I'd ever seen. You were immediately surrounded by hordes of people, and I knew that it was hopeless to wish that you would ever notice me."

"Kyle, I had no idea."

"Well, you're all mine now, aren't you?"

"Forever."

Kyle rolled onto his back, looking at the ceiling. "That's not all, you know. I'd see your parents in the newspaper sometimes. And once or twice there was a picture of you with them. When I saw you again at Bootle Home, I knew exactly who you were. You took my breath away when you entered the room."

"You acted as if you'd never met me. Why didn't you say something?"

"Like what? 'Hello, Miss Westcott. You don't know me, but I remember seeing you years ago and I've never got you out of my mind'?"

"I would rather have liked that."

He turned back to face me and put his arm around my waist. "I couldn't have known that. I didn't exactly seem like the type you'd go for."

"Do I really have a type?"

"Think about it. Beautiful socialite girls don't fancy immigrant seminarians. And in the newspaper pictures, you were always in the middle of a group of other people."

"Well, I suppose you're right."

"But still, I got to see that under all those curls and cosmetics, and inside those fancy shoes of yours, there was a girl who was softhearted enough to come see her brother and to befriend the secretary."

"Miss Ellis?"

"Of course. You know, she was not too subtle about finding one reason or another to bring up your name around me. I rather think she saw herself as some kind of matchmaker."

"And you still didn't do anything about it? I was feeling guilty because my reasons for visiting Bootle soon had more to do with seeing you than visiting Charles."

"Well, no one ever said that men aren't thickheaded. Besides, I saw you more and more in the society pages, and then the crazy bidding war broke out at the auction. Not to mention, I had my own path set and there wasn't any room for a woman in it."

"So what changed your mind?"

"The fact that I couldn't stop thinking about you, for starters. The fact that I kept one of the clippings with your photograph and told one of the other seminarians that you were my cousin when it slipped out of my notebook. The fact that when we were stranded in that barn, it took every ounce of willpower not to come over and kiss you right there. And then, when you spent those weeks with Dadaí, I realized that my heart might actually break in two if I couldn't be with you. That's when I really loved you."

"Why did you never tell me this before?"

"I guess I thought that you would already know."

"Well, I suppose I had the notion when you brought me to the gazebo."

"You mean where I did this?"

And he leaned over to kiss my neck, re-creating the moment when I knew he loved me and not stopping this time. Every touch, every kiss burned on me so intensely that I knew I would never forget this moment.

After that, he got up to shower and came out wearing his uniform. My heart leapt at seeing this man, my man, looking so suited for the role of soldier and protector. I knew then that he was going where he needed to be and that my time with him was only stolen anyway. We had agreed to say good-bye here, because going to the train station set a tone of finality that I didn't want to accept. Seeing him now made me consider changing my mind, but I think it was better this way. Except for the uniform, it was easy to imagine that he was just leaving for work and that I would see him tonight.

At least, that was what I tried to convince myself of.

Chapter
Twenty-Three

Misery loves company, they say, and if the war had brought about misery, it had also created a company of friendships that were forged through common suffering.

One afternoon while walking to the hospital, I came upon a wrenching scene that I had witnessed far too many times. What must have been forty children were in the process of boarding a bus. They all carried satchels or suitcases, wore their coats buttoned, and had the boxes carrying their gas masks hung by a string around their necks. Cardboard name tags were clipped to their clothes. They looked like miniature adults getting on the bus for work. But, in reality, they were leaving for places far away, where the lucky few would be housed with family and the rest with strangers.

Mothers surrounded them, giving them cheery good-byes and telling them how much fun they would have. The littlest ones cried and clutched their teddy bears as their mothers walked them up the steps.

After the bus drove off and the last waving child could no longer be seen, the forced smiles of the women faded. They clung to each other in tears. Leaning against a green metal lamppost, one woman crumbled into a sobbing heap as another held and rocked her.

It was a scene that was being repeated almost daily as tens of thousands of children left for reception zones throughout the country. I watched each time and never became numb to the horror of it. I imagined the complexities of moving so many children across the country and keeping track of them. I thought about the nightmares they might have and how their mothers weren't there to comfort them. How great the danger had to be if sending your child across such a vast uncertainty was the better choice. Every day I grew a sense of appreciation that my own child had left this world before knowing this particular misery.

Two women in my building had husbands who were away fighting as well, and we formed a dinner club where we combined our ever-decreasing rations and came up with creative ways to make them palatable. I was eager to learn, as I had not yet perfected the art of cooking that they had learned by their mothers' sides. And it served the higher purpose of trying to distract me from my constant worry for Kyle's safety. But there was no occupation that could eliminate even a moment of the anguish I felt over his absence.

Mary Margaret's husband was in France, as far as she knew, and Pamela's was heading to Italy. Both had sent children to Salisbury.

Dorothy joined us one evening and brought a baked vegetable hash that she'd made from carrots and ground potatoes after her meat ration ran out. She bemoaned how bland it was.

"I know what can fix that," said Mary Margaret. "A green pepper. I have one downstairs that I can send home with you."

"You're not going to use it?"

"I can't stand them myself, but I take whatever I can get when I'm at the store."

Mary Margaret was the only Catholic among us, and it occurred to me that if some good were to come out of this war, perhaps it would be the reconciliation between the two faiths that had feuded over disputes dating back centuries before any of us were born.

Dorothy remained after they had left, and I showed her something I had stashed away.

"A bottle of red wine? Wherever did you get that, Julianne?"

"My father was in town a couple of weeks ago for some government meeting, and he brought it to me. I thought I'd save it for a special occasion."

"This is a special occasion?"

"I think every day that we're alive is something to celebrate right now, don't you think?"

"Cheers to that."

I poured the wine into some juice glasses and we clinked them together, then drank deeply, welcoming the temporary dulling of our circumstances.

"Cheers to your father," Dorothy said, and we drank again. "Did your mother come down, too?"

"No, but she never accompanies him on business trips, so there was nothing unusual there. She and I write now and then. Nothing more than a few words about what we're each doing, and she still never mentions Kyle and addresses everything to *Julianne Westcott*. But in the spirit of Kyle, and all that he's away fighting for, I suppose that I can raise a glass to her good health."

"Cheers to your mother!"

"Cheers!"

It was nice getting together like this with Dorothy outside of class. We were both worn to the bone, as senior nurses had moved to military hospitals, and student nurses had taken on extra responsibilities. Abigail had married Roger and left the school to be the wife of a politician. They'd moved to Mayfair, near the new American Embassy on

Grosvenor Square, surrounded by the kinds of posh shops and restaurants that my mother liked to visit. Despite the best of intentions, we didn't get together as we'd promised.

Routine became the glue that kept one's sanity intact when so much around us was uncertain. It had become a habit to strap my gas mask case around my neck after putting on my shoes and buttoning my coat. It felt silly to wear it, day after day, but the government warned that the need for them could come at any moment. Before he left, Kyle made me promise to comply with every recommended precaution. I never missed Sunday Mass, although I still sat in the back and didn't participate when the congregation went up for Communion. The gestures and the postures were familiar to me now, and any regulars who might've noticed me would have thought me quite devoted. In truth, I was there because it was where I most felt Kyle's presence. Every moment of the day, and even in the restless nights where his side of the bed felt so desolate, I worried. But at Mass, a peace descended on me that was like the inhalation of air after drowning for so long.

Lucille and I wrote frequently, updating each other on what we knew of the whereabouts of Ben and Kyle, although our information was often a month outdated. Both spoke of missing us, but between the lines, we could see that they were enjoying their work. To the best of our knowledge, neither had seen heavy combat yet. We suspected that they weren't telling us everything, though. Ben was a radio operator away from the front lines. Kyle was an artillery loader in a tank somewhere between the Egyptian–Libyan border. I knew that he had something to do with the capture of some Italian prisoners of war, but few other details. Most of his letters were devoted to inquiring about me.

We often received each other's letters out of sequence, as they took weeks to arrive.

Kyle had been gone for ten weeks when I noticed the familiar signs of impending motherhood. When the doctor confirmed what I suspected, I did not feel the elation that I had the first time around. For one thing, my husband was not there to share it with me. I feared another miscarriage, and I was reluctant to bond with this baby in the way that I had with the first one. And again, the nausea overwhelmed me.

It was impossible, too, to feel excitement for your child when the children of all of your friends were countless miles away, leaving their mothers with broken hearts. In its place was only fear for the future of my child and uncertainty of its father ever returning.

Dorothy and I graduated from school with little fanfare, although Abigail and Roger did come out to celebrate by taking us to eat at one of the few upscale restaurants that were still in operation. My parents had actually considered coming down, but I begged them not to and accepted their note of congratulations. They would notice my drawn look and worry about me, and I was not prepared to tell them about the pregnancy. Mother's letters were increasingly warmer now that Kyle was gone. I wondered if Father ever told her of our conversation about Charles. I imagined not.

As the middle of the summer approached, I was feeling better and was beginning to believe that I might not lose this one. Every day that passed was a little victory. I finally told Lucille about the baby. My friends in London now knew, as it was becoming obvious by my tiny, rounded belly. I was showered with secondhand maternity clothes that Mary Margaret and Pamela had kept. Gone were the days of frivolous attire—another of the changes that had taken place in me in only a few years.

Kyle's letters were sporadic, still full of love and adulation, but I could also see that he was keeping difficult information from me. He gave me very few details about his duties, but he did say that the African heat in the summer was brutal and he would give anything to have a rainy English day in bed with me. I couldn't have agreed more.

I didn't tell Kyle about the baby. Although I was further along and the pregnancy was going well, I didn't want to worry him. I wanted him to be sharp and focused so that he would return to me safe and alive. Instead, my letters were full of news about dinners with my neighbors and stories from the hospital. Always light, always loving.

July and August brought news of increased Luftwaffe attacks against the RAF airfields, but the pounding did not break the resolve of England. So in early September the Führer turned his fury onto the citizens, beginning a relentless barrage of bombings on London and other cities.

The first time I heard one, it was as if fire had ripped through the sky. It was followed by another and another, the crashing sounds disorienting me. I didn't know if the building next to me or one a mile away was destroyed. I threw on my robe without tying it, left my feet bare, and felt my way through the dark to the cold, concrete stairs that led to the basement. Other residents did the same, and we stumbled faceless, nameless, scrambling to get to some semblance of safety. Even in that space, lights were discouraged, and it was only the glow of nearby bombs and raging fire that occasionally lit the tiny windows. In those flashes, I saw women and children clinging to one another, with looks of horror frozen on their faces.

For fifty-seven straight days, the nighttime sky was lit with the explosions, and the remaining citizens in London spent the overnight hours in shelters. I took to spending many nights at the hospital, where we had a downstairs area that doubled as a shelter. Many people slept in the underground stations. Our flat was never destroyed, but it did receive damage from shrapnel. Just one block away, the street no longer existed.

The bombs did not discriminate, and people across the spectrum were affected. Some buildings had chunks taken out as if cavities had rotted them away, while others had been reduced to unrecognizable rubble. The sound of a building being flattened sounded like a large crunch, and with the high and low sirens, the yelling of firemen, and the crackling of citywide fires, it formed a monstrous symphony. Sometimes, the baby kicked in response to the noise.

It was bewildering to see the everyday aspects of life go on amidst such a ravaged landscape. To see the milkman stepping over piles of debris to bring deliveries to the residences that still stood. To walk a path I'd walked just the day before, only to come upon a hole so deep that it seemed I could see down into the center of the earth. Perhaps the most unnerving sights were the few children that remained in the city, prancing among this new concrete playground and making toys out of the scraps of someone's former life. How I wished I were a child and could find joy among such agony. I thought, too, of Charles, with something akin to envy. How lonely it must be to live in darkened nothingness, and yet it served to shield him from the threats that everyday living now brought.

My midwifery skills were barely called into duty, but my other nursing skills were tested mightily. The role I had once envisioned for myself—administering injections, checking vitals, comforting patients—was a distant fantasy. We were called on to hold entrails as doctors desperately tried to stitch up patients. Or restrain a person as his leg was being amputated. The floors became caked with blood, scissors and instruments were passed from surgeon to surgeon with no time for disinfection. Screams for the limited supply of pain medication haunted what little sleep we stole. Our charges were civilians and soldiers alike. I liked tending to the soldiers. It made me feel as if I was helping Kyle. I held their hands, listened to their stories, and all too often became the last voice they ever heard.

By mid-November, I was receiving frequent implorations from my parents and Lucille to leave London, and out of consideration for the baby I realized, finally, that I had no choice. Liverpool had already faced its own share of devastation, but at least I would no longer be alone. I made plans to arrive by train on the twenty-eighth. I intended to visit with Lucille first and my parents the following day. I needed my best friend to give me the strength to see my mother for the first time since I'd eloped. I was hesitant to find out what their reaction to my pregnancy would be. Would it be the salve that would soften them to my decision? Would they become doting grandparents? Or would they see the baby as the nail in the coffin of their hopes that I would leave Kyle?

Saying good-byes to the good friends I'd made, we hugged, not knowing if we would ever see each other again. The face of London was never going to look the same, and we didn't know how many of us it would take with it.

I arrived on a late-afternoon train and squealed at the sight of Lucille. It had been so long since we had seen each other, and letters just didn't make up for that. Holding each other for what seemed like forever, I felt like we were twelve years old again.

We arrived at her flat, where she immediately set out some tea and sandwiches.

"Julianne, if it is possible, you look even more beautiful now that you're going to have a baby."

"You need eyeglasses, I'm afraid. I feel like a bloated whale about to burst. I have three weeks left, and I don't know how I'm going to make it."

"Oh, you will, darling. And I'm going to be here to help."

I smiled at her. Besides Kyle, there was no one else that I wanted to share this with more.

"Jul, you haven't told your parents yet, have you?"

"No. I've come so close—started a letter, picked up the telephone. But I kept putting it off, not knowing how they would react." I looked down at my bulbous belly. "I guess there's no hiding it now!"

Lucille giggled. "No, there's not. You *are* quite round!"

I threw a tea towel at her.

It was so good to laugh and to feel carefree again, even if only for a moment.

We reminisced over some strawberries that she'd bartered for and made plans to see *My Favorite Wife*, the new Cary Grant movie about a wife who disappears for many years. We caught up on local news and gossip. John and Maude's baby boy was now two years old, and Lucille loved going over to help. Maude was pregnant again and very excited, hoping for a girl this time. Lotte had moved to New York, following a salesman that she met while he was traveling here for work. Not surprisingly, she fell out of love with him but in love with the city, and often sent postcards from all the places that she was visiting. Blythe was working at the docks, facilitating communications between the dock offices and the naval ships that passed through.

Liverpool had been taking the same precautions as London, and I saw that my hometown's skyline was also punctuated by the now-familiar barrage balloons. Army searchlights and antiaircraft guns attempted to protect Merseyside. Bombing planes usually approached from the Welsh coast, and they used the lights of Dublin as their guide.

So far, the Liverpool area had fared better than London, but not by much. The cathedral had been damaged, children were leaving by the tens of thousands for Cheshire and other areas, and half of the docks in Wallasey had been destroyed. So much for the IRA being the thing to fear.

Birkenhead, across the Mersey, was a prime target as the largest port on the west coast. Already, the area had suffered from over two hundred air raids. Residents were creating overnight shelters in the underground stations, in their homes, and, for Lucille, in the basement of Edge Hill Training School. In fact, this was where we were to spend this first night. Lucille's flat was not safe, being on the third floor, and she had spent many nights in the basement of her teaching school, an official shelter.

After dinner we cleaned up, and Lucille pulled out a pillow and quilt for each of us. She said that it was very cold in the basement until people showed up. We also packed some food. Lucille had stockpiled her rations for my visit.

We had been so caught up in talking that we lost track of time. The air outside was freezing, and I hugged myself in my wool coat. Even my teeth were cold. It was eerie to see everything so dark. I was used to seeing London shrouded in opaqueness, but this was my hometown, and at night it looked funereal.

Rushing through the streets, along with some other stragglers, we made it to the school on Durning Road. About three hundred people were already packed in, and I could see that she was right about the body heat. After being outside, the basement was like a furnace, and I quickly shed my coat.

Cots were laid out as makeshift beds, but when a teenage boy saw my condition, he offered me his. I thanked him by slipping him a treasured chocolate bar. Lucille sat next to me, laying her pink-and-yellow quilt out on the floor. She said hello to various people, as they had become a tightly knit community in the past few weeks. Most were young ladies, many of them students at the school with Lucille.

The ways that people responded to this unnatural grouping was an interesting thing. Some were frozen in fear, even after months of hundreds of raids. Others took it in stride, using the time to play cards. The few children that were left made up games.

One little girl, maybe four years old, came over to me and stared at my belly. With curly blond hair and sunken dimples, she was adorable. She made me wonder what my child would look like. Would the baby have my blond hair or Kyle's chestnut brown? My green eyes or his brown ones?

"Did you swallow a ball?" The girl spoke through the thumb in her mouth.

"No—I have a baby inside."

"Is it going to come out tonight?"

"I don't think so. I hope not!"

"Is it a boy or a girl or a puppy?"

"I don't know yet, but I don't think it's going to be a puppy. Why—do you like puppies?"

"I have a puppy, but I'm not allowed to bring him down here. They said he's 'posed to stay at home."

"What is the puppy's name?"

"Buster."

"What is your name?"

"Genevieve."

"Well, Genevieve, when you get home in the morning, give Buster a big kiss for me, all right?"

She lit up at this idea. "I will!" she said, and scampered off.

A siren wailed overhead just then, and everyone jumped. We heard a bomb explode in the distance, and no one wanted to voice where they thought it might have landed.

Lucille and I huddled next to each other. "It's not usually like this," she whispered. "We'll get the warning sirens, but I've never heard an explosion so close."

Across the room, a woman was screaming hysterically while the policeman assigned to this shelter tried to calm her.

The siren continued, but we hadn't heard any bombs after the first.

The tone in the basement had become hushed, so we whispered.

"This isn't like a London shelter at all," I told Lucille.

"What do you mean?"

"Well, most people use the underground after the trains shut down for the night. There are so many people that many of them even sleep on the rail tracks, and others sleep sitting up on the escalator stairs."

"I suppose we don't have it so bad here."

A loud crash came from somewhere close by, and those who had managed to fall asleep awoke in a panic. Lucille and I hugged each other until the silence returned.

"What do you hear from Ben?" I spoke so quietly as to almost be inaudible.

Lucille responded in kind. "He's like Kyle. He doesn't write much about the war, probably not to worry me. I know that he's in France, but I don't know much more than that. It's irritating, isn't it, that they have to censor what they say?"

"It is, but it must be safer not to give too much away. Or maybe they're just trying not to worry us."

"I suppose you're right. And to be honest, I do the same thing. I've told Ben only a little about coming down here every night, and unless he's heard about it from the newspapers, I don't know if he knows how badly Liverpool has been hit."

"I wrote to Kyle to tell him that I was leaving London to stay with my parents. I'm sure until he gets that letter, more will arrive at our flat. I hope that he'll send new ones here. I find myself living from letter to letter, and every day in between them is just about surviving until the next one. Despite all the things I fill my days with, they're still just a countdown to his return."

"I know what you mean. But now you're here, and the wait is going to be so much more fun! Or as fun as we can manage, all considering."

Both of us grew sleepy. Lucille had studied all day for several tests, and I was weary after the long train ride. Kissing my cheek, she said, "Good night, Jul. I'm glad you're here. It's going to be just like old times. Well, except that you'll have a baby in a few weeks. But other than that, it will be like old times."

"We should play backgammon and make a deal that the loser changes the baby's nappies!"

"That's not a fair deal. You usually win, and you're going to be the mum."

"You're right. Loser gets to wash them, though."

"All right, count me in for that."

I lay back onto the cot. I couldn't lie on my back, because the weight of my stomach felt like it would sink me. I turned to the right and then tried my left before I could find a position that felt passable. Lucille had it worse, even though she wasn't pregnant. She folded her quilt in half, trying to give the tiniest bit of cushion to the cement floor, and covered herself with the other half.

About ten restless minutes passed, but as tired as we were, sleep still eluded us.

"Hey, Jul? Are you still awake?"

"Yes."

"So, speaking of mums, when are you seeing your parents tomorrow?"

"I'm meeting them around noon at a restaurant near the docks."

"It's been two years since you've seen her, hasn't it?"

"It has, poor thing."

"Poor thing? How can you say that? She's been awful to you!"

"It's that holy husband of mine rubbing off on me."

We shared a quiet giggle.

"But think about it," I continued. "Her son is born with so many handicaps. Father works all the time, and her daughter, her focus for eighteen years, has a runaway marriage and moves across the country. She surrounds herself with people, but in the middle of it all, she's lonely."

"I guess you're right."

"You know, Kyle said the same thing about me."

"What do you mean?"

"He said that I was always surrounded by people, but he could see that on my own, I was different inside."

"I could have told you that."

"And that's why I love you. You give me a lot more credit than I deserve."

An old lady shushed us, and we noticed that most everyone else had managed to fall asleep. Saying good night again, Lucille moved to a cot across the room that had become available. I closed my eyes and fell asleep almost immediately, oblivious to the ever-present sirens.

I awoke to a horrific scene.

Chapter Twenty-Four

An explosion, the crumbling of the building, and the gush of water. It all happened so fast.

When I'd gone to sleep, the ceiling above me had been a solid maze of wiring and pipes, some of them dripping. Where it had been, I could now see the sky raining debris. All around me, chunks of bricks, mortar, and glass were tossed about as if some malign giant had staged a temper tantrum, and bodies lay crushed beneath it all. The smell of gas permeated the area, and anyone still alive was coughing and sputtering. I could barely see through the ash and smoke, and my throat was on fire. Flakes of debris fell and swirled like a snowstorm. I sat up, placed my feet on the crumbled ground, and took tiny, careful steps between cots and wreckage. I could see that people were shouting, but I felt like there was a bubble in my ears, and everything was muted and distorted.

Lucille. Where could she be? I looked around frantically, but couldn't begin to judge the direction of her cot. I called out for her, but she probably couldn't hear me any better than I could have heard her. I started to shout again, but my belly contracted, doubling me over in pain. Could the little one inside hear the terror surrounding us? Instinctively, I put my hands there and rocked, humming. The pressure lessened, but I continued my miniature lullaby to calm myself as much as the baby.

Just feet away, another mother and child were wrapped in each other's arms, both lifeless. I held my hand to my mouth to stifle the nausea that was sweeping through me.

Then I spotted little Genevieve out of the corner of my eye, shaking a woman who must have been her mother. Crying, imploring her to wake up. Even from this distance, it was clear that she never would. I picked my way over to them and had begun to pick up the little girl when a terrible pain shooting through my back caused me to nearly drop her. I stooped toward her as far as I could without hurting and told her to come with me. She looked at me, confused, and I told her that Buster would want her to come home to him. At that she followed me, and we pressed on through the rubble.

Little fires smoldered throughout the ceiling-less room, and I feared the gas we smelled could ignite them at any time.

Most of the survivors appeared dazed, and many others were wailing over the bodies of their loved ones. Cards littered the floor—the solitary eye of a Jack stared at me, bewildered. As the light grew brighter, I at last got my bearings and looked toward where I knew that Lucille's cot was. I hoped that I would find it empty, and that she was looking for me, too.

But as Genevieve and I approached, I saw that Lucille's area was buried beneath a pile of beams and dangling electrical wires. Sparks flashed from the frayed ends like fireworks, and I had to duck to avoid the ones that swung down from rafters. When I turned around to make sure that Genevieve was safe, she was running the opposite direction into the arms of a man who gripped her and cried into her coat. I heard her say, "Mama's over there," as she pointed in the direction from which we'd just come.

I continued on. The beams looked like piles of broken bones, disarrayed throughout the space and bent into impossible shapes. I couldn't lift them to remove them from my path, so I stepped over them as best as I could.

Please, God, let me find Lucille.

All at once, my prayer was answered, but the response was not the one I sought. I saw the familiar pink-and-yellow pattern of Lucille's quilt, and hanging out of it was her arm, still and lifeless. I felt like I flew over, without regard for the debris or the crackling and snapping of the live wires, to the side of my friend. Pushing away scraps of wood and metal from her face, I saw that it was remarkably unscathed. But her poor body had been crushed under the weight of the beam. I turned her head toward me in a fruitless hope that she would look back at me and I could rescue her. But her eyes were closed. She appeared so restful. I didn't think she knew what had happened, and I was thankful, at least, for that.

That only lasted a second, though, and the well brewing inside of me overflowed. I cried and wailed and cursed and yelled out for her. How had this happened? This was a *shelter!* We were supposed to be safe here. And no one was safe. It looked like half of the basement's inhabitants were dead.

A thick mist started to swirl around me, but I barely noticed it. I continued my tirade against no one, screaming for my friend. The steam intensified until I couldn't help but see it, and it burned my skin. Looking up, I saw the steam was gushing from what had been a boiler one floor above, and from a severed pipe dangling from it. For a second, the vapors seemed to subside. Perhaps the boiler was spent. But then, in a blinding white flash, I saw it burst.

I glimpsed light through a haze and thought that I was dead. Fluttering my eyelids to clear my vision, I made out the shape of a woman hovering over me. She was dressed in white, but I knew that she was not an angel when I saw the nursing cap that was so familiar. A delicate gold crucifix hung around her neck.

Then there was more that I recognized. A chart on a clipboard hung beside me. Stacks of gauze. And I was propped up on pillows in a hospital bed. I saw the outline of my feet under the blanket and panicked when I felt my flattened stomach.

"Where is my baby?" I shouted. Oh, my mouth felt strange.

The nurse patted my hands, which were wrapped in gauze. I was suddenly aware that my face, too, bore the same dressings.

"There, there, brave girl. Your baby is just fine. She's in the nursery, probably sleeping. You can see her in a little while."

She? My baby had been born? I didn't remember a thing.

The nurse saw the confusion in my eyes. She pulled a chair over to my side, lifting it slightly so as not to scrape it against the tile floor.

"You've been heavily sedated for nearly two weeks now. You kept having nightmares, so we thought it would be best for the time being. But you've been sleeping better lately, so they lessened the dosage."

She leaned over to straighten my blankets. Her mousy brown hair was knotted in a perfect chignon at her neck, and she smelled like vanilla. "My name is Jane Bailey," she said. "I've been taking care of you, and I'll be here until you're all better."

I talked through the numbness, each word deliberate and labored. "Lucille. I remember Lucille. She was . . ."

And I started to cry.

The nurse took a tissue and dried my eyes, presumably so that the moisture wouldn't get underneath the gauze. I had done the same thing in London with patients.

"What happened?" I asked.

Jane proceeded to explain. The Edge Hill Training Centre on Durning Road had been bombed with a parachute mine on the morning of 29 November. About three hundred people had been sheltered there, and 166 had died. Many, like myself, were injured. Some died from the wreckage falling on them, and others from the gas that ignited and burned them. I was one of the lucky ones, if I could be called that. My burns had come from the hot water erupting out from the exploding boiler, like an unholy baptism. I was at Smithdown Hospital, down the road. I recalled that it was this hospital that had received the donations from the last festival that I had participated in.

People were still streaming in, trying to identify loved ones, and it was especially difficult with the ones that had died in the fires.

I had been found unconscious and was rescued. The trauma had brought on early labor, though, and they delivered the baby by cesarean section. She was tiny at first, but she had grown to a healthy weight under the care of the nurses and was thriving.

It was so much to take in, though I'd been dreaming things on and off that correlated with what she was telling me.

"I'm thirsty" was all that I could say.

Jane helped me sip some juice through a straw. I could barely feel it in my mouth, but I appreciated the soothing texture as it ran down my throat. She explained that the medication was numbing me so that I wouldn't feel much pain. It was also helping me with what would have been excruciating engorgement. My breasts were full, rock-hard, with the milk that had been collecting, aching to nurture the baby that I had not yet seen.

"Now, dear. Are you from Liverpool? You must have family looking for you." She lifted the clipboard from its peg and pulled a pen from behind her ear. "Let's get some information about you. Why don't we start with your name?"

I closed my eyes and turned my head. I wouldn't tell her my name, or that I was a nurse, or anything else about me. Part of me refused to believe that I was here and that this had happened. Surely this was just part of the nightmares, and I would wake up. Speaking my name to her would somehow have made it all seem real.

"Well, I'm not going to press you right now. Lord knows, you've been through enough, and you have your reasons. Why don't you take a little nap now, and maybe we can talk later."

I started to pull the pillows from my back so that I could lie down more properly, but she stopped me.

"Oh no, honey. You don't want to do that. We're trying to keep the swelling down, and that's going to work much better if you keep yourself like we had you."

Jane patted my bound hands again and left the room, pointing to a bell that I could ring if I needed her. As soon as she shut the door, I adjusted the pillows into something that had to be a reasonable compromise.

I lay back and tried to forget all that I had just been told, but it was useless. I kept seeing the fires, the broken beams, the bodies, all of the hellishness. And Lucille.

Poor Lucille. I couldn't think of her without crying, and the salty tears scorched my raw skin. I pitied her father. She had been his only daughter, the oldest above three sons. He must be devastated. I took a little comfort in the fact that they would have been able to identify her, and at least didn't have to experience the ache that came with not knowing.

But that only made me think of my own parents.

Were they looking for me? They must be. I had told them that I would be staying the first night with Lucille, and as Edge Hill was her school, it would be easy to surmise that we had stayed the night there.

But it was unlikely that they could find me. My parents would not be looking in the hospitals for a pregnant woman because I hadn't yet told them about the baby. When their searches proved fruitless, they would reasonably surmise that I had died in the attack and that my body was among the many unidentifiable remains.

I thought about sending them a message. To tell them that I was alive, that I was here. But what would my mother say? She had already abandoned one child who didn't turn out to her liking. What would she say to this one? I wasn't sure that I wanted to find out just yet. I needed to know more about my prognosis before taking that step.

Jane bustled in around suppertime with a tray containing soup and applesauce. She set them down and fluffed my pillows back into a sitting position. "I know it's not comfortable, dear, but we have our rules." She looked around and lowered her voice. "I'll tell you what. When my shift ends, I'll let you do whatever you want with them, and maybe you can get a few hours of good rest before anyone notices."

Then she pulled up a chair and sat beside me.

"Now, let's take a good look underneath these." She took one of my hands and started unrolling the gauze. I felt almost nothing, as the medicine was strong. I thought back to another time, so long ago now, where I'd unrolled my stocking after the day of the festival. I inched it down over the scrape on my leg, and I could remember how much it hurt. I could remember, too, how Kyle watched me there in that old barn, and how I knew for the first time what he felt for me. I winced from the pain of that memory. But, as to my current state, I remained numb.

Jane continued. "We've been changing these every day to keep them clean. Then we wash you down with cold water. You had a lot of blisters in the beginning, so we left those alone, and they're starting to look better now."

She kept my attention on her face until she was finished.

"All right. Now your right hand got the worst of it, so I thought I'd start there. Because after that, everything else will be better."

I looked down and shook involuntarily when I saw myself. My arm was covered with red-and-white splotches, and in some small areas, a layer of skin had been removed altogether. You could see the outlines of where the blisters had been, but like she said, they'd done well with those. There would be permanent scarring, no doubt, but not like there might have been.

When I had taken in the reality of the first one, she unwrapped the second one. It had more mobility and all of the same markings but was somewhat lighter.

"You see what I mean? This one isn't so bad."

I looked down at my formerly graceful hand and saw a void where my wedding ring had been. "Where is my ring?" My goodness, my voice sounded different. Scratchy. A few notes lower on a musical scale.

"We have a safe downstairs with everyone's valuables, and I put it in there. It's yours whenever you want it."

"Why do I sound this way?"

She put her head down a bit and shook it. "We think that you inhaled too much smoke before they got to you, and it scalded your vocal cords a bit. Truthfully, I don't know if that will improve. Time will tell. But there's nothing we can do for that."

I nodded in understanding. I suppose there were many things that I had to get used to now.

"Are you ready for the last bit?" She pointed to my face.

I shook my head. "Not yet. Please, let's wait." My voice was going to take some getting used to.

"Whatever you prefer. I do need to replace the gauze, though." She unwrapped it slowly. The air felt refreshing on my skin.

"How much longer before it heals?"

"Well, we're nearly all there. I'd say another week before we can keep the gauze off for good, and then a couple more just to keep an eye on it."

"Is it bad?"

She tilted her head sideways as she looked at me, as though she was trying to decide what to say. "I won't lie to you. It's not going to be like what it must have been before. But with some more care, no, it won't be so bad."

I decided to get the inevitable behind me after all. "Maybe I could take just a quick look, then."

"Are you sure, dear?"

"Mm-hmm." There was a hand mirror on the bedside table. I reached my right hand out for it, only to find that I couldn't grip it.

"Don't you worry, I'll hold it up for you."

I closed my eyes as she lifted it to my face. Then I opened them carefully, as if a slow revelation would make less of an impact. But my eyes couldn't help but take in the whole image at once.

My face looked much like my hands, with red-and-white markings that left large patches all around. The area under my eyes was particularly raw, where the skin was thinner. Some blisters still remained, but they were healing as she'd promised. Remarkably, my features were intact. In school, I'd seen photographs of burn victims who'd lost ears or noses. Maybe they always show you the worst cases in class.

But I was unrecognizable as myself, and I wondered aloud if I would ever be. Jane heard me and answered.

"That's hard to say, dear, but if I'm honest, and I think you want me to be, I would say no."

I took a deep breath and held back tears, lest they burn my tender skin. I could never have imagined something like this happening, and it was too much to take in. At last I spoke. "What's going to happen?"

"The markings will settle in over time and won't be so vivid, but they'll definitely still be there. Your skin will heal to the point that it doesn't hurt anymore, but it will scar into a leathery texture. We have some moisturizers for that, but they are more for your comfort than anything."

"Thank you," I whispered. "Thank you for telling me the truth."

I knew it could have been much, much worse. I knew that I was one of the lucky ones. But I was definitely mortified at my reflection. I didn't see myself in there. The face of a stranger looked back at me, the face of someone who looked like she'd been beaten. This wasn't Beatrice Westcott's daughter, who had been the most celebrated debutante in Liverpool only a few years ago. This wasn't the winner of the auction. This wasn't the wife of a man like Kyle, the wife he called gorgeous every morning.

And this certainly wasn't the face of a new mother, the face that a baby would look upon with adoration. Fear might be more like it. Fear and, later, embarrassment.

I tried not to cry. I already knew what that felt like. If I doubted before that I deserved such a wonderful man, that doubt had now been replaced by certainty. How could he love me like this? How could I even think of asking him to try? He had given up everything for me—his mother's dream, his vocation. This was not what he bargained for. Not anything close to what he deserved.

Once I had been in paradise, being married to Kyle. But now it was just the opposite. This was hell. If I'd ever harbored any doubt about God's existence, that doubt had now been swept away. There was a God, and he was punishing me for having stolen Kyle away from the priest-hood. Lucille had been right. Upstanding, righteous, precious Lucille. The memory of her pained me more than my wounds.

So no, I would not contact my parents. I wouldn't write to Kyle. It would be better if they all thought that I was dead. Then all would be as it should have been. He would not be bound to a damaged wife. He would not be tainted by my crime against God. And perhaps God would see fit to spare him and allow him to return to the life he'd been meant to have all along. The despair that gripped me robbed me of the possibility of any future happiness, but I could see no other way than this one.

As the days passed, the medicine was lessened and I gradually felt the sting of my injuries. I felt, too, the pain as my milk ducts dried, a dismal reminder that I had never seen my child. Jane was often there, and even came in when she was off duty. I learned that she was originally from Birkenhead and had moved to Liverpool with her husband after they married just over twenty years ago. Shortly after, he was shipped out with the army and died in the Second Battle of the Somme in 1918. She had never remarried, and they had not had a chance to have children.

Why did these things happen? What little exposure I'd had to church had been so formal, as if God was an unreachable deity and we his obedient subjects. Kyle introduced me to a God that was kind, and for a while I believed it. But this God, who would take Jane's husband so violently and rip Lucille from her family, punished me for having pursued love. I wanted nothing to do with this incarnation nor any other.

And yet people like Jane still believed.

I could tell that Jane loved children. When she wasn't at my side, she could be found in the nursery, and she brought me stories of my daughter's progress. I had, of course, refused every attempt she made to bring me the baby, which was baffling to Jane. What she didn't understand was that if I held this little girl, this child I'd made with Kyle, I'd fall in love with her and could never let her go. And what kind of life could I give her? I loved her too much to see her.

My bandages came off with time, and I grew accustomed to my new look. Small patches of my scalp were burned, and it was unlikely that my blond hair would regrow in those areas. My hands looked like my face, the right much worse than the left. I had lost all feeling in that one. Jane worked with me every day to exercise the stressed muscles so that they would relearn their functions. My legs were relatively unscathed, and walking was difficult only because I had convalesced for so long. When I was able, Jane would help me stand, bearing my weight on her shoulders and walking me up and down the hall to strengthen them. She knew that I did not want to walk near the nursery.

"That's a girl. One foot forward. Now the other. Oh, watch that table. Good now. You're getting the hang of it."

Every day it was like that until I didn't lean on her anymore, and then I could walk quite well on my own.

After bringing my breakfast one morning and congratulating me on my increased mobility and appetite, Jane took a deep breath, ready to tell me something.

"Dearheart," she called me, as I had still not told her my name, "I hope you don't mind, but I can't just keep calling the baby 'Baby.' Even at her little age, she is growing and becoming alert and developing a little personality. I've started to call her 'Lily.' She is so beautiful and so innocent, and she reminds me of an Easter flower."

I hung my head, ashamed that I was the kind of mother who would not look at her baby, let alone name her. Even my mother, for all her faults, had named Charles. But I had to believe that this was for her own good.

"Of course," she said hastily, "you can rename her whatever you like. It's not as if she'll remember. But for now, everyone in the nursery has taken to calling her Lily as well."

"Lily is a beautiful name. I cannot think of a better one."

Jane lit up like the Christmas tree candles from my childhood. "Does that mean that I can order her birth certificate now?"

I shook my head emphatically. "Not yet." And I wouldn't say more.

I hadn't thought about a birth certificate, but it was a reminder that I needed to make some plans soon, as I could not stay in the cocoon of the hospital or Jane's care forever. I was suddenly aware that she had to be keeping the hospital administrators at bay, putting off the inevitable reckoning for my care.

I still didn't know what I was going to do next.

On Christmas Eve, Jane brought me a package—and, without knowing it, my answer.

"I've bought something for you. Merry Christmas." And she placed the large parcel on my bed.

"You didn't have to get me anything. I have nothing for you."

"Well, your recovery is all the gift that I need. You have done so well, and the doctor has cleared you to leave on Saturday."

I opened the present delicately. My hands functioned better now, although my right one still had little feeling. The left was very sensitive, and the coarse textures of the twill binding made it throb. I concealed my pain, though. Jane was looking at me eagerly, and I didn't want to disappoint her.

The package contained everything I would need for my first day out. New leather shoes, stockings, undergarments, a skirt, a blouse, a coat, hat and gloves. They were plain and functional, a far cry from what I might have once worn. But they must have cost her plenty, and I felt unworthy of her generosity.

I choked back my emotions, more grateful to her than she could have imagined. "You shouldn't have done this."

"Well," she answered, practical as ever, "we couldn't very well let you run around in a hospital gown. *Vogue* would never approve. Not that these are *much* better . . ."

"Jane." I put my hand on her arm to stop her before she could say more. "They are perfect. Thank you."

I slid my hands up and down the gifts. The stockings were deliciously soft and smooth. But I avoided the rough fibers of the coat, as they would surely irritate my delicate skin.

A plan started to form in my head.

"And that's not all," she said. "The nursery girls have a gift, too."

Taking out another parcel, she placed it next to the first one. It was a little smaller, and I couldn't imagine what else Jane could possibly give me.

I felt my heart leap to my throat when I opened this one. Inside were clothes for Lily, nappies, and a rattle. All of the nurses who came to see me as well as the ones in the nursery had signed a card saying, "Merry Christmas, Little Lily."

"They're going to miss her, you know. I do hope that you'll bring her by to visit once in a while."

"I will," I promised vaguely.

I had avoided the anguish of seeing this perfect baby, and now she was more of a reality than she had been since I'd felt her kick inside of me. Displayed all around me was pastel clothing, chosen by those who nurtured her when I had refused to. Everything was so little—I couldn't imagine a person being so small as to fit into these. How fragile she must be. She needed the care of someone strong and stable.

Jane put the packages on the chair next to me and put one more in my hand, a tiny one wrapped in tissue paper.

It was my wedding ring. She had brought it up from the vault. I tried to slide it on to my finger, but it didn't fit, so I put it in my pocket. Maybe it was a sign, a confirmation of sorts.

During that sleepless midnight, I came to some conclusions. I was no longer Julianne Westcott, nor was I Julianne McCarthy. I was a nameless, faceless ghost, and my future was uncertain. Lily did not deserve to be brought into this. In my own way, I loved her too much for that. The embodiment of my love with Kyle, I couldn't bring her into my curse. Maybe I was no better than my own mother, although I would have liked to believe that my reasons for leaving my child were more altruistic.

I wrote a note, barely legible with my shaky handwriting, stating my intentions. I remembered the words that Father had spoken just a few years ago to me: "Julianne, wait until you have a daughter.

Wanting what you think is best for her sometimes means making tough decisions."

25 December 1940

Dear Jane,
At the same time that I lost everything I'd known, I
found you. Besides being my nurse, you have been a
comforter, a counselor, and a friend. I deeply appreciate
the gifts, and I want to give one to you, too. I am unfit
to be a mother to Lily. She needs more than I can possi-
bly give her. You have been more of a mother to her this
month than I can ever be. I am leaving the baby gifts
for you and begging you to take my Lily as your own.

Resolved, I folded it and left it unsigned. Donning the clothes from Jane, I peeked out of my room to see that the nurse's station was empty, then tiptoed past it. Out of the corner of my eye, I spotted a handbag, left unguarded, just asking for me to take it. I asked to be forgiven for this one last sin.

Grabbing it, I rushed out into the cold night.

In my hurry I nearly ran into a motorcar that was passing by. "Watch it, missus," a man shouted from the window.

Missus. It reminded me that I was nameless. I couldn't very well get on for very long like that. I would have to come up with something.

It didn't take me long to choose a name. Taking my unused first name, a reminder of the grandmother I'd never liked, matching this new, troubling face, I would be Helen. And forming an eternal connection to my new friend and to the baby girl I was leaving behind with her, the name was complete. I would now call myself Helen Bailey.

Chapter
Twenty-Five

The underground wasn't running, as it was Christmas morning, so I walked as long as I could and then huddled from the cold in a storefront doorway for the remainder of the dark hours.

For a moment I questioned the sanity of my choice, peering in the direction that would take me back to the hospital. It was unlikely that my absence had been noticed yet. But no, my decision was final. It was better for Kyle to assume that I had died than to come home to a broken, unworthy wife. Better for my parents to lose me than to have even more to explain, and to have even more disappointment to endure. Better for Lily to grow up in a loving, stable home. These thoughts warmed me from within.

I ran my fingers through my hair, a habit that would be difficult to break. I had forgotten that it sat in patches now. Maybe I would just keep the scarf over it and simplify everything.

My hands were icy, and I slipped them into my pockets. I felt my ring in there, its lonely weight. I held it up to my left hand, sighed, and put it back.

My attention rested on the handbag that I had taken from an unknown nurse. I already felt guilty about that, but I convinced myself that it was a theft of necessity. Surely, the mitigating circumstance gave me some kind of pardon. And in light of what I had stolen from God, it didn't even compare. But would anyone be looking for me because of it? I was easy enough to describe. I turned my head side to side and saw that the street was deserted.

I opened the clasp to see a little mirror, a lipstick case, a key, and an envelope with money in it. Five pounds, with a note saying, "Esther, pick out something lovely for yourself for Christmas. I wish I could be there. Love, Mum." Esther's mum had been generous, and I started to think about how I could best stretch this useful find.

As the light of Christmas morning peeked over the horizon, I started walking toward the nearest station. With five pounds, I could have found a cab and had much to spare, but I was determined to be frugal from the start. Wrapping my scarf around my face, I did not attract any attention, and I boarded the first train of the day.

I got off at Ranelagh and glimpsed the gray flats that had been, for four days, my first home as a wife. Memories flooded me—love and longing, sickness and salvation. But no, those were the memories of another girl. A beautiful girl. That was not me any longer. I shoved my hands into the pockets of my coat and walked on, bristling at the scratchy feeling of the wool against my damaged skin.

Just a few blocks more and I arrived at my destination—Saint Stephen's. It hadn't been a conscious decision to come here, but as I reflected on it, it made sense. Despite my protestations, something inside me craved anything that was familiar. I couldn't return to Westcott Manor, and I couldn't bear to go see Lucille's home. In my mind she was still my best friend, and I knew that she would never again walk through my gate and stay at my house. Saint Stephen's had seen me only a couple of times, but it was somewhere warm, somewhere I knew I could feel safe for a few hours.

The church glistened with candles and wreaths, and by eight o'clock a children's choir had begun rehearsing for the Christmas morning Mass. I stayed in a pew off to the side and smiled when I saw the procession coming up the aisle. Dear Father Sullivan. If only he had counseled Kyle to remain in the seminary. He would be serving at Mass in Durham right now instead of fighting to survive on a faraway battlefield.

At the end of Mass, I decided to try an experiment. The congregation filed out, each person shaking the hands of the priest and wishing him a good holiday. I joined the ranks and took my turn. I held on to his hand for just a bit longer than necessary, forcing him to look at me more closely. But Father Sullivan didn't recognize me. Not a flicker.

I went back in to the church and stayed for the next Mass, too, all the while considering what I would do next. I was afraid that if I stayed in Liverpool, I would be tempted at some point to inquire about my parents or about Kyle or Lily. And that only opened the door to the bigger temptation of reentering their lives. But I had brought the punishment onto myself, and I was not going to carry them down with me.

The money in my handbag—Esther's handbag—would take me anywhere that I reasonably needed to go. Julianne Westcott had nursing credentials, but Helen Bailey did not, and I couldn't turn to those skills without papers. Although, in wartime desperation, could evidence of that proficiency at least open some doors?

As if I was being sent a sign, Father Sullivan said a prayer for the citizens of Manchester, who had suffered a devastating blow from the Germans just two days before. On the twenty-third and twenty-fourth, thousands of bombs had been dropped on the city, igniting the largest fire in the war so far. In one hospital alone, they lost fourteen nurses. Surely, they could use some help from someone who could demonstrate an ability in that field.

The next morning, as thousands of people evacuated Manchester, I headed toward it.

⌇⌇

And this was how I earned a living. I followed the war from town to town, going where tragedy had struck the hardest. I would present myself as a traveling nurse who had lost her paperwork in the Blitz. It was a credible story, enhanced as I proved what I could do and by my obvious injury. When things stabilized in an area, I traveled on to another devastated town desperate for skilled, albeit disfigured, hands.

Whenever I could, I sent money anonymously to Esther at Smithdown to repay what I stole, plus a little more for the inconvenience.

People looked at me twice, which was something that I eventually grew used to. But instead of looking at me because they saw beauty, as they once did, they looked because they saw the opposite. It was just a flashing thought, I could see, because I was surrounded with the wounded and the dying, most of whom looked much worse than I did. Nevertheless, it was tiresome.

I managed to tolerate this unusual life, chasing disaster. If I died, I didn't care. I was already dead to everyone I knew and loved, and the sooner the Germans took me, the sooner this nomadic life would come to an end.

Month after month I ached to step into the crosshairs. To join Lucille, who had deserved to live so much more than I did. If I hadn't been such a coward, she might be alive today. If I had been willing to see my parents straightaway, we might have stayed at Westcott Manor, having one of our sleepovers, laughing until they told us to go to sleep. Little Lily would have broken the ice with my parents, and they might have welcomed Kyle when he returned.

That vision wasn't to be. But I'd tried to make it right, as best as I could. I died so that Kyle could live and the good God that Kyle somehow believed in had to live up to his end of the bargain. It was tragic that I had to deny Kyle knowledge of his daughter, but with no idea when, or if, he would ever return, I had to choose what was best for her. I had to believe that he would have understood.

Year after year an end was denied to me as millions died and yet I lived. Each November brought a bittersweet awareness of the milestones that must have been attained by the daughter who was in the arms of a more deserving mother. What did her first smile look like? When had she cut her first tooth? Did she wear her hair back in plaits or down in curls? With the only reverence I had remaining for anything, I found a post office and sent an annual offering, care of Jane Bailey at the hospital. A pressed flower, a doll's dress, whatever could be found or made along these sparse times, sent always with the same unsigned message:

To dearest Lily, I wish you the happiest of birthdays.

I moved to a new town after each one, so that the postmark would already be outdated by the time it arrived.

I did not make friends where I went, nor did I keep records, so the end of the war still found me without the necessary credentials to be hired permanently. As the country celebrated, I waded aimlessly through an endless shower of streamers and confetti. As the country recovered, my skills were not needed as urgently.

I was able to stretch out my unusual employment for just a few more years, going to cities that had not yet recovered from their devastation. But that couldn't last forever, and soon I was faced with dwindling funds. I had saved enough to get by for a little while, but it wasn't going to support me for long. I checked into a boardinghouse in Stoke-on-Trent for no other reason than the bus got a flat tire on the city's outskirts and I had decided to get off.

But funds were not the greatest of my problems. I began to choke on my own loneliness.

One day I picked up a knife with my right hand, which I was still trying to regain the full use of after all this time. In my left hand, I held an apple. As I applied pressure to the fruit with the blade, it slipped, cutting instead my wrist. I reached for a towel but hesitated to stop the flow of blood, mesmerized with the growing red pool on the counter. I watched the blood leave the wound, and all the sadness flowing out with it. It dripped onto the floor and onto my shoe, and still I watched.

At last I took the towel and wiped up the mess, but the image didn't leave me, nor did the feeling. I managed to bind my wrist tightly.

It happened again, a few weeks later, this time on purpose. Again I watched, detached, as the blood and sadness left my body. If only I could cut deep enough, if only I could wait long enough, that would be it. This would be over.

But something always made me reach for that towel.

That something, I discovered, was my brother. I hadn't thought of him in some time, having buried him along with the rest of my former life. But the birth of the new prince made his memory difficult to ignore. The name Charles was all over the newspapers and the trinkets and the conversations. For a little while you couldn't go a day without hearing it to the point of nausea.

"Charles, such an adorable child."

"Charles, new hope for the monarchy."

I was long past due to visit Bootle. I used the last of my money for train fare.

As the countryside grew more familiar to me, I shut it out by focusing on a *Vogue* magazine someone had left on the seat. Flipping through its pages with the eyes of a different woman, I noted that hat fashion had taken a peculiar turn. They were taller now, with creases and curves that looked unnatural. Skirts were pleated. I rather liked the pleats, but the hats I could have done without. At last I put the magazine aside, bored with its triviality, and closed my eyes, hoping to sleep through the rest of the ride.

A jerk to the train startled me, and I looked out to see that we were inching our way along.

"That's because of the new tracks they're constructing," someone next to me said. I looked up to see a squat old lady across from me holding her handbag and umbrella in her crossed hands. Her hat was saucer shaped, the practical kind, with a silk flower tucked into the sash.

"They're always building and rebuilding," she continued. "All over the country. Sometimes it seems as if we'll never recover from the war."

"Yes," I added. I'd been here, there, and everywhere in the three years since VE Day. It was the same story at each stop. Towns starting over. Life slowly returning.

"Of course, this area received such a pounding from the Germans."

"Was Bootle hit hard?" I asked. It was the one part of the country I had avoided.

"Oh yes, but no harder than any other, I suppose. I had a dear friend on Milton Street that died. Marly Conyard, poor thing. She was putting out food for a stray cat when it hit."

"I lost a friend, too."

"It's ugly business, war. I'm glad it's over."

I didn't answer her.

"And what are you here for?"

"I'm going to Bootle Home to visit . . . a friend."

"Bootle Home. Ah, that was sad."

"What do you mean?"

"It was damaged severely just before the end of the war. They lost one whole wing."

My heart froze. "I didn't know."

"You'll see when you get there. They've patched it up quite properly, although the stone wasn't from the original quarry, so you can see the new part if you know where to look."

"Was anyone hurt?"

"Oh yes, and a few died. I suppose your friend made it, though?"

"I can only hope."

I didn't feel like talking anymore. I didn't want to have to wonder if anything had happened to Charles, or imagine Bootle Home as anything other than what it had been.

We swayed back and forth as we crossed the makeshift tracks while men worked to repair the gaping crater left by an explosion.

When the train pulled into Bootle, I said good-bye to my companion and stepped out. The exhaust from the train polluted the air that I knew from memory would otherwise have smelled sweet.

"Taxi, Miss?"

A toothless man offered to take me wherever I needed to go. I pulled out my coin purse, which was nearing a death of starvation, and turned him down.

"I'll walk, thank you."

It was roughly three miles to the north, as I recalled, and the weather was pleasant enough. I took a sandwich from my handbag and ate it along the way.

I'd prepared myself for the worst, based on the comments of the train passenger, but Bootle Home looked relatively untouched. Now that I knew to look, I could see a slight discoloration on the left wing, but I might not have noticed without her commentary.

I walked up the familiar steps, ten years estranged. Before I could open the door, a couple of the residents came out with an orderly. All three were laughing, bundled in their winter coats, with cherry-red noses and cheeks. One resident was a little girl, just about the age that Lily would be. She wore a knitted pink hat with matching mittens, and I thought I might make one in time for the next November package, Lily's eighth. I stared longer than I should have and wiped away a cold tear that escaped.

I turned away and looked up at the intricate carving atop the threshold. Complexities immortalized in lacquered wood. I sighed and entered. The hallway was the same, as were the sofas, which looked as untouched as when I was here before.

A young woman with dull brown hair pulled into a frighteningly severe bun sat behind the desk. Her eyes widened when she saw me, but then she looked down and shuffled her feet beneath the metal chair.

"Where is Miss Ellis?" I inquired.

"Miss Ellis?" She put a well-chewed pencil into her mouth and looked up into nowhere. "I'm not sure. I replaced Mrs. Hainsworth. But I think Miss Ellis was before that. She left to live with her daughter or something."

"I don't believe she had any children."

"Or maybe it was her sister. I don't know." The pencil came out of her mouth, but she held on to it. I saw a deck of cards lying next to her, displayed by suit in a setup for Patience, or some other useless diversion. "Anyway, what do you want?"

"I'm here to see Charles. Charles Westcott. Is he here?"

"Yes. Charles. Are you a relative?"

"I'm . . . I'm a friend."

"You have to be a relative or get special permission."

"I have permission. From his sister."

"I didn't know he had a sister."

"He did. But she died. In the Blitz."

"I'm sorry. I can't let you in without permission."

I had not come this far to be dismissed by such a mindless little twit. I leaned in so that she could get a good, hard look at my face. I saw her quiver a bit.

"Look. It was his sister's dying wish that I come here and check in on him. Surely you wouldn't deny a dead girl's final request?"

"No . . . I suppose I wouldn't."

"I didn't think so. Now, where is his room?"

She pulled out a register and pushed a pen toward me. "Here. You have to sign in first."

I sighed but went through the little charade. Helen Bailey. It came naturally now. It had taken almost a year not to start my name with a *J*, longer than it had taken me to write my married name without thought. She looked at my name and appeared satisfied. "He's in room 203. It's just down the hall, on your right."

The same room as before. It was comforting to think that there were some things that didn't change, even if they were insignificant ones.

I walked to Charles's room, and it felt as if it could have been just yesterday since I'd been there. I found it empty, but it was unchanged. The bed linens were still the stark white ones, but it wasn't as if that were likely to change. The same brocade curtains lined the windows and looked over the same gardens, still well tended by someone other than a McCarthy.

Only one thing was different. The colorful pots still lined the windows, but like the memory of the gardener who had brought them here long ago and stolen my heart with his kindness, their contents were withered and brittle, covered by a canopy of spiderwebs. I traced my finger along one of the sinewy strands, pulling it like taffy.

"Excuse me." I wiped the cobweb on my skirt and turned around. An orderly—a thin, young man with the beginnings of a mustache—had peeked his head in. "Can I help you?"

"I'm here to see Charles."

"All right. He's just coming now."

I held my breath, and then I heard his plodding footsteps.

He hadn't changed a bit. He appeared to have been frozen in silent time. As the orderly walked Charles to his chair, I stepped back, almost afraid to touch him. This had been a bad idea. What right did I have to come back here, to disrupt the little part of the world he occupied?

I turned to leave but stubbed my toe on the corner of the bed frame. I put my hand out instinctively to catch myself, and it landed on Charles's arm. Seeming not at all surprised, he reached out to my hand and squeezed it, three times in rhythm.

I was too startled to move. Our little form of communication. But he'd done it first. Did he recognize me? Was he able to sense that I was here?

He kept holding my hand, stood up, and walked me to the windowsill. He felt around until he could touch the pots. He patted them and frowned.

"That's amazing."

I turned to see that the orderly was watching us. "What's amazing?"

"Those old pots. He usually refuses to touch them. But whenever we try to take them away, he screams bloody hell. So we just leave them there, sad as they are."

I looked at Charles. He still held me with him and touched the pots.

"Yes, Charles. They're still there. But everything must have died. We'll have to plant some new ones."

I walked him back to his chair, took off my jacket, and rubbed my hands together. I picked the pots up, one at a time, and dumped their lamentable contents into the nearby waste bin.

"Now," I said and turned to the orderly, "what must we do to put something new in here?"

"I'm on my break in fifteen minutes," the young man said, eyes shining. "I could go find some soil and some cuttings and see if that will work."

"Perfect. We'll see you back here then."

I stayed two nights at Bootle Home, using the dying wish bit as long as I could stretch it and securing an empty room for sleep. Charles seemed happy, as far as I could tell, when we watered the plants and stroked their soft leaves. But this was not a permanent solution. I had to leave before he became used to my presence, and the place held too many memories for me, exactly the kind I was trying to escape.

But before I left, I swiped the handbag of the secretary and found enough money for train fare. I had no plans to pay her back.

The next train was leaving for Birmingham, so I bought a ticket for that one.

Chapter Twenty-Six

We'd been traveling for about two hours when the conductor ran through each car, asking if there was a doctor on board. I looked around at the other passengers, whose reactions ranged from panic to disinterest. When no one seemed to be able to answer the call, I stood up and volunteered to help. Looking me up and down with a suspicious eye, he shrugged, as there was no better offer. He guided me down the narrow corridors to the first-class cars, where an elderly woman had fallen.

Hastening to her side, I saw that her leg was broken and badly swollen. I called for a dowel or a strong stick—anything I could use to set it—but nothing could be found. At my recommendation, we made an emergency stop in the next town, Stone.

The train left us behind after we disembarked, eager to bring the rest of its passengers to their destinations on time. With a porter's help I created a makeshift bed on the bench at the station and placed her on it. Taking a blouse from my bag, I tore it into strips and used it to secure a thin board that the stationmaster brought to us. The woman cried out as I set her leg on it, and I fumbled in her handbag to retrieve the aspirin she'd begged me to find. A call was made for a doctor to come from Walsall, but by the time he arrived, the work had been done.

After she had been transferred into the backseat of the doctor's motorcar for the trip to the neighboring town, she grabbed my shirtsleeve.

"Thank you so much. You're an angel." She smiled beneath her pain-furrowed brow.

"It's what anyone would have done if they knew how to."

"Here, I want to give you something." And she pulled three pounds out of her purse. "It's all that I have with me except for what I will need to finish my journey. But here is my address in Birmingham. Please write to me of your whereabouts, and I will pay you properly."

"You really don't have to. It wasn't anything."

"I insist." She pressed the money into my coat pocket, and then the doctor closed the door.

Watching the car recede in the distance, a new idea formed in my head. Maybe the big cities were not where I should be going to look for employment. With no license, I would be able to find only menial work there. But these small towns might be different. The services of a nurse and midwife might be appreciated, and it would certainly cost less to get by in them.

So the traveling nurse continued, visiting towns too small to have a doctor, staying for months at a time, tending to the ill and delivering babies. I found success most often by speaking to a local chemist, who was more often than not glad to have the help. I became used to the stares that I would receive upon my arrival, but I quickly won them over with my work. I stayed only as long as my restlessness would allow and always left before I could make any lasting friendships. My sentence was to journey through this world alone, perpetually atoning for my sin, patient by patient.

I sent chocolates to Charles every time we shared a birthday, through the lanky young orderly who had been so kind to him. I'd leave an address and wait for an update before moving on to the next town. He was doing well, I was assured. But he had let the plants die once again.

Six more of our birthdays passed—and six more of Lily's. She was fourteen now, so the gifts became more appropriate to her age. A lipstick and compact. A hat that I smartened up with a little embroidery.

It was around this time that I found myself in a tea shop on the far outskirts of London. I picked up a *Sunday Times* and saw a photograph of Abigail and Roger in the social section. Roger was running for office, and informed opinions saw him as the favorite. How distinguished he looked; how different my fortune might have been if my heart had loved him as my mother would have wished. But that was not the life I wanted to live. Beautiful, brash Abigail was at his side, playing the role she was born for. I envied them nothing.

Two more birthdays brought me to the town of Alcester, and the country saw the intervention of British troops in the Suez Crisis. I sent a Union Jack brooch to Lily for her sixteenth birthday in a show of patriotism and tried to keep myself from thinking of when Kyle had fought in the same part of the world. To keep myself from thinking of where he might be now. It was another life.

One more year saw me in Oakham and brought the unveiling of a plan to allow women to join the House of Lords for the first time. These events caught the attention of the people in the countryside, but most other times they were focused on the daily tasks of living and farming and surviving. I liked that about the country. The hardworking people were not easily swayed by fashions and politics. I had become such a simple person, such a different person from the girl living in luxury next to Newsham Park.

The people paid me for my work in different ways. When they couldn't afford money, I was compensated with clothing, food, lodging, or whatever else they could muster up.

In Bedworth I was paid most unusually for an equally singular task. I had been there for two months, after the departure of their doctor for bigger opportunities. I heard a knock on my door and opened it to find a small boy, no older than five years. I recognized him as being the son of a farmer down the road.

"Are you the doctor?" His faced was scrunched and his head tilted.

"No, I'm a nurse, but I might be able to help you. What do you need?"

"I need you to come with me."

His look was so pleading that I couldn't help but follow him. "What is your name?"

"I'm Arthur. I live over there." And he pointed to the house in the distance.

Arthur led me past the house, though, and into the nearby barn. "She's in here. I hope you'll be able to help her."

I looked around for a woman but didn't see her. Then he opened the door to a stall. I erupted with laughter, a rare thing for me, at the sight of a border collie lying on her side. I thought it funny that a child had called me in to deliver puppies. Until I noticed the dog's distress and realized that something was wrong.

I ran my hand along her black-and-white coat, damp with sweat. Two puppies had already been delivered, but she seemed to have given up. Her breathing was heavy, and the white fur around her nose indicated an advanced maternal age.

She seemed to be suffering from uterine inertia, in which her muscles weakened and could not push without assistance.

Arthur kept his back against the stall, equally repulsed and fascinated as one by one, four more puppies emerged from his beloved pet. I released each one from its sac, making the labor happen manually, and laid them by the teats of their mother. She licked them clean, and it was the happiest sight I recalled seeing in a long time. I washed my hands at the nearby pump just in time for Arthur's father to return from the fields.

"What do we have here?" He looked at me, then at his son, and back to me.

"Needa had her puppies! There's seven of them!" Arthur was full of the news, and he recounted every detail. "Can we keep them?"

"Well, son, we might be able to keep one or two, but we're going to have to find homes for the rest."

The boy looked at me. "Do you want one?"

I hadn't yet been offered a puppy for my services, and I wasn't sure that I wanted one just now, as I didn't intend to be in this town much longer. But Arthur was so enthusiastic that I couldn't turn him down. I heard myself say, "I would like that."

Without asking my opinion, he selected the runt of the litter for me, a black-and-white bundle. "What are you going to name him?"

I hadn't named my own child, and now I was on the spot to pick one for this little mutt.

After some consideration, I said, "I think I'll name him Ellis." Maybe he would love me like my old friend had.

Ellis kept me in Bedworth for a few more weeks, as he grew stronger on the milk of his mother. Arthur delighted in bringing updates to me every day, and a few times I went to see him for myself.

As soon as he was weaned, I left without saying good-bye to the boy.

Ellis was a delight, though I was reluctant to admit it. Wherever we lived, he found a corner to make his own. He greeted me enthusiastically when I entered and licked my otherwise untouched face. No one had shown me such affection in decades, and I welcomed it, even though it was from a dog. Sometimes I brought him to the bedside of patients and was intrigued at the difference that his attention made in their demeanor.

Besides Ellis, my one indulgence was the television. Of course, being always on the move, I did not own one, but I was fascinated every time I had a chance to see it. By the end of the decade, most of the people I visited had tellies in their homes, save for the poorest of them. I imagined my father must have a number of them. We had owned several telephones long before most households had even one.

It was in 1961, Abertillery, the old ironworks town, that I received a package from Bootle. I read the note from my faithful correspondent that accompanied it:

> *Dear Miss Bailey,*
> *I am sorry to have to write this to you. Charles suffered*
> *a heart attack this week, one that I'm afraid was fatal.*
> *He appeared to have been having chest pains for several*
> *weeks and may have had a congenital issue that went*
> *undetected. His belongings are being sent to his parents,*
> *but I was able to sneak away this little pot for you. I*
> *hope that it arrives without damage.*
> *Respectfully, Andrew Bosch*

I opened the package. It contained one of the blue pots with small green dots painted along the top edge. It was split on the side, but just a hairline fracture that didn't jeopardize its purpose. I clutched it to my heart and cried. It was the first time I'd cried in as long as I could remember, and the tears poured not only for Charles but also for everyone else that I'd lost. He'd been my last tie to Julianne. Now I was truly alone.

I threw the pot at the wall, startling Ellis, and breaking it into large pieces. It was ruined now, just like me.

I set the fragments on my table. And went to buy the pills.

They sat there for days, weeks. I'd hold them in my hands, the dye staining my skin a sickly ochre color. I'd take one but spit it out. It had an awful bitter taste. But they were the means to my end, and I was determined, sooner or later, to swallow them all.

One night I laid out fourteen of them, about twice what it would take to do the job. Surely, twenty years of penance was enough. Ellis looked at me with his big brown eyes, and I think he sensed that something was awry. He laid his chin on my knee as I sat on the bed, hunched over in despair. We looked at each other for what felt like hours. Every time I moved, his tail wagged along the floor, only to settle again when he realized that I was only shifting my position.

I followed the first one with a large drink of water, forcing it down my throat. One down. I thought of Charles and of Lucille. I wanted to see them again, but I was heading in a different direction. They had been angels on earth. I was not.

One more drink of water, and the second one was finished. Two down. I thought of my parents. I wondered how they reacted when they learned of Charles's death. Was it with sadness? Regret? Did they think of me?

Three down. It wasn't getting any easier. God, they were awful. I didn't feel anything yet, but maybe it was too early.

What would happen to Ellis, I wondered? He was a good dog, though. Someone would take him in.

I opened the drawer of my nightstand and pulled out a picture. It was the one I'd sneaked of Kyle, taken from the window in Bootle. I was already in love, and we'd spoken only a few times. The silver frame had tarnished through all of my travels. I hadn't looked at it in a long time, other than to stuff it in a bag before moving again. But I wanted to gaze at it one more time.

This was how I wanted to remember him. Whistling, working in the gardens that he loved. I showed it to Ellis and then set it on top of the nightstand.

This was going to take too long. No need to draw it out, make a ceremony out of it. I picked up three more pills, sighed, and reached for the water.

There was a knock at my door. Ellis barked madly. I couldn't see the clock in the dark without my glasses, but it had to be late. Very late.

Let them knock.

Ellis quieted, and I thought whoever it had been had given up. I washed down another of the pills and was about to swallow the next when the knocking picked up once again, more urgently now. Ellis erupted again, and as I reached for him, the pills fell to the floor. He was frantic now, as the knocking continued. I set the water on the table and brushed the picture frame with my arm. It tottered, then fell back faceup.

This wouldn't stop until I answered the door.

"What's the damn hurry," I said in a low voice that no one could hear. I flipped the light and ran my hands through my hair, a habit of a long-ago vanity. I avoided the mirror that came with the rented room. I already knew that my blond hair was paled by many grays. I knew that the years had rounded my figure. And that the scars on my face, though having mellowed over the years, still gave it the look of splotchy leather.

The knocking at last stopped. Whoever it was must have heard me coming.

It was one of the Campbell kids. Thomas. Tommy. Timothy. Whatever. There were so many of them.

"Miss—"

"What do you want at this hour?"

"It's my mother. She's sick. Bad."

"Is it the baby? It's not her time for another few weeks."

"I guess God thinks differently. It's coming. But something isn't right with Mum."

"God has nothing to do with it."

He ignored my blasphemy, as most did when their need for my services outweighed their shock at it. But they were not being punished by a God that I had long since expelled from my life.

"I brought the truck."

I told him to wait while I got dressed, then came out with my carpetbag of tools. The pills would have to wait.

⚜

Mrs. Campbell died while the priest was hearing her confession. I could tell because I'd met Death in the hospital, in the war-torn cities, in the faces of villagers during all my years of roaming. I envied the woman lying there after having escaped the pain of living.

The priest didn't realize it at first, so zealous was he to assure her salvation.

"Exaudi nos, Domine sancte, Pater omnipotens, aeterne Deus: et mittere digneris sanctum Angelum tuum de caelis, qui custodiat, foveat, protegat, visitet atque defendat omnes habitantes in hoc habitaculo."

I fought back the memory of a similar night in a third-story flat long ago. When Kyle had explained the ritual to me, step by step, as his father lay dying.

"Domine, non sum dignus, ut intres sub tectum meum: sed tantum dic verbo, et sanabitur anima mea."

With my good hand, I dipped the towel in the hot water, recoiling a bit when my skin touched it. I shifted it to my right hand so that I wouldn't feel the heat on my fingers. Steam wafted off it, reminding me of the incense that was supposed to carry our prayers to heaven. Funny how the presence of a priest kept bringing these memories to the surface.

"Accipe, soror, Viaticum Corporis Domini nostri Jesu Christi, qui te custodiat ab hoste maligno, et perducat in vitam aeternam. Amen."

I hated that old language. The cadence of the Latin was taking my thoughts to places that I did not want to visit. Flashes of Kyle studying in the garden. Kyle driving me through Anglesey. Kyle with the perpetual grin on his face.

I shook the towel until it was cool enough to wring with both hands.

Touching the little one's eyes gently, I then moved around her cheeks, the crown of her head, down her neck.

I found a dry towel next to me and prepared to dress and swaddle her.

"Oremus. Exaudi nos, Domine sancte, Pater omnipotens, aeterne Deus: et mittere digneris sanctum Angelum tuum de caelis, qui custodiat, foveat, protegat, visitet atque defendat omnes habitantes in hoc habitaculo. Per Christum Dominum nostrum."

Mr. Campbell had left the room to be with the other children. I heard the clink of what must be a small glass bottle, and I knew that the priest was anointing the woman with oils—meant, if I remembered correctly, to cleanse her of her sins. I prepared the baby in front of me for life, as the priest shepherded her mother into an eternity with the good God that they believed in. Such dreams ahead, such dreams behind.

Carefully I pulled the delicate hands through the sleeves of her babysuit, doing the same with her toes. Snap, snap, snap. Close up the sleeper. I looked around for a blanket in time to see that Mr. Campbell had returned, and his stricken face told me that he knew she was gone.

"Ego facultate mihi ab Apostolic Sede tributa, indulgentiam plenariam et remissionem omnium peccatorum tibi concedo et benedico te. In nomine Patris, et Filii, et Spiritus Sancti. Amen."

The priest continued anyway. What was the point of that? Her body would soon be cold, so how could the prayers do anything now? Well, it was none of my business if they wanted to waste their time. If the ritual brought reassurance to Mr. Campbell, confident that he had assisted in his wife's salvation, I suppose that it served some purpose after all.

I found what I was looking for and folded the blanket in half, forming a triangle. I placed the baby in the middle. Bottom corner to the chin. Left and right corners tucked in under her back. It was automatic to me.

I felt dizzy again and steadied myself on the mantel. I gripped the baby tightly so that she wouldn't fall. She slept soundly, secure in her tight wrapping. Babies like the confinement. It reminds them of the security of the womb.

Nestling her in the crook of my arm, I turned around, cautiously hoping that they were finished. The priest was standing now, his back to me, leaning over and blessing her head with his thumb. It was then that I noticed the ring on his right hand. It was gold, with a silver band running through it.

I'd seen that ring before or, rather, one just like it. It was just a coincidence. It meant nothing.

A sigh of acceptance escaped from Mr. Campbell's lips, and he hung his head before speaking.

"Thank you, Father—"

"Father McCarthy."

At the sound of that name, my mind crumbled the useless barriers that I had tried to put up when the Latin stirred the memories. It hovered in the air, just like it had when the boy had spoken it in the truck.

I shouldn't have let it paralyze me like it did. There were thousands of McCarthys in the world, weren't there? But it used to be *my* name, it used to be a beloved name. The sound of it on his lips seized my full attention as much as it would have if he had said, "Julianne." I listened to their exchange, one voice sounding like a phantom to me.

"Father Trammel was called elsewhere tonight. I am his houseguest and was available to help."

Mr. Campbell put out his hands, which Father McCarthy went to shake. But suddenly, overcome with emotion, he put both of his hands around those of the priest's. "I know it meant a lot to Agnes that you were here."

Head bowed, Father McCarthy stayed where he was, his hands being held, until they were released.

The moment was so touching, I was transfixed. My mind was clouded, battling the flashes of the past that kept trying to break through. I felt like I had already intruded too much, but I couldn't move until it at least occurred to me that the baby provided the perfect reason to excuse myself. She was dressed, and her anxious siblings were no doubt sitting outside wanting to see her.

And fervently awaiting news of their mother's condition. I wasn't going to be the one to tell them. They should hear this from their father, not some ragged-faced stranger.

Just as I took a step toward the door with the child, the priest stepped back and turned around. We were face-to-face at last.

The eyes, the voice, the name. He was standing in front me. There was no doubt. I felt dizzy again.

Kyle. *My* Kyle. Here. A priest, after all. A rare rush of joy flooded me as I realized that my sacrifice had not been in vain.

I stumbled again and held the baby tighter.

His hand took my elbow to steady me. As if anything *could* steady me. My chest was pounding, my breathing was quick and heavy, and my blood pulsed at his touch.

"My fault," he said—still, after all these years, so quick to claim blame for his own. But yes, he should accept fault for being here. For conjuring things that I had buried. For disrupting the plans I had to end this life of mine.

But these were just the musings of a bewildered woman. And inside her was resurrected the spirit of an eighteen-year-old girl, flittering at the proximity of the man she loved. The girl overpowered the woman.

He released me and stepped back when it was apparent that I was not going to fall. I stepped out of the room into the next, where several children continued to sleep and others were weary-eyed.

"Your sister," I said, knowing no words of comfort for the loss of their mother. Emily stood up, with tear lines staining her cheek, but she smiled at me as she took the girl from my arms.

"Thank you," she whispered and softly kissed the fuzzy head of the baby.

I returned to the room to find the priest gathering his belongings into his little black bag.

"Wait, Father." The word left a strange feeling on my tongue, one that I didn't care for.

He turned to me, halfway through putting his hat on. I remembered the feel of his warm cap on my head as we strolled through rows of Christmas trees. He was so young then, so carefree. The man in front of me was weary.

"Yes?"

"You've come all this way. I was going to make some tea. Why don't you stay for a cup?"

"I would like that, thank you."

Replacing his hat on the table, he walked with me into the kitchen.

As I heated the water and searched for two cups, I stole glances at him. He was the same Kyle, almost. The sandy hair was now speckled with gray, and it made him look distinguished. He wore round wire-rimmed glasses that made him look scholarly. But his smile was missing. His ever-present smile.

So much to say, none of which I could without letting on more than I wanted to. When had he heard the news about the Edge Hill bombing? Why did he decide to reenter the seminary?

Unfortunately, I was limited to less revealing inquiries. "So, you are a houseguest here?"

"Only for the week. Father Trammel and I are old friends from school. I came to see him before heading to my new assignment."

"If you don't mind me asking, isn't Father Trammel much younger than you?"

"Yes, but I entered the seminary later than most."

"Why was that?" I was entering delicate territory, probing further and wanting to ask things that would be considered too familiar in this circumstance. He must have thought so, too, for he looked at me in a questioning way.

Still, he answered. "I was in the war, and after that, I was—searching."

The words *For what?* started to form on my lips, but I held them back when I saw that it wasn't a subject that he seemed to want to discuss.

Searching. I pondered this as I turned the stove down and steeped the tea. Was he searching for himself in the life he had to create as a widower? Was he searching for something—our home, our lost belongings? Was he searching for *someone?* I dared not to wish for that. He must have accepted the common belief that I was lost in the bombing in Liverpool. But without evidence, what if he had looked for me? How futile that would have been. I had made a clean break and not left any trails.

I ached to reach out to him and tell him that I was here. Julianne was inside the shroud that he saw. But of course that was out of the question.

As I pulled out a chair with my foot, he stood to take the scalding cups from my hand.

"I'm sorry," I said. "They are still very hot." My right hand barely felt its heat, but the steam wafted ferociously above the rim.

"That's all right," he said as he reclaimed his seat. He picked up a spoon and twirled it in the amber-colored drink, releasing the steam like incense.

I wanted to hear his voice again. It sounded the same, just a little more mature, and I wondered if my voice sounded familiar to him. Though of course it wouldn't, as the scorched vocal cords had taken on a deep, gravelly tone. Did anything about me stir up ghosts in him the way he stirred them in me? By the look of him, there was no hint of recognition.

"Where is your new assignment?"

"Outside of Liverpool, in a little church called All Souls."

All Souls! I remembered that place, of course. The remote little church attached to the sprawling cemetery in which we had laid his father to rest. Why was he going there? Kyle had told me that some priests liked it for the solitude while others were drawn to its ministry to grieving families, but either way, after a few years, they moved on, all too ready for a transfer. Had Kyle been assigned there, or had he requested the isolated place?

Of course, I wasn't supposed to know any of this.

"Is it a large church?" I asked nonchalantly. I stirred my own cup.

"No, it is a little country church."

"Oh, I like those. The ones made of stone, with a little rectory split in two for the priest and for a housekeeper."

"Yes, this one does have that, as I recall. But this one usually houses a groundskeeper, as it sits on many acres. However, I was told that the grounds are now kept by a professional company in the city, so I suppose I will be living alone."

"Will you not have a housekeeper?"

"No, I don't believe so. I've been told that there is not any money for one."

"I hope that you are a good cook."

He smiled—not a full smile, but one that showed he was at least somewhat comfortable with me. To me, it was the most brilliant thing I had seen in twenty years. The sunshine breaking through the gloom.

"I can find my way around in a kitchen," he said. "I can even darn my own socks!"

"Well, a priest and a housekeeper for the price of one, then? What a lucky church."

"I suppose so."

A possibility entered my head. No, it was too, too presumptuous. Wasn't it? But how incredible if it could happen. I couldn't let the idea go unspoken. "You say that there is no budget for a housekeeper?"

"That is what I was told."

"I have been thinking of coming up north to find work. But I am alone, and all that I really need is a roof over my head and food on my table. Would you consider taking me on as a housekeeper?"

Perhaps that was too direct. He had just told me that there was no money. I needed to modify what I said. "Of course," I added, "only temporarily, until I find other work."

There. Let him think that he was doing me a favor. I didn't want him to know that I wanted this more than anything. That the seeds of hope, of a life, had been awakened in me.

"I don't see why not, if it's only going to be vacant otherwise. I have to warn you, though, I am not very good company."

"What do you mean?"

"I just want you to know that I am not usually one for talking, and it could be a very solitary existence for you."

"Well, seeing as it is just a temporary situation, I don't suppose that it needs to matter much."

"So be it."

Then I remembered Ellis. "I have a dog. Do you mind? He's not any trouble."

"That won't be a problem."

He took a sip of the tea and then a larger one. He found a piece of paper and scribbled on it. "Here is the address of the church. I plan to be there in two weeks. You are welcome to come, but if you change your mind, I understand. I pray that you have a safe journey wherever you go, and I ask you to pray the same for me."

Standing up and finishing the tea in one drink, he put his black hat on and made his way to the front door.

I spoke, hoping for him to linger for even one more second. "Thank you for being here for the Campbells."

"I was glad to be able to stand in for Father Trammel. Have a good evening."

He left, and my heart was afire with anticipation. I was moving back to Liverpool. And I was going to live with Kyle.

Chapter Twenty-Seven

In a fairy tale, I would tell Kyle who I was. He would kiss me, and his kiss would be a magical one, restoring me to a more enchanted time, one in which we would live happily ever after.

Of course, I knew that this was just a fantasy. I did not make this move with some misguided hope that we were going to be together. Kyle was a widower, as far as he knew, and now a priest. I was to be his homely housekeeper, a safe female attendant for a man living otherwise alone. I was being given an enormous reprieve from heaven, a stay of execution. Kyle had told me once about purgatory. Maybe that was what this was after all: a place to atone for my sins, but always with the knowledge that paradise was waiting one room over. Not the hell that I'd deluded myself into. It would take the kind of fatherly God that Kyle believed in to make this reunion take place.

I came home and flushed the rest of the pills down the toilet, grateful that I hadn't taken any more than the three. I drank four glasses of water in rapid succession, hoping to dilute whatever remained in my system and quell the dizziness that the first few had caused.

I left for Liverpool the next day, determined to make up for every day that I had lost. I found lodging in a shabby boardinghouse that was willing to take on a tenant for two weeks and even my dog for only a few pence more. Ellis was used to a nomadic existence, and he didn't seem to take notice that this might be any different. He would love the grounds at All Souls. So much open space. I rubbed his ears, and he wagged his tail in response.

My first stop was Newsham Park and the proud manor that sat on its border. It appeared to be undamaged from the war, unless repairs had been made that I couldn't see.

It took two days of walking by at all hours before I saw either of my parents. I saw my mother on a Monday morning as she met her gardener and pointed out her instructions. She was such a creature of routine. Mondays were gardening days, even now.

Mother herself appeared little changed. She had the same bony frame. Still smartly dressed, she was only an older version of the one whom I remembered, even from a distance, I could see that wrinkles had set in. I was tempted to talk to her, and I even took a step forward. But I hesitated. It was too painful. So I just watched her instead as a passerby. Before long she left in her car. It was older than I would have expected—she and Father had always enjoyed the latest things. I had heard that the war was very lucrative for the docks and warehouses in Liverpool, but in the last decade they had seen a sharp decline due to increased air travel. The father I knew would have found a way around the problem, even starting a brand-new business if he had to.

After the gardener left, I slipped through the gate and walked the grounds. The gazebo was neglected, in need of a fresh coat of paint, but it was beautiful to me. I ran my hand down one of the beams, closed my eyes, and inhaled the memory. Kyle holding me as we cried in each other's arms. Kyle kissing my neck and moving his way up to my lips. I recalled the sensation that had run through my body as if it were happening now.

Waking from that dream, I walked around the flower gardens, and my eye rested on a large, engraved stone. It read:

IN MEMORY OF OUR BELOVED DAUGHTER, HELEN JULIANNE WESTCOTT
BORN 3 MARCH 1920
DIED 29 NOVEMBER 1940
MAY SHE REST IN PEACE.

It's not every day that you read your own memorial. It only made sense that they would have done something like that, but to see what was essentially my own tombstone felt rather macabre. And yet I had not been Julianne Westcott in so long that it seemed as if the monument belonged to someone else. It had not escaped my attention that the name inscribed did not have McCarthy added to it. Nor did it surprise me. The charade had been maintained. If they couldn't accept who I was then, how could I expect them to do so now?

On another day I visited Albert Dock. They did, indeed, look as if they had seen busier times. I strolled by Father's warehouse, hoping to see him as he left for lunch, but I did not. The third day brought some success, though. He came out around noon, carrying a sack lunch, and sat on a bench overlooking the water. My heart was overwhelmed with love for him. He hadn't been a perfect father, but he had tried. Recklessly, I approached the bench.

"May I sit here?" I asked, taking the chance of meeting his gaze, though without fully facing him. Part of me wanted him to look in my eyes and see familiarity there. Part of me was afraid of it. Of course there was nothing to worry about. My green eyes had grayed over the years, dulled by hard work and loneliness, and God knew my face as a whole bore no resemblance to that of the beautiful young daughter who'd broken his heart. Ellis sat attentively at my side, watching the gulls on the pier.

"Um, yes." He slid to the edge of the bench, leaving plenty of room for me, and never looked my way.

He didn't say anything else, and I was afraid that I would cry if I opened my mouth. So we sat there, each staring out over the water. Its smell was unchanged, fish and industry, although both languished, along with my father. I could see that he, too, looked like an older version of himself, but not a sharpened version as Mother was. He looked like a man beaten by life, not even putting on the pretense of conquering it. Poor Father. I could imagine that he took my loss with great difficulty, and I recall thinking that he might have been the one person for whom my new appearance would have made little difference.

I wanted to put my arm through his, rest my head on his shoulder, and whisper, "Oh, Papa." But of course I resisted for a dozen reasons, not least the fact that the shock of it might have killed him.

He ate noisily, or maybe I noticed it because we were otherwise quiet. When he was finished, he stood and, with a brusque "Have a good day," walked back to the warehouse offices and disappeared through their revolving doors. My eyes remained on those doors long after they stopped turning.

I came by for the next three days, sitting in different places and watching him eat his lunch in supposed solitude. On the last day, I sent a kiss into the wind and asked it to find its way to him.

I played sleuth for the remainder of my time in Liverpool, looking for information about other people that I had known. Sometimes I found things in public records and old newspapers, and other times I found it by starting a conversation with someone.

Lucille's grave was in the corner of the church graveyard. Several withered bouquets leaned against it. I added my own, a fresh one full of daisies.

I learned that Lucille's father had passed away about ten years ago and that one of her brothers still lived in their house. Ben had returned from the war, missing one arm and his beloved bride, but was otherwise intact and decorated for his achievements. He had remarried in 1950 and had two little boys.

John was still the pastor of the church, and Maude had gained a pleasant, round shape after the births of three more babies, all boys.

Lotte never returned to Liverpool. She had made her way from New York to Hollywood, where she had landed some walk-on movie roles before finally becoming a publicist. How appropriate for her. She must have been in her element, being paid to talk and gossip. I wished her well.

Blythe had died during the war in May 1941.

All that remained was finding out about Jane and Lily, a task that reduced me to near immobility. Jane alone knew the map of the red-and-white scarring on my hands and arms, and that threatened my anonymity. And yet the opportunity to see my Lily was a stronger force than fear.

I sat by the lake in front of the hospital and took it in, delaying the moment when I would step through those doors. The building was engulfed in reddish-brown brick, with rows and rows of dormers and turrets looking down on me, its windows concealing the unseen eyes of the sick and dying. I had once been among them but was spared, a fact that I'd spent two decades resenting.

My legs carried me, just barely, up the steps and through the door to the main hallway. Its white walls enveloped me, and the sounds of hurry echoed from places above and around me. I approached the main desk.

"Excuse me."

The woman behind the desk looked up, and her eyes took on the look of pity that I'd grown immune to.

"I'm inquiring about a nurse who once worked here," I said. "Who might work here still. I was hoping that you could help me find out where she is."

"Yes, of course. What is her name?"

"Jane Bailey. She worked here about twenty years ago."

"Oh yes, Miss Bailey. I know exactly who you are talking about. Such a lovely woman. But no, she isn't here anymore. Miss Bailey left Liverpool when her daughter graduated a couple of years ago. Let's see—where did they go? Oh, yes, I think it was somewhere in London. Something about her daughter going to art school. I'm afraid I don't know any more than that, though. I'm sorry."

"No, that is enough. Thank you."

I turned to walk away, but a thought came to me and I returned. "If I may ask. Do you know anything about her daughter?"

"Miss Lily? Oh yes. She'd come by now and then. A beautiful thing she is, so stylish."

"And she was happy?"

"Happy?" She cocked her head just perceptibly at that. An odd question from an odd woman but, she seemed to decide, a harmless one. "Oh, my word, yes. Adores her mother, that one, and vice versa. There is nothing that Jane wouldn't do for her. When Lily became interested in photography, Jane spared no expense to find the perfect camera for her. Then she moved on to painting, and Jane turned their parlor into a studio full of canvas and brushes and easels. Some children might turn rotten with so much attention, but not Lily."

I smiled and felt a joy more profound than any I'd known could exist. My daughter was happy and loved and flourishing. It was all a mother could hope for.

"Do you have a forwarding address for them?"

"I'm so sorry, but I don't. The administrator would likely know, but he's on holiday right now. I could have him ring you."

I declined, thanked the receptionist, and felt happy that at least this news existed among all of the sadness left behind in the hometown of Julianne Westcott.

Charcross lay ahead of me, and I hired a cab. It was still remote, although as we left Liverpool, I noticed how much the borders of the city had expanded. What had once been fields now boasted rows and rows of housing, bland little streets lacking the character of history but tidy enough to be home to some. Soon enough, though, the countryside came into view, lonely in comparison but so very welcome. As the steeple of the church appeared on the horizon, I realized that today was 18 August. Our wedding anniversary. I wondered if Kyle recalled such things as this, or if he'd immersed himself so thoroughly in his vocation that such things were no longer of significance.

Kyle met the cab and helped me with my bags, no more or less friendly than two weeks ago. He was clearly a little surprised to see me, as if he still didn't understand why I would want to take this nonpaying position all the way out here, with the company of only a sad priest and the tombstones of the departed.

All Souls looked just the way I remembered it, and now it was going to be my home.

The first few days were uneventful. Kyle was still unpacking and organizing. He blew the dust off the books in the rectory and arranged the titles by some method of classification that I could not detect. He would get easily distracted when he pulled one from the shelf and thumbed through its pages. He had always loved to read, and these were going to be his companions for the duration of this assignment. He wore little spectacles now, and he peered closely at the books to see them better.

I was to live in the other side of the rectory, and it was clear that a woman had not been there in ages, if ever. Contrary to what I had told Kyle, I intended to be there for as long as he was. If I couldn't be his wife, at least I could take care of him. I still loved him, achingly so, and would take the scraps that this chaste occupation offered just to be near him. And so I set to work.

As I beat out rugs and polished floors, my senses were ever aware that my husband was just feet away from me on the other side of a wall. I felt sprightly, like a new lover. How had I come to deserve this reversal of fortune?

His name was always present in my mind, which made me realize that I must be very cautious when I spoke. To Julianne, he was Kyle. To Helen, he must be Father McCarthy. In fact, to think of him in such a way might subdue the romantic feelings that I couldn't help but harbor. It was as good a time as any, here in the beginning, to set that straight in myself. I made a concerted effort to think of him as the priest that he now was.

That was easier to do than I realized. Although he looked the same, with some extra years, this was not the dynamic young man that I had married. Kyle smiled all the time and was quick with a joke. Father McCarthy was strained, introspective, and private. I pitied him in this state, and every day I was more grateful that I was here to look after him. We had vowed to grow old together. And now, if the God who had given me this reprieve was indeed benevolent, we would.

Father McCarthy and Kyle did share one enduring quality. Both were exceptionally kind. Through the first weeks, as I tended his house and cooked his meals, he was always appreciative. He opened up his humble library for my use and never said anything that wasn't amiable.

We settled into routines as we grew accustomed to life in Charcross. He celebrated Mass every morning in the chapel for the few residents that came by. On Saturday evenings, he prepared sermons with fervid dedication. I marveled at his passion for preaching, especially as there was almost no one to hear it. I made the habit of lingering over Saturday night's dishes so that I could listen to him as he talked it out to himself. He would pace as he held the papers, a pen in his mouth, at the ready for a revision. I enjoyed this rehearsal, as I was not yet ready to attend Mass and see him in his vestments, fully inhabiting his priesthood. He was still Kyle enough in my mind that I couldn't face that.

The primary purpose of All Souls was still to manage burial details. My side of the home became a kind of church office. I opened the front room whenever I heard a car pull up and was the first contact that people made here. I pitied them for having to see me in the moment of their bereavement. I hurried through the administrative necessities of the work and ushered them in to Father McCarthy as soon as I could. He did have a calling for this work and was the compassionate ear that they sought. In contrast, I was used to two decades of keeping people at bay, and it was difficult to soften that exterior. I was determined to try, but it would take time.

If they had no priest of their own, he also conducted the funeral services. The bells, in their solemn tones, echoed mournfully through the lonely valley.

When Father McCarthy wasn't counseling or studying, I would find him in the long-neglected garden. I marveled at his talent for reviving it. Trimming hedges and making plans for the spring, he seemed almost happy when he was there. Save for the black cassock, he seemed like Kyle to me more often than not, and it always brought a rush of emotions. Reconciling the two people in one was challenging.

We never spoke more than necessary, though. We had each become such solitary people since our shared tragedies.

When November came, I sent Lily the carved peacock that Kyle had once made for me. Without knowing where in London they might be, I sent it to Smithdown and left its route to my daughter to fate. And I wrote the same unsigned message that I had twenty times before:

To dearest Lily, I wish you the happiest of birthdays.

I disregarded the guilt I felt, knowing that I was with her father and they knew nothing of each other.

The Advent season approached, and I decided to surprise Father McCarthy with an assortment of boughs with which to decorate the church. I still had some money saved. As all of my necessities were met, save for an occasional plain frock to replace a worn one, it was easy to indulge in this. I wrote up an order and paid a local farm boy to pick some up for me. When they arrived, their evergreen scent took me back to the tree farm in Wallasey.

I ventured into the church when I felt certain that Father McCarthy would be occupied in the garden for some time. I had researched Advent and Christmas customs, and hoped that there might be a storeroom with the appropriate supplies.

I was right. In the sacristy, I found a closet with many such things. I pulled out a large gold ring and five pillar candles that were meant to rest on it. Three purple and one pink would be arranged around the ring, and the white would be placed inside of it. Kyle once told me that the purple represented repentance and the pink stood for joy. The white was reserved for Christmas morning. I added some boughs around it and stepped back to look at my handiwork. It occurred to me that it was a perfect metaphor for my life—a majority of repentance, with scant punctuations of joy.

Finding a ladder, I got to work on the rest of the chapel. I hung swags of evergreen from the altar and from the columns, and highlighted each with tasteful red bows.

Father McCarthy entered just as I was hanging the last one, and I could see that he was stunned by the results. He was not talkative to begin with, but now he was positively speechless. I hoped that meant that he liked it.

"I hope I didn't do anything wrong," I said. "I read about the liturgical seasons first so that I didn't do anything incorrectly."

He approached the altar and looked at everything closely. One candle in the wreath had fallen, and we both reached for it at the same time, brushing the sides of each other's fingers.

Our eyes locked briefly. *See me,* I suddenly thought, and just as quickly I brushed those words from my mind. I turned away before my gaze could tell him more than I wanted him to know. His touch had lit a fire in me, and I was thankful when he took his hand away.

He turned around once more, taking it all in, and finally spoke.

"No, you didn't do anything wrong. It is perfect." He walked up and down the aisle, hands folded behind his back. "You know, I never see you here at Mass. Now you have to come so that you can see how beautiful it is with the decorations."

"I can see it here without the Mass. But thank you anyway."

"I'm sorry, I didn't mean to pry. I guess it's just odd that you do so much here, and yet you don't attend any services. Perhaps my sermons are even duller than I thought."

"Oh, that's not it, I promise. In fact, I've heard you practice them sometimes, and they are quite good. You put so much work into them. But you are a pastor of souls that have departed. Why labor over them for the few living souls that show up?"

"If I can speak to the heart of even one person on a Sunday, isn't that worth it?"

"I suppose so. But you are very gifted. It's a waste to exile you here."

"I am not exiled here. I requested this assignment."

I looked at him with surprise.

He leaned back against a pew. "I have dedicated my life to praying for loved ones who have died. Now I can do the same for the loved ones of others."

The words were right there, on my lips, and I had to bite my bottom lip to keep from asking, "Who are your lost loved ones?"

He cocked his head and looked at me oddly. I suddenly remembered the times when he teased me about my habit of nipping my lip when I was lost in thought. Had it triggered a memory in him? I almost wanted it to.

But he looked aside, appearing to shake it off. "You know," he said, "my father is buried here. I also liked the idea of being near him and spending time at his grave."

"Is that why you take those morning walks out to the west part of the cemetery?"

I knew the answer, of course, but I wanted to keep him here, to keep him talking.

"Yes. It's a nice way to begin my day."

"He is a lucky man to have such a devoted son."

And any prayers you might spend on me are useless, since I am standing here right next to you.

"Well, he was a good father." With a sigh, he stood straight and went to the sacristy to set up for tomorrow's Sunday Mass.

My heart delighted in the exchange—the chance to talk with him again.

I heard from the scant parishioners as they exited Mass over the next four Sundays that they loved the decorations, so I made use of Father McCarthy's library to learn about other liturgical seasons. I laid out green altar cloths on regular days, and red ones on the feasts of martyrs. White on days of celebration, and black on days of funerals. I covered the crucifix during Lent and uncovered it on the Vigil of Easter. I enjoyed delving into the symbolism and could see why Kyle had been attracted to it. Everything had a meaning, a place, a purpose beyond itself. Some traditions came from the days of the early Christians, and others were developed over time.

I read that the Vatican was poised to review some traditions in light of a movement toward modernism. The following Christmas, the pope announced his intentions to convene a council that would address these and many other issues. If I had been Catholic, that would have been monumental to me. But Father McCarthy never seemed affected by outside issues, and he continued to live the life of a humble country priest.

So we lived season by season, day by day, growing comfortable in our habits. Father McCarthy never questioned why I stayed on, why this had never been temporary. He enjoyed evenings reading by his fireplace, and I spent mine by the small television that I had bought. I indulged in *Coronation Street* along with just about everyone else in Britain, enjoying the ongoing drama of the working-class characters. Some nights I sat at my window, waiting, although I didn't know for what. Save for Lily, everything I wanted was here.

As time went on, there were many days when the name of Kyle never even entered my mind, so fully absorbed was I in my daily duties for Father McCarthy. There were reminders, though.

In late 1963, Father McCarthy fell ill with a terrible fever and was unable to get out of bed for several days. The doctor said that he would improve with time, but I was still frightened. I resolved to tell him everything—about me, Lily, the bombing—when he was better, because I couldn't bear the thought that he would never know the truth. I covered his duties for him except, of course, the priestly ones, which were left neglected out of necessity. I tended his garden. I had never had a green thumb like Kyle did, but as I held these flowers and watered their roots, I felt close to him. Their velvety petals left their scent on my hands. I remembered that day I'd first met him, when he smelled like earth.

I took up his morning walk, visiting his father.

"Dadaí," I'd say, "wherever you are, please do what you can to help him recover. I'm not ready to let him go. But if your God takes him, then tell him to take me, too. Because I don't want to live in a place where he doesn't exist."

I delivered meals to him, coming closer to his private space than I ever had. I sat by his door once, laying my head and hand to it. I closed my eyes and recalled the times that we had shared a bedroom.

One evening he didn't respond to my knocks, so I entered cautiously to make sure that he was all right. I had made a pot of chicken soup, fresh bread, and herbal tea. The room was neat, with the next day's clothes laid over a chair the way that I used to do it for Kyle. A dusty easel rested in the corner, on which sat one of the pictures of Ireland that his father had painted. As I marveled at this sanctuary, I nearly forgot why I was here. I turned to look at his bed. I saw his form under the blankets and made out the tiniest hint of rhythmic breathing. He must have been so deep in sleep that he just didn't hear me at the door. I looked around for a place to set the food, and I nearly dropped it when I saw what was on his bedside table.

I was face-to-face with a framed photograph. The sepia tones could not hide from me the dancing green eyes of the lovely, young blond girl sitting in the window of the ruins of a church and smiling for the man behind the camera. I remembered Kyle taking that picture on the evening of our wedding day. In front of the picture sat a small votive candle, burned almost to the nub.

I gasped audibly, and Father McCarthy woke. I must have startled him, because he sat straight up. His gaze met mine, and he saw where my eyes had rested. Immediately he took the picture and placed it facedown. I looked at him, a question in my eyes for which he gave no answer. Apologizing for the intrusion, I set the food on another table and asked if he needed anything else. He shook his head through a fit of coughs and waved me out.

I closed his door and leaned against it. My hand flew to my heart in a vain attempt to calm its rapid beating. He had a picture of me on his nightstand. I was next to him as he slept. Every morning he woke up to me. It was all so dizzying. My love for him felt overwhelming. Love because he still had feelings for his wife. Love and pity because she was gone. I wanted so much to run back in and tell him that I was here. I was here, but I was changed. I was here, and I loved him more than he would ever know. But would he love me back? I had bet my last twenty years that the answer would be no.

When he recovered, he avoided conversation with me for nearly two weeks. From his point of view, I'd seen him as a priest with a picture of a beautiful girl at his bedside. What must I think of him? Since we weren't going to discuss it, I went out of my way to be extra kind, extra solicitous, just so that he would know that I passed no judgment.

And I reneged on every good intention to admit my betrayal.

But fate, God, destiny had other ideas. We had just settled back into normalcy when the new Advent season brought a surprise visitor to the church.

Chapter Twenty-Eight

I was immersed in my third year of decorating for the holiday season. Each year I tweaked it a bit, and this time I was wrapping luxurious ribbons around the candles, matching their color. Fluffing them up, I turned at the sound of the door opening. I expected to see Father McCarthy or one of the old parishioners that dropped by to light candles now and then.

Instead, a young woman entered. She wore a lime-green tunic accessorized with a thick white belt. A matching caped coat was wrapped around her shoulders, and she clutched a shiny gold handbag. Her taupe heels click-clacked as she walked up the aisle toward me. If I were twenty-five years younger, this was exactly the sort of ensemble that I would have worn.

"May I help you?"

"Yes. I am here to make arrangements for a wedding."

What an odd request.

"A wedding? Are you sure that you are at the right church? We're more accustomed to funerals here."

She tilted her head back and smiled. "Yes, I know. My mother said that I should come take a look. She came to this village a few weeks ago and told me that it would be an ideal spot to consider. You see, I grew up in Liverpool, as did my fiancé, so we wanted something close by. But we also fancied a wedding in the country."

As much as this possibility was surprising to me, I looked around and saw that this could, indeed, be an ideal place for nuptials. The ominous black altar cloth that often adorned the church could be replaced with a brilliant white one. I envisioned flowers and ribbons and a white carpet that was rolled down the aisle. Yes, it could be just right.

"It's the perfect size," she continued. "We don't want a large wedding, just some family and close friends."

"I'm sure it will be no problem, but you will have to be patient with me, as I'm not accustomed to the details of planning a wedding." *I was a runaway bride myself,* I thought.

"Oh, I know exactly what I want. I'm sure we can work together to make it happen."

I gestured for her to sit in a pew, and I joined her. Up close, I was struck by the brilliance of her malt-colored eyes and the shiny texture of her long blond hair. What a lovely, polished young woman. Ready to get to work, she laid down a notebook and pen, and pulled her hair into a thick ponytail. I couldn't help but see the inch-long birthmark under her ear as she did so, and just as I thought to myself that it looked remarkably like Kyle's, she said, "First things first. My name is Lily Bailey." She put her hand out to shake mine.

Lily. Jane Bailey's Lily. *My* Lily.

The realization swept through me, and I felt cold. I couldn't breathe and looked away. I coughed until I could get air back into my lungs.

"Are you OK?" she asked with some concern. She moved her vacant hand around me and patted me on the back.

"Yes." Cough. "I'm fine. I'm not sure what came over me." Cough, cough.

Jane. She said her mother had been here recently. My pulse raced. I had worked so hard to keep my whereabouts unknown, fearing her anger, or worse, facing her untarnished saintliness in comparison to my great sins. Perhaps this was all some great coincidence, though, and she knew nothing of me. I might be worried without cause. I hoped that Lily would decide that the church was inadequate for her needs and I would never need to find out.

And yet now that she was here, I never wanted her to leave.

When I had composed myself, she continued. "Well, all right. So, again, name is Lily Bailey. My fiancé is Albert Howell. Would it help if I wrote this down for you?"

I searched her eyes, innocent of what she had stepped into. Having no way of knowing what or who was before her.

Picking up the pen and notebook, I replied, "No, I can do that. And by the way, I'm Helen." I neglected to reveal our common surname.

"Helen. It's nice to meet you. Now, we are looking at a spring wedding . . ."

As she continued, I took notes, but the information wasn't really sinking in.

Lily was here. The baby that I had never laid eyes on. The baby that I had chosen a mother for. The baby that was created through the deep love of Kyle and myself. She was so enthusiastic with her plans that she didn't notice how my eyes traced every detail of her face. She looked, actually, very much like my mother, and she carried herself in the same way. Poised and chic, she embodied the latest in fashion and style. Her attention to detail also reminded me of Mother. Her eyes were Kyle's, and her hair was mine. I saw no trace of our fathers, and I imagined that the few unidentifiable features might have come from his mother.

When she was finished, she relaxed a bit, and in her smile I saw her father's face.

"Miss Bailey, I am sure that we can work out everything that you are asking for," I said. I was still in disbelief that my daughter was sitting before me, inviting me to participate in her wedding.

"Thank you, Helen. I'll be by again in a few weeks with Albert and my mother. Should I make an appointment?"

"That's not necessary. I am here every day. You'll be able to find me at any time." I cleared my throat. "So your mother is coming, too?"

"Oh yes. In fact, she'll really take over most of the details, because I've been caught up in a project I'm working on for university. As I said, it was her idea to consider Charcross in the first place. She had planned to be here today, but the poor dear sprained her ankle getting off of the train from London. She's back at the hotel icing it down."

"Give her my best," I whispered, but already I was thinking about the day coming soon when I would again see Jane Bailey.

"I will." She stood up and smoothed her dress. Cleanly ripping out what I had written, she handed the pages to me, then tucked the notebook under her arm. "I will see you in a few weeks. Thank you for your help."

Her heels tapped again along the tile floor, and she left the way she came. I watched my baby as she walked away, a smile on my face and a sudden lightness in my being.

The weeks of Advent rolled by, and Lily did not return. I found myself looking for her every time the church door opened or the bell of my home was rung. I knew that she would come back, though, or at least send a note if she had changed her mind. She appeared to be a very thorough young lady.

The last few months, starting with Father McCarthy's illness and culminating with my introduction to Lily, had stirred the past like a cauldron. I didn't know what magic would come of it, but I hoped it would be good. If it was, indeed, God giving me a second chance, maybe he deserved the same from me.

On Christmas morning I put on my best dress, gloves, and a hat, and I walked the few yards to the church.

All Souls did not have a choir, although it did have an ancient organist who probably wouldn't live to see Easter. As he started with a slow rendition of "O Holy Night," I took a seat in the back and watched people file in from the cold. The church was not full, by any means, but was more so than usual. Some townspeople had visiting relatives and brought them to church on the holidays, and others were too busy on Sundays but wanted to at least celebrate once a year. I had no room to criticize. I had first ignored, then resented God for most of my life, and I was here to amend that.

Mass began, and Father McCarthy came up the aisle, led by an attendant bearing the thurible of incense. Finally, I faced what I had been avoiding: Kyle in the vestments of a priest. Kyle in the role that he should have played all along. And he played the role well. The parishioners, joyous in the season, smiled at him as he made his way up the aisle. I knew that he had spent hours preparing the sermon, highlighting the need for peace of soul and hope for salvation. I prayed to find it.

Surprisingly, the motions of the Mass came back to me. I found the rote posturing easy to keep up with and some of the Latin responses vaguely familiar. I looked at Father McCarthy as little as possible and turned my attention to the details of the liturgy for distraction.

However, I couldn't keep my eyes from him as he delivered his homily. As he preached, it was as if I were hearing the words for the first time, the recital surpassing the rehearsal. In front of his congregation, I recognized Kyle. The old Kyle. The one who smiled and laughed and taught with every breath. At the pulpit, he was in his element, and for the first time I truly reconciled the two identities that I knew in him. He spoke of the innocence of the Christ child and of how we are called to be like children. To believe simply, to leave complications behind. I knew about complications, and I was here to set them aside. It was as if these words were intended for me. He spoke as if he had lived it. I had always seen the strength of Kyle's faith. But surely that faith had been tested. War. Death. Loneliness. How did he conjure the strength to still love God as much as he did?

The Mass continued, and I saw him consecrate and lift the host for the first time. I bowed my head like everyone else, and my chest started pounding. Pain shot through my left arm. Feeling faint, I sat down and rested my head on the pew ahead of me. I stayed like that and realized that if anyone took notice of me, I must look like someone lost in prayer. When I recovered from that strange spell, I wiped the perspiration from my brow in time to watch everyone entering the Communion line.

At the final hymn, "Joy to the World," I left and sucked the crisp, refreshing air into my lungs.

When the second Mass of the morning started an hour later, I was sitting at my window when I saw Lily enter the church, accompanied by a man and a woman who must have been her fiancé and Jane. Lily was as vibrant as she had been four weeks ago, in a tight red sweater and gray trousers.

Feverishly, I cleaned the house. I kept it immaculate every day, but the idea of Lily being here made me find dust and spots that I had never noticed before. Soon enough, Mass was finished, and my bell rang. Ellis barked, as he always did, but in his advancing age, he didn't get up from his spot. Putting the broom back in the kitchen, I ran my fingers through my scarce, graying hair and answered.

"Hello, Helen?"

"Yes, Miss Bailey. How are you?"

"Good, thank you. I'm sorry to intrude on Christmas Day, but you said that you were here every day. With all of us in Liverpool for the holiday, it seemed like the perfect time to show Albert the church."

I opened the door wider and showed them to the sofa. Lily was followed by a tall, dark-haired young man and by a woman that she introduced as her mother.

But she needn't have. I recognized Jane Bailey at once. Her hair was gray now, and her hands had taken on the faint brown spots that begin to decorate our skin as we age. But her face was unchanged, as gentle as I remembered.

As I busied myself with offering them a drink and biscuits and gathering up the notes that Lily had left for me, I was aware of Jane watching every move that I made, and I delayed the little tasks as long as possible. Jane had nursed every inch of my face and hands back into life, and she had worked with my muscles to restore their functions. It had been her job to know me inside and out. Time hadn't changed that. Our eyes met, and she could see that I knew her, too. I had skipped out in the middle of the night, stolen her friend's money, and left her with a baby without asking her permission. All this after she had given up her days, her nights, her life to care for me.

But there was no anger in her eyes. Saintly Jane. I should have known. And I welcomed it more than I had anticipated.

She turned her attention to Lily, though, as Lily let Albert in on the details of the ceremony. Albert was quiet and gentle and willing to do anything that Lily wanted. They appeared to be very well suited for one another. What a lovely couple. What a nice young man for my daughter.

The affection between Jane and Lily was equally clear. Lily included her mum in everything and accepted suggestions without conflict. She certainly listened to her mother far more than I had ever listened to mine. Then again, she had Jane for a mother. I was more confident than ever in my decision of long ago.

Who would Lily be now if she had been my child? Dashing into danger, following cities that had been destroyed, traveling from town to town and never setting down roots. What kind of life would that have been for a little girl?

Thanking me for the hospitality, they rose to leave. We made plans to meet again in February, setting a final wedding date for 4 April. As I shut the door, I noticed that Jane had left her gloves on the table. As I picked them up, I heard a meek knock at the door.

Jane was there, returning for the gloves.

"Helen—"

"Yes?"

"Well, it's finally nice to attach a name to you after all these years."

"So you recognized me."

"Well, yes. But I already knew you would be here."

I looked at her, dumbfounded. "How is that?"

"You certainly didn't make it easy," she said, laughing. "In fact, I came to believe that you were evading me altogether!"

I shifted in my seat. This was exactly what I had done all these years.

She continued. "It started with the first package, on Lily's first birthday. You sent it to Smithdown. A pressed flower and a little ribbon for her hair. Her hair wasn't long enough to use it just yet, but I saved it for her. Your note wasn't signed, but of course I knew who sent it."

I remembered that ribbon. I had found it in some rubble in Manchester, surprisingly unharmed among the ruins surrounding it.

"And then, every year, I began to anticipate the little gifts you'd send. The doll clothes. The children's books. The lipstick. The peacock."

"Her father made that," I said under my breath.

Jane didn't hear me. "At first there was no way to find you, but sometimes you sent them from towns so small that I thought there was a chance. I'd correspond with the local postmaster there, but the message was always the same. They knew who you were, but you had just disappeared and you'd left no forwarding address."

"Why would you want to find me?" I asked.

She reached out and took my hands in her own, and considered the contrast. Mine, ravished by burns; hers discolored with age. But we shared something beautiful—a girl who rose above ashes and time and brought us back together.

"Dear, don't you know?"

Our eyes met. Tears began to form in mine.

"Lily is as much a part of you as she is of me. I knew what anguish I would feel to never know what had become of her. I wouldn't have encroached upon your privacy. I just wanted to write to you. To tell you how she was. To thank you for sacrificing such a gift to my care. But you'd always vanished."

I hung my head as she pressed on.

"It wasn't until recently that my hope in finding you was renewed."

"How is that?"

"Charcross. This is the fourth year in a row that the postmark had the same stamp. I'd begun to think that you were finally settled."

"But I always sent it to Smithdown, and you aren't there anymore."

"Lily and I come back every year for Christmas, and as I'd come to expect your packages every November, I just asked them to hold it for me if it would arrive."

In my comfort of my life next to Father McCarthy, I had not thought about the postmark being from the same place. After so much time, I'd doubted that anyone would have still cared to find me.

"And so you came to Charcross to find me?"

"Well, I'm no Poirot or anything," she laughed. "It's not more than a village, and it wasn't too difficult to write and ask if there was someone of your, well, distinct appearance." She shifted in her seat. "When the postmaster responded and said that the housekeeper at the cemetery matched your description, I had to come see for myself. So I came out a few months ago. I didn't see you at the Mass, but I did see you sweeping the front steps."

"Why didn't you come over?"

She sat back into the chair. "I nearly did. I wanted to. But I chickened out, as Lily might say. After all this time, there you were. I just lost all my words."

"But you sent Lily here?"

"Yes. She and Albert met in school when they were much younger, and although we've all moved on to London—Lily will be graduating soon—they wanted to get married back in Liverpool. We looked at some churches around there, but they kept saying they wanted something simpler, something in the country. I remembered All Souls."

She looked out the window. "It's really peaceful here, you know. Beautiful in its own way, with the rolling hills. I knew that Lily would just love it. And she did."

I glanced where her gaze had taken her and nodded.

She turned back to me. "I told her I'd sprained my ankle, as I didn't want to come here and stir something up by my presence. I figured if Lily agreed with me and liked the setting, then I would decide how best to move forward. But I should have counted on my girl jumping right in and talking to the woman who runs the place."

I smiled. "So she told you about me?"

"Yes and no. She mentioned meeting a woman who could help her make the arrangements, but I had to ask some, well, pointed questions to determine if it was you that she had met with."

"What do you mean?"

"I asked her what you looked like."

"Oh."

"Do you know what she said?"

I looked up.

"She said, 'Well, she had the prettiest green eyes, and she looked at me as if she'd known me all her life. I liked her.'"

I smiled. My daughter had seen me through the mask of my face. "And so here we are."

"Yes," she said. "Here we are."

We stared at each other in silence, questions unspoken, but certainly thought.

"It's a long story," I finally said.

"You were never one to give up information easily."

I laughed. "I'm sorry about that. I suppose that I became a very private person."

"Well, I'm sure you have your reasons."

"You have no idea."

We sat like that for a second. I wasn't going to offer up any more just yet, and she didn't press the point.

"Lily is wonderful," I said, filling the space.

"She is. She is the best Christmas present that I ever received. I have you to thank for that."

"No, you've done it all. I had no idea how to take care of myself, let alone a baby. I'm so grateful that you kept her." As I said the words, I realized how true they were. All those years I had suppressed thoughts of my child and the natural imaginings of her life.

"Oh, you know, we had already started bonding in the nursery. It was an easy decision."

I handed her the gloves. "Here. Don't forget these."

"I didn't forget them. I left them here so that I could have an excuse to come back in." She stood up, and I joined her as she turned toward the door. "Listen," she said.

"Yes?"

Jane placed her hand on the knob and looked down. "Do you intend to tell Lily—well, you know?" Jane looked uncertain as to what she wanted my answer to be.

"Not at all. Lily is all yours."

I saw a flicker of relief. "She knows she's adopted, of course. She just doesn't know that it's you. I don't know what I was thinking even coming out here in the first place. Curiosity. Gratefulness. I can't say, other than I felt I had to see you. You know, maybe in time, we can tell her the truth."

I shook my head. "There is no need for that. She's already got a saint for a mother. No need to tell her that she has a sinner for one as well."

Jane touched my arms with her familiar, reassuring way. "Oh, Helen. You are far too hard on yourself. Whatever you have done, you surely had your reasons. And you have certainly atoned." She slid her hand over mine. "I hope you can believe that yourself and find the peace that I have always wanted for you."

I sniffled. Jane was the only person ever to have loved me as Helen.

"I have. I am. I mean, I'm sure that I will. Find peace, that is."

"Good. I will be thinking of you, as I always have, and I will be sure to come with Lily for our meeting in February."

"I look forward to that."

"Me, too. Take care, Helen." She squeezed my hands, the ones that she had rescued.

"You too, Jane. Happy Christmas." And I closed the door.

The pounding in my chest started again, but was quickly resolved with some deep breaths. It was only noon, and I had packed more emotion into the day than I could bear. I took a cup of tea upstairs to my bedroom and lay down for a nap.

※

The return of Lily and Jane to my life left me giddy. Jane generously sent me notes in the post telling me stories of Lily's childhood. I read and reread each one of them, placing them in a little wooden box for safekeeping when I was finished. I found myself humming and smiling, and even Father McCarthy noticed the difference. My joy must have been contagious, because he became more cheerful as well. I cooked with extra care, paying attention to what he liked and calling on my memories to re-create his favorites.

I became reckless, relaxing my usual caution in concealing myself. This was a fact that I realized one day when I spent the morning baking. Carrying a hot plate into the garden, I saw Father McCarthy pulling weeds.

"I made some cinnamon rolls. Would you like to take a break and eat one?"

He took off his thick gloves and wiped his hands on his garden apron. "Cinnamon rolls? I haven't had those in years."

"Well, they're fresh out of the oven. I've brought plates and napkins, and a fork if you prefer not to eat it with your fingers."

"They are rather dirty. I think I will use that fork. But first, I'm going to wash up at the hosepipe."

I sat down on the stone wall of the church courtyard, swinging my legs like a schoolgirl. The sun was making an appearance today, rare for this time of year.

It took him a while to scrub the caked dirt off his fingernails. He used the time to initiate the conversation, something that was quite out of the ordinary for him.

"So I've seen you at Mass for the past few Sundays. It's the stellar quality of my preaching that keeps you coming back, isn't it?"

"Oh, undoubtedly. It's not enough anymore for me to hear you practicing on Saturday night. I have to come see the full show."

"Well, it's certainly not sold out, and I'm glad to have one more in the audience."

"Maybe I'm that one soul that you're supposed to be reaching, as you told me some time ago."

He finished with his right and started with the left.

"Whatever it is that brought you, I'm glad you're there."

He was glad that I was there?

He continued. "The shepherd loves when his sheep return."

Of course. He was happy that I was there because it was one more soul returning to his God. Still, my presence made him smile, and I was grateful for that, whatever the cause.

"I'm not all the way there, but I do find some comfort in it. You know, I'm not Catholic."

"Yes, I noticed that you are not in the Communion line. Why not be confirmed in the faith and be able to participate fully?"

"I almost did, years ago. Then this happened"—I pointed to my face—"and I never went back. I guess that I was angry at God."

"How did it happen?"

He'd always been far too polite to bring it up, but now I had.

"In the war." Any more, and I might let slip more than I should.

His shoulders slumped. "Yes, there was much lost during the war. On both sides of the fighting." He looked at me and lingered. *See me, Kyle,* I willed. *See me.* He blinked and turned to shut the water off.

I returned to our conversation, both dejected and relieved. "You told me once that you served in the army."

"Yes. It took me all over. I spent the beginning of it in Egypt with the Desert Rats, as we were called. And later we fought in Italy, stormed Normandy, returned to Britain, and finished in Germany."

"It's amazing that you survived."

"It is. I asked God so many times why he took some and left me behind."

I had felt this sentiment myself. "I guess we'll never know why things happen the way that they do."

"Yes. We just have to make the most of what we are given." He dried his hand on a clean spot on the apron and hopped onto the wall next to me. "Well, it's time for one of those cinnamon rolls. We wouldn't want them to get cold now."

I handed him his plate and fork. He took a bite, and I saw his eyes widen before even swallowing.

"What is it?" It had been ages since I'd last made them, but I didn't think they could be that bad.

"Nothing," he said through a mouthful. Finishing that bite, he added, "It's delicious. Perfect, in fact. They are just like the ones that—that I used to have."

"I'm glad that you like them."

He took a second bite and a third. "It is very unusual to put lemon in the icing. How did you think of that?"

How reckless I had become. What was happening to me? "Oh, I just like the sour taste with the sweet taste."

"Me, too."

After he'd eaten it, he reached for another. I was still working on my first when he'd finished his second.

"Thank you, Helen, for making these. They've—I've—they are wonderful and bring up equally good memories."

I have equally good memories of the last time I made these. I grinned at the thought. Is that what he was remembering, too?

"What's so funny?" he asked.

"Nothing. I'm just glad you liked them. I'll go clean up the kitchen now."

He hopped down from our perch and reached for the hosepipe again. "Do you want to wash the icing from your hands?" he said.

"Yes, thank you."

With one hand, he turned on the hose lightly so that the water trickled out. With the other, he took my fingers and placed them under the water. Using his thumb, he slowly rubbed off the stubborn icing. He didn't seem to be bothered by the flaws and the markings, the red-and-white splotches. Even through the scars, I felt heat at his touch. No one had touched me like that in decades, and now it was him. I held back tears, carefully guarding my reaction. He was so close. I could say his name. My lips parted, and the roll of a *K* sound formed in the back of my throat.

"There you go, you're all done." He turned the hosepipe off and stood up, unaware of the landslide that I nearly started.

"Thank you. I'm going to go in now," I mumbled.

"And I have some corn cockles to wrestle with. They're trying to strangle my roses." He held up one of the pink blossoms with black lines. It was hard to believe that such a pretty thing was a weed. "You know," he said, "corn cockles were once used as primitive medicine, but now they're considered poisonous."

That was just like him to know that kind of thing.

"Well, good luck with them."

"Thank you." He turned back to his work.

Watching him as I left the garden, I smiled.

Chapter Twenty-Nine

Lily arrived first thing in the morning on 4 April, followed by Jane and three girlfriends. I opened up my side of the rectory as a dressing room. I enjoyed watching them primp and prep as they took up my parlor. It reminded me of my days with Lucille and what it could have been like if we had been there for each other's weddings. I felt her there with me, celebrating my daughter. She would have found twenty thousand details that needed to be managed.

Mandy, Lily's university roommate, applied her makeup and styled her hair. Her dress had clean lines and an empire waist. It was not embellished with lace or pearls as was traditional, for Lily was thoroughly modern. The veil was sewn on to a wide cotton band that encircled her head.

The attendants' dresses were light pink with white trim but were cut in the same clean, modern lines.

Jane devoted herself to it all, fluffing the dress and putting Lily's stray hairs in their place. Her dress was light blue with a short matching jacket. There was a little lace on the edge of the sleeves, no doubt a nod to her more traditional tastes. More than once, she pulled me aside and begged me to join them at the reception in town. I declined, saying that I had given up that right long ago but was so pleased to be asked. I would, however, attend the ceremony.

Our organist, still playing away by some miracle, pounded out the wedding march, one of the few compromises toward convention. She had brought her own priest, but as a courtesy, allowed Father McCarthy to concelebrate the Mass. It was not every day that a wedding took place at All Souls, and he didn't want to miss out on that.

He had asked me earlier, upon seeing Lily's name, if she was any relation to me. I told him that I had no family. I lied to a priest. Well, it was probably the least of my sins. Though the nagging temptation to tell him the truth had returned. Now that they were in each other's company, the guilt of my deception burned each time I saw them. But I easily convinced myself that this was not the right time for this revelation, that the focus should be on Lily's wedding, and I postponed it once again.

I took my usual seat in the back, tucked behind a column, and peeked out through my damp handkerchief.

"Do you, Lily, take Albert to be your lawfully wedded husband? To have and to hold . . ."

I closed my eyes at the words. Today I heard my daughter speak the vows that I had once made. I looked at Father McCarthy, sitting up at the front, and wondered if he was remembering the same thing.

"For better or worse, 'til death do us part."

Kyle had kept up his promise, and I had not. I realized this now as I hadn't before. When I chose to disappear, I never considered my vows. Would I have loved Kyle and stayed with him if he had come home injured from the war? There was no doubt. I had been injured in the war, and I didn't give him a chance to make that decision. And I had no doubt now as to what it would have been. So "worse" had found us. And I had fled.

"'Til death do us part." Kyle had more than kept up his end of the bargain. There were several years between his return from the war and his entrance into the seminary. He had told me that he was "searching." Somehow I knew for certain that he was searching for me. He didn't accept that I was gone, and he didn't return to school until he had come to terms with my death. Faithful always, like the story of Saint Dwynwen that he'd told me on our honeymoon. The patron saint of lovers.

I felt so ashamed. We had each said "I do" to these vows. And later I said, "I don't."

I had convinced myself that I was making the choice for everyone else. Kyle would be better off without a scarred, broken wife. My parents would be better off without an embarrassment of a daughter. Lily would be better off without a migratory mother. But that was not what I had vowed, and I realized the truth of it now. It was I who did not want to feel like the lesser part of the marriage. It was I who didn't want to return to my parents without pride. It was I who chose to break every tie, even with my precious daughter. I was too wrapped up in my vanity and my desperation to consider the other people involved.

I teetered back and forth between joy and sorrow. Happiness at the return of my loved ones and contrition at my part in hurting them. Suddenly Kyle's faith made sense to me. It was not for the perfect; it was for the repentant. A faith for those seeking healing and salvation. Every Sunday they dropped on their knees to ask for answers, offer thanks, and beg forgiveness.

I found myself wanting this forgiveness more than anything, and I knew where to find it. Tomorrow I would tell Father McCarthy that I was giving in. I wanted to join his church and to hear the words of absolution for my sins.

He looked resplendent in his vestments, white instead of black. I flipped through the Latin missal and followed its translation, thinking of the days when Kyle had showed me how to use it. But as I turned each translucent page, the years fell away and the priest's voice of today drowned out the boy's voice of yesterday.

Dominus vobiscum.

The Lord be with you.

In spiritu humilitatis, et in animo contrite suscipiamur a te, Domine.

Accept us, O Lord, in our spirit of contrition and humility of heart.

Haec quotiescumque feceritis, in mei memoriam facietis.

And as often as you shall do these things, do them in memory of me.

Albert and Lily sealed their promises with a kiss, and a shout of congratulations broke out in the church as friends applauded the couple. They had their lives ahead of them, and with any luck the world would be easier on them than it had been on us. They left in a shower of rice, and I trailed behind. Such dreams ahead of them. The bells tolled, their usual dirge replaced by peals of celebration.

Jane lingered before leaving. She was overcome—her baby was all grown up. The baby that she coaxed during her first steps. The child that she picked up from school. The adolescent that she guided through first love. The young woman that she embraced as her own.

She wrapped her arms around me, kissing my cheek, and I held her as well. We smiled from the sentiment of the wedding and our shared motherhood. I was indebted to her forever.

After watching her drive away, I stooped to pick up a grain of the rice. My chest contracted again, so I rose slowly and held the rice up to the sun. *All my dreams could fit in this little grain,* I thought. But Kyle's beliefs promised that faith the size of a mustard seed could move mountains. And this rice was larger than a mustard seed.

I tossed it away, where it was retrieved by a waiting sparrow.

I paused at Father McCarthy's stoop, rested my cheek against his door, and traced the knots of the wood with my right hand. The faint light of dusk cast a shadow on the earth along the wall of the rectory. The elongated version of myself hovered on the ground like a dark and menacing angel. I closed my eyes and knocked.

"Come in," said the voice that I had loved for so many years.

Father McCarthy was seated at his desk, engrossed, I presumed, over the homily for the following Sunday. He stood when I entered.

"Helen," he said, surprised to find me here at this unusual time. "Please close the door and have a seat." He gathered papers that were strewn upon the sofa and gestured for me to take a seat. "Tea?" he offered.

"No, thank you." I could hear every sound in the room. The tempo of the wall clock. The low volume of the classical music from his radio upstairs. The chair as he slid it over by my side.

"All right, then," he said as he sat down. He folded his hands and rested his elbows on his knees as he leaned in toward me. "What can I do for you?"

His nearness made me feel faint, and I almost forgot my purpose. I looked at him at last and cleared my throat. "You asked me several weeks ago why I don't participate at your Mass."

He leaned back. "Yes, I remember."

"I'm ready now," I said.

"I see. May I ask what changed your mind?"

"I suppose I would like to be able to be a part of it after all. I thought I should tell you so that I didn't just show up for Communion one morning."

He smiled. "Well, I'm glad you came to me, then. It's not as simple as just getting in line."

"What do you mean?"

"Well, when you receive Communion and say 'Amen,' you are assenting to everything that this faith embodies. Not just that moment.

It usually takes a year of study. Catechism. History. Theology. And then the catechumen receives the sacraments for the first time at the vigil of Easter Sunday."

Time was not my enemy. Here in Charcross, the calendar crawled lazily, marked only by funerals and sparsely attended feast days.

"So how do I get started?"

He threw his hands up and smiled. "If you'll have me, I can be your teacher. A poor one, I'm sure, but as they say, beggars can't be choosers. And we don't exactly have a resident catechist nor a wait list of students."

The possibility of spending so much time with him delighted me immeasurably, and I quickly agreed.

This began months of study and a new routine that filled me with anticipation throughout the day. We went about our regular duties and spent most evenings bent over books or reviewing lessons. Often we'd get lost on tangents, though we never shared anything too personal, each keeping our guard.

But there we were, two otherwise lonely people, sharing meals, talking and laughing. We settled into a comfortable friendship once again.

It occurred to me that if the war had not entered our lives, this might be the picture of how we would have ended up anyway. Of course, there was not the affection of a marriage nor the sharing of goods and a bed. But twenty-five years of marriage would probably have looked something like this.

One of the greatest joys of this time together was the rediscovery of the kind and loving God that Kyle had never doubted. His faith stayed true through such sufferings. Mine had not, but I saw now that it was I who deserted God. Not the other way around.

By midsummer, though, I noticed a change in him. Our lessons continued, but they became perfunctory in nature. Father McCarthy wouldn't meet my eyes and began to sit across the table from me instead of next to me, as had become his habit. I wondered what I had done wrong.

On the first evening in August I knocked at our usual hour. I had made a cranberry-and-walnut loaf to share, and I could feel its heat through the foil.

"Miss Bailey," he said, reverting to a formality that we had long since discarded.

I looked at him as I found my seat. He held a letter in his hand.

"Miss Bailey, I hope you know that I have enjoyed these months of study with you, and your years of service at All Souls has brought life into this otherwise desolate place."

I braced myself for what might follow the setup of these kind words.

"I have just received word from my bishop that I'm being transferred. As you know, priests rotate through here every few years, and now it is my turn to move on."

"Yes," I protested, "but you received a letter like that several years ago and were able to defer it. You said that no one wants to be out here." My heart beat faster. What was to become of me now? What would become of the new "us" that had just begun?

"You're right, of course," he continued. "But the time has come, and in hindsight we're often able to see the wisdom of these things."

The bread escaped my trembling hands, and we bent down in our seats to pick it up at the same time. Our hands brushed, but he moved away faster than I did.

"I'm sorry," I whispered, pulling the loaf into my lap.

"I've already corresponded with the new priest on your behalf, of course." He got up to walk over to the stove and busied himself with the teakettle as he spoke. "Father Brown from Merseyside will be taking my place. I've told him that you are an excellent cook and housekeeper, you don't ask for much, and it would be my recommendation that he keep you on. If you prefer that, naturally."

I nodded out of mirrored politeness. "And where are you going?" I asked.

"Crosby," he answered. "It's north of Liverpool."

"And just beyond Bootle," I murmured.

His head snapped to look at me. "Yes, Bootle." Our eyes locked. *See me,* I thought once again. But he looked away.

"The transfer is almost immediate, I'm afraid. I'm leaving next Saturday. Father Brown will be here in time to conduct that Sunday's Mass."

"And there is to be no good-bye?" I asked. "To your congregation, I mean?"

"You mean the trickle of people who come for their weekly obligation or the few regulars who are just one step away from becoming permanent residents?" He looked out the window at the vast graveyard and turned back to me. "No, Miss Bailey. I don't expect to be missed here, and as long as it's for the best, it might as well happen now."

"And my studies?"

"Yes, I have already spoken to Father Brown about that, too. Your progress has been excellent and will no doubt continue under him. He is a very learned man, from what I gather, and you will be in good hands. You'll still receive your sacraments on time in the spring."

He said this with the dismissive tone that told me there was nothing else to speak about. I stood up and pushed in my chair. It echoed in our silence. I couldn't speak, lest the tears that had gathered behind my face make an unwanted appearance. I gave him a curt nod in farewell and left to my side of the rectory.

I paced the room before I crumpled into a heap on the floor. My hands balled into fists, and I covered my head as I cried.

Surely this wasn't the end. To have lived so long in despair. To have found hope and even happiness. To have my daughter restored to me only to have my husband taken away. Was there no place in this world where all could be right, if only for a little while? Was there some great balance that had to be righted by pairing grief and joy? Kyle would have told me some drivel about true happiness being found only on the other side of life. Was it so wrong to hope that happiness could be lived on this side?

I stayed in the house for three days and didn't emerge for any of my regular duties. Twice I saw from behind the curtain that Father McCarthy came up to my door and paused, but he never knocked.

By Friday my bags were packed. I didn't know where I would go, but the nomadic lifestyle had served me well enough in the past. There was no way that I could stay here in this place without the presence of this man who was my everything. Father Brown would be an imposter, an interloper, and I could not stick around to live a charade of contentment.

A charade. I stopped when the word entered my mind. Hadn't that been what I'd been living for decades now? Had I believed that coming to Charcross and living as the housekeeper to Father McCarthy somehow mitigated the lie I'd begun on that Christmas morning in Liverpool? Was it not a charade to stand near him day by day and to keep this secret?

I thought again of Lily's wedding and the vows once spoken and broken by me. I was not merely seeking absolution from a priest or a church or a God. My penance had been great, but it was not complete. My confession needed to be made to my husband.

Chapter Thirty

Father McCarthy liked to hear confessions on Fridays. Some churches did it on Sundays, where one priest celebrated Mass while another heard the sins of the faithful. But there were no other priests here. He liked Fridays, though, in remembrance of the sacrifice on the cross.

The day drew the same faces every week. He told me once that hearing the sins of the elderly who came so devotedly was like being pelted with feathers. Their transgressions were so minimal, so scrupulous, that nothing merited more than a couple of Hail Marys as penance until they returned the following week.

I left my two suitcases, dusty from disuse, at the foot of the door of the church. Ellis had followed me outside as I locked my house for the last time.

"Stay," I said, and he lay down and rested his head on his paws.

I opened the door. The church was dim, save for the streams of sunlight that illuminated specks of dust, which danced like glitter. The confessional stood at the side of the church. I'd cleaned the nooks of its carved scrolls so many times, and I knew the imperfections of its wood as well as those of my own hands. It had always looked mysterious to me, this depository of wrongdoing. But at this hour the light from the windows poured on it and I understood how people saw this as a kind of gateway to salvation.

I did not know if salvation or condemnation awaited me on the other side of its curtain. But for certain I would at last lift the shroud of lies that I'd told.

Three people stood in the queue before me, standing far back from the confessional itself, offering privacy to the penitent who knelt in front of the maroon curtain that separated him from the priest on the other side. Father McCarthy had told me that the changes happening at the Vatican might include a more informal, face-to-face sacrament in the future, but for now the guise of anonymity was safeguarded. For this, I was grateful. To speak these painful words to the person against whom the hurts had been committed would inflict a pain I had not known since my hands and face had felt the first rush of scalding water.

Two people remained, examining their consciences with booklets that helped them recall their shortcomings. One stepped forward. Then the next.

Then I was alone. My arms shook and my heart quaked as I approached the kneeler. I looked back at the door to see if there was a last-minute arrival who could spare me this agony just a few minutes longer, but none came.

My knees bent as my hands rested on the wooden ledge. The thick velvet curtain was hung on rods that rippled its fabric. I could hear Father McCarthy breathe behind it. I imagined him there, waiting for yet another mundane admission. He might be tired, taking off his spectacles, rubbing his eyes. Looking at his watch and counting the minutes until the last person had been heard. This was my final chance to back out. My suitcases were at the door. I could spare the priest from this purgation, and I nearly convinced myself that it would be selfless to do so. But it was false altruism that had led me here in the first place, and it had to end. Now.

"Bless me, Father, for I have sinned," I began, in the words that Father McCarthy had prepared me for in our studies.

"And of what do you accuse yourself?" he asked routinely.

"I have lied," I said.

"Mm-hmm. And are you speaking of a venial lie or a greater one?"

"A greater one, Father. Much. I have lied to my family, my husband, my friends." I paused, then whispered, "My child."

I heard him shift in his seat.

"No sin is greater than the forgiveness that can be bestowed upon the sinner. Now, what is the nature of this lie and whom did it hurt?"

My pulse rushed, as I said the only word that needed to be said: "Kyle."

The silence on the other end was total.

"Kyle," I said again, this time through the tears that would no longer be barricaded. My head fell to the mantle, and my shoulders heaved.

I felt the curtain flutter, and I looked up. His hand slipped out beneath it and searched until it found my own. He squeezed it tightly and didn't let go. The feel of his hand on mine was overwhelming, sending tremors throughout me as I tried, poorly, to keep my composure.

"Kyle," I cried again. "I'm so sorry. I'm so sorry for what I've put you through. I don't know what else to say."

All the words I'd prepared. The litany of offenses I'd rehearsed. Every thought left me as our hands explored one another's.

Then he pulled away suddenly, and I heard the creak of the floor as he stepped out of the confessional.

I was hunched over the kneeler, but turned to him as he stood next to me. He fell to his knees and pushed my hair away from my face.

"It *is* you," he said. "I had imagined it before, but thought that I was going mad. I thought I was seeing a ghost."

He tucked a lock behind my ears and brushed his fingers down my ruined cheeks. I blinked as I saw him through water-filled eyes.

We reached for one another until our hands, our arms, found one another and, at last, our lips.

Our kiss was a frantic one, and I sank into the familiarity of Kyle that had haunted my dreams for over half of my life. Our breaths were one, hurried and demanding, and interrupted only by the sound of the church door. He jumped back. I leapt to my feet and smoothed my hair and face. But the door didn't open, and I realized that it was only Ellis scratching to get in.

We looked at one another and laughed. He leaned on the pew for support, and I wrapped my hands around my stomach.

"Oh my goodness," I said at last when our breathing had returned to normal. "Just imagine if someone had walked in! The priest and the housekeeper!"

Kyle smiled and stepped back toward me. This time he reached his arms around me and I nestled my head into his shoulders.

"My gorgeous girl," he said. "My sad, my broken, my darling girl." I felt the heat of his breath in my ear as he whispered, "What happened to you?"

Ellis scratched again.

"Maybe we should continue this at your house?" I suggested.

"Let me lock up. I'll meet you there." He placed a gentle kiss on my forehead.

I nodded and walked outside. Ellis jumped up to me.

"Silly, unromantic dog," I said. I picked up my suitcases and walked over to Father McCarthy's side of the house. I waited at his kitchen table and looked down at my nails. How I'd let myself go. I'd sunk wholly into this dowdy persona I'd created. Once I had cared about setting my hair, painting these nails, wearing colors that complemented me. Through the years I'd lost myself so entirely.

He arrived a few minutes later and, without speaking, closed the curtains of all the windows. He pulled the white collar from his cassock and set it on the table. Then he walked over to me again, pulled me to my feet.

"Julianne," he said as he wrapped his arms around me again. He held me there, our bodies swaying gently as we stood. At last, he stepped back. He looked at my face and down at my hands. He placed delicate kisses on each and then led me to the sofa. "Please tell me everything."

I shared with him, then, the story of Helen Bailey. I talked and talked. He listened and looked at me with those malt-colored Kyle eyes that were changed only by the slight wrinkles that encircled them. He held my hands the whole time, rubbing his thumb along their scars. I told him about Lucille and my parents and Charles and Roger and Abigail, and even about Jane and Lily. His hands tightened and his face hardened when I told him about our child, and I even confessed that it was her wedding that he'd presided over.

"A daughter," he said.

He stood up, running his hands through his hair, and walked around the room several times before joining me again. He sighed, deeply and wearily, assimilating this great new hurt.

"How could you do that?"

"Kyle, I'm so sorry," I pleaded again. "I didn't know if you would come back from the war, and it seemed like the only chance I could give her. You have to believe me that it was the most difficult thing I've ever done." I started to cry at the thought of what might have been and how my decision had separated them all these years.

He walked over and took me in his arms. My tears wet his shirt, and he brushed his fingers through my hair.

"Shh," he said. "I know you did what seemed right at the time. I was just not expecting anything like that." He kissed my head before stepping back. "I'm partially to blame, though. I knew it. I looked for you for several years. I wouldn't believe that you were gone. I thought that if you were gone, some piece of me would sense it. And there was no body. But there you were, all along, in that hospital. I *went* to that hospital. And every hospital in the area. How could I have missed you?"

"You missed me because I didn't want to be found. I thought that I was being punished for taking you from the seminary, and I thought this would let you go back to what you were supposed to be in the first place. And I was right. Look at you!"

"Look at me? Julianne, did you never hear anything I said to you? I was meant to be with *you*. *You* were my vocation—do you remember me telling you that?"

I looked down, speaking softly. "I do. And now everything has changed because of me."

Kyle gripped my arms. "Nothing has to change. Nothing has to be different."

"How can you say that? Look at you! Look at me!"

"Do you see my collar over there?"

I looked in the direction that he was pointing, and I saw the stark white tab gleaming against the old dark wood of the table. I nodded.

"I couldn't be a priest now even if I wanted to be. I'll have to write to my bishop, and he will tell me that my marriage is an impediment to Holy Orders. That through no fault of my own, those vows are invalid."

"Invalid," I repeated.

"Yes. Believe me. I don't say that casually. It's been a good life. Serving like this is a privilege that few men are called to, and it's something I take very seriously. And perhaps I pleased my mum and da somewhere up there."

"And what about Crosby? You were going to be transferred there."

"I asked to be transferred, but that's moot now."

I looked sharply at him. "You *asked* to be transferred? You told me that your commission here at All Souls had come to an end."

He grinned sheepishly. "Well, that was nearly true. I was due to get another letter about that. But yes, I asked to be transferred."

"Why? I thought you liked it here."

"I *love* it here. I love it too much. That was exactly the problem."

"I don't understand."

"Our dinners. Our studies. The time we spent together. You reminded me of my love of long ago. Your cinnamon rolls. The way you bite your lip when you're nervous. All these things. I began to have the kinds of thoughts that a priest shouldn't have. So I asked to be removed from this place. I needed to leave before I crossed a line that I shouldn't have."

I was speechless. To think that he could have loved me even as I was, that in this state I could stir such emotions in him. Enough that he felt he had to leave.

As if reading my mind, he said, "Look." And he traced my face once again. "I knew when I married you that we would grow old together. See this?" He pulled at the gray hairs at his temples. "And this?" He rubbed a finger over the wrinkles around his eyes. "We're both getting older. I'm not the robust young man that I was when you first met me. I'm going to have to have faith that you're not going to leave me for some university-aged buck when you think I'm too much of an old man for you."

I smiled. "I don't know. What if he's tall?"

Kyle stood and pulled me to my feet. "Then I'll just have to find other ways to compete with him." And he kissed me in a way that made me glad the curtains were closed.

Epilogue

Helen Bailey was born on 23 November 1940 in a flood of hot water at the height of the Blitz. She died on 5 August 1966 in the confessional of a remote church in Charcross. Her life was sad, friendless, and dotted with memories that were filled with remorse.

I, however, was reborn in that same little church when Kyle reached out to take my hand and forgive the sins that had been committed against him.

As predicted, the bishop dissolved his commitment without incident, expressing regret at losing such a dedicated priest. Having great admiration for Father McCarthy's years of service, he recommended him for a teaching position at a small parochial school on the Isle of Man.

We left Charcross after Father Brown had been there for a few days, and we kept the nature of our relationship quiet for fear of causing scandal to those who didn't need to hear an explanation. On the Isle of Man, we would start out again as Mr. and Mrs. McCarthy, and our strange history would be known only to us.

Our years there were happy and quiet. The same heart condition that had stolen my brother took me eventually, but I'd outlasted him by many years. I credited the love of a devoted husband and our daily walks along the coast of the island. I was an old lady by the time my heart finally gave out. My funeral was attended by Kyle, Lily, Albert, their two children, and three grandchildren, who had all traveled from London. And, of course, the many friends we had made. Jane's health was too poor to travel at the time, but she and I wrote up until the very end and exchanged pictures of this family we shared under most unusual circumstances. Early in our correspondence, we agreed that Lily had a right to know about her parentage, and Kyle and I had a joyous reunion with our daughter when Jane invited us to a Christmas celebration at her house.

Kyle was the last to leave the graveyard. When all had gone, he knelt down and kissed the freshly dug dirt. His hand traced the length of it as he whispered, "Good-bye, gorgeous. I'll see you soon." He propped himself back up on his knees and then stood with much effort. His white hair glistened in the sunlight like the collar he had left behind so many years ago. He wiped the dirt from his hands and walked from my grave.

Book Club Questions

1.   How might Helen, looking back over the years, identify with the life cycle of the caterpillar that Kyle finds for Charles in chapter one?

2.   Lucille is the voice of reason as Julianne struggles with Kyle's impending ordination to the priesthood. Would you have given Julianne similar counsel or encouraged her to pursue him?

3.   Julianne loves that Kyle takes her to the ruins of Saint Dwynwen on their honeymoon. What is the most romantic thing you have ever done that required thought over cost?

4.   Was Julianne's abandonment of baby Lily the ultimate sacrifice of a mother or the self-serving action of a distraught woman?

5.   Julianne has witnessed the last rites at the deathbed of Mr. McCarthy, and later as Helen at the side of Mrs. Campbell. How has her character evolved between the two events?

6.   Why does Julianne choose nursing as a career, and how does that decision shape her life?

7. Before Helen goes to Charcross to work for Father McCarthy, she stops in Liverpool and observes her parents. Should she have revealed to them who she was? Or did she spare them from further grief and shock?

8. How might Kyle's and Julianne's lives have played out if he had never left for the war?

9. How does the author weave the concepts of heaven, purgatory, and hell into the story?

10. What scene or character most resonated with you personally?

Acknowledgments

I have always thought of writing as a solitary event. But I've never been so happy to be wrong. Many people have been a part of this journey.

To my agent, Jill Marsal. Thank you for taking a chance on me and for encouraging me to be better. Your first phone call was one of the best days of my life!

To my editors, Danielle Marshall, Catherine Knepper, and David Downing. Danielle—thank you for believing in this book so ardently and for your unwavering advocacy! Catherine—your comments made me smile and you helped take this book to another level. David—I appreciated your insights that gave the final polish to the story.

To everyone at Lake Union Publishing, I am grateful for all of your hard work and support on my behalf—Gabriella Dumpit, Tara Parsons, and the many others who make up an extraordinary team.

I am blessed to have wonderful friends who suffered through my early drafts. A few of them made some specific suggestions that I took to heart or offered just the right word of encouragement at a moment when it was needed: Elmie Guidry, Sarah Remmert, Julie Alexander, Jennifer Salamon, Myra Garza, Fr. Ed Hauf, Melody Escobar, Patty King, John Michael Ruiz, Sarah Weaver, Kathy Cucolo, Amy Castillo,

Magda Pretorius, Leslie Sawaya, Magda De Salme, Jim and Kristen Peterson, Carol Taylor, Melanie Stovall, Beverly Lamoureux, Melissa Stack, Melissa Wittman, Tracy Remmert, Cece Smith, Carolyn Taylor, Yvonne Russell, Megan Homan, Judy Kennedy, Jennifer Eichelbaum, Bianca Sanders, Julie Williams, Joe and Laura Ilsley, the whole Solis family, Julie Reyna, Julie Di Maio, Inge Di Maio, Jessica Bernstein, Francine Chapa, Cindy Comfort, Anne Wright, David and Ann Dreggors, Norma Alvarez, and Marie Cook. And to Erin Chipman— my original Anglophile friend and sharer of banana splits.

To Amanda Tidmore, Lorraine Zavala, Lianna Patterson, Francine Wong, Julie Hardin, and Ashley Zimmerman: thank you for helping with real estate tasks so that I could write. And to everyone at Keller Williams Legacy for being so enthusiastic!

To Aunt Cheryl, for being my role model in strength, humility, and generosity. Thanks for making so many dreams come true. And to Uncle Travy, who inspired more than anyone knows.

I am here because of all the great writing that has captivated me ever since I could read. Thank you to my writer friends—your work and your own journeys are very inspiring to me: Stephanie Cowell, Leila Meacham, Eileen Palma, Jeanette Schneider, Melissa Romo, Les Edgerton, Melissa Roske, and Ann Sullivan. And to the members of SARA, WRW, WFWA, and the other LU authors, who are all continual supports for the craft and lifestyle of writing. I look forward to reading your future books!

To my brother and sister, Paul and Catherine Remmert. They make a cameo appearance in chapter ten. I couldn't write about siblings and not think of how blessed I am that they were given to me. They are the best! Paul is the genius behind my book trailer.

I won the offspring jackpot with Claire, Gina, Mary Teresa, and Vincent. You have been patient and helpful for much of your lives while I wrote this book. My prayer is that you will discover your own vocations and develop the individual gifts that you were given. You have had a front-row seat to what it means to achieve a goal—through frustration, elation, rejection, and celebration. I can't wait to see what life has in store for you. You are all amazing and I *love* being your mom.

To Sir Paul McCartney: thank you for your innovative music. My story of a priest and his housekeeper was greatly inspired by your lyrics.

And, most especially, I am grateful for the faith that was given to me. The metanoia of the past few years means more to me than anything else that could ever happen. All things are truly possible with God, and I am living proof. Thank you to Mary, Therese, and Philomena for your intercessions.

I know, I know. If this were an Oscar speech, they would have cued the music by now.

Author Bio

Camille Di Maio has always dreamed of being a writer and has had pieces published in various regional and parenting magazines. When she's not delaying sleep in favor of reading "just one more chapter" of a great book, she and her husband homeschool their four children and run a real estate office in San Antonio, Texas. Camille also regularly faces her fear of flying to indulge her passion for travel. She is inspired by the concept of "sucking the marrow out of life" and, to that end, trains in tae kwon do, buys too many baked goods at farmers' markets, and unashamedly belts out Broadway show tunes when the moment strikes. *The Memory of Us* is her debut novel.